Leaving Ardglass

Leaving Ardglass

William King

THE LILLIPUT PRESS
DUBLIN

Published in 2008 by
The Lilliput Press,
62–63 Sitric Road,
Dublin 7, Ireland
www.lilliputpress.ie

ISBN 978 1 84351 135 9

A catalogue record for this book is available from The British Library.

10 9 8 7 6 5 4 3

Typeset by Linden Publishing Services in 11 on 13 point Bembo
Designed by Susan Waine
Printed in England by MPG Books, Bodmin, Cornwall

I

'TIME TO RING THE BELL,' I remind the sacristan as I settle the green chasuble over my shoulders.

In the mirror beside the vesting bench, I can see him grip his walking stick and shuffle to the back door of the church; his shadow stretches out over the ancient flagstones. 'For whom the bell tolls, Monsignor.'

For whom the bell tolls: the same routine every morning. He brushes along the gravel path, and a gloomy succession of strokes invades the vestry. Roused from his sleep, a neighbour's collie barks in anger.

The sacristan's arthritic hip is a legacy of his days digging trenches in London. 'You wouldn't treat an animal like that. Out in all weather,' he said to me once when I visited his house soon after I arrived here in Kildoon under a cloud. He was rummaging for biscuits, even though I had assured him that a cup of tea would be fine.

While he spoke, I was in a time warp: every street corner and café in Kilburn and Camden Town I had come to know so well forty years before came alive. He was shining a torch too on a summer in London which had changed me, on a chapter of my story which I had wrapped up and hidden away in some dark cupboard.

'Any chance you'd help me around the church. Nothing heavy, just to put out the chalice, the cruets and so on,' I had asked him.

'Glad to, Monsignor.'

To be honest, I could have managed these chores myself, but I needed company. Around here, apart from meeting a few old people who come to the morning Mass, I might not see another soul for the rest of the day. And yet, after all I've been through in the past couple of years, I have found peace. Peace or refuge – I'm not sure which.

Just off the motorway for the North, where the traffic begins to pick up after leaving Drogheda, Kildoon has two pubs, a Londis and a service station: here lorry drivers stop for breakfast rolls, or burgers and greasy chips on their way to Belfast. Against the advice of the planners, the service station owner gained access to the main road. The locals claim that brown envelopes had been slipped to councillors. Since the new housing estate has been completed, a bottle bank has appeared where the old creamery used to be. The two pubs are jam-packed on a Saturday night and are at full pitch when the sacristan and I are locking the church. Later, the thunder of Range Rovers, Cherokees and Pathfinders wakes me and the neighbour's dog when customers are on their noisy way home long after closing time.

Now, through the open door leading to the church, I hear the stragglers arrive: the two old ladies who run a haberdashery and who will whisper to each other until I appear in the sanctuary. Close by one of the radiators, Kevin the bell-ringer, a one-time seminarian, will be working through his faded novena leaflets. The day before his ordination, he took off accross the football pitch at the back of the seminary, spent twenty years in England and then returned to the village where his mother runs the post office. 'Mammies are great, aren't they, Monsignor?' he informs me one day when I am buying stamps.

'They are. Great.'

When the sacristan returns, we bow to the crucifix, and enter the sanctuary where the usual half a dozen or so are scattered thinly about the church, one or two continuing to say their rosary during Mass.

Although they must know that I was once Bishop Boylan's right-hand man and a candidate to succeed him or be given another diocese, they never raise the subject when I visit their homes, nor how Boylan's successor, Bishop Nugent and I had been at loggerheads. They would have picked up the diocesan rumours also – I am still sore at being turned down for a mitre. My argument with Nugent was nothing more than sour grapes, some of the priests had said, and the best decision I took was to bow out gracefully, and not cause a division in the diocese.

When we cut logs with the chainsaw at the back of the house, the sacristan confines himself to describing his daughter's children in Margate, and how he and his wife can't wait for their next visit. Learning that my brother is M.J. Galvin, and that I, as a student, had worked in north London, he resurrects a patchwork of memories: dances in Holloway Road and Cricklewood; fights in the Crown; the drenching they got in the back of open lorries at six in the morning, heading out to Guildford or Reading in the driving wind and rain. 'No one will ever know except us what it was like when we slaved behind the mixer,' he says while he holds back a branch, and I sink the screaming chainsaw into a log and send up a shower of amber chippings. ''Twas savage,' he adds as the log drops on a bed of sawdust and I shut down the throttle; the neighbour's dog goes silent. 'Our own were the worst,' and then he rushes in with a sweetener, 'although your brother, by all accounts, was fair.'

He grimaces as he stretches his back, and looks away towards the main road where articulated trucks and jeeps are rumbling past a hoarding that shows a laughing couple tripping along by a blue sea's edge. The caption says that the Costa del Sol is the place to buy your own villa at a knockdown price.

'We were neither fish nor flesh. Branded as letting down this ould country by going across to John Bull. Sure we'd have starved to death if we'd stayed.' He flings another log on the pile. 'And not wanted there because we were the drunken Irish.'

In the evening, when my housekeeper has left and I settle down to the newspaper and Lyric FM, a hoard of memories begins to stir. I put aside the paper and take a sip from my doctor's advice: 'A glass of milk at night, Monsignor. Good for an ulcer. Try not to be worrying; what happened is beyond your control. Look, take one of these tablets, if you feel anxious; they're not strong but they'll calm you, and try to stay off the hard stuff.' She smiles when she hands me the prescription for tranquillisers.

The field in front of the presbytery reaches down to a disused railway line; beyond the line, boys, with 'Keane' and 'Ronaldo' on their backs, chase a ball around the soccer pitch, filling the air with their cries. But the sacristan's words keep tugging at my elbow, drawing me back to London – pointing out men in turned-down wellingtons and hobnailed boots. The paddy wagon is screeching to a halt on the glistening cobbled streets outside M.J.'s pub, The Highway. A queue is forming in front of Willesden Post Office; I see them, as clearly as 'Keane' and 'Ronaldo', clutching five-pound notes for money orders to send home.

I switch off the radio. Write it. 'No one would believe what we went through in those days, especially with all this wealth. Not even if you swore on the Bible!' The sacristan's words circle my brain, looking for a landing. Maybe they would believe, if I tell the full story as I remember it.

Although I no longer take the occasional Valium, I still have scars from my fight with Nugent about the way he pilloried innocent priests. I need some project to lift my gloom. Earlier one of my golfing foursome had rung to tell me the latest gossip – they thrive on gossip. We were ordained together, and, apart from my three years in Rome doing a doctorate, we have been meeting almost weekly for the past forty years: golf on a Thursday and then the week after Easter we spend in one of M.J.'s villas outside Málaga. Since I came to Kildoon, I have more time on my hands, so I join them for cards on a Friday night. And to be honest, I too relish the clerical gossip.

My golfing confrère tells me that another priest who had been accused of molesting a child has been cleared by the Director of Public Prosecutions. 'But the harm is done, Tommy.

Nugent visited the parish and announced at all the Masses that he was withdrawing him from the ministry. You can't clear your name after that. But sure what did the Church ever care about us?'

I go to the Jameson bottle at the weekend, yet I know full well where that leads. Working for two bishops over thirty years, I have seen priests – and indeed bishops – who had gone too far out and would stare at me with defeated eyes or turn away when I tried to talk to them about their drinking. Easy for my doctor, however, to issue prescriptions. She doesn't have to live in an old Georgian house surrounded by stone walls, a field away from the nearest neighbour.

2

I BEGIN CLOSE TO THE END. In my room in All Saints Seminary, one Sunday morning last September, I am mulling over a way to defend a priest whom Nugent wants expelled from the diocese. While on a parish holiday to Italy, the priest had been caught in bed with a married woman; her husband is claiming that the priest has ruined his marriage, and is talking about suing the diocese. 'Do your best for me,' the priest pleads. 'I'm no saint, I know, but I was hitting the bottle then. Big time, Tom.'

'I'll do my best,' I say.

The phone interrupts my trawl through his file.

'Monsignor Galvin,' the operator says, 'a call for you from London.'

'Thanks, Eamon.' I can hear M.J. clearing his throat. 'Are you busy, Tommy? I want a word.'

'Fire away.'

Through the window I can see Nugent below me pacing around by the fountain at the centre of the cloister. With him are the two other priests who, with me, form his kitchen cabinet: Father Henry Plunkett and the lanky cut of Father Vinny Lynch, known since his student days as Dr Hackenbush from the way he boasted about the three generations of doctors in his family. 'Here cometh Dr Hackenbush,' said a college wag one day while students were idling by the tennis courts.

'Did you see the papers?' M.J.'s voice sounds more gravelly with the passing years.

'Not yet.'

'I'm called to appear at the Heaslip Tribunal.'

'Sorry to hear that.'

'The Revenue are claiming I had an offshore account. Sure I left all that to Seery. I didn't know half the time where my money was going. That's what I was paying that bastard for. They've nothing on me.'

'No, absolutely not.' Soothing words come easily after years of listening to cries for understanding.

'I'll be over in Dublin for a few days. We might meet for a bite.'

'Sure.'

'Brownes on Thursday, one-ish.'

My day for golf, but I say, 'Right. See you there.'

I watch Nugent ambling back towards the college. He was once regarded as the most handsome-looking man in the diocese, with prospects of a diplomatic career at the Vatican. When he was a student at Maynooth College, girls from the village used to attend the public Mass just to gape at him. Now he wears a hangdog look – the visible effect of his fights with what he considers to be a world out of kilter. Plunkett's head is tilted in a listening pose, and Lynch is throwing a tennis ball for Caesar, the bishop's Alsatian.

True to form, M.J. gets off the phone as soon as he's got what he wanted. He makes a passing reference to the Church's difficulties. 'You've a lot on your plate. I see another unfortunate on TV last night.'

'Hard times, M.J., but we'll pull through.'

'I hope so. Thursday then.'

I put down the phone and glance at the empty cloister. Once, when the seminary was full, this time on a Sunday was special. A few of us who taught theology sorted out our lecture notes for the following week and then met before lunch for a gin and tonic.

Since the last student was ordained two years ago, my work consists of attending the bishops' meetings in Maynooth, advising Nugent on moral issues and hearing priests' grievances in the front parlour of the bishop's house. And unless they ask specifically to see Nugent, I listen to their confusion about a world that is banging the front door in their faces.

Ever since the seminary closed eight years ago, we have Sunday lunch in the bishop's house. Standing defiantly on top of a hill, and across the main driveway to All Saints, this granite miniature of a Roman palazzo had been built towards the end of the nineteenth century. Sometimes visiting bishops or cardinals from Italy or Germany, or theologians on the lookout for a mitre, join us for the meal; this Sunday we are on our own.

After Nugent has blessed the food in Latin, his valet, standing at the sideboard, lifts the lid off the soup tureen, releasing a cloud of steam.

'Tom,' Nugent says as he removes his napkin from its silver ring, 'you didn't manage a walk. Lovely out today, thank God. Indian Summer.'

'I'll take a stroll by the river later.'

The media becomes the object of his rage once again. 'That wretch on the television distorted my words,' Nugent is saying in reference to an interview he has given. Behind him on the wall is the broad figure of the smiling Pope and himself in a double handshake.

'She doorstepped you that day you were flying to Rome.' Vinny Lynch fusses around the table filling wine glasses. 'I can't for the life of me understand what has got into these people who are bent on destroying our Church.'

'Power,' says Plunkett, 'that's what they want. And they're ashamed of being Catholic.'

I too make agreeable sounds. Like supporting actors in a long-running play, each of us knows when to speak our lines. Lynch fidgets with his knife and fork; Plunkett parrots the bishop's dissatisfaction about young people not going to Mass and drinking to excess – too much money and no discipline.

When his anger has spent itself, Nugent revisits the good old days when he had been a professor at the national seminary and six hundred students filled the chapel every Sunday for morning Mass.

After a couple of glasses of Chardonnay, I am able to flow with the tide, and nod like Plunkett as if hearing all this for the first time. The bishop's valet serves our coffee and we relax in the delicious aftertaste of good food and wine. Then small talk until I excuse myself: I have to work on files and take that walk by the river. They understand.

And each of us follows the time-worn habit for Sunday. The bishop will go for his siesta, a Roman custom since his student days at the Collegio Irlandese. Vinny Lynch will walk Caesar, and then visit his maiden aunt for tea and scones. Plunkett will disappear to the house he got at a cut-price from an old woman he used to visit with Communion every Friday.

In my room I search through the Sunday newspapers until I come across the piece on the Heaslip Tribunal, and, right at the centre, photos of my brother M.J.: one taken nearly twenty years ago at Fairyhouse Racecourse; beside him, Donaghy, the government minister, who has also been called to give evidence. In a panel at one side, a journalist had resurrected a piece about a farm near Naas when M.J. was accused of bribing Donaghy, through his bagman, Seery, to have the land rezoned. That case fell through for want of evidence. The headline spells it out: 'Multi-millionaire has questions to answer.'

I read the opening paragraph:

One of Ireland's most successful builders will appear at the Heaslip Tribunal during the coming week. Mr M.J. Galvin, who left his native Kerry in 1952 for London, is a self-made man, and has been carrying out major building contracts both here and in Britain: one such contract was an extension to Heathrow Airport. Mr Galvin has been summoned to give evidence about one of his companies, Ardglass Trust, and its connection with a Cayman Islands bank account.

At the bottom of the page are more pictures of M.J.'s house in Terenure and of housing estates he had built around Dublin and County Meath.

I put down the newspaper and stare through the window. Instead of the empty cloister, another theatre spreads out before me. Laughing crowds are romping outside Quex Road Church in north London during Sunday Mass; hands are clutching shillings and half-crowns, and reaching out above the milling crowd towards the stalls that sell the *Donegal Democrat*, the *Connacht Tribune* and other provincial papers. I see M.J.'s roguish smile and shock of wavy hair, girls in flared summer frocks and mother-of-pearl necklaces. The music of Brendan Bowyer and the Royal Showband is streaming through the open doors of the Galtymore Ballroom.

3

M.J. SENDS A CHEQUE the year I do my Leaving Certificate – Barclays Bank in copperplate print – with a note attached: 'Travel like the swanks – get a flight from Shannon.' In the boarding school, also paid for by copperplate Barclay, I keep the cheque in my locker, beneath a 45 record: Ray Peterson's 'Tell Laura I Love Her'. My future is secure: I would go on to study engineering at the university and then join M.J. in the firm. He had been in London for nine years and already was employing over a hundred men, and had bought a pub on Kilburn High Road.

When the neighbours in Ardglass see our new house going up, they satisfy their jealousy by spreading the rumour that when M.J. is clearing away bombed-out buildings, he helps himself to safes and jewellery. 'Far away from boarding schools and two-storey houses the Galvins were reared. Only the crows nesting in the thatch.' My father is still trying to get the feel of the new house and never uses the toilet, preferring instead to chuck his coat over his back and hunker near a hedge behind the cowhouse. 'Go by boat, Tomásheen,' he tells me, 'you'll see what's happening to this oul country of ours with all this emigration.'

The morning I leave, we have to squeeze our way to the ticket office at the railway station.

'Make sure you don't lose Hanna's address, Peg,' a woman says to a girl of about sixteen or seventeen who is crying openly.

'No, Ma, I won't.'

'And talk to a priest if you need anything.'

They kiss on the lips, the girl rushes for an open door of the train and disappears inside, dragging her case behind her. Without looking back, the woman gathers about her three other children who are sobbing loudly, and shepherds them out of the station. With belts or twine around their suitcases, a gang of men makes a noisy entrance: they laugh loudly and jostle their way through the crowd, one or two are carrying hurley-sticks. Dressed in the faded jacket of the Local Defence Force, a boy with a forlorn look stands near the Eason's kiosk. His shovel blade is wrapped in old newspaper; beside him stands an elderly woman in a black shawl. They are silent, except when, now and again, the woman looks up at him and speaks; he nods and throws a hooded glance around the station, a sheepish grin on his face.

My mother talks to the girl at the hatch and returns with a ticket. 'Put that in a safe place,' she says, and buries her hands deep in the pockets of her coat – a relic of her days in America. As an only child, she had to return from Chicago and look after the four cows when her father died in the County Home. 'Wasn't I the fool to bring that drunkard into this house, instead of going back to America for myself?' became her lament whenever my father returned maudlin from a fair and had to be put to bed.

Now he is greeting people he has never seen before. 'Soon there won't be anyone left to bury us,' he jokes with a porter.

'Old stock,' says the porter, taking a pocket watch from his waistcoat, 'same every week. We're losing the flower of the crop. Nothing here for the poor devils.'

'Look out for yourself over there.' My mother turns to me. 'My poor son Mossie would be alive only for that place.' At every opportunity she blames M.J. for persuading another brother to join him in England: Mossie disappeared one rainy night in Kentish Town, and was found floating in the Thames a week later. 'Death consistent with a severe beating to the head' was the coroner's report. Our neighbours in Ardglass got a different version: Mossie had slipped and fallen off a ladder. There was no mention of the row he had started earlier that night in a pub.

'I'd better be getting a seat,' I say.

My father begins to sob: 'Goodbye, my son. Write to us.'

'I will.'

'Phone Eily,' my mother is already tightening the scarf around her head, 'and tell her to keep an eye on that sister of hers.' Even now, she won't relax the bitter tone when she talks of my sister Pauline, who ran from the convent and joined Eily to train as a nurse in Leeds.

'I'll be back in no time. Sure I'm only going for three months.'

'Don't let him work you too hard.' Her handshake is hard and dry.

'No. Goodbye so.'

As the carriages begin to shunt, plumes of smoke fill the station, and a guard's whistle pierces the sad air; my father waves and hobbles along the platform. A mournful cry rises from the girls I had seen earlier. Caring little for those around her, the woman with the shawl screams through the open window. 'Come back, Mike, if 'tis too much for you. You'll never be short of a bite at home, boy.' Her voice breaks and she lets out a pitiful cry: 'You'll always have a roof over your head as long as I'm alive, d'you hear me, Mike boy.'

Her son casts aside his wary look and calls out: 'I hear you, Mam. Goodbye so, and I'll be back at Christmas. Mind yourself.' He is calling so loud to his mother, a vein stands out at the side of his neck.

Sunlight floods the carriage as the train gains the open countryside. The clatter of a horse-drawn mowing machine catches the attention of the men with the hurley-sticks. Now they stand in the corridor, swaying to the train's regular motion; they have bottles of Guinness they had brought with them. 'No more slavin' for oul John Farmer anyway,' says one, indicating the half-cut meadow. Fragments of their conversation reach me. 'An uncle in Wallesey – a subbie.' And for the first time, I hear the password: 'He'll give you *the start.* Ask for *the start* – you'll find him at The Lion's Head in the Whitecliff Road. He has the shout.'

We are packed so tightly together that when the train jolts, we lurch as one; across from me a middle-aged man wearing a tweed cap and a black tie is in conversation with a young woman: their knees are touching. 'Lemass and his crowd up there in the Dáil are doing nothing for the likes of us who have to take the boat.' He had been over for a friend's funeral in Abbeyfeale: 'No shuttering – the trench caved in.' He takes out a packet of Sweet Afton and offers one to the woman, who holds the cigarette in a clumsy way and coughs when she inhales.

'That's Irish subbies for you – saving money. Man, mind thyself.' He draws on the cigarette.

'And woman likewise.'

Each station repeats what we have already seen: girls in high heels, and scarves patterned with the Rock of Cashel and the Lakes of Killarney, lean against older women before they join us; men with peaked caps stand on the platform staring at us, and turn away when the train begins to move off with their children.

I stay out on deck as the boat pulls away from the North Wall. Others I had seen on the train are fixed on the receding harbour. A cluster of girls are crying, their arms loosely around each other. The youth with the shovel scans the shoreline with brooding eyes.

In the lounge, the air is heavy with smoke and the faint smell of cattle rising from the hold. Around the tables, covered with glasses and empty bottles, groups are singing raucously.

> *You'll get no promotion this side of the ocean,*
> *So cheer up me lads bless them all.*

'Up Dev.'
'Fuck Dev.'

'*Fuck 'em all, the long and the short and the tall.*

An accordion player starts up, and a small man sings 'The Green Glens of Antrim'. They shout for more. By now some of the young women have dried their eyes; one or two are sitting on men's laps. As one might with a child, a man is rocking a girl on his knees and singing:

> *Speed, bonny boat, like a bird on the wing;*
> *Onward, the sailors cry:*
> *Carry the lad that's born to be king*
> *Over the sea to Skye.*
> *Loud the waves howl, loud the waves …*

He is nestling his face in her hair; they are both laughing. Sitting on his own, the youth still guards his shovel, and out of a canvas bag he takes a bottle of milk and a sandwich – two thick slices of bread with wedges of bacon between them. Slowly and deliberately, as though lost in thought, he removes the soggy paper cork and puts the bottle to his lips. He takes stock of his surroundings and bites into the sandwich.

A man with a Guinness bottle lying idle in his strong hand makes room for me; his foot taps to the rhythm of the music and he speaks without taking his eyes off the singer.

'Your first time, boy?'

'Yeah.'

'A well-fed lad like you will get work, no bother, but you'll be hardened by John Lang before many moons.' He stands and puts a hand on my shoulder: 'Stay away from the Irish subbie, unless you're badly stuck. They'd drag the heart and soul out of you, boy.' He indicates a suitcase at his feet: 'Mind that for me, boybawn. I'll be back soon.'

I pick up a newspaper that lies on the slatted bench. Yvonne de Carlo is smiling out at me, her curves stretching a low-cut dress. *Nine out of ten film stars like me use Lux Toilet Soap.* Five Sligo men have been fined at Bury St Edmund's Crown Court for starting a row over a barmaid outside The Jolly Roger. A youth from Cavan is recovering in St Andrew's Hospital. The judge fined each of the men £10 or three months in prison. 'Let this be a lesson for your countrymen,' he said. 'This is a civilized country. You come over here and behave like hooligans. Whatever you do over there, you'll most certainly not do in my jurisdiction.'

The man who hates Irish subbies returns, picks up his suitcase, throws his gabardine over his shoulder and peers through a porthole. 'It'll be dark soon,' he announces. 'When you see daylight again, boybawn, we'll be on our way to Euston. Take a fool's advice: look for factory work, boy, and go to school. Plenty of them in England. The Irish would skin you.'

By now the accordion player is silent; girls are asleep on the benches, their heads resting on each others' shoulders. A stale smell of porter is lingering in the night air. I had reserved a bunk, so I decide to hit the sack as tiredness sets in, but first I climb up on deck for a last look. In the distance, a knot of people are gathered around a woman who is holding the railing with one hand while she sings; a man with a cap is sitting on a suitcase and playing soft and low on the fiddle. Some have bottles of stout in their hands; all are silhouetted against light from the ferry. I move closer. The woman's face and tangled brown hair glisten with spray while she sings to the dark sky. Her coat is thrown open by the wind; her breasts rise and fall with the rhythm of her breathing:

> *Oh, well do I remember the year of '48.*
> *When Irishmen, with feeling bold, will rally one and all …*

A couple have their arms around each other while the boat cuts through the water like a scythe through young grass.

> *I'll be the man to lead the van beneath the flag of green,*
> *When loud and high we'll raise a cry – Revenge for*
>   *Skibbereen.*

Later, dozing in my bunk, I can still hear the plaintive music of the fiddle player above the steady sound of the boat and the occasional bellow from the exiled cattle down in the hold.

At some time in the night, I become aware of cigarette smoke; men are talking in the cabin.

'A young fella, out of the nest,' one of them says.

'Always a first time.'

I hear the sound of shoes hitting the floor and belt buckles brushing against a bunk frame. 'I wouldn't mind givin' a first time to that fine heifer from Wexford.' Someone strikes a match. More cigarette smoke. 'She's goin' to Manchester – herself and the other two – to be nurses.'

'Majella from New Ross can nurse me anytime.'

I drift off again and am woken by a nudge on the shoulder.

'Get up, young lad, we've landed in Liverpool.'

Beneath the lamps that line the quay, we hurry for the train; men with tousled hair and shirts carelessly open down the front shout 'Up the Republic' until someone says to keep quiet or we'll all be deported.

Then the drowsy journey to Euston – yawning, stretching and the smell of cigarettes; the rustle of chocolate wrapping paper and sleepy throwaways about the size of fields. The train rattles on from one town to the next: street after street of red-brick, people making tea in their kitchens. Then the open country again.

4

AS THE GREY LIGHT OF MORNING gradually fills the carriage, the train rattles its way into London. With much hissing and releasing of steam and grinding metal, it comes to a halt at Euston. A big round clock with Roman numerals shows the time to be at a couple of minutes after six. Doors are thrown open. I join the flow heading for the exit: faces from yesterday, from a faraway land. The girls have renewed their lipstick; some of the men have put on neckties – a few carry bundles wrapped in brown paper.

The high arched roof amplifies the shunting and clanging of other trains in the vast station. Men with loud Cockney accents are pushing trolleys loaded with the morning news-papers along the platforms, the iron wheels of the trolleys grating on the concrete. Near the exit, a priest is standing on a stool and is talking nineteen to the dozen about work and lodgings to a group who had been on the train from Liverpool. They are handing him scraps of paper and he is giving directions about buses and the Underground; all the while his hands are gesturing rapidly. At the edge of the crowd and straining to hear is the youth with the shovel.

'You must be Tommy.'

I turn to see a woman in a tight-fitting black dress and high heels.

'I'm Bonnie Doyle, a friend of your brother.' Gold bangles jingle when we shake hands.

'How did you know me?'

'A chip off the old block. And then the elbow patches – sure sign of a student.' Her perfume softens the bitter smoke from the trains. 'M.J.'s caught up in a cable-laying job out in Putney, so you'll have to do with me.'

A burst of laughter erupts from the group who are listening to the priest.

'Father John,' she says with a wave of her hand, 'never fails to get a job or a place to stay for anyone off the boat. Come over and meet him.'

The group is thinning out; a couple of men are talking into the priest's ear while he writes in a notebook. His whole body is restless.

When they have gone, Bonnie approaches him. 'Harty, shouldn't you be in your bed.'

'Bonnie, girl,' he straightens, and puts the notebook in the side pocket of his jacket, a playful look on his round face. 'No rest for the wicked, you ought to know that.' He slips an arm around her waist, and winks at me, gestures very different from the priests in my boarding school – gaunt, and walking the grounds with measured steps.

'This is Tommy, M.J. Galvin's young brother,' she says. 'Over to help the boss.'

'Wise move, Tommy. You'll be rolling in it in no time. Welcome to London.'

'Thanks, Father.'

'John. My name is John.' His blue eyes are dancing. 'You're lucky to have a tour guide like herself here.' Again he is drawing her close; this time tickling her so that she laughs loudly, and tries to wriggle out of his hold. 'I never had anyone to look after me when I came here.'

'Oh, go on.' She nudges with her hip.

Two young men rush up to him. They have just come off the train; one has a tattered piece of paper: 'Where's the Seven Sisters Road, Father?'

'Where're you from, lads?'

'Askeaton.'

'Know it well.' He talks to them about work and digs and

directions to the Seven Sisters Road. We leave with a promise to meet some night at the Irish Centre in Camden Town.

Outside the station the air is warm and grey and rumbles with the sound of London. Bonnie has parked her Mini Austin beneath a hoarding: a giant Yeoman of the Guard in bright red offers me a glass of Beefeater's Gin. A transit van with Murphy printed on the side is parked by a footpath where men in navy dungarees are digging a trench; taxis, lorries, black Ford and Hillman cars fill the morning with the heavy smell of oil.

On the way to M.J.'s house in Chiswick, Bonnie gives me a potted account of her life: left Athenry at seventeen, worked as a chambermaid in different London hotels – The Imperial, The Royal and The Grosvenor. While there, she attended a catering college, eventually becoming one of the assistants to the manager at The Victoria in Holloway. 'I'd the misfortune to meet that brother of yours in the Galtymore one night,' she says while we are stopped at a junction.

M.J.'s house gives no indication of his growing wealth; like all the others in the reserved street, it has the standard bay window at the front; the walls are half redbrick, half pebbledash. 'An old army officer owned it along with fifty acres at the back,' Bonnie says as she pulls up into the driveway. 'He has to get the borough council on his side for permission to build houses, but that man' – she stretches for her handbag in the back seat – 'he always gets his way.'

After she has gone to work, I lie on my bed and drift off with London fading in my head. When I awake to the smell of frying and the click of smart footsteps from somewhere below, the room has grown dim. In the slanting sun, I survey the slated rooftops at the back, the fifty-acre field so level and well-trimmed and stretching away into the distance; suddenly, the noise of a heavy engine invades my thoughts.

When I go downstairs, M.J. is holding the newel post for balance while he removes a pair of clay-encrusted boots. He is tanned, and his wavy mop is sun-bleached.

'Bonnie look after you?'

'Yeah, she did. Great.'

Settling into the habit of each other, we talk about the good spell of weather in Ireland and how, if it continues, the neighbours will have the turf out of Hogan's bog by July. Then we take refuge in the crossing to Liverpool.

'You should've taken a flight. Anyone would say I'm a miser. How're they at home?'

'Fine.'

'The girls were down for a couple of days. Pauline is' – he glances towards the kitchen and lowers his voice – 'she's well. Yeah, she's fine now. Ah, too much life in Pauline for places like convents.'

He talks while he washes in a small toilet beneath the stairs and then brings me to meet his housekeeper. 'Vera makes the best bacon and cabbage in London. Home away from home. She'll be a mother to you.' He winks behind her back.

'Enough of that, Mr Galvin. In here both of you.' She sashays ahead of us and indicates the open door of a room where a table has been set.

'You want to work with the men,' he says. 'Sure, why don't you take a rest after all the studying?' His shoulder muscles stretch the white shirt and he gives the impression of someone who is always at the starting blocks. 'Take a holiday, why don't you? – wander around London. Fine city, although God knows I haven't had time to see much of it. "Have you been to Covent Garden, Mr Galvin, or up to Stratford?" says one of them smart-alecky bastards of town planners to me one day … . What's at Stratford, Tommy?'

'Shakespeare plays.'

'Oh. Is that all?'

He takes a potato from the willow-patterned dish. 'Go up to Leeds to see the girls.'

'I will, but I'd prefer to do a bit of work first.'

'Long enough you'll be working on the site … . How's himself?'

'The same.'

'Any sign of the new apples yet?'

We laugh at a shared memory.

' "Come out till ye see the size of these lads".' He mimics our father's excitement every September, when we were all expected to look in amazement as he picked a handful of crab apples off the tree at the side of the house. ' "Look at them, did ye ever see the like a' them"?'

' "Never. No never".'

' "I'll bet ye the big people," ' pointing up the hill towards Healys' mansion, "I'll bet ye oul Matty with his orchard and his pear trees won't have as good as them this year." '

' "No, he won't." '

Then, to fall in with his high spirits, we would bite into the crab apples and suffer the bitter juices while we chewed, and tried to swallow.

Occasionally, our mother, if she were slackening her grim hold on life, stood at the door and looked at us all, shaking her head and grinning.

'Mammy, come here and see the lovely apples,' was enough to send her back into the house, muttering that she had more to do than listen to nonsense.

' "We'll make money out of them this year, ye'll see. People in town make lovely apple pies out of them." '

' "We will, Da, we'll make money out of them this year." '

M.J. is doing another take-off. ' "That crab tree. D'ye see the shelter it gives to the house. Wouldn't a fella pay any money for shelter like that?" '

' "Oh, he would. Great shelter." '

'The trouble was,' says M.J., 'he believed they *were* apples.'

5

FOR A FEW DAYS I learn the different Tube lines, take in the cold glances of the teeming masses, laze around Piccadilly and Trafalgar Square, throw scraps to the pigeons, and take stock of red buses, Buckingham Palace, and policemen on horseback. Delighting in the sweet taste of freedom, I scramble to the shops on Charing Cross Road for books that are banned at home: *Room at the Top*, *Saturday Night and Sunday Morning*, *The Catcher in the Rye*. One wet afternoon I sidle off to see Sophia Loren in a long-running film called *Two Women* showing in a small cinema off Leicester Square. And all the while M.J. is coming and going from the house, leaving messages for Vera that he won't be in for his dinner. When he does turn up, he devours his steak, or bacon and cabbage, wipes the plate clean with a crust of bread, then out the door again. I become accustomed to the heavy throb of the jeep pulling up in front of the garage in the small hours of the morning. Even when he is on time for the evening meal, he has to answer phone calls from subcontractors about prices for roofing or bricks in Finchley or Milton Keynes. Rolled up maps and drawings lie on the hallstand and on armchairs.

Once or twice I wake to the sound of muffled voices, and after a moment, make out Bonnie's stifled laugh. In the morning they have gone, and through the half-open door of his bedroom, I notice the black dress she had worn when she collected me at Euston; nylons are draped across the back of a chair.

Towards the end of the week, I am ready to begin. 'And I'll move out tomorrow so that I'll be near the pick-up point,' I tell him while he gulps down his breakfast.

'But I can run you there.'

'Ah, no. Easier if I stay at The Highway.'

'That place can be a rough house at times. Will you be able to sleep?'

'No bother.'

'Come here for the weekends. You'll have a bit of peace. They can be noisy bastards.'

'Right so.'

'I'll get Sandra the barmaid to make your dinner every evening.'

Despite his protest, I feel he is relieved. He would be saved the bother of driving me to Kilburn in the mornings when he needed to be out at Dunstable or High Wycombe. And Bonnie wouldn't have to suppress her giggles when they returned late at night.

Soon after five o'clock the following Monday morning we drive in the jeep to Camden Town. At Swiss Cottage, the traffic gets heavy: in black Vauxhalls with gleaming fenders, solemn-faced men in stiff collars and ties hold a firm grip on the world.

Camden Town is a cattle fair. The footpaths swarm with men in baggy trousers, and shirts hanging loose: they are slamming the doors of trucks, rushing across the street, shouting – it's uncanny to hear Irish accents in these foreign streets.

Red hairs stand out on the back of M.J.'s powerful forearm when he points towards a convoy of lorries parked on one side of Mornington Crescent: 'Green Murphy,' he says, 'and over there towards the Kentish Town Road, Pateen Lowry's gang from Connemara.' He steers towards a kerb and parks.

Men are spilling out of cafés, mixing with those who are standing in a ragged line. Some are slouching against the front of the Westminster Bank and Dolphin's Hardware. Many are over six feet tall; they walk with long loping strides and give the impression of untamed energy. Others leaf through the *Daily Mirror* and keep a baleful eye on the world. 'The same every morning,' M.J. says. 'Close on three hundred men; you wouldn't be long saving hay in the Hill Field with a few of them lads.'

One or two, wearing creased shirts and loose ties, shout to get into the fucken trucks, that they have to go out to Leighton Buzzard. The men have a ruffled look: dried clay on their turned-down wellingtons or hobnailed boots. A thickset man is walking up and down inspecting a queue of men; he looks mostly at their shoes; every now and then, he lifts his cap and wipes his bald crown with a piece of navy cloth.

'I've to check these fellas,' M.J. says and hops out. 'Stay as you are 'til we're ready to go.'

Across the street is a line of trucks with Galvin Construction on the driver's door; some of these M.J. had bought from the army. A man sidles up to him, rubbing his hands: 'Any chance of *the start*, M.J.?'

'Where were you until now?' He is hurrying away so that the man has to follow.

'Wimpy. Up near Manchester. A bypass job.'

M.J. studies him. 'You were with us last year; you let us down.' He begins to move off again.

'The oul lad died, M.J. I had to go back home.'

M.J. hesitates. 'Hop on one of the wagons. Report to Batt Muldoon.'

'You're a dacent man, M.J.'

'Dacent my arse. If you let me down again, you're finished.' He turns back, makes a pistol with his hand, and cocks it towards the man.

They both grin. 'Thanks, oul stock.' The man rubs his mouth in a shy gesture, and like many men who are self-conscious about their height, walks with a slight stoop to the nearest army truck where others are sitting in two rows. Down the road, boys are jumping in the air and kicking around a paper football, jostling each other for possession.

'Come on here,' M.J. shouts. 'I'll give you plenty to tire you out behind the mixer.' They desert the ball like schoolboys and climb into one of the trucks. Above the thud of their boots, a big red-faced man with a head of black hair shouts abuse at them. Did they think they had all the fucken day? Such a crowd of lazy fuckers he'd never met in all his life.

M.J. returns.

'Who's your man?' I ask.

He follows my gaze.

'That's the one and only Batt Muldoon – Horse Muldoon, as he's known all over London.'

The smile fades. 'There's trouble at Reading. Some hothead floored a ganger. I'll have to get out there. Will you go with Jody to Stevenage? You'll see how they lay the cables.' Already he is striding along the footpath where a sandy-haired man in a lumberjacket stands near the door of a Transit. I get out of the jeep and follow.

Jody's casual smile and easy manner is a contrast to the commotion. His handshake – a surprising gesture of courtesy – is at odds with the rough-and-tumble, the shifting of gears, the smoke and the heavy smell of diesel as the trucks pass.

'So you're goin' to study engineering.' He is keeping a peeled eye on the trucks.

'That's my plan.'

'You'll have it made.'

A muffled rise and fall of voices comes from the back of the van. 'The trade is booming now. London needs flats and houses, and Paddy is the man to build them.' He has to raise his voice to be heard. 'Will you join the firm when you qualify?'

'Yeah. That's probably what I'll do.'

We drive behind Horse Muldoon and slow down again after a few hundred yards on the Inverness Road where another group of men stands waiting. Horse hops out of the wagon and, shouting at the top of his voice, bundles the men into the back, his arms raised like a demented herdsman. He whips a newspaper out of a young fellow's back pocket: 'Is it for readin' the fucken newspapers you came to England, lad? Into the fucken truck or you'll find yourself back in the bog, or up to your arsehole in rushes.' He keeps on roaring as they clamber into the wagon, like cattle for the market. 'We've trenches to dig out in fucken Stevenage.' He looks over towards us, winks at Jody and lopes up to the van, wiping perspiration from his glistening forehead with the sleeve of his jacket. 'You've a helper today, Jody.'

'M.J.'s brother, Tommy. Here for the summer.'

His mood softens. 'Ah, good man. Learning the ropes, boy.' Yellowed buckteeth show when he grins, and the smell of stale sweat reaches me when he leans into the van. But I am forgotten while they talk about shuttering and sub-stations and a new dumper that should have been delivered the day before. Jody goes to check with another foreman about the cable-pull at Stevenage. The cable-pull, as I later learn, is a special event requiring extra help: men enticed the night before by the sight of a roll of notes appearing out of Horse Muldoon's pocket in The Highway.

Two red-haired youths are jumping to tip a barber's pole down the street, but when they spot Horse getting into the wagon, they run to him. Above the sound of the engine, one of the youths calls out in a pleading tone, 'Mr Muldoon, give us *the start*. We only came over yesterday.'

With one arm resting across the open window, Horse looks back at them: 'Hah, only yesterday.' An ugly grimace shows on his face.

'Mr Muldoon, give us *the start*. We're from Tourmakeady.'

'Hop up so, lads,' says Horse, but the wagon is gaining speed. The youths break into a trot. One of them manages to get a hand on the tailgate and tries to gain a foothold, but he slips and falls, tearing the knee of his trousers. The other youth goes back and drags him along. A milk van ahead has slowed them down, so they catch up. Again they try to climb the tailgate, but fail.

'Yerra lads,' shouts Horse, 'ye'er not able for this work. Too much cabbage water in Tourmakeady.'

Those in the back guffaw, someone flicks a cigarette butt that barely misses one of the youths. Horse's arm disappears inside the cab, comes into view again as he throws a few copper coins in the air and drives off.

Blood oozes from the youth's knee; downcast, he limps to

the footpath and rests against the wall. The other youth stands glaring after the wagon.

When Jody returns, I tell him what has happened. 'That's Horse.' He shakes his head and turns on the ignition. 'Don't worry about them. They'll get taken on by some subbie, if they're any good. No shortage of work in this town.'

At Stevenage we stop behind the other wagons and I take in a sight that is to become commonplace that first summer in London. All along Albert Grove is a mound of earth, and beside it a trench that stretches to the top of the road and disappears around the corner. Doors and tailgates rattle, and, with a thud of shovels and pickaxes on the mustard clay, the crew set to work.

Horse resumes his shouting: 'Am I payin' you to scratch your arses? Down there, boy, and start diggin',' he bellows as he strides towards a giant spool of cable.

Jody rummages in a shelf beside the steering column, throwing aside screwdrivers, pieces of wire and a torch. Eventually his groping fingers find a bulky notebook that hits off the gear lever as he draws it from the pile. A sheaf of ten-pound notes spills onto the floor. He looks at me for a second and gathers up the fallout. 'I've to see this gaffer from the borough council. I'll be back in a while. There's a park near here if you want to stretch your legs.' He nods in the direction of a bald man in a tweed jacket and well-pressed flannel trousers, who is leaning over the edge of the trench, making sure to pick his steps as he does an inspection. Every few yards he stretches a metal measuring tape across the top of the trench.

Jody ambles towards him; they shake hands and speak for a while, looking down at the trench, before they cross the road to a green Vauxhall where the bald man lays out a map on the car.

Farther up the road, two men are straining to unwind cable from the spool on a wooden stand. Grunting and swearing, the trenchers pull the leaden cable like a tug-of-war team, one behind the other.

'Pull you fuckers!' Horse roars. He pushes aside a youth and, with a lot of bluster about what he wouldn't do if he was ten years younger, joins the team of trenchers. 'Look, that's how you pull. Use your fucken legs, boy; take the strain!'

I get out of the van for a closer look. The men heave the cable as far as a sub-station and then a man in navy dungarees connects the end with another cable by means of a metal sleeve that screws one section into the other.

Ahead of the spool, in a haze of sunshine, a line of men, some stripped to the waist, are digging into the earth. Every time they raise a pickaxe, the muscles ripple in their backs and then slacken when the pickaxe comes down with a dull sound. Close by, a man is knocking chunks out of the concrete with a jackhammer so that the hedges and the rows of maples are covered in a chalky dust and the mannerly neighbourhood is now a harsh mixture of grating sounds above the steady beat of the generator.

Self-conscious about idling in the face of their back-breaking work, I hurry up the road as if with a purpose. A ganger is marking with chalk the amount each man has to dig that day. I take a side road to the left, leaving behind the rattle of the jackhammer, and the swearing of the men.

'Who's he?' someone asks.

'Who?'

'The young lad with Jody.'

'Galvin's brother. He's in some college.'

'Out of our fucken sweat, I suppose.'

The thumping and the banter of the men fade as I go deeper into the estate with its prim box hedges and manicured gardens. A man in a straw hat is talking to his marmalade cat. Next door another man is reversing a gleaming Austin Cambridge out of his driveway. Wearing a floral apron and bed slippers, a woman calls to him: 'Don't forget the chutney from Bateman's, Philip.'

'No, dear.'

'And the mint sauce.'

'See you, love.' 'Philip' waves and returns to his driving. She throws me a suspicious glance and, when she closes the door, the drop leaf falls with a hostile clatter.

The road leads to a public park, where a man is running a mower over a bowling green, leaving uniform swathes on the trimmed surface behind him. Mindful of the hum of the mower and the scent of fresh grass, I sit on a bench and open one of my banned books, which I had hidden from the men, and read until the sun is high in the sky. In the distance, men in whites are standing on a clubhouse veranda; some are resting on deckchairs and sipping out of teacups. I mark my book and return to the trenchers.

'Pull, Leitrim! Fuck it, you're leavin' it all to me,' I hear Horse long before I get back.

'I'm pullin'.'

'Yes, too much fucken pullin' and too much thinkin' about them whores over in Richmond Street.'

The coarse snort when he laughs shows that Horse is in control. They pull with all their might, knowing that his word determines whether they can buy steaks and pints when they hop off the lorries at Kilburn High Road later on.

A smell of cooking is heavy in the air. A youth with a long-handled fork is turning sausages and chops. The frying pan — the sawn-off base of a tar barrel — rests on a brazier.

Clouds of smoke and dust have formed a haze above the men in the trenches. They are silent now, saving their strength for the work ahead as the sun beats down: dark patches of sweat stain the armpits of those who have kept on their shirts. Shovels of earth rise from the trench. 'Dig deep and throw it well back,' the ganger barks as he paces by the growing mound of earth.

Above the digging, and the creaking of the spool releasing its cable, a door slams across the road and a woman with a Helen Shapiro beehive trips down the driveway; her head in the air, she is dangling a coloured umbrella.

'Look,' says one of the lads who is guiding the cable out of the spool. Heads appear above the trench. 'A fine bit of stuff.' He does a curving motion with his hands to describe her figure and struts in imitation of her walk. The men guffaw: 'She wouldn't let you sniff it, boy.' But he pretends to go after her, unaware that Horse is stealing up behind him. One of the men tries to gain his attention by coughing, but the youth is too absorbed in his act to notice.

Horse grabs him by the hair. 'You want a ride, is that it? Go after her then. Go on. Can't you see you're holdin' up the work because of your dick.'

'But Batt … .' Wriggling like a fish at the end of a line, the youth catches hold of Horse's arm.

'No fucken excuses,' Horse snarls, swollen veins on his bull neck. 'Now fuck off outa here,' he gives him a kick up the backside, 'and don't look for work in this outfit again.'

One of the men has jumped out of the trench and is helping to get the spool moving, and, like fearstruck pupils, the rest bend over the cable, hauling it back and laying it on the track at their feet.

A safe distance away, the youth seems on the edge of bursting into tears, but he still puts on a face-saving act, and mutters about what his brothers won't do to Horse in the Crown that night. In a helpless rage, he whips his jacket off a load of shuttering planks and makes off down the road. When he is well away, he turns and shouts: 'You're only a fucken Roscommon gorilla – Galvin's fucken gorilla.' But Horse is now taken up with the cable-pull, watching the men straining and sweating and putting in an extra effort so that they too aren't given a kick up the backside, and have to make their own way to Camden Town. 'Jaysus,' Horse is shouting, 'is that all you've done since we started? Pull it. Come on, pull it.' The absurd grin on his face and the derisive snort are signals that his appetite for cruelty has now spent itself. He stands talking to one of the gangers and then lopes across the road, the pick-up dipping to one side when he throws himself into the driving seat.

Just as the cook is calling out in a Cockney accent: 'Right-eeo, food's up,' Jody returns in the Vauxhall with the man in the well-pressed flannels. The men fling down their pickaxes and shovels and stretch their backs, the spool comes to a halt and farther up the jackhammer goes silent. The dust settles. They gather round the load of timber shuttering and sit on the planks with plates of chops, sausages and roasted potatoes. One of them glances in my direction: 'What are you doin' on your own? Will you have a bite with us?'

'Right. I will so.' Even though Jody has mentioned that we might go to a café later on, I'm afraid a refusal would cause offence, so I'm handed a tin enamel plate and eat the sausages and chops. I remain at the edge of their small talk.

'Great weather for saving hay,' says one of the carpenters, as he shields his eyes from the sun.

'Ah fuck you and your hay,' comes the reply. 'All the farmers' sons can think about is savin' fucken hay.'

'Shag off and throw us over the loaf of bread,' says the farmer's son, settling himself on the load of timber.

The food has a calming effect. Some stretch out on the mound of earth, their peaked caps shading their eyes; others play cards on the wooden planks. Thoughts of Gaelic football and hurling matches in New Eltham, and women at the Galtymore give them a moment's release from drudgery, and Horse, and pulling cable. 'Bridie Gallagher and her band are coming to the Glocca Mora. You might get your bit, Nealie,' says a man to a lad beside him with a pimply face and spiky hair. 'Sure that young fella thinks 'tis for stirrin' his tay,' says another, rolling a cigarette between his callused hands. Nealie blushes and shows crooked teeth when he grins. They are only beginning to laze when the ganger blows a whistle and orders them into the fucken trenches, and is it fucken Butlin's they think they're in?

I help the cook to tidy up the plates. His silence gives me a chance to sort out the strange world of which I may one day be a part: the savage look on Horse's face, the suppressed tears and the put-on swagger of the lad he had brutalized, the indifference of the others.

Jody returns. 'Come over a minute, Tommy,' he calls from the open door of the van. 'You may as well get to know the ropes.'

He lays a map on the driver's seat. 'You see here.' A stout

finger runs along the paper, creased where it's been folded. 'This is the stretch of ducting and cable-laying for the Electricity Board.' He looks up and down the road and back to the map. 'This is Albert Grove, and we go around that corner up there.' He points towards a cloud of dust and smoke raised by the jackhammer. 'Down Nelson Avenue – about a half-mile of cabling. I had to convince that latchico from the borough council that there's hard rock for half that distance.' He looks at me and grins: 'Hard rock, more money. Are you with me? Three or four times the price for clay. No flies on Paddy.'

I force a laugh.

'He has to be looked after though.' He folds the map. 'That's how things are done around here. A few quid today and M.J. will put him and the family up in a good hotel in Killarney later on. It pays. He's mad for fishing, and thinks the Irish are great gas.'

'I'd say so.'

'A jungle, Tommy. Jungles have their own laws. The strongest always survive. D'you follow me?'

'I do.'

He winds a piece of string around the notebook and puts it back by the steering column. 'Now let me see. I've to go over to a site in Hitchin. You may as well come along. We'll be back to pick up the lads in the evening.' He switches the motor into life and Johnny and The Hurricanes fill the cab with 'Crossfire'.

On the way to Hitchin, Jody has a string of stories about grafting. It's the way things are done. If we don't do it, we'll be left behind. There's the haulage guy in Watling – a Mayo man – who makes his money out of selling the same load of sand or gravel three or four times in the one day.

'How?'

'I'll tell you how. It's simple. The lorry driver pulls into the site: "I have your sand, sign here." The usual. He doesn't unload, just drives around and out the other gap. An hour later he's back with the same load. Of course, your man at the gate has to be looked after.'

'Of course.'

At Hitchin, Jody pulls up at a gap in a whitethorn hedge: deep wheel tracks rock-hard on the passageway leading to the site – a field of over a hundred acres. Inside, the field is littered with scaffolding, mounds of topsoil, wheelbarrows, planks and loose bricks thrown alongside heaps of sand.

'A thousand houses to go up there,' Jody says. 'Wimpey got the job, but he subcontracted, so M.J. Galvin has two hundred and fifty.'

We get out of the van. Ahead of us are rows and rows of houses, at different stages of development, some only beginning, others at wall plate, and others with fresh timber beams ready for the roofers. Carpenters are hammering into struts and rafters. I wait while Jody disappears into the site office: a tunnel-shaped hut in the shelter of a row of sycamores. Two men are shovelling sand into a mixer. Another man slashes a bag of cement in two with his trowel – he grimaces and turns away while a cloud of dust rises into the air.

Down farther where the houses are more advanced, a man is mounting a ladder with a full hod of mortar on his shoulder; above him, two bricklayers are tapping bricks into line with the handle of their trowel. Jody appears at the door of the hut and beckons to me. 'Come in and meet this gangster,' he shouts. 'He'd make the Kray brothers look like the Legion of Mary.'

In the hut, a man with a few strands of hair stretched across his crown is barking about fucken sand being late, and what is he to do if it doesn't turn up in an hour.

'This young man is looking for *the start*,' Jody says.

'Better put him in Horse's crew then.'

'No,' he chuckles. 'I think he's had enough of Horse for one day.'

The sand arrives. The lorry driver stands at the door, and draws a pencil from behind his ear: 'Sign here, Pat,' he says to the site manager, who scrawls on the docket.

'What the fuck kept ye?' the site manager asks.

'I had another delivery to a site in Dunstable, hadn't I, mate.'

'Well, don't be late tomorrow.'

A dog-eared photo of the Cork hurling team is pinned to the wall. Beside it, stretching her plaid shirt and blue jeans to their limit, Jane Russell reclines on a bale of hay. And nearby is a group taken in front of the Lourdes Basilica; circled by a red biro is the site manager's glistening head.

The driver walks heavily down the ramp to his lorry. The site manager impales the docket on a spiked stack. 'That's the second time the fucker was late this week.'

'We won't need him much longer.' Jody rests his backside on the table that serves as a desk, 'The boss is buying a sand pit out in the West Country.'

'A whole pit?'

'He'll need it when the Heathrow job comes through.'

'A lot of shillings there,' says the site manager, and turns to me. 'This brother of yours will have his own bank soon.'

6

UNLESS HE IS WORKING LATE or trouble has cropped up at a site, M.J. drops into The Highway a few times a week to count the takings, around the time when Sandra the barmaid has finally succeeded in clearing the pub and is washing glasses by one of the amber globes. Most Friday nights I drive with him to Chiswick.

One night I help him take the bags of coin to the upstairs safe of The Highway, and in a silence broken only by the occasional shout from the street below, we arrange the notes in bundles for the bank. All the while, a succession of images is becoming a jumble in my brain: gangers shouting abuse and sacking lads who have failed to reach the chalk mark, sheaves of bank notes falling out of notebooks, and fishing holidays in Killarney. And despite my admiration for my brother, and indeed my indebtedness to him, I am now seeing the foul underbelly of his success.

While he is filling in a lodgement slip, I leave the table and saunter to one of the windows. Groups of men are still hanging around the street, washed clean after a downpour. Some are staggering, one makes a feeble attempt to snatch at women passing by, but they escape his clutches and, shrieking with excitement, click along in their high heels. A raucous version of 'Kevin Barry' reaches us:

> Lads like Barry are no cowards
> From the foe they will not fly
> Lads like Barry will free Ireland
> For her sake they'll live and die.

When he is finished, the singer looks up and down the street and shouts at the top of his voice: 'Up the Republic! Up the fucken Republic!' He flicks a cigarette butt on the pavement and slouches out of sight.

M.J. turns the key in the safe, tests the handle and rises from his knees. 'How did you get on today?'

'Alright. But that Muldoon … .'

'What about him?'

'He's a savage.'

The smile fades and, as I've noticed, when his hackles are raised, he runs his hand through his wavy hair.

'Explain yourself.'

I describe Muldoon's cruelty. 'And the young fellow was only joking. No harm meant.'

'A brute. Is he now? Tomásheen, you know fuck all about what goes on here. Muldoon is a good foreman. And good foremen are hard to find. Fellas I can rely on.'

'For kicking lads up the backside.'

He is now glaring at me. 'Look, you need eyes in the back of your poll if you want to make it over here.' He strides across to the window. 'Come over here a minute, Tommy. Come over here and I'll show you something. Look down there.'

The street is now bare apart from a man who is shadow-boxing in front of a plate-glass window, and whose shirt is hanging loose over the waistband of his trousers. 'I didn't take the boat to join up with them eejits holding up the street corner and singing "Kevin Barry".'

He goes back to the table and starts flicking through the lodgement book: 'I looked around, boy, and saw where money was to be made, and I needed men like Muldoon.'

'Right.'

He keeps checking a bundle of dockets, and after a while, without raising his head, offers an olive branch: 'Any chance you'd have a look at these figures? And you might go to the bank on Monday morning with Sandra if you're around.'

'Sure.'

And from then on I try to impose commonsense on my

private debate – this is life in a rough-and-tumble world. We're in a jungle, Tommy; jungles have their own laws. I've been sheltered too long in a boarding school.

One Friday evening, M.J. grants himself a half-hour's breathing space after supper; we chat about Ardglass for the first time. He had received a phone call from Con, one of the twins in Chicago. 'They're in real estate.' He does an American take-off. 'Bill is going out with a lassie from Lixnaw.' While he is speaking, I have the feeling he could have been talking about uncles, or older cousins, so wide does the gap seem between me and my brothers and sisters.

'Do you remember when they left?'

'Barely.' The scene comes back misty around the edges. I hear hushed voices in the bedroom; a lighted candle in a sconce is moving about in the darkness. My head is being tousled; someone is whispering 'Come on, Con. Leave the child sleep – the train won't wait.' There's a bar of Urney's chocolate on the pillow when I awake in the morning. They all seemed to leave like that: Mossie soon after M.J., Eily to Leeds to be a nurse, and Eddie to the depot. Of nine children, only one – Gerry – remains in Ardglass. Then parcels stamped with the Stars and Stripes arrive from Chicago: American bobby socks for the girls; showy jackets with 'The Bears' on the back for Gerry and me. Very soon they are calling me 'Yank' in the playground. Pauline refuses to wear the socks, and gets another thrashing with a sally rod one morning before she goes to school. 'But Mammy,' she cries, 'they're laughing at me.'

'Notions of yourself, you have. Is that it? You'll wear them, and be glad to have them. The Cruelty Man, that's who I'll send for.'

The Cruelty Man was her most fearsome weapon to scare the living daylights out of us. The Cruelty Man had been called to a neighbour's cottage and three children had been taken off to a home, and were never seen again. On our way from school, especially in winter, we used to huddle together until we were well clear of the cottage.

'Mammy, don't send for The Cruelty Man. I'll wear them.'

'My name is mud with the mother because of Mossie,' M.J. is now saying.

'She doesn't talk much about that,' I hedge, keeping my gaze on the framed photos on his sideboard: a black-and-white one of my father thatching the roof of the old house; Mossie in his First Communion suit, a rosary beads around his joined hands. And beside them on the polished surface, my father's pocket watch. But in my head I hear her recriminations: 'Himself and his money and his building.'

I was in the study hall when the Rector called me to his room: 'I'm sorry to bring you bad news. It's about your poor brother, Maurice.'

M.J. reads my thoughts. 'Mossie, God rest him. Too hot-tempered. And I warned him to stay clear of that gang he hung around with.' He pushes away his plate and rests his head in his hands. When he looks up, his eyes are red. 'How did you get on in Leeds?' he asks.

'Fine. Very strict rules. Suits Eily fine, you know the way she always had her copybooks neat and tidy. So, no complaint.'

'The sums always right for the Master.'

'But Pauline says she may as well be back in the nunnery.'

'How is she?'

'Looks much happier. Likes being a nurse, but she's giving out yards about the mother and how she pushed her into that convent.'

'She *did* too.' He starts drumming his fingers on the table's edge, tapping into a shared family wound: the shouting in the kitchen that wakes me one morning during the summer holidays: 'I won't have a wretch like you bring disgrace on us.'

'But Mammy.'

'I'll give you "Mammy".'

Then the scurrying and the slapping and Pauline crying: 'It was nothing, Mammy; he only asked me to go home with him after the dance.'

'Dance, is it? Up in Relihan's shed you were, you wretch, and don't tell me lies. I'm here slaving, and the young fellas of the parish after you like dogs.'

'Ah, leave her; she's only young.' My father's plea is puny against the sound of the beating.

'Shut your mouth, and go out and do a bit of work for a change. My brothers would have a day's work done by now.' More smacking and crying for mercy then, and when I go down to the kitchen, Pauline is sobbing in a corner, her beautiful face covered in red blotches. Then the following summer, when she has done her Leaving Certificate, we go with her in a hired car to a convent outside Limerick; my father sits in front beside the driver, my mother says the rosary, and Pauline keeps her face turned towards the window, weeping quietly into her handkerchief.

'They live in the nurses' home – a huge redbrick,' I tell him. 'On their day off, they have to be in at ten, nine in the winter. The matron interviewed me in her office, and wagged her finger: "Young man, even if you are their brother, don't imagine that you can come and march into this hospital whenever you like, as if you were the Lord Mayor." '

'Poor Pauline.' Smirking, M.J. stretches and then yawns. 'What's she going to do at all?'

'She'll be fine. By all accounts, she's very popular with the young doctors, whatever the matron thinks.'

'That's our Pauline.' He laughs. 'Is Gerry making any shape?'

'Yes. He's doing OK. Has the milking machine now.'

'Them heifers I bought him, I believe he sold them off at the January fair.'

'He's going to a farm school in the creamery, every Friday night.' I am painting the best picture of Gerry, to whom our mother had given the few rushy fields M.J. desperately wanted.

'And the Summerhill House crowd?'

'David is in the university, going to be a doctor. And Bernard is an agricultural instructor. Richard is at home.'

He chuckles. 'D'you remember what the mother used to say? "Only for their oul grandfather finding some mine out in Montana, 'tis far away from grandeur they'd be. All the Healys ever had was two goats and a donkey on the side of a hungry hill." '

Back from America, Matty Healy's father had greased the palm of the landlord, who rented out and eventually sold him Summerhill House and three hundred acres of the best land in the parish.

'Every St Stephen's Day, we used to watch at the big gate.' M.J. is staring into the past. 'Mossie, the twins and myself. You'd hear the horses stamping on the cobblestones up at the house, all shiny in brass and buckles, and the maids with pinafores rushing around with a tray of glasses.'

He returns to the Healys after Vera has cleared the table. 'And her ladyship, Miss Grace, as oul Matty made the servants call her – is she a nurse yet?' He picks his teeth with a match.

'I met Miss Grace on the Green Road before I came over. Jodhpurs, riding cap – the lot. She was taking Scarteen for a trot before the County Show. She's coming to London for some course when she finishes at St Vincent's Hospital. Queen Alexandra School of Nursing, I think, she said.'

The picking stops. He is now waiting for every word that comes from my lips. Then, like someone coming out of a daydream, he places his hands on the table, raises himself, and begins to gather up maps and drawing plans.

'Old Matty, the bastard,' he says, 'wouldn't give Eddie time off the morning I left. "Cows have to be milked, no matter who's going to England." A month later Eddie told him he could shove his cows up his hole; he had passed the exam for the guards anyway.' He takes the plans to the hallstand and bounds up the stairs, leaving me in the slipstream of the winter's morning he had departed for England.

'I'm going over to meet a chap called Seery in The Stag's Head. A Clare man,' he says when he comes back down with a floppy briefcase. 'He was a schoolteacher for a year or so, but gave it up. Clever bucko. Will you come and meet him?'

'Sure.'

'This fella has notions; he's young – late twenties, at the most – wants to do well for himself. He looks after my lodgements at Barclays, and I'm hoping he'll come and do the books for me. I had a great woman do them, but she's having a baby and then she's off to Australia with the husband.'

The Clare man is reading *The Guardian* when we arrive at the pub. In his navy suit and polka dot tie, he fits in with the groups of men, some of whom stand at the counter talking loudly. Others are sitting around in cane-backed chairs: wearing check shirts and tweed jackets, they could have stepped out of *Horse and Hound*. A man is seated at a low table; in front of him is a plate of ham and tomatoes. While keeping an eye on the TV high above the till, he twists the cap of a YR sauce bottle.

M.J. doesn't waste much time in small talk. 'I'm prepared to top what you're getting at Barclays by two quid a week.'

'Make it three. You won't be sorry,' says Seery.

'Two and a bonus at Christmas and August.'

'They were right – they told me you're a hard man.'

'And did they tell you I keep my word?'

'Weekends for a start off, until I finish at Barclays.' Seery's shrewd eyes recede when he grins.

'Right. And welcome to Galvin Construction. What's your poison?'

'A single malt should seal the bargain.'

M.J. strides ahead of him to the counter and beckons to the barmaid, who puts a whisky glass to the optic. The two of them talk while they wait, Seery raising himself up on his toes.

From a wooden beam hangs a tattered Union Jack; beside it a picture of the Queen looking away towards her far-flung Commonwealth. On the other walls are pictures of English rugby teams.

'Why did you hit John Bull then, Christy, with your secure job?' M.J. hands Seery his Glenfiddich, puts a glass of Watneys in front of me, and, without waiting for an answer, raises his tumbler of whisky in a toast. 'Good luck, lads.'

'I didn't want to stare down at forty years of teaching snotty noses the difference between a noun and a pronoun, M.J., or, "I will arise and go now, and go to Inishfree." Two weeks in Bray each summer walking up and down the promenade while the little woman does her window-shopping. Ah, no.' An impish grin spreads across his face. 'Anyway, half the secondary schools in Ireland are staffed by spoiled priests.'

'You were going for the Church then?' says M.J.

'The Brothers.'

'Right, well, I'm sure you know best yourself.' They discover a mutual interest in horses, and are both surprised that Psidium won the Derby; his form as a two-year-old didn't indicate any great promise, and he was left far behind at Longchamp. Both agree that Lester is the greatest. M.J. is excited about a two-year-old he has running at Newmarket at the latter end of July.

'Right-eeo,' he says and drains his glass. 'The sooner you can start the better, Christy.'

On the way back, he is silent behind the wheel, until suddenly he says: 'You know the first time I ever tasted tomatoes, or saw YR sauce?'

'When?'

'A threshing day at Summerhill House. They had two dinner tables – the big shots ate in a separate room from the rest of us.' Graze of stubble when he rubs his jaw. 'Lovely sunny weather towards the end of August. I was on the reek of straw that evening, when I noticed Grace going across the lawn in her uniform. The prettiest picture I'd ever seen in my life.' He checks his dreamy tone and laughs. 'I thought she stopped to look at me, but sure, I suppose that was my imagination. Anyway, oul Matty was taking her back to some convent school in Galway. I remember the cloud of dust when they were driving off down the avenue. They had one of them big American cars at the time.'

'I remember. Like a funeral car.'

'I wanted it all.'

'What?'

'The whole bag of tricks: the ivy house, the slated stalls and to be at the big shots' table.'

Two weeks later Seery starts working for Galvin Construction. When the bank closes each Friday afternoon, he comes to one of the site offices and is still bent over documents long after the men have departed for the Crown, and the dumpers and generators are silent. He takes invoices from the spike and makes entries in the hard-bound ledgers. The following morning he is back and working on until the four o'clock stopping time.

Since Seery is one of the few who has gone beyond national school, we form a friendship of sorts. We visit an El Greco exhibition in the National Gallery, and after that to the pictures or for a drink to The Stag's Head. More often than not, he goes through an act of tapping his pockets at the ticket office, before the stock excuse: 'You won't believe this – left my fecking wallet behind in the flat. I'll pay you back.' It's the same routine when we meet in the pub: when his turn comes, we sit there with empty glasses while he spins out stories of women he's bedded after a night at the London Irish Rugby Club, until eventually I go to the counter.

'This is my office,' he says with a twinkle while I bring two glasses to the table one evening. 'Where I do my business. Good luck.'

'Good luck.'

'Advising Irishmen with brains,' he taps his temple, 'how to put their hard-earned money to good use and make sure Harold Macmillan gets as little as possible. The Isle of Man. Guernsey. Channel Islands. You'll know all about it when you join the brother.'

A horse race has ended on the black and white television; the *Horse and Hound* set cheer in a polite way and order more pints of bitter.

'I stay away from Kilburn,' Seery says, the hint of an English accent creeping in. 'They're going nowhere.'

'Poor devils.'

'Don't mind your poor devils. You've got to look out for number one in this cesspool. In two years I'll have my own accountancy firm. Can be done you know. Then when I'm well-established, I'll return to the oul sod and settle down. But first,' he rubs his hands together, 'there's a rake of skirt in the Buffalo and the Galtymore. Have you sampled yet?'

'No,' I reply and hope he doesn't see me redden.

'No?' He's surprised. 'You'd have no bother.' He leans in and lowers his voice. 'Loads of skirt.' He reels off a list of fast things – nurses at Whittington Hospital and the Royal Brompton with their tongues hanging out for it. 'I can fix you up any time you like.' A sly grin on his face, he leans back to study my reaction, but just then a man wearing a grey pinstripe suit with a cheroot in his hand, touches his shoulder. Seery listens while the man whispers into his ear.

'Excuse me, back in a jiffy.' His accent has become more English. They both leave the pub by a side door; I watch them get into a white Hillman. The man in the pinstripe is talking, Seery is nodding.

I lose interest. Across from me a stained-glass window showing a hunt floods an alcove with golden light; beneath the hunt two men are wrapped up in a chess game.

Seery is humming when he returns.

'That seems to have gone well,' I say.

'Tommy, the only lesson in life fellows like us need remember,' he taps his forehead: 'Up here for making dosh,' and then points to his feet, 'Down here for dancing.' Casting sly looks around the bar, he leans towards me and opens his jacket to show a bulky envelope in his inside pocket. 'That's what I call using your nut.' He whispers: 'The magic words, Tommy – Guernsey, the Isle of Man.' For a while then, he is lost in thought, until he notices the chess players. 'Two things I thank the Brothers for.'

'What?'

'How to play chess.'

'And the other?'

'The morning I'm leaving the monastery, the Head Brother says to me: "Mix only with fellas who are making something of themselves. Stay away from them who are propping up the street corners. You don't want to become like the Tech boys."'

He had become a novice at fourteen. A broad-shouldered Brother in a black soutane had visited the two-roomed school above the village. The girls played in the yard while the Brother beamed down at them and spoke about the fine big college out by Dublin Bay: hurling and football every evening, a film on Sunday night, roast chicken three times a week. And when they got their Leaving Certificate, it was off to university.

'Like winning the Hospitals Sweepstake,' he says, 'too much to refuse for a boy like me from a county council cottage.'

'How long did you stay?'

'Eleven years. In at fourteen. I left two years ago.' He shakes his head, 'Ah no, the monk's life not for me. Unnatural. No bit of fluff. You know yourself.' His glasses catch the light when he blows smoke rings into the air. 'From now on, Tommy, everyone will be looking for an accountant who can keep his gob shut and prevent the revenue boyos from getting at the pot of gold.' He is going to have the time of his life for the next few years and then find a professional woman – maybe a doctor. 'And sure if it doesn't work out, so what? Plenty of fish in the sea. What about you? You'll go to college, I suppose, and then join the big man.'

'Very likely. Engineering probably.'

I keep to myself another voice that has lately been faintly calling, and that has persuaded me to make tentative enquiries to All Saints, in the Oriel diocese, which also trains priests for the foreign missions. The president of the seminary replies promptly: as soon as I matriculate, I'll be welcome for an interview. He encloses a brochure about All Saints and a prospectus: one black lounge suit, one black hat, seven white shirts with detachable collars, seven sets of vests and shorts, seven pairs of socks, one black soutane, one Roman collar. On the front cover of the glossy brochure, students in soutanes are resting in front of Doric pillars leading to a doorway: one or two are smoking pipes. The back has a picture of students jumping for a football: goalposts stand out against a blue sky.

But I don't reveal to Seery my wish to become a missionary, lest I spoil a summer's freedom or jeopardise my possibilities with nurses from the Whittington, their tongues hanging out for it.

7

IOPT FOR THE BUILDING SITE at Hitchin, rather than the pipe-laying job at Stevenage.

'If 'tis too much,' says M.J., 'come back to Chiswick and take a proper holiday. Play a bit of football up at New Eltham. With all the oul emigration, they have good Gaelic teams there; you might get a run out with one of them. Or why don't you go to Wimbledon? An old English gent I bought land from is always offering me tickets. Now wouldn't I look nice at a tennis match?'

'No. I'll give the building a try. Harden me up.'

'The navvy's job is no picnic.'

'I'll take a week at the end.'

'You're as stubborn as a mule.'

'A family trait.'

I know now I wanted to pay him back for the Barclay cheques that kept the rector of the boarding school smiling whenever we met in the corridor. So I tend bricklayers, keep the mixer going, make sure they have enough mortar, or *compo*, on the scaffold when the walls rise. Even though it grates, I throw out the odd *cunt* or *bollix*, or *who took the fucken pickaxe?* in order to merge with the herd. In a short time, I know about headers and stretchers, the difference between English and Flemish bonding, and about pointing and bedding. Three parts sand, one part cement disappear into the mixer: a crust of mortar around the mouth, clean as a washing machine on the inside. Wearing a dirty white shirt that he will throw away on Saturday evening when he buys another drip-dry, Kilrush, a foreman, stalks the site. 'Work till you drop, you fuckers,' is his mantra. He winks at me – secret code that we're on the same side.

My hands blister, and my thighs, where I rest the shovel for leverage, are raw and sore at night. In bed my whole body tingles from struggling with bags of cement, tilting the mixer, and filling the hod for Sputnik, one of the navvies, to climb the ladder and slide back down, his two feet clinging to the outside of the horizontal bars. Some evenings I am so jaded after having my dinner in The Highway that I trudge up the stairs before nightfall, collapse on to the bed and fall fast asleep with my clothes on until the alarm clock explodes in my ear. (Nowadays when a dog barking or a car starting up can keep me awake for half the night, I look back and wonder how I drifted off despite the shouting and the crash of breaking glasses below me, and the mad scramble when Sandra the barmaid had to call the police.)

Occasionally the uproar wakes me with a start and draws me to the window: there I watch a blur of flailing fists, wild savage shouts and blood pouring down shirt-fronts. And then, as if they are only playing a part in a film set and some invisible director shouts 'Cut,' the fighting stops and they fall silent when a paddy wagon comes screaming down Victoria Road.

Later that summer, M.J. and Jody pick a gang to swing into action at the first sign of trouble. They all stand well over six feet, most had wrestled at the Holloway Road Gymnasium – one or two are boxers. After that, the paddy wagon is seldom seen.

Bonnie calls a couple of times a week. In a low-cut dress, she pulls pints if Sandra is short-staffed and the bar is crowded, especially at weekends. When M.J. comes to empty the till and take the money to the safe upstairs, she leaves with him.

The Highway is the first Irish pub to sell bacon and cabbage every evening just as the men are hopping off the lorries after a two-hour journey. I watch while a man puts a cheque on the counter. 'Cash that for me, Sandra, like a good girl,' he says, settling himself on the high stool and breaking open a packet of Craven A.

'Sorry old china.' With one hand on the Watneys pump while a head of foam rises to the top of the pint glass, Sandra surveys the bar. 'There's a line of blokes ahead of you, but I'll give you a few quid on it now.' A replica of other evenings: by closing time the cheque will have a deep hole. I return to another banned book, *Lolita*, I had bought that day at Charing Cross Road, and devour the pages until, suddenly, Bonnie is standing over me, a glass in her hand. 'How can you read in this bedlam?' She turns over the book to look at the cover: 'Well, of all the sleeveens. Our scholar is only a wet week in this pagan country and now he's reading dirty books.'

'Educational purposes.'

'Education, my arse. Move over in the bed.' She slides into the corner seat beside me. 'I'm jaded from humouring people all day.' A pearl necklace hangs over her red summer frock.

'I thought yourself and M.J. were going to the White City.'

She inclines her head and a mane of hair falls over her sullen look. 'M.J. suits M.J. No one can come in the way of that boyo's plans.'

'What happened?'

'Trouble out at Stevenage. One of the foremen could've looked after it, but I can be thrown aside like an old dishcloth whenever he likes.' Her hurt becomes an angry outburst. 'He's hail-fellow-well-met, life and soul of the party, but there's ice in his heart – that's if he has any. And do you think he would apologize?' She settles loose strands over one ear. 'Selfish bastard.'

A violin player begins to run the bow along the strings and to tweak the tuning pegs, saving me from her fit of temper. He leads in a man who sings in the manner of professionals: one hand up to the side of his face.

> *Irene, goodnight Irene.*
> *Irene, goodnight.*
> *Goodnight Irene, goodnight Irene,*
> *I'll see you in my dreams.*

Bonnie's anger falls away, and, while she is speaking close to my face, I catch the whiff of drink from her breath: 'In ten years he'll be one of the richest bastards that ever set foot in Liverpool, but he'll still be a bastard. And I don't mean to offend you – he's your brother.'

'I'm sorry he let you down,' I say, and when I turn, her hair brushes against my face, promising an excitement that is dark and sensuous, and, as yet, unknown to me.

Veins stand out on the singer's weather-beaten neck; the men urge him on as he comes to the final verse. He has no sooner finished than another man, swaying and holding on to the counter tries 'Someday I'll Go Back to Ireland' in a hoarse voice that is out of tune. A shout goes up. 'You'll never go back to fucken Ireland. Neither will I. We'll die in John Bull. They don't fucken want us back there.'

Sandra screams: 'And I don't fucking want you here, mate. If you don't shut it, I'll call the rozzers, and you'll spend the night in the clink.' But no one takes any notice and the fiddle player drowns out the singer with a dance tune.

Sandra comes outside the counter to collect empty glasses and the drunken singer makes a grab for her sturdy hips, but she gives him a push with such force that he lands on a table where men are playing cards; pint glasses spill all over the players, and smash on the floor. He is called the biggest fucken eejit under the sun.

Seated at the bar, Leitrim Joe, whose shoulder muscles strain his crumpled jacket, takes a last drag from his cigarette butt, raises his head and does a recitation for one of the ceiling lights:

> *I remember, I remember,*
> *The house where I was born,*
> *The little window where the sun*
> *Came peeping in at morn ...*

'You know somethin', Leitrim, you're a fucken poet,' says one of the men drinking near him.

His party piece over, Leitrim hangs his head, and rests his turned-down wellingtons on the brass rail that runs along at the base of the counter. 'Schooldays, the happiest days of our lives. Amn't I right, lads?'

'Ah, fuck you, Joe, and your schooldays.'

Just then a stocky man with a head of tousled hair staggers towards us; his face is half-hidden in the gloom and a cloud of cigarette smoke. He rocks on his feet at our table and peers at me. 'Who the fuck are you? Fucken books. Readin' fucken books,' but his concentration lapses when he notices Bonnie. The baleful look softens. 'Ah jaysus, if it isn't wan of the finest-lookin' mares. Give us an oul kiss.' He spreads out his arms and almost falls on top of her as he bursts into song:

My Bonnie lies over the ocean,
My Bonnie lies over the sea …

'Garryowen you bastard, get off me,' she wriggles out of his clumsy embrace.

'Don't be like that. Wan, wan oul kiss, the best-lookin' girl in London. *Bring back my Bonnie to me.*' One of his wellingtons strikes the table and knocks over my book and my glass of Tizer. A throaty roar goes up from the men who are standing nearby. 'Go on, Garryowen, you boyo, you're a glutton for your mutton.' While still trying to canoodle Bonnie, Garryowen half-turns to them: 'No mutton here, boy. This is spring lamb.' The reply draws another guffaw from the gang of drinkers.

Bonnie finally succeeds in pushing him away, and wipes his spittle from her face. Garryowen gives up, and, breathing heavily, peers at me.

'Who's he?' he asks her. He has to steady himself with one hand on the table. A rolled-up copy of *The Limerick Leader* falls from his back pocket. 'Sure he's wouldn't be able for a mare like you, Bonnie.' His drunken gaze tumbles towards my book, now lying on the sawdust. 'Books. I can't stand anyone readin' fucken books. Thinkin' he's fucken better than the rest of us. When I was your age, boy, I was ridin' women.' He moves closer. His face is dark and his deep-set eyes are mad with drink and aggression.

'He's M.J.'s brother,' says Bonnie, smoothing down her dress at the hips.

'M.J.'s brother?' He gapes at me; his body slackens.

'Tommy,' she adds. 'He's here for the summer. Going to college to be an engineer, and he'll be your boss some day, so be nice to him.' She touches my elbow.

'I didn't know, boy, I didn't know.' His tone is now subdued. 'Put it there, put it there. If you're half the man your brother is, you'll take over London.'

I shake his hand, as coarse as sandpaper.

'I'll have to get you a drink, Tommy boy. What'll you have?'

'A glass so.'

'Yerra a pint.'

Bonnie intervenes: 'No, a glass will do fine. Do you want to make him as drunk as yourself?'

On his way back from the counter, Garryowen knocks into the men who had been urging him to have a go at Bonnie. 'Ignorant bastards from Connemara,' he says, putting the glass of Watneys, and a gin and tonic on the table. Then he slumps into the seat beside us.

'What's up with you tonight, Garryowen?' Bonnie asks.

He ignores her and rakes the bar with peevish eyes. 'Man is only a unit of production.' Placing a hand on her knee, he leans over. 'Do you know who said that, Tommy?'

'No, I don't.'

'You don't? What are they teachin' you in that college, boybawn?' He sits back. 'Karl Marx, that's who said it. And do you know what? He was fucken right.'

His eye catches a yellowed picture of the leaders of the 1916 Rising to the right of us. 'God rest you, Connolly.' He raises his glass to the picture. 'You were the best of them. The rest were only oul poets.' In a mocking tone, he quotes the Proclamation: *cherishing all the children of the nation equally.* 'Look,' he says, picking up his sodden newspaper from the floor and wiping off the sawdust with his sleeve. 'Look.' He straightens out the front page, showing a picture of President de Valera, beneath it a banner headline: 'Bronze Statue to the President Unveiled in Clare.'

'An oul fraud, if ever there was one.'

'What did the poor man ever do to you?' Bonnie asks.

'What did he never do *for* me?' He sweeps his hand over the room. 'Does Dev or his crowd give a curse about any of us poor bastards here in John Bull?'

'Didn't he give you the dole?' She nudges me.

'Dole my arse,' Garryowen says. 'Thirty bob a week. Any Irishman worth talkin' about, girl, wouldn't stick his paw out for the dole. Townies maybe. A countryman would work at the shovel till he drops.'

To make his point, he stretches across her: 'Tommy, they can say all they like about M.J. Galvin or the Murphys or Pateen Lowry; God knows where we'd end up without them. If you're fair, they'll treat you all right.' Then, satisfied with his speech, he lapses into silence. On the table, Dev's picture lies soaking in beer and Tizer. Garryowen's head sinks into his chest, and he begins to snore, but a shout from the card table causes him to jerk, and like a mongrel dog frightened out of his sleep by lice, he opens his eyes. 'What?' He stares at us for a moment and calms down again, picks my book off the floor, wiping the cover with his calloused hand. 'Stay at the books, boy.' A fringe of dried ale clings to his chapped lips. 'I had no chance, even though I was better than the fella that was put on for the scholarship – no pull, you see. He's now a schoolmaster; I'm here in Kilburn.' Dark cavities show when he laughs.

'Doyle, you're a great-lookin' mare,' he says and struggles to his feet. 'I'd go all the way with you. The full fifteen rounds.'

One of the men near us shouts: 'Give us "Dan McGrew".'

Garryowen sways, and, without taking his eyes off Bonnie, declares in a loud voice: 'The Shooting of Dan McGrew.'

The men guffaw and call for attention: 'Go on, Garryowen. Go on, boy.'

'A bunch of the boys were whooping it up in the Mala- mute saloon … .'

Someone slaps the counter. Sandra shouts that she'll call the police. The men cheer.

'You never lost it, Garryowen.'

'He'd be quare without it.'

'Shut up, let ye.'

The kid that handles the music-box was hitting a jag-time tune;
Back of the bar, in a solo game, sat Dangerous Dan McGrew,
– And watching his luck was his light-o'-love, the lady that's
known as Lou.

He reaches out to Bonnie and this time she suffers his clumsy attempts to kiss her. The men drown him out with their cheering when he tries a second verse. Grinning, he gives up: 'Ignorant fuckers like you give our country a bad name.' He puts the pint glass to his lips, drains it and slouches off to the bar. Bonnie watches him go, a look of pity on her face: 'It's true for him. I believe he was at the top of his class at school. Brains to burn.'

We talk for a while beneath James Connolly and the 'oul poets'. By now she has forgotten her anger at M.J., and I want to share with her my impressions since I've arrived: maybe get a balance or knock into shape the whole crazy picture, but it will have to wait. I am growing jaded and have no wish to revisit scenes of brutality. But I do mention the notebook.

'Happens here all the time. You'd better wise up, kid – as they say in the pictures. That's how money is made. Those officials turn a blind eye. M.J. Galvin puts them up in Killarney; M.J. Galvin becomes a millionaire.'

The din is getting louder. The globes along the counter show clouds of cigarette smoke piled up beneath the ceiling. I pick up my book, fan the pages and do a stretching act of tiredness. Bonnie gets the message. 'If you want anyone to tuck you in … .' She gives me a roguish glance and stands up, smoothing down her frock. 'Joke,' she adds, and laughs. 'Don't look so shocked. Only a bit of gas.'

She is picking up her purse when the door opens and

Horse Muldoon's large head appears above his cronies. For a moment the noise falls away; the fiddler puts down his bow, the card-playing comes to a halt. Even Sandra stops. Horse struts to the far end of the bar where he stands with his back to the wall, and takes a roll of notes from his trouser pocket. 'Right,' he shouts. 'Cable-pull out at Maida Vale in the morning. I'm lookin' for two dozen skins. Good men, not slackers or hobos.'

A few of them leave their pints and rush to him, and, like yearlings at a fair, each gets the cattle dealer's once-over. He peels off a few notes from the roll, hands them to some, others he tells to fuck off, that he's seen too many of their kind. 'I'm lookin' for men, not fellas draggin' their arses after them.' Then, with one of his henchmen pushing a way ahead, he storms out again.

'*The sub*,' says Bonnie. We are both standing as if to get a better view of a set piece on a stage. 'They'll get a few quid now so they'll have to be on the lorry in the morning, and for the next few days. But if Horse doesn't like them, he'll kick their arses by midday and they'll have to make their own way back from Maida Vale.'

8

THE FOLLOWING MORNING, arriving in good time before most of the lorries at the pick-up point, I go into one of the cafés on Cricklewood Broadway, and find a place at the end of a long table. A swarthy man with an apron around his waist shouts at me from behind a stainless steel counter. 'The same, Paddy?'

'The same?'

He is getting impatient. 'Double eggs, sausages and bacon, Paddy,' he spells it out as if I'm a dunce.

'Yes. That'll do fine. Thank you.'

'Thank you, thank you,' he jeers. A broad grin spreads across his glistening face and he shouts into the cooking area behind him. 'Double everything for posh Paddy.' The cook, a black man, wipes sweat off his forehead, shows a set of white teeth, and explodes into a squeaky laugh, shaking his head and repeating 'Posh Paddy' to himself as he throws more sausages on a huge grill.

In the crowded café, the warm air is mixed with cooking smells, cigarette smoke and the occasional wave of sweat when the men throw coins on the table and amble out. The mood bears no resemblance to the previous night in The Highway. They are now like monks vowed to silence: the only sound comes from the scrape of a knife and fork, the rustle of a newspaper. Someone is stirring his tea, the spoon glancing loudly off the inside of the mug. The swarthy man is calling out for 'another double eggs, bacon and sausage over here, mate'.

Some have pushed away their plates and are rolling cigarettes or have their heads buried in the *Daily Mirror*. On the wall, Marilyn Monroe is cooling off over an air vent, her white dress billowing up to her elbows.

After a while the heavy sound of Galvin lorries on the road outside breaks the silence; Horse Muldoon is shouting, 'Stop playing with your goolies and get into the fucken truck.' He starts blowing on a whistle. Newspapers are stuffed into back pockets, cigarettes are thrown on the flagstones and stamped on. A quick sign of the cross – a bookie's tick-tack – and they stamp out the door, chewing as they go. I finish my breakfast and follow them to the lorries.

Unlike the previous day, the sky has clouded over and drops of rain are sprinkling the footpath. A ragged figure with a matted beard stands with his hand out; as he trundles along, methylated spirits, jutting out of his torn gabardine, sloshes around in a bottle. 'A few coppers for a bite to ate, boy,' he growls. I give him a threepenny bit. 'God save you, boybawn,' he says hoarsely after squinting at the coin. 'Blessins 'a God on you, boy.'

Jody is standing by the driver's door of a Transit while a crew, with much loud talk and shuffling of boots and good-humoured jostling, are climbing into the back. I sit in beside him.

On the way through streets of red brick, I notice the hated sign on the lace curtains: 'No dogs. No blacks. No Irish,' and try to make light of it. 'We're like the Jews. Downtrodden.'

'The same old story. Give a dog a bad name.' He switches on the wipers. 'They piss in the beds – then we're all tarred with the same brush.'

At Camden Town, like every other morning, the men are crowding around the lorries now parked ahead of us. One man has the trace of dried blood on his shirt-front. Jody pulls up in front of Corkindale's Select Victuallers: pork, bacon, and sausages slantwise at each side of the signboard; at the centre, a laughing pig is jumping over a wooden fence.

With a rumpled tie loose around his neck, Kilrush has hopped off a truck and is counting the crew. A lanky youth rushes up to him: 'Any chance of *the start*, Murty?'

Kilrush looks down at his shoes: 'Is it fucken tennis you're goin' to play? Go home, boy, and get a pair of boots, and I'll see you here tomorrow.'

'Murty, I'll work hard.'

'Look, lad, I'll give you a root up the hole, if you don't get out of my way.'

Kilrush's bald head moves among the men; he picks out the strongest and those who have boots or wellingtons, then shouts to a driver across the road: 'Five more skins and we're away.'

His hands deep in his pockets, a youth mooches around the road with three or four others until he notices a Batchelors peas can on the footpath, and, like a footballer lining up for a free kick, he takes aim. The empty can soars into the air and just misses a man who is drawing out a striped awning with a long pole. The man stops and glares across: 'Ey, Paddy, kick your rubbish somewhere else.'

'Ah, fuck off and mind your own business.'

'This is my business, Paddy, and this is my country.'

The youth makes to cross the road, but the others grab him.

'Bloody Paddies,' the man mutters to himself and disappears into his shop; the awning remains lopsided over the window and the signs on the wooden frame: Price's candles, Goddar's soap. Brushes, kettles, pots and pans.

'Lads,' comes a shout from somewhere behind the vans: 'Green Murphy is lookin' for a few skins for a job in Putney.'

Like runaway horses, dodging and weaving between cars, they thump on bonnets, and charge down the road towards Mornington Crescent; the rasp of their boots and their shouts are at war with the angry hooting of motorists.

Jody returns: 'Let's go in God's name.' He checks the side mirror and joins the convoy. The men at the back stamp and thump and whistle whenever we pass an attractive-looking woman. Jody raps on the back window of the cab: 'You lads, save your strength – we've houses to build.'

About halfway down the Kentish Town Road, Jody slows down and stops where a fellow in a bedraggled check shirt and blue jeans is resting against the front of a hardware shop. 'A student in Dublin,' Jody explains. 'Trying to put himself through the university. Good worker.'

The men tease him as he gets into the back. 'Deano, I'd say the dickey was lookin' up at you this mornin' with a red eye.'

'Was that the barmaid from the Tara you had at the Galtymore? Headlights like a Morris Oxford.'

'Yeah, and what none of you bastards will never know is that the gearbox is even better,' says Deano.

They laugh coarsely and make room for him on one of the stools. 'You'll never be a vet if you get on her every Sunday night.'

I look through the back window and see a lazy smile on Deano's sensitive face.

M.J. is anxious that I take out a driver's licence. Back in Ireland, I had driven the Ford Prefect, but this is London and now I'd be driving a pick-up or a Transit. After a few runs to Stevenage, Milton Keynes and Hitchin, however, one Sunday when the traffic is light, I am able to find my way with little bother. So every morning I collect a crew outside the Galtymore or on Kilburn High Road near the Schweppes factory and take them as far away as Leighton Buzzard or Bury St Edmunds. During the day if the carpenters are out of nails or other bits and pieces, I do a run to the suppliers. Sometimes, when the men have drunk too much and a lump of their wages has made its way into the till at The Highway, I drive them to their digs. Before long, I could do the journeys blindfolded: Camden, Willesden, and occasionally as far as the Seven Sisters Road.

I get to know the men in all their moods: at six in the morning when they are trying to shake off a hangover, and late at night when they rehash their wild plans to go home – this summer, next year. 'Pocketfuls of green, boy. I'll be back in Tournafulla, get myself a tidy bit of land, my own fireside by next Christmas.'

'And a mare.'

'Oh, a mare.'

They are always going back; always building castles in the air, and they know it. When the drink puts them in bad form, they curse Dev and 'them hoors of politicians who are only all talk'. Now, when I can't remember where I put my breviary or glasses, those men, some of them – more youths than men – come back to me whole and entire. Leitrim Joe, Sputnik, and Hill of Howth – the last given the name because he used to boast of a second cousin once removed who was a parish priest there.

Keeping the mixer going and filling the hod for Deano and the others becomes my daily chore when I'm not called to go to Carling's Builders' Suppliers. Whenever the list is long, Deano travels with me to load the pick-up. We form an easy friendship; on the way to the suppliers, he tells me how he got his name. At a break one day he was idling with the shovel across his shoulders like James Dean with the shotgun in *Giant*. 'Jaysus, lads,' says a Dublin plasterer who had been to the film a few years before in the Metropole, 'would you look, James fucken Dean.'

'So that's how Paddy Conway became Deano,' he tells me with a grin.

After returning in the pick-up one day, we sit on a load of sand with two mugs of tea. Now and again a whiff of cooked meat carries from the dying embers of the brazier where the tea-boy is cleaning out frying pans. I scan our section of twelve houses; we are well ahead of the roofers, so the bricklayers playing a game of cards in the hut can afford a breather until the next storm when Kilrush will appear around a corner blowing a whistle and shoving his hand inside his trousers to scratch himself. Garryowen has disappeared across the railway line to The King George.

We cast away the dregs of our tea and lie back on the sand. Pigeons coo high up in the rich foliage of the chestnuts along the old boundary wall of the Alcott farm that will soon become Alcott Village. Our broken conversation is played out at a lazy rhythm. Deano is calculating the amount of money he will make as a veterinary surgeon in the scheme to eradicate tuberculosis in cattle.

'Is your father a vet?' I ask, working the warm sand into my body's shape. He laughs, and the newspaper he is using as a sunshade falls from his face. 'My father, oh, he is, all right. A vet of the village pub, The Hole in the Wall. Never did a stroke in his life, but that's for *your* ears only.'

'Your secret is safe with me.'

'The lads here have no time for fellas on the dole. They're strange that way.' He settles the paper again. 'No. I got a county council scholarship, but the grant only covers the essentials.'

He doesn't want to be empty-handed with well-off farmers' sons from Meath and Kildare when they are having pints in Hartigans or O'Dwyer's in Leeson Street, and going on about their fathers' prize cattle and hunters. We sit up and he throws a crust of bread to the crows. 'Another year and I'm home and dry. A brass plate on my door on the Athlone Road. As good as the best of them.'

Across the road a team of men are digging trenches for sewerage and services; others are spreading gravel on a rough path to the site – a wide expanse of land stretching as far as a cluster of houses with brown roofs. Beyond them the bell tower of a Protestant church.

Deano studies the trenchers. Along a line marked out by a cord, they are thrusting the spades into the earth, stepping on the lugs to drive them deeper and lifting out a neat sod, grassy on top. Like a colony of giant moles, they bob up and down, bare backs glistening in the sun.

'Slavery,' Deano says after some time. 'Some of these lads will spend their lives digging and drinking. Digging and drinking, and finish up in the doss-house. Poor bastards ending their days with winos and lunatics.' With a look of contempt on his face, he turns away. 'There'll be a quare few bob made out of *dead men* over there.'

'Dead men. Come again?'

His upturned shirt collar, Elvis-style, is frayed beneath the fold. 'All the subbies do it.'

'What?'

'The big shots sub-contract, say forty men to do the footing.'

'So.'

'The subbie will hire thirty-five and put five men's wages in his pocket. They don't exist. That's why they're called *dead men*. Three or four pounds a day for each dead man. That's a tidy sum at the end of the week. Thirty-five will do the work of forty. You got a sample of the cable-laying out at Stevenage. What else do you think all the chalk marking is about and the roaring from Horse Muldoon and Kilrush?' He glances at me. 'You're surprised, well, don't be. It's been the same since time began. That's the way it has been and the way it'll always be.' He settles back and makes a tent out of the newspaper. 'You know the road we drive up every evening in the wagons; where we drop off the lads at the Crown?'

'What about it?'

'It goes through Kilburn and Cricklewood and then north through Stratford and ends up – guess where? Holyhead. Built by the Romans about two thousand years ago. The very same road that our crowd took. Digging and slavery don't change a whole lot in two thousand years. Some make it in this life, Tommy, and some don't. And there's no more to be said about it, except to make sure you're not with the galley slaves.'

The whistle blows and the men pour out of the hut, still arguing about a hand of cards – 'and you shouldn't have played the joker so soon, you fucker'. One of them makes a playful swipe at his cards partner, and for a moment they act the part of two boxers circling and dodging and poking the air, their boots scuffing against the loose gravel. 'I'm a pure Cassius Clay,' says one of the men, dancing and ducking to avoid his opponent. But then, as quickly as they have begun, they burst into false laughter, their arms dropping to their sides, both knowing that a stray punch could rouse a sleeping giant. For always beneath the banter is touchpaper that could suddenly explode into flames. Like the day Sputnik, out of devilment, squeezes the spout of the hose to increase its force, and tries to shower those of us sitting on planks for the morning break.

'Better than any bath,' he cackles. 'You lads are smelly anyway.' Except for Leitrim Joe, who is about to bite into two wedges of bread with strips of bacon between them, we all jump to safety. Water dripping from his face and peaked cap, Leitrim throws aside the sandwich and lunges at Sputnik, his fist crashing into his face.

Covered in dust and lime, they roll and kick on the ground close to the mixer, which is still running. 'Ah, come on, lads. Come on, Joe, 'twas only a bit of oul fun. An' oul joke.' Garry-owen rushes in, but fails to pull them apart. Blood is pouring from Sputnik's nose. An English lorry driver delivering timber to the site calls from the cab to his mate who is clearing the passageway of planks. 'Harry 'ere, over 'ere. See the Paddys are killing each other again.' Chortling, they watch until the fight ends.

Now Kilrush is blowing the whistle and banging on the door of the hut: 'Come out, ye fuckers. Is it for playing cards ye came here?'

When Deano yanks the starting handle, the mixer shudders into life, at first, belching out quick blasts of smoke and then moving into a steady rhythm. The bricklayers remove their trowels, clean as surgeons' knives, from a bucket of water, and climb the ladders. I split a bag of cement in two and stand well back while a cloud of grey dust rises.

The routine is second nature: I stretch and thrust the shovel into the sand and feed the mixer while Sputnik turns on the hose and directs the flow into the revolving drum. Then I heave the cement into the open mouth and watch the wet concrete slosh around until it is ready; together we tilt the drum and fill the hod for Deano to hoist onto his shoulder and climb the ladder.

On the scaffold the bricklayers tap the solid bricks with the handles of their trowels; now and again, they hold a spirit level up against the rising wall and run the trowel along the side to clean off any excess plaster. Their conversation carries in the clear air: 'Who's this Elvis Preston fella anyway?' one of them asks.

'Say that again.'

The man hesitates, aware now that they have stopped and are watching him. 'Elvis Preston.'

A loud burst of laughter follows. 'What friggin' mountain are you from?'

'A friggin' mountain the same as you're from.'

Discovering his mistake, a slow smile appears on his face, and he laughs with them. They resume their tapping.

As if our conversation about scams and dead men is still kindling in his brain, Deano speaks in a low voice while Sputnik is relieving himself at the back of the hut. 'I did a rough calculation,' he says. 'A subbie can make a hundred and fifty a week out of dead men. About the same as Woulfe the doctor in Granard makes in a month.'

He doesn't need to spell it out. M.J. had taken the same route to reach the top of the pile: money that went to the new house at Ardglass, the Ford Prefect, and to keep me in a college with merchants' and doctors' sons.

'Most of the lads have no books or stamps or a pension. Buckshee they call it. But I shouldn't complain; it has paid for my pints at Hartigans.' Lifting the full hod on his shoulder, he throws me a James Dean smirk: 'And remember Charles Darwin, Tommy boy: the fiercest ape is king.'

Anger and confusion at M.J. and what he is doing keep me away from Chiswick that weekend; and also some guilt that I am heir to his dishonesty. Over the pub phone he says something about going for a drive down to Maidstone on the Sunday with Bonnie and himself, but I can't make it out with the din all around me.

'I'm playing football at New Eltham, so it'll be easier to stay at The Halfway,' I tell him. 'See you next week.'

9

ON THAT SUNDAY MORNING during the twelve
o'clock Mass at Quex Road, I sit on the low wall
across from the church. Dead men, Darwin and
Deano's Roman Road, and the clever ones making money out
of the slaves are becoming a mishmash in my head. Over the
granite arch of the front door is a megaphone broadcasting the
Mass to those who can't get room in the church, or, who, like
myself, stay outside and fill the yard. The road is mobbed. Some
have lingered after the previous Mass to meet friends, others
because they have nothing else to do. Now they stand in
groups, or flock around the stalls that sell the Irish newspapers.
Light-hearted boys are pushing at the back, others are reaching
over shoulders, clutching a shilling or a half-crown. Girls
scream in a flirty way. Inside the stalls, men with Pioneer pins
are handing out *The Cork Examiner*, the *Sligo Champion*, and
The Kerryman; they drop coins and notes into shoeboxes behind
them.

The overhanging beech trees are casting random shadows
on the green canvas of the stalls. While the priest intones the
Latin prayers, a youth with a shock of wavy hair falling over his
forehead is playing with a girl's ponytail and slipping his arm
around her waist. A hush descends on the crowd while the
notices are being read: marriage banns – anyone with object-
ions should inform the parish priest. Deaths, and set-dancing
competitions at The Banba. A Legion of Mary outing to South-

end-on-Sea – if you need a ticket for the bus, you should call to the sacristy. And Father John Harty will be in the office at the back to see anyone who needs work or a place to stay. A whiff of cigarette smoke or waves of perfume carry in the warm breeze. On the Feast of the Assumption of the Blessed Virgin, says the voice-over, a procession will begin at the church after the last Mass.

As the crowd parts for a couple of cars going towards Kilburn High Road, I catch sight of Deano surrounded by a group of girls. He has on a herringbone jacket and flannel trousers – inside his open-necked shirt he wears a maroon cravat. He waves and comes across: 'Best place in London to pick up a woman. You see the bit of goods in the dark slacks?' I search the giddy swarm and find a blonde woman whose red lipstick sets off her full mouth.

'Isn't she a pure Kim Novak? I'm fixed up for tonight at the Galtymore.' He rubs his hands. 'Why don't you come, Tommy? Butch Moore and The Capital Showband are over.'

The megaphone crackles, and the clear fresh voices of a children's choir float over the noisy crowd:

> I'll sing a hymn to Mary, the mother of my God,
> The virgin of all virgins, of David's royal blood.
> O teach me, holy Mary, a loving song to frame,
> When wicked men blaspheme thee, to love and bless thy name.

Near one of the stalls a girl's teasing laugh – like a mating call – soars above the sunny conversations, the pushing, the good-humoured shoving, and the grabbing of newspapers.

'I will. I'll go, yeah, sure.' And I silence the confessional advice in the college chapel: 'Stay away from dances and company-keeping if the priesthood is on your mind. You'll only make it more difficult for yourself.'

That evening, as soon as I turn a corner and see a crowd already gathered outside the dance hall, I have to hold back from running up Cricklewood Broadway to join them; many of the Quex Road faces are there. They form a medley of restless colours: white shirts and tiepins and the whiff of excitement. Women in high heels, flared dresses, yellow, blue and green, and mother-of-pearl necklaces with matching earrings. And whenever the red doors open, the thrill of the dance floor spills on to the street. Deano and Kim Novak emerge out of the sea of faces. His arm is around her neck.

We have to jostle our way through the breezy swarm at the ticket office: a hole in the wall big enough to show a glistening head framed in the light of a naked bulb; behind the head, conversation and the clink of coins. I insert my five shillings through the hole and clutch the ticket that is thrust into my hand.

Two men, arm muscles straining their dress suits, stand in the foyer: they tower over the laughing stream hurrying to get into the hall. 'Aisy there now, lads. Plenty for everyone,' they joke as they take our tickets.

'I wouldn't tangle with one of them fellas in a hurry,' Deano says. 'Not unless I wanted to end up in hospital. They're wrestlers.'

Suddenly we are standing at the open door to pure pleasure. The revolving crystal bowl sprays the dancers with specks of light which cause the women's jewellery and spangled dresses to glitter. Swags of red, blue and yellow bulbs along the side walls cast a soft glow around the hall. Behind the stage, little lights like stars shine out against a navy backdrop; the lead singer, Butch Moore, is fondling a microphone while he sings:

> *Sugar in the mornin', sugar in the evenin',*
> *Sugar at supper time;*
> *Be my little sugar, and love me all the time.*

Like him, all the members of the band are dressed in royal blue blazers with gold buttons and beige trousers; in a line, they move forwards and backwards in time to the music: one step out, one step back, one step out, one step back. Trumpets, trombones and saxophones are glinting in the movement. The floor heaves to the rhythm of the dance; the light changes: now orange, now a shade of red, now indigo. Girls are throwing back their heads and laughing. This is heaven. 'Butch Moore,' says Deano, who has to shout into my ear. 'Lucky bastard, he has all the girls mad after him. Look. And the same back at home.' Along the front of the stage women are reaching out, waving with handkerchiefs, and calling the singer, who smiles down at them and continues to fondle the microphone:

> *Put your arms around me and swear by the stars above,*
> *You'll be mine forever in a heaven of love;*
> *Sugar in the mornin'....*

'Terrific song for jiving,' says Deano, leading his girl out on to the floor. He turns back. 'Don't waste any time. Life is short. Get yourself a wench, Galvin.'

At one side of the hall women are standing, some with their arms lightly on each other's shoulders, handkerchiefs tucked inside the strap of their wristwatches. Across the dance floor are rows of men, whom I had seen playing football at New Eltham or hopping off lorries in the evening, covered in dust and lime. Now they are clean-shaven, and wear sports coats or shiny suits with narrow-legged trousers.

When a waltz comes round, I pluck up courage and ask out a girl who has a Tara brooch on her green dress. 'I'm Maureen,' she says. 'From Claremorris.'

She's chatty. No one left now in Claremorris. She had come to an aunt in Ealing, but is headed for New York, where the Irish count for something. Who do I work for?

'A builder. M.J. Galvin.'

'You don't look like a navvy to me. And you don't have the maulers of a builder, so pull the other one.' She smiles easily.

'Only here for the summer.'

'A student. I thought so.' The previous summer she had gone out with a student who worked for Grey Murphy, one of the biggest of the Irish builders. The student never stopped complaining about someone called Elephant Jim.

'John.'

'What?'

'Elephant John, a hiring-foreman for Murphy.' Wholesome scent of her body when I shout into her ear: 'John.' She still can't hear me. Who cares? I'm holding the prettiest girl in the dance hall.

We have lemonade and biscuits and stand on the balcony looking down at the swaying couples as they circle the floor. Like snowflakes, the specks from the crystal bowl caress their smiles.

'Paying your way through college, is that it?' Strands of her hair brush against my lips.

'Something like that.' I venture to put an arm around her.

'I like that in a fella.'

Deano passes by, holding hands with Kim Novak. He whispers in my ear: 'You boyo, Tommy. She's a bit of all right.'

I dance again with Maureen; this time it's a slow waltz. Like the other couples, we are barely moving; she rests her head on my shoulder. The overhead lights are dimmed, so that the little stars behind the stage shine out bravely. Butch Moore is smiling, and swaying, while he sings:

Just you know why, why you and I will, by and by,
Know true love ways.
Sometimes we'll sigh, sometimes we'll cry and we'll know why,
Just you and I, know true love ways.

'It's a change to meet someone who isn't blind drunk or has his paws all over you.' She looks up, and I feel the pressure of her warm body.

'You don't think I'd be like that.' I give her a sidelong glance.

'Not half. Students are the worst of all.'

The set is coming to an end. Butch Moore is wiping his forehead, and laughing as he returns a handkerchief to one of the excited women. I hold on to Maureen's hand, and rush out with: 'Later, before it's over, will we dance again? Just one more.'

'Down, boy, down. I'm not going anywhere.' She saunters away, turns and then winks. I dance with others but keep an eye out for her, even when I am talking to Deano and his girl. Maureen is asked out for every set by fellows I'd come across over the weeks. One of them has such a firm grip around her waist, a length of lacy slip shows below the green dress. Near the end of the night we dance again. Time is running out. 'Would you ... I mean.'

She looks up smiling, while I struggle: 'Lemonade? They sell ice-cream here too.'

'More lemonade? No. But I'll go out with you, if that's what you're up to.' She waits for an answer.

'That's exactly what I'm up to.'

'You're not going to try anything ... students can't be trusted. Take advantage of a poor little girl from Mayo now, are you?' She gives me a dig in the side.

'Not if I can help it.'

'Right. Mind this while I get my cardigan.' She puts a small purse into my hand.

The wrestlers in monkey suits are now relaxed and moving through the shrinking crowd. 'Don't do anything I wouldn't do,' they say to couples who are making for the front door. But I'm interested only in Maureen from Claremorris, and keep my eyes fixed on the door of the ladies' cloakroom.

The night is soft and warm when we step out. A weedy little man with a stained shirt open down the front is staggering all over the footpath and offering to fight any man in London. 'I'd fight fucken Jack Doyle this minute.' He tries a Doyle impression. With a notional woman in his arms, and swaying to the movements of a waltz, he bursts into the boxer's song: 'When Irish Eyes Are Smiling'. Then he pokes the air with drunken jabs and uppercuts. 'I'd down The Gorgeous fucken Gael this minute,' he shouts. Chatting groups laugh and step out of his way.

Over her shoulders, Maureen wears a white cardigan, buttoned at the neck. Couples are nestling in every doorway and secluded spot along Cricklewood Broadway. 'Around here,' she says and slips her hand into mine, leading me to the rear of the hall, where cigarettes glow red and then fade. The murmur of voices, a fit of giggling or the rustle of clothes trickle out of the sensual darkness.

Here also, every nook and cranny is occupied, so we cross the street to Eddington's Lane which leads to a glove factory, and search until we find a niche beyond the reach of the street lamps. My contact with girls until then has been confined to a few clumsy kisses in a neighbour's hayshed and a chance meeting with a girl from Eccles Street Convent School during the previous Christmas holidays.

The first feel of Maureen's eager body inside the summer dress scatters any lingering traces of guilt from talks about purity and purgatory and being temples of the Holy Ghost. As soon as I feel the moist pressure of her open lips, a powerful desire that needs no coaching takes hold. My heart is thumping in my ears as one hand begins to explore her silky thigh, and, meeting no resistance, continues until elastic gives way to my probing fingers. She lets out a faint moan and tightens her grip around my neck.

Afterwards, while settling down her dress, she laughs: 'You must be learning more than sums in that college.'

'Ah, no. I'm a fast learner.'

'You can say that again.'

We kiss, but this time she grabs my hand: 'Show's over. I've to meet my sister.'

'Sorry.'

'It's OK. Usually fellas want much more.'

'There'll be other times.'

'Other times? No other times.' She is running a comb through her hair, a gesture that sets off another wild impulse to go back to the doorway. I catch her combing hand and draw her close: 'Can't we meet next Saturday night?'

'Not unless you're in New York.'

'New York?'

'I've enough saved now, so I set sail in the Cunard on Wednesday. Here, you're only a slave if you're Irish.'

'We can meet tomorrow night.'

'No. Anyway, you're a student. Students go back home and become doctors or engineers. No time for the likes of me.' This is said in the same steely tone that declared that she has enough saved for the liner. She takes in the crushed look on my face and her voice softens. 'I've come across a good few here – you're a bit different, but I have to look after myself.'

'Just once more. Just once.'

'Come on.' She kisses me again before drawing me out into the light where the crowd is now milling around the front of the Galtymore. We stand in the bright streetlights, arms around each other until suddenly she stiffens: 'There's Bridie. I've to go. Goodbye.'

'Who?'

'Bridie. My sister.'

'Oh. Well, I hope you get on all right in New York.'

'Right. Goodbye, Tommy.'

'Don't go yet.'

'I have to. Bridie is waiting.' She looks amused.

'Another five minutes, Maureen.' Against the clock, I'm desperate for the right words: that she can't go to New York, because we will have a great summer around London, dancing and going on boat trips up the Thames every Sunday. She is my girl now. But all I salvage is one more hurried kiss and then she slips through my arms.

The following morning, I bury my face in the shirt which is saturated with Maureen's perfume. She is the most beautiful girl I have ever seen. I love her more than anyone else in the whole world: her face, the feel of her hands around my neck, her dark eyelashes. I'd give up everything for her. Her lack of real interest, too, makes me a slave to her charms. She doesn't sail from Southampton until Wednesday. I still have a chance, but I have no name, no address – nothing, except that she works for Smith's, the clock manufacturers in Cricklewood.

I phone Jody. 'Slight hamstring injury at New Eltham.'

'No bother. I'll get one of the lads to drive.'

That day and the next, I catch a bus to the factory and wait for hours in the rain until all the skittish workers have spilled out through the main gate. Slouching back to Kilburn, I pass by a Galvin man on his merry way into the Crown. 'Jaysus, you're a right-lookin' eejit.' He bursts out laughing. 'Like a drownded rat. You'd need the head examined, boy.' He is tapping his forehead and leering his way to the pub door.

By the weekend my fever is subsiding; her perfume too is wearing off the shirt I've held back from Vera's wash. I now go to the Galtymore every Saturday and Sunday night, alternating between the back ballroom for a céilí and the front for jive, foxtrot and quick-step. Once in a while, I catch myself looking out for her – the Tara brooch, the satin dress. Occasionally, on the dance floor, my invitation to lemonade or ice-cream meets with a flat refusal. A Cavan girl whose breath smells of drink glares at me. 'Do you think I'm a child? Lemonade and fucking ice-cream!' She turns away in contempt, leaving me empty-handed in the middle of the swaying dancers. When, however, success comes my way, in the dimly lit balcony above the flowing river of couples, or in Eddington's Lane beyond the reach of the street lights, I live again the fortunes of the first night with Maureen from Claremorris, and, with probing desire, wallow in the dark recesses of a woman's body.

'Play the field,' Deano advises, when he splits up with Kim Novak. 'We're too young to be tied down.'

I do. I play the field, take my pleasure and move on to the next girl who likes lemonade and ice-cream. And while I am swept along on a carousel of pleasure, my resentment against M.J. and dead men and hard rock evaporates.

Again a place beside him at the table beckons. 'You'd be rollin' in it in no time,' he had assured me during a flying visit to Ardglass the previous Christmas. With the engine of his Corsair running, we were standing at the driver's side before he set off for the ferry. In the frosty air, the smell of petrol mingled with farmyard manure. 'Come over in the summer, hang around the sites – the best university you could go to,' were his parting words before he sat in and drove in a low gear down the boreen to the main road.

Now after discovering the rare pleasures of Eddington's Lane, I try to bury the rector's words of a mild evening in early May: 'If you have a calling, then at least put it to the test, but, don't foreclose on your interest in engineering.' We are pacing the gravel apron in front of the college; one of the caretakers is weeding flowerbeds around a flagpole. 'You'll be better placed to decide after your summer in London. One shouldn't make hasty judgments about such matters. But it's a noble calling to follow in the footsteps of the fishermen. And remember, Thomas, an imperishable prize is in store for those who sacrifice everything for the sake of the kingdom.'

'Yes, Father.'

From the playing fields comes the smack of a cricket bat. 'Yes, go to London, Thomas. But remember: the fishermen left their nets and followed the Lord without delay.'

I manage to suppress all thoughts of fishermen and their nets as I thrust and throw shovels of sand and cement into the mixer and fill the hod with wet concrete. Whenever I'm not playing football with Erin's Hope in New Eltham, I catch a train to Leicester Square with Deano. Sometimes we go to a film or visit one of the art galleries or just mingle with the sightseers and the strollers: a planet away from headers and stretchers, and Garryowen, and the rumble of trucks and diesel fumes. Over the summer both of us have toughened up and are well able to keep up with the frenetic pace; of course, we are working in the knowledge that we are not prisoners to this drudgery. At times I am on the point of revealing to Deano the dilemma that faces me, but fear that any talk of seminaries and priests would pull the plug on the sight of spangled dresses and the magic of Galtymore nights. So I try to convince myself that I am made for the rough-and-tumble of life on a building site. The doubts, however, like weeds between flagstones, keep pushing to the surface.

And they are fed constantly by moments that set my teeth on edge. Like the evening I pull up outside The Highway and the men are jumping off the pick-up and heading for the double green doors. Deano remains chatting with a few of the men who are in a weekend mood while I park up a side road. When we go in, the men, like homing pigeons, have settled themselves at their regular places at the counter, others at one of the round tables where one man is shuffling a pack of cards. Too jaded to talk, Deano and I sit near a window and sip glasses of lemon-and-lime. The smell of cooking drifts from the kitchen when one of the staff appears from the back with steaming plates, causing the men at a round table to shout at Sandra to hurry on with their 'mate and cabbage'. Indifferent to the scattered rise and fall of voices from the men playing cards, we sit there, letting the fatigue drain from our tired limbs.

'Look who's coming now!' says Deano. He is pointing to the front yard where Horse Muldoon has driven up and reversed a truck just outside our window. We watch him storm through the front door and stride across the floor towards the counter, kicking sawdust as he goes. For a belt, he has a necktie around his wide girth. Midway he stops and looks around. The card players stop too until Horse's red face creases into a ridiculous grin: 'Great for some people that can sit drinkin' pints and playin' cards.'

At his usual spot near the far wall, Garryowen taps the side of his head: 'You have to be able to use your nut, Batt.'

'Pity you don't use your nut as much as you use your nuts over in Richmond Street, Garryowen,' he shouts across, and makes a snort when he guffaws. Some of the men join in. Sandra places a pint of Watneys in front of Horse; he raises it to his lips and drains it, then he wipes his forehead with the loose sleeve of his shirt. 'Blessin's 'a God on you, Sandra,' he says while she is filling another. Nearby, a youth of sixteen or seventeen is standing at the counter; he is protecting between his shiny brown shoes a paper parcel tied up with twine. Horse saunters over and takes his measure. After a while, he says: 'You're out of the nest, young lad.'

'I am.'

'Where are you from, boy?'

'Roscommon, sir.'

'Roscommon,' Horse roars, and thrusts his sweaty head in

front of the boy's face. 'Roscommon is a big place, boy. Where?'

Wide-eyed, the youth draws back. 'Strokestown.'

'Dacent people. Have you a place to rest your head tonight?'

'I was to meet a fella from home, but he's gone off to Manchester.' The youth blushes and a nervous grin appears on his face.

Horse stoops down and picks an empty Sweet Afton packet from the sawdust, tears it open and scribbles on the back with a pencil stub he has taken from behind his ear. 'Now,' he says, handing the youth the torn packet. 'Go down to that woman. She'll give you a bed.' He turns to us and winks: 'Maybe more than a bed, if you play your cards right.'

One of the card players shouts: 'Ah Batt, you're a boyo.'

'Have you a job to go to?' Horse asks the lad.

'A fella in the boat told me I'd get work in a glove factory across the road from a dance hall. Around here somewhere.'

Horse snorts: 'Don't mind your glove factory. That's only for women. Be outside this pub tomorrow morning at six and I'll give you plenty work.' He turns to Sandra. 'Pull that young fella a pint, like a good girl.'

'Ah no,' the boy protests.

'Don't mind your "ah no" or I'll change my mind.' While Sandra is pulling the pint, Muldoon rests his two hands on the counter. 'Is there anyone at all left in that fucken country now, boy?'

'Only the oul people.' The youth smiles in a shy way and raises the glass to his lips.

'Tomorrow mornin' at six, young lad,' says Horse over his shoulder as he saunters towards us, holding the glass in a careless way so that the beer is spilling down the side and dribbling on the sawdust.

'You're leakin', Batt.' Emboldened now by Horse's good-humour, Garryowen calls across and points to the glass aslant in the big red hand.

'Ah, fuck you and your leakin'.'

Horse sits with us and chats. The Hitchin site is near

completion and the flats in Islington are making good progress. 'M.J. Galvin,' he says, raising his glass, 'best fucken outfit in town.' The card players overhear him and shout, 'Murphy.'

'John Lang,' says a man who has one foot resting on the rail at the base of the counter. He turns his ferret eyes towards us: 'Irish subbies would fucken crucify you.' Ferret Eyes inhales, and the cigarette smoke drifts up to the yellowed ceiling. But this evening no one feels like fighting. Through the open door a breeze raises a spiral of sawdust into the air. We talk football and good weather and racing. 'Put a few bob, lads ... hold on, a fella gave me this.' Horse draws a scrap of paper from his pocket, peers at it, and, after a short silence, throws us a sheepish grin: 'Here, Tommy,' he says, 'the oul eyes are ... you read it.'

'The Chancy Man for the Ebor Handicap,' I read out.

Deano jots down the name on a corner of the *Daily Mirror.*

'Where do they get them names?' says Horse, and very quickly recovers from his failure to read the words on the scrap of paper. 'Goin' back soon, Tommy?' he asks.

'In three weeks. Paddy here is staying until September.'

'You're lucky bastards to be goin' home. As soon as I have the price of a good farm, I'll show the fucken Master at home who's a pig.'

'A pig?' says Deano.

'Kicked me up the hole he did. Made me walk like a pig on my hands and knees, because I didn't know my catechism and the bishop was comin' to the school. The children didn't know if they should laugh or cry. One of them pissed in his pants. I could see the piss drippin' beneath the desk when I was crawlin' around the room. "What are you, Muldoon?" the fucker kept sayin'. "A pig, Master." "Grunt Muldoon. Grunt." And the bastard made me go around the whole school gruntin' like a pig.' Hair extends from his wide nostrils. ' "Out and clean the lavatories, Muldoon, and make sure you bury it properly," he orders me every Friday evenin'. "You won't need algebra when you're swinging a shovel for McAlpine." '

He lets flow a tide of bitter memories. At fourteen, he had worked for a farmer who had made him sleep in the hayloft;

the same farmer who stole to the servant girl's room every night, and got what he wanted while his wife was in a nursing home having a baby. 'He has a son now goin' on for the Church.' He grins, 'Holy Ireland. Holy, my arse.'

In the same casual way in which he'd joined us, he ambles off again to the counter where men are coming up to him and asking for *the start*.

My interest lapses and I turn to look through the window at the passing traffic. Men wearing hats and starchy looks are making their journey home to ham and tomatoes and Yorkshire Relish. My attention wanders until, out of the corner of my eye, I notice a twitching, jerking movement in the brown sacks thrown on the back of Horse's pick-up. It puts me in mind of an evening on my way from school when I met a neighbour heading for the river with a bag of kittens.

'Look, Paddy,' I nudge Deano. 'The sacks.' He cocks his head and looks out, then sits back with a grin. 'Horse's way of putting the hunt on lodgers. You know those ramshackle houses M.J. owns in Finsbury.'

'Yeah. What about them?'

'We picked up the Connemara lads back there a few mornings.'

'I remember.'

'They're for the wrecking ball. London wants flats, but our friends from Paki land don't want to move.'

'So?'

'So. Two or three bags of hungry rats let loose in the attic will put the hunt on them.'

I stare at the twitching sacks. 'Jesus, how could anyone do a thing like that?'

'No. Well then, welcome to London.' He raises his glass in mock celebration. 'They did the same in Hendon last year and before that out in Leighton Buzzard.'

While he speaks, I see in my mind's eye the yellowish-brown woman with the pink spot on her forehead, folds of cotton and silk in orange, gold and brown. In her soft voice, she tries to dissuade her children from climbing on the running board while I wait for the Connemaras.

'Please, Mr Irishman, Mr Tommy, a ride on your lorry.' Sets of brown shiny buttons looking up at me.

'Not today; I'm in a hurry. This evening. Not now.'

'Only down the road, Mr Tommy.'

'All right. But hold on tightly.'

Their mother smiles her apologies.

The calm voice of old Shanai sitting in a rickety chair outside his door. 'Some evening I make Indian meal. You eat with me, Tommy.'

Then the customary handshake before I set off for the site with the Connies shouting in the back.

10

ON THE FOLLOWING TUESDAY, M.J. arrives at the Hitchin site with a quantity surveyor, and while the surveyor is chatting to a foreman, he comes over to where I'm affecting a close scrutiny of the mixer.

'Anything wrong?' he asks.

'A bit of a rattle from the drum – just a loose stone.'

'You didn't turn up for the weekend.'

'I had a match in Luton.' I resume my shovelling into the mixer, and very quickly he senses my offhand manner. I speak my mind.

His anger flares up. 'You don't know them blasted Pakis; they're like fucken leeches. They'd never leave.'

'But the children! If the rats bit them. Hungry friggin' rats.'

'Well they didn't and Horse put down poison after the Pakis left.' His colour has risen, but he is keeping an eye on the quantity surveyor who is waiting at the open door of the jeep. 'I gave them three months' notice. Plenty of time to get another place.' Suppressing his rage, he speaks in a low voice. 'I'm not the fucken Salvation Army, you know.'

'Whatever you say.'

'You don't know what you're talking about, Tomásheen.' He turns on his heel.

'What was that about?' the surveyor asks him.

'Ah, a young fella who's talking through his arse.'

The two of them get into the jeep, M.J. banging his door.

Deadlines and fresh contracts, however, and The Royal Showband at the Buffalo dictate the rhythm of life in London. And whatever is smouldering inside about bribes, hard rock and hungry rats, I bury deep, lifting bags of cement and feeding the mixer.

We are ahead of schedule at Hitchin, which puts the men in good spirits. They know that their pay packet, whether from the site office each Friday evening, or from a roll of notes taken from the hiring-foreman's trouser pocket in The Highway later, will be supplemented by a good bonus at the end of August: more five-pound notes to flash around in Ireland and show how well they are doing in London.

So the pressure is on to make more money. We are working at a scorching pace: twelve houses in each section. Horse is making sporadic raids and striking fear into the younger men, who have seen others failing to reach the chalk-mark and being hustled off the site before the midday break without a penny for the train back to London. 'He'll get what's comin' to him before many moons,' they swear with impotent rage over pints, or in high-spirited moments on the Tube to New Eltham: football boots and togs in Caltex bags at our feet, and, across the aisle, disdainful looks over newspapers when our Irish accents rise above the clatter of the wheels.

Deano has the same news. 'Do you see him?' he nods one evening in the pub towards a raw-boned man with dark eyebrows – known as The Lone Ranger – who always sits on his own with his pint and packet of Woodbines. 'He's going back next month. Bought a bit of land near Labasheeda, but he swears he's going to get Horse.'

A few days later it happens without warning. Horse has driven behind a lorry load of concrete to floor one of the sub-stations for services. As always, he curses and swears his way onto the site. He doesn't have all fucken day. 'Back up,' he roars at the driver, 'or I'll have to back the fucken thing myself.' In his haste he nearly trips over a pickaxe. 'Who the fuck left this here?' He flings the pickaxe against a stack of bricks; the iron bar flies from the handle, glances off the stack and barely misses

The Lone Ranger, who is working with a group of men putting down a kerb. The Lone Ranger throws him a menacing look, but Horse grins and strikes the side of the lorry with a lump hammer. 'Come on, back up. Whoa!'

The pins jingle when he gives them an upward tap; the guard-rail falls and the hydraulic shaft slowly raises the front of the load, causing the wet concrete to flow smoothly into the open mouth of the sub-station and to give off a smell of lime and cement. Down below, a student from Sligo is levelling off the bottom of the pit with a shovel. Wet pebbles like hailstones rain down on him and dance on his shoulders. His shirt and trousers are covered with grey splashes and the concrete is rising around his ankles.

'Bottom the fucken thing. Come on, bottom the fucken thing!' Horse keeps shouting down. 'Too much playin' with yer goolies is what's wrong with ye student fellas.' From where I stand by the mixer, I can see the student's blond head and the laboured movements of his body as he wades through the concrete and starts to climb the ladder.

'Do you see what I see?' Deano moves up beside me. 'Look'. The Lone Ranger has stopped kerbing, and, like a jungle cat that has seen its prey, he glowers at Horse. Concrete sloshes in the forgotten drum of the mixer. 'Get back down there and level off the fucken thing,' Horse roars and waves the lump hammer threateningly at the student.

'My clothes are destroyed.'

' "My clothes are destroyed." ' Horse mocks him. ' "My clothes are destroyed." Is it Savile Row you're wearin', you little bollix? Jaysus, what am I paying you for?' His shouting has attracted the attention of the bricklayers, and the roofers, who rest on one knee against the felt and the battens and look down.

The student shades his face with one hand and keeps on climbing despite Horse's abuse: 'Get back down and bottom the fucken thing.'

As soon as the student reaches the top, Horse makes a rush at him, but he dodges and weaves out of his way. Remarkably nimble for his size, Horse closes in and makes to grab his shirt but again the student parries the attempt. Terror on his face, he keeps shouting. 'Leave me alone, you fucken animal,' but he gets trapped in a corner formed by two stacks of cement bags; and now, as if he were a rag doll, Horse wheels him around and draws a kick on his backside. 'There,' he says, breathing heavily, 'get the fuck outa here.'

While he is catching his breath and looking around for approval, he fails to notice that The Lone Ranger has grabbed the pickaxe handle and has stolen up behind him. With a dull thud, the handle comes down on Horse's back, his knees buckle and he collapses; on his upturned face is a frown of confusion as if he has a question to ask and is lost for words. For a moment, The Lone Ranger stands looking down at the struggling body near one of the lorry wheels, vibrating with the force of the hydraulic. Then he throws the handle aside, picks up his jacket and saunters off down the passageway.

The site has come to a standstill, except for the concrete, still sliding into the open mouth of the sub-station. One of the bricklayers steps forward: 'Are you alright, Batt?' he asks, picking up the sweaty hat from beneath the lorry.

Horse raises himself, blinks and looks around, all his actions in slow motion. 'What the fuck? What happened me?'

'The Lone Ranger,' says one of Horse's lackeys.

With a scowl, Horse turns around: 'Where's the fucker? He's done for.'

'Gone,' says the lackey.

Horse rubs his large curly head. 'I always knew he was a mad bastard. I'll see he never gets a day's work in this outfit again.' He stands, a bit groggy at first, and feebly puts his hat on his head. They gather round: some only up to his shoulder. 'Your man. Always drinkin' on his own. He's gone in the head, Batt.' But as they return to their posts, I notice one or two grinning and winking to each other. Leaning against his shovel, Deano smiles at me and clenches his fist in triumph.

Keeping the mixer going, however, is the main agenda; that and buying silver watches for the holidays. And like desperados, the men take risks in order to meet the August deadline.

Wearing an old cowboy hat and slapping the side of the loaded dumper, Sputnik steers in and out of the sun-hardened ruts, missing by inches the tea-boy lighting the brazier. One day, Hill of Howth swings around with a plank on his shoulder and flattens a bricklayer who is standing back to admire his work. I run to The King George and phone the ambulance. For a while the sight of their fallen comrade, his forehead cut open and blood streaming down his face, sobers the men. Sputnik eases off on the dumper, but thoughts of a bulging wallet, a new suit and a cigarette case to impress those who didn't have to take the boat is too much to resist, and, by evening, the men on the scaffold are shouting for more fucken compo.

With just a couple of weeks left, we are on the home straight: the twelve houses in our section are up to wall plate. The tilers are already on the previous lot – so close to us, they shout as they work their way, supple as monkeys, over felt and battens: 'Get off your arses, you fucken latchicos.'

We get our breath back during the morning and midday break when the purr of the compressor is the only background sound to the idle chatter. The arguments continue. There was no one like Seán Purcell. You're talking through your arse. The best man that ever laced boots in Croke Park was Mick O'Connell. Fucken eejit, didn't he leave the cup in the train? I saw it in the newspaper. Fuck you and your newspaper. 'Tis far away from newspapers you were reared, except to line the holes in your shoes.

After pints in The Highway, such crossfire would have led to blows, smashed glasses, and to Sandra phoning for the police. Not now. They had slaved together. The prize is in sight.

A few days before we finish, Deano saunters back from his lunchtime snooze in one of the trucks and throws himself beside me on a heap of sand. To boost his earnings, he has taken a part-time job in a pub, and is jaded by break-time. We laze in the sun watching Sputnik return from The King George.

'Why do they call him that name?' I ask.

'Sputnik.' Deano yawns and rubs his eyes. 'Well, not because of any interest in space travel. Fastest man in and out of

Richmond Street on a Friday night. D'you follow?' Resting on one elbow, he scoops sand with an open palm, and lets it trickle through his fingers. 'The women get their money; Sputnik gets his cocoa, so no complaints.'

'You won't be sorry to finish here,' I say and sit up to survey the site; a loud cheer rises from the card players in the hut. Kamal, the Indian boy, is scouring the frying pan; while he scrubs, the shining metal glints in the sun. For over three weeks Greenwich has recorded unusually high temperatures, so between frying steaks and chops, Kamal has been running to and fro with bottles of milk, Cidona and Tizer.

'I'll be down to Barclays for my pot of gold and then out to Euston as fast as the Tube can take me. And I don't ever again want to see a mixer or a dumper. I'll be in Glenamaddy for the opening of The Dreamland Ballroom or else my name isn't Paddy Conway.'

'When're your finals?'

'May. The brass plate on the front door this time next year.'

'I might visit you.'

'I hope you will.'

As soon as the half-hour is up, Kilrush storms out of the site office blowing a whistle and scratching himself. 'Come on, you lazy bastards, move your arses,' he shouts. 'Is it a shaggin' holiday camp you think you're in?'

Brickies climb the ladder; the mixer chugs into life and coughs up smoke, and I split open another bag of cement.

Raising a blanket of grey dust, a lorry pulls in with a load of sand; the driver calls me: 'Hey Paddy, sign here.'

'Sure.'

Approaching the cab, I overhear their put-down: 'Can the blighter write his name?'

'He can do an x, can't he?'

They both snigger and the driver hands me down the slip through the open window. 'Ta, Pat.'

'My name isn't Pat.'

'Oh, is it not?' They snigger again as I hand him back the book of invoices.

I return to the mixer and, to expunge the hurt, shovel all the harder. When the concrete is right, I stop the motor and tilt the drum onto a wheelbarrow. And all the while I rehearse in my head the crushing replies I should have made, but gradually my anger gets lost in the rattling pace: the tapping of trowels, and Deano whistling as he climbs the ladder, a full hod of compo on his shoulder.

We work in a contented silence, broken only by fragments carried in the breeze about fast women, or crops of hay and turf saved early in Sligo because of the good weather.

Then, without warning – like all great misfortunes – out of the sky falls a nightmare. A dreadful cry pierces the air; a cry that still, on occasions, works its way into my dreams, and causes me to start up in the bed.

'Maaaam!'

My head shoots up and I see what spreads a pall over my world for months afterwards, changes even the course of my life's path. Deano's two feet are kicking against an indifferent sky, his hands are clawing and scratching in a futile effort to break his fall. With a sickening crack, his head hits the edge of a dumper and his body is hurled on to the pitiless clay: a shudder from his hands; a half-kick from one foot. Blood oozes from his mouth and ears.

Trowels and buckets are thrown aside, men are running. Garryowen cries out: 'O sweet Jesus.' His boots scrape the gravel when he falls to his knees; he puts a hand around Deano's limp head, and, in a trembling voice, cries into his ear: 'O my God, I am heartily sorry for having offended thee, and I detest my sins above every other evil because they displease thee, my God, who, for thy infinite goodness, art so deserving of all my love … .' His head sinks, and I throw myself on the dry earth and supply the forgotten words: 'And I firmly resolve with the help of thy holy grace never more to offend thee and to amend my life. Amen.'

Pale-faced, Garryowen turns to me: 'Run, boy, run for Jesus' sake. Run for the ambulance. And a priest.'

I dash over long grass and strips of wood, empty Tizer

bottles and rusted hoops that nearly trip me up: down the railway track to The King George to phone. My frenzied mind argues against the horrid truth of what I've seen: if I run faster, the doctors will be able to make him all right again. Racing over the wasteland, I say Hail Marys: please, Blessed Mother, help Deano. *Please.*

The rest is a series of horrifying snapshots passing in front of my bewildered stare: the white sheet that covers the patches of blue on his face and neck, the head twisted in a dreadful manner, and the stretcher disappearing inside the back of the ambulance. The priest with a violet stole around his neck. Garryowen's hand resting against the back of the ambulance until the driver very gently says: 'Excuse me, sir.' Bloody fingerprints left on the door. The tyres crunch the gravel passage and the siren fades as the ambulance races down King's Row. I stand looking after it until I feel vomit rising to my throat.

With one hand against the back of the hut to steady myself, I retch into the nettles. A police car drives through the entrance, jolting over the rough ground until it comes to a halt beside a stack of cement bags. Like every site accident, self-preservation comes first: those without cards, and others who have fictitious names and are claiming for a wife and several children back in Ireland scurry into the dark cavities of the nearly completed houses.

Once they are satisfied that no treachery has occurred, one of the policemen closes his notebook and fastens it with a rubber band; the other winds up a measuring tape. 'Right then.' The notebook officer turns to Garryowen: 'Sorry about your mate. Poor chap. Too young to die. You may be called on to testify at a later date.'

As soon as the police car has swung on to the main road, men start to appear at doorways, others from the backs of houses with empty wheelbarrows. 'What's one poor Irish gorsoon less to them boyos?' says Sputnik, fumbling with his cap.

A frightening silence has descended on the site. Kilrush picks up a shovel, thrusts it into the heap of sand and, in a tired voice, says: 'That's it for today, men. I've phoned the boss. We'll go home in God's name, but let us say a prayer for the boy's soul and for his poor father and mother.'

The tilers join us and every man on the site gets down on one knee beside where I have swept Deano's blood into the sand. 'What a story for his poor family,' says Kilrush as we rise. 'Load up, lads.'

Frame by frame, every detail of that awful day comes back as if it had happened only yesterday. No shouting now at attractive women as we drive back to Camden in silence, no talk about the greatest footballer. Even the motor seems hushed. Eventually one of the men speaks: 'Who's at home?'

'The mother and father. Poor oul father.' In the mirror I see him do a drinking motion with his hand up to his open mouth.

'God help us.'

M.J. phones me that night at The Highway. 'We'll get a coffin in the morning and go back with the body when 'tis released.'

The next couple of days I spend at The Royal Hotel, or out with Deano's family in their single-storey farmhouse with small windows and a corrugated iron roof, rusted in places. Cups of tea with too much sugar and milk, and Nice biscuits are put into my hands. Even now the sickly taste of those biscuits can bring back that bad time. I sit beside his mother at an open fireplace and speak in a grown-up way: 'Everyone liked Paddy, Mrs Conway. And he was my best friend.'

'Was he, boy?'

His father and other men, with bottles of Guinness in their hands, stand near the stairs at the gloomy end of the long kitchen and speak in low voices; women buttering currant bread, pause and wipe away tears.

'Too good for this world.' Without raising her head, Deano's mother speaks to the fireplace, letting the rosary beads lie idle in her lap. She looks up at the grandfather clock. 'Before the priest brought the news, I knew. A mother knows, boy.' I glance at the silent face, the dead pendulum and the black hands stopped at five past three. 'A shiver went through me, Tommy. I knew something had happened to Paddy, and I'd just stopped the clock when the priest was standing at the front door.'

On the day of the funeral, as I'm climbing the lichen-covered steps to the village church, bees are humming in a fuchsia hedge at one side; a cock crows in a neighbouring farmyard. My father would have removed his hat, because that's the sign of a soul going to heaven, he always said. Though the weather is sultry, a cold damp smell fills the sacristy where I volunteer to serve the funeral Mass.

'And where did you learn Latin, young man?' Over his glasses, the parish priest takes my measure.

I mention the boarding school.

He laughs. 'Oh, the Jesuit Fathers, no less. And I thought you were a navvy in John Bull. What is someone the likes of you doing over there?'

'Working for the summer, Father.'

'It takes a tidy penny to go to that college. Who are you?'

I tell him.

'The young brother.' He laughs again. Dandruff lies on the shoulders of his soutane, and he gives off a smell of pipe to-bacco. Leaning against the vesting bench, he turns the pages of the Roman Ritual. 'Thanks, young man. But we've our own altar server here.' He nods towards a stout boy in a corner who is struggling to pull a surplice down over his soutane.

'Right so, Father.'

The people are gathering for Mass in the main body of the church: men are talking at the back and clearing their throats; women are huddled in the pews, a doleful tone to the rise and fall of their voices. I tell M.J. what had happened in the sacristy. 'Don't worry. I'll settle this,' he says. He leaves, and through the diamond-leaded windows, I can hear his footsteps on the gravel path beside the church.

In a minute, he is back, looking pleased with himself. 'Every man has his price, Tommy. Never forget that,' he whispers.

'Twenty quid goes a long way in helping a parish priest to change his mind. He won't be getting that much for a Mass around here for a long time.'

The priest appears in the sanctuary, scans the congregation and beckons to me. 'I didn't know you were young Paddy's best friend,' he says in the sacristy. 'You should have told me. You'll serve the Mass. Good man.'

After the burial service, in the graveyard above the village, the priest replaces the ribbon markers, closes the black-covered Roman Ritual and removes the purple stole from around his neck. With Garryowen and Sputnik, I fill in the grave. The clay hits the coffin with a dull sound; there is a sharp crack when pebbles strike against the brass plate. Dust rises from the dry earth while we work. We kneel for a silent prayer before the men head down the road to the two pubs. The women, who form a wailing huddle around Deano's mother and sisters, remain staring at the mound on which we have placed the shovels in the shape of a cross.

I mooch around the graveyard, studying the headstones as if they hold some explanation for this hammer blow to my expectations about life, and Deano's dream of being a veterinary surgeon and owning a big house on the Athlone Road. Election posters are wrapped around the poles: Vote for the party that cares. A plate-glass window of the village shop advertises the opening of The Dreamland Ballroom in Glenamaddy. Grand extension until 1 am. Admission five shillings. Music by Doc Carroll and The Royal Blues.

In the pub, the schoolmaster is standing at the counter with M.J. and Seery. 'The poor fellow worked so hard for that scholarship,' the Master is saying. 'He used to arrive at my house every evening on a donkey. A donkey. Imagine.' The watch-chain across his waistcoat shakes when he chuckles.

'Great little worker,' M.J. adds. 'Never missed a day, and he was with me right through his college years.' A brandy in his hand, Seery is taking it all in. He had got a one-way sailing ticket and planned to return with us in the ferry. When he wasn't fawning on the young teacher who told us that she and all the girls were mad about Deano, he was in the back of the car with a ledger on his knees and dockets on the seat beside him.

A couple of sticky papers covered with flies hang from the ceiling laths. In a bizarre way, a catchphrase of my English teacher echoes in my head: 'As flies to wanton boys are we to the gods; they kill us for their sport.' Chalk on the wings of his soutane, he paces the schoolroom, giving the class a few minutes' grace before he fires questions on the previous day's lesson.

Fragments of the conversations rise and fall: someone has the last of his hay saved and is cutting a bit of oats; there's a slight increase in the price of heifers. And the oul bovine TB is nearly cleared up, thank God. A burst of laughter comes from a group of young men who are standing by an empty fireplace, their pints resting on the mantle. The Master apologizes: 'They can only take so much of death. Too frightening.' He returns to his pipe and his topic: Lemass is putting Ireland on its feet at last. Dev has had his day. The Master is becoming more voluble as he lowers one glass of whiskey after another. M.J. is nodding, but I notice him glance at the round clock beside a picture of the Pope. Eventually he looks at his watch and affects surprise at the time; he stands, shakes hands with the Master and turns to a few men who had tried to buy him a drink earlier. 'So long, lads, and if you decide to head to London, there'll be no shortage of work. You'll find me through The Highway pub on Kilburn High Road.'

At the outskirts of the village we stop at a Caltex pump where a chap about my own age is lying on an old car seat reading a Zane Grey western. He was in the same class as Deano's younger brother. 'Brains to burn, that family had. Deano would be a qualified vet next year, did you know that?'

'Yes. I knew that.'

He talks while he fills up the petrol tank. As soon as he finishes his metal work course in the Tech, he is heading for New York. All his class, apart from the sons of well-off farmers, have gone away. While we chat, I can hear Seery talking figures and schemes to M.J. 'Guernsey', 'the Isle of Man' and 'blasted tax' escape through a chink in the nearest window.

Two cows are grazing on the roadside in front of Deano's house when we call to say goodbye before setting off for Dublin. In an empty shed, children are taking turns on a swing: two ropes tied to a crossbeam – a hay sack for a seat. Barking and jumping, a mongrel races around them. 'I have a few hundred here,' says M.J. reaching into a pocket in the dashboard. 'By the look of things, they'll need it.'

'M.J.' Seery stops turning pages; his tone is rigid. 'I know it's very sad, but if you give that,' eyeing the bulky envelope, 'you could be seen as accepting liability.'

The starched collar of his shirt strains when M.J. turns round and studies him. 'Have you any screed of feeling, man?'

'They're nice people, M.J., and we're all sorry for them and for Paddy, but when the dust settles, they might have that as material evidence that you were admitting liability and take you for thousands.'

By now the children have left the swing and are grinning at us through the warped bars of a gate. 'If you want to give a few hundred,' Seery continues, closing a ledger and smiling out at the children, 'pitch in when the benefit dance is held in the Galty. No one need be the wiser then.'

M.J. studies the envelope: 'You might be right,' he says and hands it to Seery. 'Look after that. I'm goin' in for a minute.' He jokes with the children, giving each of them a few coins; they refuse at first, but then take the money and run to the shed, comparing their good fortune.

I I

A TEAM OF GARDENERS has already begun on the first
section of houses when we return from the funeral. For
a day or two the Galvin men work in long periods of
silence so that whenever the mixer is turned off, we can hear
the carpenters hammering the door frames and smoothing
down the wood inside the nearby houses. Each evening they
sweep out the sawdust and the curled shavings, filling the air
with the smell of fresh timber. Some have by now gone to
another contract, so that life seems to have drained from the
site.

Sitting on a load of roof tiles during the break, I stare down
at the spot where Deano crashed to his death, and hear again
his last desperate cry. One of the carpenters settles himself
beside me. 'Deano,' he says, as though reading my thoughts, 'was
he on the beer the night before?'

'No. He was *not* on the beer the night before.'

He looks up in surprise, and then continues to roll a cigarette. 'I was only asking.'

'That's all right.' My anger cools. 'No, some fucker removed
a plank by mistake from underneath the tarpaulin, so when
Paddy took a step on the scaffold, he had nothing ... well, you
know the rest.'

He strikes a match against one of the tiles; he wants to talk,
I want to be alone. 'Sorry. I know he was your friend, and if these
things didn't frighten us, sure we'd have no nature at all.' But he

himself has grown hardened to life's casualties: trenches caving in because the foreman was cutting down on shuttering – shuttering costs money and a carpenter's time. More money. He has seen bricks falling from the sky and splitting open a man's skull. And the day a lorry backed up against a wall and crushed two men who were having their lunch in a suntrap. As always, of course, they deadened the pain of life's misfortunes on the high stools of the Crown or through visits to Richmond Street.

I too try to shelve my discontent by returning to the Galty every Saturday night and groping for satisfaction with whomever will provide comfort and ease my confusion. While London is sleeping, I pick up the men at Camden Town and at Kilburn High Road. Gradually the banter returns: the fine bit of stuff that Seery got off with on Sunday night; the best man in Ireland right now to take a free is Mattie McDonagh; but Cassius Clay will never have the punch Jack Dempsey had.

'You're very quiet these days,' says Jody when we are settled in to double bacon and eggs at a café one morning.

'I can't get over what happened to Deano. Have you seen much of that, Jody – men losing their lives?'

'Indeed I have. Up in Coventry, a young bloke, racing on a dumper.' He is dipping a crust of bread into one of the eggs. 'Same old story. Flash the few bob around when he went home – show them that he was doing well. Anyway, he was emptying concrete into a tunnel – twenty feet deep – and pulling right up to the edge. "Slow down," we told him. "For Christ's sake, slow down, you mad bastard." No use. Well, one time he drove up too fast and the force carried him over the top. Awful. By the time we dug him out,' he shakes his head, 'the poor lad's face and body were as grey as them floor tiles.' With his deep blue eyes, he looks out through the window where men are shouting and hopping on trucks. 'You get used to it. Lads lose their footing. You don't think too much. Go mad if you did. And you hope you'll get out of here alive and maybe come by a few acres back home.'

'How did you end up here?' I want to understand; the plan to join M.J. is now finally unravelling.

'A friend of mine. We had spent a year together in the Tech. He came home one Christmas with a wristlet watch, and he used to tap his fag against a silver case before he lit up. He was one of the Pincher Laddies – McNicholas's crowd. I thought I'd be made in London.' He had to hide the cardboard suitcase from his mother and father in the hayshed. 'Strangest thing of all: the old sheepdog was howling around the yard the morning I left. I told them – the Da and herself – that I was going to the hurling final in Croke Park.'

As we are leaving the café, Horse Muldoon comes tearing around the corner cursing and swearing that six of the Hitchin crew – the fucken Connies – hadn't shown up and he would burst their goolies.

'I'll take the pick-up and collect them,' I say. 'Jody can take some of my gang.'

By now, I am well-used to the short cuts: down Camden High Street, then left at Old Street where the traffic gets heavy around seven o'clock.

The address on Horse's torn-off Wild Woodbine packet leads me to a cul-de-sac off the Seven Sisters Road. When the knocker won't budge, I call through the letterbox, and wait. Tall grass and weeds cover the tiny garden. One of the upstairs windows has a broken pane of glass; inside, a drip-dry shirt on a wire hanger is stirring in the breeze. I call again; this time a dark-skinned man in a long beige shirt over cream trousers answers the door. The smell of India pours out through the open door. 'O yes,' he says as if delighted to see me. 'Irishmen upstairs. Noise. Very noise.' He grins and puts both hands up to his ears. 'Oh yes, very noise. Every night.' A brown-eyed child clings to his trouser leg, smiles up at me and then hides.

Some of the banisters in the stairs are broken or hang as-lant. As I reach the landing, a man in a torn singlet puts his head out the door, then swings around and shouts into the room: 'Jaysus, get up! The college lad.'

'Who?'

'The boss's fucken brother. Get up, you bastards.'

I hear a thump on the floorboards: 'Get up, fuck you!'

They fill the quiet street with loud talk and the smell of stale beer.

'Nice morning, lads.'

They grunt and hop into the back.

A tall sinewy man, a few years older than the others, sits in beside me. His red hair stands out, and on the side of his face is a trace of dried blood. He catches me looking.

'A bit of a scrap in The Maid of Erin,' he says as if by way of an apology.

'Ah, sure, it happens.'

Silence in the back. I glance in the rear-view mirror. One of them is puking over the side: the green vomit splashes on the mudguard and slides down to the road. At a set of traffic lights, two women in gabardine coats glare at us. One of the men shouts. 'What are you fucken lookin' at?'

The women look away. 'Disgusting. Those Irish,' says one of them. She makes a face.

An older man, his hand on the sick youth's shoulder, raises his tousled head. 'Ah, go and fuck yourself, you dry old bitch. 'Tis how you never had a good ride in your life.'

The lights turn green.

'The oul bitch,' says the man beside me. He rolls down the window and sticks out his head, so that his long hair is tossed about wildly. 'An bhuil tú ceart, a mhic?' he asks.

'Tá mé all right, a mhic.'

They let out a roar at the women, who are now falling back from my side-view mirror.

For a couple of nights I go upstairs to my room in The Highway and stare out the window at rows of terracotta chimney pots and the slated roofs of houses, trying to impose order into my thoughts. I would be insane to give up the newly found pleasures of the Galty, or the promise that lies ahead with M.J. Galvin Construction to go into a seminary.

The insane voice, however, has me in its grip. I begin to visit Quex Road Church and kneel beneath stained-glass windows; my mind wanders along the grain of the dark wooden pews to the brass plaques: 'Pray for the souls of Francis Dolan and family. Remember Joseph Egan. R.I.P.' I look up at the tabernacle – and for the soul of Patrick Conway. On my way out, I light a candle at the shrine to the Sacred Heart.

'To be a priest?' M.J. laughs when I break the news to him before I leave. He is removing boots caked with dried mud in the red and black chequered hallway, supporting himself with one hand on the newel post of the stairs. 'Pull the other one, Tomásheen. A priest? Did the sun get to your brain or something.' He looks at me; the smile fades. 'You mean it.'

'Yeah, well, give it a try anyway.'

'What would make you do a thing like that, boy?' A frown shows on his tanned face, he flings the boots into the press beneath the stairs and slams the door. 'And throw away the chance of a lifetime.' He glowers at me and keeps running his hand through his wavy hair.

When Vera has gone to her ballroom dancing with her husband, he brings it up at the dinner table.

'Where did this notion come from anyway?'

'I've been speaking to a priest in school. He thinks I should give it a go.'

'What? A priest in school. What do they know?' He shakes his head. 'Sure all them fellas do is play golf and eat scones with nuns. And walk around with shiny shoes. Waste of a life, if you ask me.'

'If you think so little about the whole thing, why do you go to Mass?'

'Go to Mass. Of course I go to Mass!' His anger is rising again. 'What has going to Mass to do with anything. Doesn't take much to go to Mass; didn't all belonging to us go? Are you out of your mind, boy?' He pushes away his plate, and begins to tap the table. 'For the life of me, I don't know why a fella would want to do a thing like that when he could have it made in no time. And you want to go to Africa, you say.'

'I'm not being ordained tomorrow. I'll have seven years – if I stay – to think about it.'

Usually, when he has cleaned his plate, he is out the door

to some meeting with a quantity surveyor or borough council official. Not this evening. Instead, he is in and out of the sitting-room, pulling out drawers, looking at maps. I switch on the radiogram and pick up the *Daily Mail*, and behind the newspaper I'm trying to shape a defence for the next attack. Yes. I'm searching for something. Answers. Why did Deano …? Something beyond Muldoon shouting and throwing youths around like rag dolls. Better not to take that line – Muldoon is a trusted foreman. Fragments from school retreats, and films showing priests strolling around schoolyards, black children grinning broadly and looking up at them. Gregory Peck going off to China in *The Keys of the Kingdom*. The young priest back from Uganda who said Mass in Ardglass chapel one Sunday, and talked about digging wells, and giving people a chance to live. And a current of something close to arousal was racing through my veins. In school the following day, he showed films and asked if any boy would sell *The Far East*.

'Yes, I will. I'll sell six, Father.'

The periodic reminders in *The Sunday Press. Would you like to devote your life to God? No greater love…*. In a photograph, clerical students in soutanes are having a grand time in front of a seminary throwing snowballs at one another.

'And tell me, how are you going to keep your paws off the young ladies? You'll be going to bed on your own for the rest of your living days. By all accounts you weren't sitting in a corner on your own in the Galty.'

'Haven't priests managed for the last nine or ten hundred years?'

'I know nothing about these things, Tommy boy, but I know 'tis not natural.' He is rolling up ground plans that don't need rolling.

After much mindless activity, he grows calm again: 'I'd make you a director in no time, if you got the engineering. Even if you didn't get it. I never had the oul education, and sometimes 'tis hard to keep up. You know, at dinners, and meetings, these architects and engineers talking about their university days and classical music and Covent Garden. Doesn't bother me too much because they know I could buy the lot of them, but still... . And to have one of my own, that would be great.'

I lower the music on the radiogram. 'I have to give it a try.'

'We're not to your liking over here.'

'No. I enjoyed the work.'

'That's the way things are.'

He gives in and we flit over territory now well-known to me: the flats in Dunstable, the Heathrow job, the sand pit at Sundon. He was getting out of cable-laying: the demand for houses would hold for a long time yet. Then suddenly I step on a mine. *Dead men. Subbies pocketing wages.*

His colour rises. 'So we're con men, is that it?'

'Ah no.'

'No? All right for them that have dreamy notions about how things should be, while us poor bastards paw the shit.' He glares at me: 'I got no help from anyone when I came over here, but I didn't waste my time scratching my arse. I copped on very soon and saw where I could make a few bob. And every brand of a hoor out there trying to do me.' He slams the door behind him. Stunned, I slump into the armchair as the jeep thunders into an angry roar.

The same thunder wakes me some time after two o'clock and, before I drop off again, my fear of another confrontation in the morning returns. When I come downstairs, however, he stands, filling the doorway to the kitchen, a mug of tea in his hand: 'I've a plate of rashers for you in the oven.' He puts me in mind of a bricklayer's remark one day in Hitchin: 'Your brother – I may as well tell you the truth – he's as thorny as a fucken porcupine, but he never keeps up a grudge.'

'Where're you off to for the day?' he asks me.

'Charing Cross. I'll hang around a few bookshops, stroll by the river. The day looks promising.'

'You can't be reading any more of them dirty books from now on, Father Galvin.'

'No. I suppose not. Have to be very holy from now on.'

Steam rising from his mug of tea, he sits opposite me and hangs his head while I eat. Then he says: 'You've been a topping worker. Here's something to keep you going whatever you decide to do.' He takes a bundle of notes from his trouser pocket and places it beside my plate. Then he grows silent, lowers his head again, and, this time, explodes into a fit of crying that startles me. 'Sorry about last night, Tommy. There's too much oul spite and bitterness in our family. I don't want to be fighting with you too.'

'It was nothing.'

'Fucken emigration made strangers out of us. And then the way things were at home. The two of them not talking half the time.'

He dries his eyes with the back of his hand. 'Look, you'll need a few bob in one of them priest colleges too. I'll be late tonight, so enjoy yourself.' He gives me a light poke on the shoulder, sits back, and takes a mouthful of tea.

'What's funny?' he asks when he sees me smiling.

'What they say about you is true: that brother of yours is a thorny bastard, but he doesn't hold a grudge.'

He leans in again. 'A lesson I learned in life if you want to succeed: never keep up a spleen, because it'll eat you up. And another thing, Tommy: never lose your rag with the fella who's against you – same as a boxer. If a boxer loses his rag, he's finished. He has to keep his mind on the job of getting the better of the other fella.' He places his hands on the table as if he is about to rise, but is reluctant to go. 'Anyway, you're the one with the education round here.' He cocks his head: 'Do you know anything about dreams?'

'Not much.'

'Strange oul dream last night.' He talks from the kitchen where he's washing his mug. 'I dreamt my bank manager at Barclays called me in. "Sorry, Mr Galvin," he says, "but mice got into the vault." Then he brings me down to the main safe, opens the steel doors and says: "Look, sorry, all your money. I'm afraid, all of it." And I stand there looking down at a heap of pulp and a mouse nibbling at a ten-pound note. And the worst of all is our mother is standing a bit away from me, laughing.' He shakes his head. 'Ah, oul dreams. I suppose they don't make any sense.'

12

BACK FROM LONDON and with only two weeks to prepare for All Saints Seminary, I search the house for the president's prospectus, and the brochure with the laughing students smoking their pipes in front of pillars.

My mother is in a peevish mood when she rummages in cupboards. She finds my open wallet on the kitchen table and goes through it, but all she finds is a clipping from a newspaper showing a sultry Marilyn Monroe in a tight-fitting blouse, her blonde hair resting on the upturned collar. She peers at it: 'Who's this Marilyn Monroe when she's at home?'

'She's a film star.'

'Well, faith, a film star.' She makes a tongue-clicking sound. 'And you have her picture in your wallet. I'm sure she'd be delighted if she knew that.'

Still searching under seat covers, she continues to grouse: 'How is it that you could lose the prospectus, but you wouldn't lose Marilyn Monroe?' I sense, however, from the odd glance of concern that her testy mood is a mask to hide her sinking heart. 'Of all the foolish young fellas.' Muttering to herself, she lifts a pile of clothes off an armchair. 'You'll never be kept in that college if you don't smarten yourself, boy.'

With a Hitchin tan, and wearing the prescribed black suit, white shirt and black tie, I climb the steps of All Saints in mid-September. The other first-years and their families seem at ease as if sauntering through the ornate doors is a commonplace event in their lives. They are chatting and smiling by the grey pillars mottled with age; one of them simulates a golfer's swing and follow-through, a hand up to his forehead becomes a visor so that he can keep an eye on the ball's trajectory. He says something that causes the others to burst into laughter.

Cars are pulling up and parking in a circle around a flowerbed of Celtic cross formation. With the satin cape of their soutanes lifting in the breeze, priests are conversing with men wearing well-cut suits, or tweeds and flannels, and women with pillbox hats.

My father looks awkward. When he strains his neck to admire the canopy above the door and the concrete urns on the top step, I can see stubble on his scrawny neck where he has missed with the open razor; his collar stud has come unhooked, so his tie is loose. I redden when his thick country accent causes a woman with a fur stole to glance in our direction and smile.

'Frightful high ceilings ye have here, Father,' he bellows.

The president, whose smooth black hair is parted down the middle, allows a smile to form on his thin lips. 'Quite so, quite so,' he replies. 'Your son, Thomas, has a wholesome complexion. Has he been abroad?'

'England, Father,' my mother says.

'Oh, beautiful country this time of year. When I was a student, a few of us used to cycle around the Cotswolds. And one year we went as far as Bath – such a splendid city. I can tell you we felt it in our joints afterwards. Did you cycle, Thomas?' A fold of pink flesh rests on his shining Roman collar.

'No indeed,' my father rushes in before I can answer. 'Workin' the shovel, and drivin' men to their buildin' site.'

When they catch the light, the president's rimless glasses conceal his eyes, but I know he is taking stock of us. 'My word,' he says and begins to rub an earlobe. And despite his polite small talk and my father's brave efforts, two social orders are colliding, so that, now and again, the conversation founders.

'Must be a job to paint them high ceilings.' My father is

thrashing about in the engulfing silence. He launches into a soliloquy about the lovely grounds and the 'goalin' pitches' as he calls the playing fields. 'Sure anybody would be glad to be here.'

'Yes, Mr Galvin,' says the president, whose earlobe is itching again. 'We make sure our seminarians are fit in body as well as spirit. *Mens sana in corpore sano.*' When he goes on to speak about rugby and soccer in winter, croquet and tennis in summer, my father loses interest and begins to rummage inside his jacket. He unfastens a safety pin from the lining and removes a roll of notes from the pocket.

'I'll pay you now, Father. For Tomásheen ... for Thomas.'

The woman in the fur stole throws another sly glance.

'Well, it isn't strictly necessary.'

The president's glasses twitch and there is a whiff of aniseed when he covers his mouth with a white handkerchief and utters a muffled 'by all means, if you wish, Mr Galvin.'

My father's knobbly thumbs peel off one hundred and thirty pounds. 'And here's a fiver to say Mass for us and the holy souls, Father.'

'Thank you. Thank you so much, Mr Galvin. Very kind. Well now,' he says, looking at his watch. 'My word, look at the time! We'll be going for tea in Egan Hall in a moment. Lovely meeting you; we'll chat later.' Leaving a jet stream of aniseed, he hurries off to greet another family who have driven up in a big black car.

'I suppose', my father says, as if we are deaf or he is talking to us from the far end of a long room, 'he'd be very learned.'

'Very learned.' I watch the president in the distance, pointing in the direction of the playing pitches. He seems more relaxed now, telling the new family, no doubt, about croquet in the summer.

After tea, we all, including the president and some of the teaching staff, stroll to the front again with our families, and stand aside as they are getting into cars and cruising down the sweep of driveway. Mine are in the back seat of a hackney for the train. My mother looks straight ahead; my father, wearing dentures that seem too big for him, gapes out, and when he finds me, waves as if he is cleaning the window. I raise my hand, and in the flurry of goodbyes, am crushed by an overheard remark: 'Where did they get your man?' Nearby, two first-years are sniggering, one of them – the golfer – is dressed in a smart three-piece and is carrying a leather portfolio.

I bury the insult, and trudge up the steps with the others. Inside the main door, an unsmiling student, in a Roman collar and a soutane with a row of small buttons down the front, informs us that he is the head prefect and we are to follow him to Egan Hall where the dean of discipline, Reverend Doctor Quirke, is waiting for us. Walking tall, with his heels hardly touching the floor, the prefect tells us that he had been an army cadet, before he entered All Saints. We pass oil paintings of stand-offish bishops in lace. One bishop seems peeved that his prayer has been interrupted: his index finger is inserted between the pages of a breviary that rests on a roped mahogany table.

Seated behind a table on a platform, Doctor Quirke looms over us and, above his horn-rimmed glasses, eyes each student as we move along the benches. After a short prayer in Latin, he reminds us that we must submit our university fees to his office within three days.

Then the rules. He covers everything: weekly confessions, table manners, personal hygiene, 'and the decorum that is fitting to a pontifical seminary shall be observed at all times'. Students should always bear in mind that only those who conform to the rules are fit for the sacred ministry. He looks up from the rulebook and fixes on some point far off in the high ceiling.

'On no account, gentlemen, is a student to enter another student's room. No mercy will be shown to any student who breaches that rule.' Again he rakes the hall – a mannerism we shall come to dread.

'If any man here considers these rules unfair or unjust, he would do best to leave his bags packed and return to his home forthwith.'

All shall pay strict attention to the ringing of the bell which marks the beginning and the end of the various public actions of the day.

All shall observe strict silence except at times when speaking is permitted.

All shall regard this observance as an indispensable means of acquiring the virtue of obedience and custody of the tongue.

Whether in procession or alone, each student shall raise his biretta in reverence to the statues that are located in alcoves throughout the college.

He closes the rulebook, wipes his red face with a handkerchief and stands, his massive girth straining the soutane to its limit.

With perfect timing, the president, in a trailing cloak with a gold chain at the collar, sails into the room. Scowling, the dean jerks his two hands upwards for us to stand while the president mounts the dais and beams at us: he indicates that we are to sit. We are aware, he reassures us, that the rules are not drawn up to frustrate us in any way, but rather to help us in the formation of our character so that we may be good priests. He quotes some saint: Keep the rule and the rule will keep you. If any student fails to observe the rules, he will be showing the college authorities that he is not suitable material for ordination. 'He may have a vocation for another diocese,' he adds with a smile, 'but not this one.' Then he wishes us well, and, swishing his cloak, leaves as quickly as he had entered.

The dean of discipline, who has been standing aside, again climbs the platform and glares at us. He announces the programme for the rest of the week, including a visit to the university where we shall be studying for the next three years. Every morning after housework has been completed, the prefects will convey the dean's instructions from the foot of the main staircase. In a fear-stricken silence, we listen.

'He's a prick,' someone beside me whispers.

The dean of discipline stops. 'You.' He points at the student. 'Did you have the temerity to whisper. Stand up. Were you never taught manners? What's your name?'

'Séamus Meehan, Father.'

'Mr Meehan, you're from down the country.'

'Yes, Doctor Quirke.'

'I thought as much. Mr Meehan. In All Saints your place is to be seen and not heard. Sit down.'

After a cup of tea and a biscuit, we have permission to go for a walk around the grounds before Night Prayer. The sturdy figure of Meehan in a soutane that seems too tight for him sidles up to me as we all drift out by a back door where a Romanesque colonnade forms an ambulatory lit up in amber. Lining the alcoves of the ambulatory on two sides are mosaics that glitter under the spotlights: each alcove contains the names of priests, dating back to the nineteenth century, who died while on the mission fields of Africa, Pakistan and South America. At the centre is a flowing fountain. The grass has been cut; summer smells linger in the cloistered air. 'Did you ever hear such bullshit in all your life?' Meehan says.

'Ah, I wouldn't take much notice of that.'

When he hears I'm from Kerry and I tell him a bit about the Galtymore and playing football in New Eltham, he opens up about the great time he had in New York over the summer, carrying bags for rich old ladies in a Manhattan hotel and getting off with college 'chicks' who were also working in the hotel.

Ahead of us are a group who are listening to one of the prefects – a little guy with a high-pitched voice; he is parroting what the president was saying: rules are for our formation, to make us good priests, and the dean is not such a bad old skin, his bark is worse than his bite. They nod.

'We'll organize a tog-out tomorrow,' says Meehan. 'Although some of these pricks, with their fancy accents, probably play croquet or some other drawers game. Do you know what one fella said to me in the refectory? "I can't understand a word you're saying." The pasty-faced little bollix, I should have … .' His voice trails off when the prefect glances in our direction.

Meehan's candour is endearing, and even though jaded after a long day, I warm to his chatter. He tells me about his uncle, a Holy Ghost missionary in Papua New Guinea. They go fishing whenever he's home. Great guy. Got on the Meath football team back in the 1940s. 'I only came to All Saints to try it out, or maybe to please him.'

'Same here. To try it out.'

'And sure if it doesn't work out, we'll have a degree in our arse pocket; my parents couldn't afford to send me to university. I don't know about you.'

'Much the same, although my brother is doing fairly well in England and he gives me a few bob.'

Those ahead of us are now like a touring group, stopping and turning when the prefect points out the Pugin chapel, the neo-classical façade of Pio Nono House, and the gothic windows of the oratory – features that would become my daily landscape for many years to come. We have almost caught up with them. The prefect, in his squeaky voice, is giving a run-through of the following day's programme. He mentions housework every morning after breakfast, and laughs; the others join him in a polite chuckle. 'Nothing heavy, just sweeping the corridors and washing out the toilets – *The Ritz* we call them.'

Meehan nods in their direction. 'Would you listen? They could get the cleaning women to do that, but they want to stick our noses in it – make us humble. Pricks,' he says between his teeth. 'I was in a minor seminary, Tommy, a feeder for Maynooth and here; I know what goes on. I may be from the bog, but I know my arse from my elbow.' The arched roof fills out his bursts of laughter, and he seems oblivious to the looks we are getting from the prefect and his group.

'Let's take a walk over this way, Séamus,' I say. We head towards two massive gates with the diocesan and papal heraldry decorating the wrought iron. And here, for the first time, we fix our gaze on the Roman palazzo. 'Remind you of home, wouldn't it?' Another loud laugh from Meehan. But he is interested only in telling me about 'chicks', and especially,

Siobhán, a student teacher from Galway, who worked with him in the Manhattan hotel, about the days they spent at Greenwich Village, and out at Staten Island. And then, coming back in the ferry with people from every nation under the sun.

As young men often do in army barracks, most of us adapt to All Saints and learn how to keep in step; and, like soldiers, we gain support from each other in coping with the regime. At the same time we grumble: some about the food, others about the silence or being forbidden to mix with lay students at the university. Our shared dream, however, becomes the driving force. One day we shall break new ground: love will replace sin, dark confession boxes and the fires of hell. We'll help to usher in a new age: priests will no longer live in big houses and drive expensive cars. Reports from Rome give us encouragement: the Pope with the face of an old peasant is spring-cleaning the Vatican. What is more: a Catholic has made it to the White House – and he is Irish.

Our country too is leaving behind a long dark winter: ballrooms are opening up; girls have on flared dresses like they see Connie Francis and Sandra Dee wearing in the pictures. People are buying cars and television sets, and some can even afford to send their children to university. Farmers no longer rise at four o'clock to drive cattle to the fair. Instead, they chug along at nine or ten to the cattle mart in their Massey-Fergusons.

So we slip into a routine of attending lectures, football or basketball in the afternoons, and films on a free day. And, apart from wearing priests' clothes and getting up to pray on dark November mornings, the programme differs little from boarding school. The frequent reminders from the dean of discipline that we lack the proper attitude for seminarians, we learn to take in our stride; the rebukes too, while he wipes his forehead: 'For the life of me, I don't know how some of you got in here.'

13

LADEN WITH BOTTLES OF SHERRY and whiskey and a basket of groceries with the Queen's head on pots of jam, M.J. turns up at Ardglass that Christmas, only his second since our brother Mossie's body had been dragged out of the Thames. In a new Wolsey he drives into the yard as Gerry is watering the cows at the trough. His visit, however, is much more than a homecoming for the festive season. He has got word of a manse and a hundred acres for sale outside Killarney. By St Stephen's Day he is restless, and asks me to go with him to view the property.

'Gerry, you go along too,' my mother says in a loud voice.

Reeking of drink, Gerry throws himself into the back and lies there, a ridiculous smile on his flushed face.

'Very little to do to the house,' says M.J. as we wave good-bye to the Protestant minister and crunch our way back along the gravel driveway. 'And that old bloke hasn't much to live on.'

'They were built to last,' I say. Already, Gerry is beginning to snore in the back.

M.J. relaxes behind the wheel. 'Nothing like having a stake in your own country, Tommy.'

'No, I suppose not.'

'Anyway, we're only getting back from that crowd what they took from us.'

We traverse common ground: Seery, Horse Muldoon, and Garryowen, the goings-on at The Highway. 'Not a bit of trouble now since I brought in the heavy gang.'

'Good.'

'And Jody is over in Bristol with his other woman.' He gives me a sidelong glance. 'I shouldn't be talking like this now to a fella that's going on for the Church.'

'I'm much the same since you saw me last.'

'He'll go home to the wife and kids for a few days before the New Year. The wife wouldn't live in England, wanted to be near her mother, and Jody couldn't find work around Galway. He sends on the money order without fail.'

Gerry suddenly comes alive as we are approaching Farranfore: 'Tomásheen is right, M.J., they were built to last.' He leans forward, 'Will we have something, lads? 'Tis Christmas and the three of us don't meet much.'

'One then.' M.J. glances at me.

A wrenboys' party is in full swing in the pub: dancers tap the wooden floor with their Christmas shoes; twirling skirts rise higher, showing stocking tops and suspenders and causing shouts from the men seated on the high stools. The air is thick with the smell of drink and cigarettes.

Those home from England are easy to pick out: they wear shiny suits and gold watches and throw pound notes on the counter. And they are good at jiving. Some of them know M.J., and, swaying on their feet, try to stand us drinks.

'Have something stronger, Tomásheen, for Christ's sake, and don't be like an oul lady with your bottle of lemonade, ' says Gerry, eyeing my glass.

M.J. rounds on him: 'Don't you think there's enough topers in the Galvins already? And by the way, when are you going to give up being a drunkard?'

'You see this, M.J.' He lifts his glass: 'After the first of January, as God is my judge, not another drop will touch my lips.'

M.J. glares at him and looks as if he might slap the glass out of his hand, but Gerry rambles off to talk to the shiny suits. As soon as he has gone, M.J. edges in with the other reason for his visit: would I go over for a few days – some of his workers didn't get home – just to give them their Christmas box?

'I don't know.'

'I'm up to my eyes getting books in order with Seery. And I've to see some people about the Heathrow job. You'd be doing me a big favour. Just to give them a few quid. They're in bad shape, but they're good lads.'

'I suppose I could manage it.'

'And there's a big do at the Irish Club on New Year's Eve. I'd like you to be there. I'll get you an oul dress suit.'

The mother puts on a scowl when I tell her: 'I suppose I've no say in this house any more. The big man with his money decides everything.' Then, as if with the slightest touch of a button, she unleashes a torrent of abuse. 'My son Mossie would be alive today only for him. He sends you to that college with the big nobs, and your father crying his eyes out every time you went back after the holidays, and saying "Why isn't the Christian Brothers School good enough?" I'm to be pitied if ever a woman was.'

'Only for three or four days. I'll have another week's holidays when I get back.'

In a taxi from Heathrow, I watch people hurry along the wet streets, umbrellas tilted against the driving sleet, fringes of snow by the kerbs. Pink and yellow and blue neon streams run down the taxi window as we pass the Odeon cinema on Gloucester Road.

Vera is rushing from the kitchen to the dining-room and back. 'Have to meet Bertie, me hubby. We're going to Bayswater, Tommy. Victor Sylvester's playing at the Palais.'

'Fine, Vera.'

Envelopes behind the radiogram. Back tomorrow, M.J. has scribbled on the back of a cigar box left on the hallstand; beside it, the keys of the Corsair. I take the batch of addressed envelopes to the dining-room where Vera is now placing a casserole dish on a green and red tablecloth.

'I've ice-cream in the fridge for you. Your favourite.' She

pauses for a moment at the table, a neat apron over her skirt. 'That brother of yours, he'll run himself into the ground, he will. Doesn't half-finish his meal, and he's gone. See you tomorrow then. Ta ra, love.' On her way to the kitchen, she can't resist preening herself in the mirror.

'Thanks, Vera.'

The sleet turns to snow overnight; small drifts lie against the garden walls and on window ledges as I drive at a snail's pace up Magenta Drive the following morning. At a slope in the road, children are taking turns on a sledge; cries of excitement fill the pure air when a snowball smashes against a child's woollen hat and dissolves into a shower of white powder.

The roads are almost free of traffic, so I stop now and again to check the addresses. A boy on a three-wheel delivery bike appears above the brow of the hill and then freewheels down the slope whistling Perry Como's 'Magic Moments'. On the basket carrier is a metal plate: *Hammond's Sausages, a cut above the rest.*

In the first lodging house, a woman peers at me through a chink in the open door.

'Yes?'

'I'm here to see a couple of friends.'

'Are you family, Pat?'

'A friend.'

Reluctantly, she stands aside, and, with a look of contempt, points upstairs: 'Tell them they're out if they don't stop pissing in the bed.'

'I will.'

'Their last chance. Do you 'ear, Pat?'

'I hear.'

'Second landing, the door on the right.'

As I climb the cold stairs, a man's barking voice rises from below: 'What was that all about?'

'Another Paddy. Filthy lot. I should never 'ave taken them in. Only for you.' The door bangs shut.

A murmur of voices leads me to a door with peeling paint. I knock.

'Who's there?'

With caution, I turn the doorknob and catch the dense smell of sweat and stale beer. A gas fire casts a reddish glow over the dark room. After a moment I make out three mounds on rumpled beds; another man in a string vest and shorts is hunched in front of the gas fire.

'Close the fucken door,' says one of the mounds.

'I'm Tommy. M.J. Galvin's brother.'

'Even if you're the Lord Almighty, I'm goin' out to no fucken site on a day like this.'

On the fireguard are shorts and socks that look like dried bits of sticks or strips of cardboard, standing rather than lying on the network.

I close the door and the draught causes a string of tinsel to loosen its hold on the window and flicker as it falls.

'I've a few Christmas presents.'

The men raise themselves and peer at me. Then, with low growls of contentment, they tear open the envelopes and count the notes: thirty-year-old children with dark stubble seeing what Santa has brought.

'The blessin's 'a God on you, boybawn. You'll have a drop?' says the man in the string vest; already he is making towards the bottle of Powers on the windowsill.

'Thanks, but I've a few journeys to make. And the snow.' I'm searching for the doorknob behind me.

'Good man.'

'Right so.'

'Thanks, boy.'

'Dacent man, M.J.'

'Happy New Year, boybawn.' One man is already tucking the envelope beneath the pillow and pulling the bedclothes about his head.

Garryowen's one-room flat in Maitland Park is my last port of call. The flat complex, a functional building of windows and pebbledash, looks old and dirty above the white carpet. Melted ice and slush trickle down a drainpipe. On the opposite side of the street, a man is shovelling snow off the footpath in front of a dull brown building. He calls out: 'Hey mate, over 'ere.'

I cross the street.

'The body's in the fridge, mate. I'll take you up.'

'The body. What body?'

He looks closely at me. 'Aren't you from the undertakers?'

'No.'

'O Jeez, mate, I thought you were, you know, here for the stiff. The black tie and the white shirt.' He breaks into laughter.

'Sorry, mate, and he's one of your countrymen too. Poor bloke, brought to the morgue only yesterday.' With a nod, he indicates the front door. 'No one to claim the poor blighter. Life can be shitty, Pat.'

'It can.'

He talks while shovelling. The body had been found on a disused ground behind a Catholic church. 'Only a skeleton, mate, d'you get me? In rags. Been staying at the same spot for the past seventeen years, mate, the locals told the rozzers. Awful smell, Pat. Rats, d'you get me? A few children playing hide-and-seek found him. Mayo – the only name he ever had. Always singing the same song: something about Mayo. Pity no one claimed him, Pat, because the cops found over two thousand quid in a tin box. And some Irish prayer.' He checks his watch. 'The padre and the undertakers should be 'ere any minute. I got to be back to me missus by three. Ta-ra, Pat.'

I climb the stairs to Garryowen's flat. 'You didn't make the journey home,' I say while he is clearing a crumpled heap off a chair and throwing it on the bed: a necktie, the knot still on, falls onto the worn linoleum.

'Have a drop, boy. 'Tis freezin'.'

Before I can stop him, he pours whiskey into tea-stained mugs and puts a glass of water on the table: the blue Formica top is pockmarked with cigarette burns.

'Happy New Year, boy. I hope '62 is better than the one gone out. And the Lord have mercy on the dead.'

'Amen. You didn't get back for Christmas.'

'No.' He shakes his head and smiles: 'Ah, a crowd of us went to Holyhead, but sure, while we were in the pub, doesn't the fucken boat go out without us. Yerra boy, when you're not doin' much for yourself over here, you don't want to go home. Wouldn't give them the satisfaction.'

Springs creak when he sits on the bed. 'I believe you're goin' to Maynooth College now.'

'All Saints.'

'Never heard of that place. Foolish man. You could be a millionaire.'

He takes a swig from the mug and breaks into a fit of coughing from deep in his chest. 'I may as well tell you: I never had much time for priests, or all this talk about heaven and hell. When they throw you down, that's the end, Tommy. And hell? Sure, Jaysus, aren't we livin' that every day.'

He reaches across with the whiskey bottle, but I cover the mug.

'The priest, when I was a gorsoon, only wanted the company of the dispensary doctor or farmers with big creamery cheques. Oul snobs.' On the mantelpiece are two Christmas cards and a bottle of Aspro. 'Although I've met a few good ones over here. Father Harty – he's a dacent man. Likes his comforts. An eye for the women too – small blame to him.' He tilts the bottle of Powers over his mug. 'Maybe we can do nothin' right in our own fucken country, includin' religion.'

In a recess in the wall are a few books: among them *An Introduction to the Basics of Engineering*, Zane Grey novels, a hardcover copy of *The Art of Self-Defence* by Jack Dempsey and *Songs of a Sourdough*.

'You're back to work on Monday,' I say, to get away from talk of snobbish priests.

'And thanks be to God for that, because if we don't have a shovel in our paws, we'd go mad. The site and the pub, boy – that's all we have.' He spits in his hands and rubs them together; his face creases when he grins. 'A twelve-storey block in Slough, bright and early on Monday mornin', rain, hail or snow. Thirty pounds a week isn't bad. Teachers at home aren't makin' that for all their oul go on.'

And few of them will leave it in the Crown or in Richmond Street comes to my lips, but instead I gesture towards the books: 'Have you read them?'

'Ah, I had plans when I came over. Oul night school. Make my money and go home to buy a bit of land.' He offers me a Sweet Afton; more coughing when he lights up and inhales. 'Yerra, you'd be a laughin' stock on the site if you were caught with books. We brought the oul begrudgery over with us, boy.'

'Pity.' The night in The Highway when he staggered towards Bonnie and myself and threw a baleful eye on my novel comes winging back.

Darkness is falling as I return to the house with the scattered fragments of human wreckage floating around in my head: Garryowen missing the boat, 'Moonlight In Mayo', 'the site and the pub, boy'. The snow has now turned to slush, except for little white hills on pillars and at sheltered corners. Figures in tightly belted overcoats and carrying umbrellas pick their steps and smile if they brush or collide with one another.

Outside a cinema, a queue is forming to see Charlton Heston and Sophia Loren in *El Cid*. A man in a trilby and a mackintosh is stamping his feet; the woman beside him checks the seams of her nylons and then glances at the drivers waiting for the green light.

M.J. rings to say he'll be late and to apologize to Vera, and would she put his dinner in the oven? 'He'll give himself a heart attack, he will,' she says as she places a plate of steak and chips in front of me. She is off again with Bertie, to a party in Kensington. She touches up her perm: 'I believe,' she says without taking her eyes off the mirror, 'that you are studying to be a priest. The Reverend Mr Galvin.' She laughs.

'Trying it out anyway, Vera.'

'So you'll never get married then?'

'Yes, that's the way it is.'

'Bit of a waste if you ask me, but then as my Bertie says, "Each man to his own." '

Before leaving, she returns, wearing a red coat that matches her lipstick, and carrying a floral umbrella.

'The big dance tomorrow night, Tommy.' She fills the room with the scent of her perfume. 'I'll get Mr Galvin's dress suit from the dry-cleaners in the morning, and I've rented one for you. Hope it fits. Okey-dokey, I'm off. Ta-ra, love.'

The New Year's Eve dinner and social is held at the Irish Club in Eaton Square. Guests of honour are the two McMorrow brothers from Sligo, one of the biggest firms of road builders in Britain: they have done long stretches of the M1, as well as bypasses and major intersections. From time to time they have featured in *The Irish Press* and the *Irish Independent*. Another success story. With only two rented lorries, they had begun clearing up rubble in post-war London. Now they have winners at Doncaster and Ascot, their sons have gone to Stonyhurst and acquired clipped English accents. 'Slave drivers,' Garryowen had called the brothers: 'They'd hang their mother for the last penny.' Some of their workers had joined M.J., hearing that the boss 'has an oul way about him'.

The function is held in a long banqueting hall with a bar lit up in a golden arch at one side: white linen cones, tall glasses and the sparkle of silver cutlery on the long rows of tables.

As the guests are crowding into the hall, M.J. calls me aside; he is flushed and restless: a boy at his first dance.

'Guess who I met earlier.'

'Man or woman?'

'Woman.'

'Her Royal Highness, the Queen.'

'Close. Grace Healy.'

He draws on a cigar: 'She's doing one of them swanky nursing courses. Queen Alexandra, I think she said.'

'I told you that last summer.'

But he is not listening: 'Look. There she is. Over there.'

A group of men and women are chatting in one corner of the hall where a man is pulling back a chair for Grace to sit on. Unlike the pint drinkers who stand at the bar, they give the impression of being at home in dress suits and cufflinks, with women wearing taffeta – the men hold tumblers, the women sip sherry, or gin and tonic with a slice of lemon.

'Her doctor friends from the hospital.'

While he speaks, I watch her: wearing a royal blue dress, and a string of pearls around her neck, she has the same ice-cold look and starchy gestures I'd remembered from seeing her at Ardglass chapel.

'Turned out to be a fine-looking woman,' he says. 'Anyway, I'll see you later.'

Galvin men who work in the trenches and keep the mixer going look out of place and clumsy; they have never been in the Irish Club before and most likely will not be again. So they keep to themselves and throw brooding looks at the cigar-smoking quantity surveyors and engineers.

'I tried to get them to join us,' M.J. says when we are called to take our places at the long tables. He leans over. 'You might stroll round to them later. This is all beyond them.' He throws his eyes towards the cornices: ''Tis far away from chandeliers any of us were reared.'

We stand to attention when His Eminence, John Cardinal O'Hara sails into the room as if on castors, his crimson cloak of washed silk trailing behind him. A young priest sweeps ahead, clearing a passage, like a fussy waiter; then, with a stylized gesture of his hand, guides His Eminence to the top table beside the McMorrows. The Cardinal recites a prayer in Latin and blesses the room.

Bonnie is at the other side of the table; next to her, the bald man with the pipe I had seen that first morning at the cable-laying out in Stevenage: the chap who is mad for fishing in Killarney.

His head tilted in a listening mode, the Cardinal nods, while a flow of words comes from Harty, whose hands are darting and plucking the air like a highly strung conductor. Sometimes he laughs so loud, those nearby turn their heads in surprise, and then smile: the Cardinal smiles too, takes a sip from his wine glass and casts a shrewd eye around the hall.

Earlier Harty had given me a blow-by-blow account of his latest project: he is buying up old houses and converting them into flats for Irish families. 'Your brother has a big heart. Sure I'd never have got the damn thing going only for him. But keep that under your hat. M.J. does a good turn but he wants no talk about it. Confidence, Tommy, that's what they need.' His whole body is involved in the telling: hands coming to life again. 'To go into a bank and get a loan. We bring an oul fear of these places with us from across the pond.'

During the meal, Bonnie, with a discreet sidelong shift of her eyes, indicates the bald man, who has ignored his blue-rinsed wife and is leaning towards herself. After the main course, his wife leaves the table, and, when she returns, gives him a playful thump on the shoulder. 'Right, Denis,' she says in a Scottish accent, 'I want to have a chinwag with this lovely Irish girl. Move over.' Like a sulky child, he does as he is told.

As soon as the waitresses have finished pouring tea and coffee, the president of the Emerald Society stands, places his cigar in an ashtray, and taps the side of his wine glass with a spoon. His Eminence heads the list of dignitaries he addresses, then a government minister from Ireland, a Labour MP, the chairman of the Luton Borough Council, and others. After bestowing much praise on the McMurrows, he invites the Cardinal to present them with a Waterford Rose Bowl and honorary life membership of the Irish Club.

'You have made an inestimable contribution to the restoration of this great city,' the Cardinal tells the brothers, 'and to the development of social order after the ravages of war. This applies also to the many professionals among us: doctors, nurses, engineers and building contractors from the shores of Ireland.'

Then he addresses the wider audience. 'You are privileged to be Catholics and should be grateful for the fine religious upbringing you have received. You have a missionary role in a foreign and largely non-Catholic country.' The Labour MP removes his glasses and rubs his chin. 'Living up to your faith will impress those among whom you live and work, and will bring many converts to the Church.' Seery, Horse Muldoon, Garryowen, bricklayers from Islington, cable crews I'd driven home many a night to Finsbury or the Seven Sisters Road when they were too drunk to find the Underground, all have their eyes fixed on the Cardinal. 'Conversely, failure to live and worship as Catholics will scandalize and turn away many searching for the truth.

'Your abiding love of your country, and your unswerving commitment to our heritage of the one, true, Catholic and apostolic Church make you exemplary.'

Word goes round that His Eminence would like to meet other builders, including M.J., so after the speeches, we line up to kiss his ring.

'A future recipient of the award, I've no doubt,' says the president when introducing M.J. 'And this is his brother, Thomas.'

'My goodness.' The Cardinal smiles and takes our measure: 'What great ambassadors for Ireland.' He passes on to a huddle of Galvin men.

'Now who've we got here?'

As if remembering how he should speak when the parish priest visited the school, a youth gives his name in a mannered way.

'You didn't go home for Christmas, young man.'

'The summer, Bishop,' another one of the group answers bravely, but his hand, holding a cigarette, is trembling behind his back.

The Cardinal delivers a short lecture about writing home and sending support. 'And I hear Mr Galvin is an excellent employer.'

'He is, Cardinal,' says the brave one, shifting his weight from one foot to the other.

'What do you earn, young man?'

'About twenty-five to thirty quid a week, bishop.'

'Did you hear that, Father?' He turns to his fussy acolyte. 'My goodness, not even a Cardinal earns that much.'

As expected, the priest laughs, and others join in.

'You do practise your faith, young men, don't you?'

'O yes, Cardinal,' they chorus.

Looking ill at ease, the president of the Emerald Society touches the Cardinal's elbow and spirits him away to meet the group of doctors and their friends.

'You do practise your faith, young men, don't you?' Bonnie, who has been standing by, does a take-off into my ear. 'So what did Scarlett have to say to the young priesteen?' She takes a sip from her glass.

'Who?'

'Scarlett O'Hara. I saw you kissing his ring.' Her eyes are glazed: 'As the posh lady says to the bishop. "May I kiss your ring, My Lord?" "Well, you may," says the bishop, "but the way it is, I keeps it in the arse pocket of me trousers." '

'I told him that I'm a seminarian.' I joke: 'He said, I might be a bishop one day.'

'You wouldn't be a Galvin if you weren't ambitious.' The smile dies and she lowers her voice: 'Who's this stuck-up one, Grace Healy?'

'Oh, her. She's just a neighbour from home.'

The attempt to sidetrack, however, fails to relieve the pout. I follow her gaze to where M.J., an attentive look on his face, is now bent low while listening to Miss Grace sitting upright in a chair. 'You'd tell me, wouldn't you, if anything was going on between them?'

'Of course.'

'I met her earlier. Such a high and mighty bitch. She looked me up and down and said: "Aren't you lucky to have that little job in the hotel." She has some creep with a pencil moustache – a Doctor Roger something. "What part of the bog are you from?" the creep asked one of the waitresses.'

'Don't mind them.'

Bonnie's instincts are right: M.J. has only one interest. From time to time, he strains to check on the doctors' table and even when the Cardinal was talking to his men, he was still keeping a weather eye open for Grace Healy.

Just as the musicians climb the stage and begin to tune up, the Cardinal, with a final wave and a gathering of his silk cloak, leaves with his mincing priest. Fortunately, I had learned to dance in the boarding school: a whole gymnasium of coupled boys on Sunday morning after Mass, stumbling and trotting their way around the floor to the starchy voice of the scholastic 'one-two-three, one-two-three'. Crackle from the gramophone on the stage playing 'The Blue Danube'.

Even on the dance floor, Bonnie keeps searching the hall, and remains indifferent to my attempts to praise the meal, the band, and the big turnout. We dance again when 'The Walls of Limerick' is called; then we get separated.

At an interval the bandleader asks for singers. A request goes up for Harty; he doesn't need to be asked a second time. 'Done more for us than the crowd at home in their big houses,' says one of M.J.'s foremen as he passes by with three pints balanced between his hands. Harty coaxes the crowd to join him in 'Come Back, Paddy Reilly' and other songs: 'Galway Bay', 'The Kerry Dances' and 'The Star of the County Down'. Delighted with himself, he trips down the steps and joins the others at one of the tables. The band leader reads from the back of a John Player cigarette packet: 'A special request now for a lovely young lady. Miss Grace Healy on the piano.' The doctors and their companions cheer as she gathers yards of taffeta about her and links Doctor Roger to the stage.

First she plays 'The Vale of Avoca' and then 'Believe Me if All Those Endearing Young Charms', finishing up with a few lively dance tunes. While he sips his brandy, M.J.'s eyes never leave the stage. A wave of cheering, clapping and shouting of 'Bravo' and 'Summerhill House forever' sweeps over the hall as she descends the steps; Roger holds her hand lest she trip. The doctors break into the Blackrock College rugby song and stamp their feet on the wooden floor. The foreman, who had passed earlier with pints, is off again to the bar; he stands and looks at them for a moment: 'That fucken crowd will never carry the hod, Tommy.'

'That's for sure.'

M.J. invites Grace to join us for a drink; Roger and two other junior doctors from Dalkey and their girlfriends come with her. His pencil moustache forming a sneer, Roger says it is great to be among real men who are doing an honest day's work, building up Britain. The back-slapping and 'we're all from the same oul sod' to one of M.J.'s bricklayers is overdone.

He turns to me: 'Another Kerryman, what? Ready to take on London. Do you know the Furlongs – they live just outside Tralee? Legal family. I can tell you, Gwen Furlong is a tricky character on the tennis court.'

'No. Don't know them.'

'She's a smashing dancer too. Spent many a good night in that town. And the Hilliards, the Killarney Hilliards.'

'I wouldn't know those people. I've passed by their shops.'

All this seems lost on M.J. Like a schoolboy on a first date, he keeps praising Grace's performance, stands and offers her a place to sit, and when he hands her a gin and tonic off the waiter's tray, Roger throws a shifty glance in their direction.

'Right, chaps. Action stations,' says Roger. 'We'd better be getting back, lest we'll be carpeted for our bad manners.' His slit eyes recede when he grins. 'So glad you lads are doing well. Keep the old flag flying up there in Camden,' half-turning to one of the Mayo men, known as The Bruiser.

'We always try our best,' says The Bruiser.

Roger chuckles: 'That's a good one – we always try our best.'

One of the doctors has a camera and he goes around trying to bundle us into position for a photo. The Mayo men begin to sidle out of range, but M.J., who has come out of his trance and has positioned himself between Grace and Roger, calls them back: 'No, lads, all of us. We're all Irish.'

'Hear, hear, M.J. Well said. We're all Irish,' says the doctor, adjusting the lens. 'Come to a rugger game with us some Saturday; we're playing Quins next weekend.' He stands on his toes, and, in a matey way, reaches up to throw an arm around The Bruiser. 'And loan me your man here for the team. Ever played rugger?' He looks up at the sweating giant.

'Ah no. Gaelic I play.'

'Ah, Gallic, New Eltham, Croke Park.' He pronounces the words in a broad accent, much to the enjoyment of his friends. 'Ah, yes the GAA, tear into them, boy. Lay into them, isn't that it?'

He flails his arms and makes jabbing movements with his fists, causing the camera to swing around his neck; the whole performance has his friends in whoops of laughter. And in the manner of a stand-up comedian, he goes through a routine. 'I was in Croke Park once.'

'Go on, we don't believe you,' the medics chorus.

'Honest to God. A few of us from Belvo were playing cricket on the school pitch and our ball soared over the wall, and, of course, muggins here had to climb over and retrieve it. And that was my visit to Croke Park.'

While they are laughing, I see a cloud deepening on The Bruiser's face, his great fists forming into sledgehammers. Then, as in The Highway, over Gene Tunney or Jack Dempsey and the greatest-boxer-ever debate, it all happens in a flash. The Bruiser catches the laughing photographer, and chucks him over a table as if he were a sack of hay: a fresh leather instep shows when he sails through the air. Those nearby freeze. A woman screams and a string of pearls crashes to the floor. Now others farther back are straining to see what is happening. In a moment The Bruiser has torn asunder the veil of good manners.

M.J. rushes in and helps the doctor, who looks stunned and, in an abstracted way, begins to examine his camera.

'Of all the savages,' says Roger. 'Mr Galvin, you'd need to put some manners on that brutish fellow.' And he turns to The Bruiser: 'You're not in the Crown now, or those wretched places up in Camden Town, my friend.'

The Bruiser looks as if he'll lunge at him, but M.J. gets in between them. He winks at The Bruiser and indicates the bar.

The band strikes up a waltz, the doctors and their friends retreat, with much shaking of their heads and words of comfort for their hapless colleague. In the distance M.J. is in conversation with Bonnie. I go towards them, but then realize from the angry set of her body that they are having a row. He reaches out to touch her arm as if to talk her round, but she slaps away his hand. They see me before I can get lost in the crowd.

'Bonnie has to go, I'm afraid. I'll take her back. Hold the fort while I'm away,' he says as he comes towards me.

Already she is storming off towards the front door, but she stops and turns back: 'See you, Tommy, before you go.' Her eyes are red-rimmed.

The lights dim, the crystal bowl sprays the dancers as the band strikes up 'The Tennessee Waltz'; Harty glides by with a woman who had come to sit beside him as soon as the Cardinal had left.

A couple of days later, when I am coming out of Willesden Post Office where a line of men and women are buying postal orders, Harty pulls up at the kerb and lowers the window of the Austin Cambridge. His woman from the night at the Irish Club is at his side. Leaning in, I catch the smell of fresh leather from the seats; the dashboard is made of polished wood. I remark on what I've seen in the post office.

'Same every week,' he says, the fingers of one hand tapping the steering wheel. 'These fellas and girls are putting the roofs on houses back at home. Will they get any thanks, Tommy?'

He catches his friend's hand.

'You met Mary.'

Mary leans over and smiles.

'Mary's from Limerick. I'm showing her the sights.' He winks. 'There's a shindig in The Maid of Erin Friday night. We'll see you there.'

'Afraid not. I'm going back this evening.'

'You'll be missing a great night, Tommy.' Already he is easing the gearshift into position. Fumes from the exhaust thin out in the frosty air as they join the stream of traffic; through the open window, Harty raises his arm: 'See you next summer.'

14

THE FOLLOWING SUMMER I return to London, mindful of the first steps I've taken on another road that leads away from ground plans, quantity surveyors and site listing. Many of the faces are new to me, and in so far as they are prepared to accept the boss's young brother who is going for the Church, they give me the freedom to hover at the margin of their banter and drunken plans. 'Next year I'll be back in Ahamore with my own trucks, and fucken London won't see me again, boy.' Nothing has changed – except for me. I had chosen All Saints, and, according to the mantra of the time, I had made my bed – a single one – and now I would have to lie on it. So the throbbing dance floor and the thousand sweeping stars of the Galty are out of bounds.

The president had laid down the law for me a few days before the holidays. 'I'm not happy with your going to that godless country. Make sure you stay away from dances. You have set your hand to the plough. And remember, Thomas: custody of the eyes.'

'Custody of the eyes, Monsignor.'

I sit at the side of his bureau while he lectures me on the temptations that can come my way in London. Then he places on the draw leaf a slip of paper. Ratio Mensis is a chart that will guide my spiritual programme, and keep me safe from girls who like to snuggle up and kiss in the dark of Eddington's Lane.

Horse Muldoon still bursts in on the site without notice.

He lopes over the rough ground like a primitive monster and shouts at the men that they are dragging their arses, or calls to youths to whom he had given *the sub* only the night before to 'go across the road, and get me a packet of fags', and no sign of paying them when they return. Some of those I'd worked with in Hitchin had gone to Birmingham or Sheffield or across into Wales.

'Where's Kilrush?' I ask one of the men.

'Kilrush is up north. Big bypass job near Preston. Gone to follow the shillin', boy.' And pushing a wheelbarrow loaded with compo up a ramp, he breaks into song: '*Way up north, north to Alaska, goin' north the rush is on … .*'

Building close to two thousand houses in Luton, McAlpine has farmed out sections to sub-contractors: to M.J. Galvin Construction he gives over four hundred. The wide expanse of land is an anthill: groups of houses are at different stages of development. Teams of men are putting down services and access routes, foremen are abusing navvies to dig the fucken drain and 'stop giving suck to the shovel', when one of them rests for a moment to catch his breath. The rasp of gravel when a lorry empties its load, dust rising into the blue sky and the constant beat of compressors fill the swarming site. Caravans appear selling bread, chops and sausages: among them is Peggy from Scunthorpe. Each day she stands inside her caravan, hands resting on her sturdy hips and calls out: 'Right then. Come and get it.' She swaggers from the shops with an armful of loaves, wearing high boots and a tight-fitting skirt, giving as well as she gets from her drooling audience.

After a few days I notice Sputnik hanging around Peggy's caravan and being ever so helpful: hitching the generator on to the back of her caravan, or lifting trays of meat when the butcher's boy arrives.

While one of the men is back in Limerick for his mother's funeral, I do odd jobs: drive to the builders' providers for bits and pieces, take orders for sand, cement and timber if the site foreman is elsewhere.

When the heat rises about midday, the hut smells of tar and

fresh timber, and is strewn with rolls of wire, pieces of window frames and batches of handles for shovels. The wooden floor is stained with oil and dried clay, and sounds hollow when the men tramp about looking for nails and pickaxe handles. A shaft of sunlight through the open door shows up clouds of cigarette smoke while they are fumbling through boxes.

At one side, a half-partition separates the office from a cubicle big enough for a bed where one of the navvies rests if a delivery of timber or cement needs guarding overnight. I come in one morning to find Sputnik asleep and Scunthorpe Peggy in her slip beside him.

Sitting behind an old table that acts as a desk, Jody hands me a thick roll of notes. 'Pay the drivers out of this. They want cash on the nail, but get a receipt. Be careful with that. The lads aren't light-fingered, but there's no point in putting temptation their way.'

Then, as always, he checks that the coast is clear, and lowers his voice. 'Now I hope this doesn't trouble your conscience.' He studies my reaction. 'You'll be signing invoices when they bring the gravel or cement.'

'OK.'

'We've an arrangement with the drivers. Every time a load arrives, you get the driver to write out an invoice for, say, a hundred and twenty, and you pay out a hundred. Are you with me?'

'I am.'

'So at the end of the year that'll be a nice penny saved and we won't have to be working our arses off for the Chancellor of the Exchequer.' A grin of devilment plays around his mouth. 'Of course, the drivers have to get their quid. Twenty out of each load of gravel, cement thirty and timber fifty; that's our way of getting round the taxman. Are you with me?'

'I'm with you.'

'Seery can set it against John Bull's tax bill.'

'Right.'

'We pay enough already, God knows.'

'We do.'

'And another thing. Make sure the drivers don't pull a fast one.'

'How do you mean?'

'Pulling in one gap and out the other without emptying the load. Then back an hour later with the same gravel, and so we pay twice or maybe three times. Black Mick from Rathkeale, he's a bastard. Watch him.'

From the roll I peel off notes and give the drivers their cut, sign the invoices, and fasten them to a wire that hangs from a stanchion. 'Thanks, Pat.' The English drivers hand me a receipt. I keep a close eye on Black Mick, and try to convince myself that Jody is right: that M.J. is paying enough already to John Bull. Jody had laid down the rule of thumb: 'A jungle, Tommy. Jungles have their own laws. They need us Paddies and our sweat; we've built their skyline. Everything is hunky dory.' Graft is second nature to them. And like the previous summer, what M.J. is doing leaves a sour taste, but I still carry the traces of a child's admiration for his big brother, who carried me on his broad shoulders one glorious summer's day when we had set off for the lower reaches of Mount Brandon and my legs would take me no farther. The fun we had together – such as the night we were walking up Ardglass from the village and I thought the full moon was following us. 'Right, Tomásheen,' he says, 'we'll be home before that moon.' And he begins to run, allowing me to get ahead until we reach the wicket gate of our house. He was in England only a year or two when he sent money for my first bicycle: a dark green Raleigh with a gear case and a bell.

He is now going out with Grace, yet whenever I stay at the house, I notice Bonnie's dresses lying across a chair in his bedroom. And he is getting me to back up his deceit. 'There,' he says one Thursday evening, handing me the keys of the Corsair. 'Bring her for a meal – some good place. Tell her I'm delayed and there's no use in waiting.'

But he's not delayed. Grace has a free day from the hospital, and the weather being so fine, she wants to go on a boat trip up the Thames to Wapping where, she heard, there is a first-class fish restaurant. That, as far as I can remember, is the only day off he takes during those two summers, apart from the odd Sunday.

Bonnie is waiting outside The Victoria on Holloway Road: a lone figure all done up in expectation. 'He has to meet the foreman of the job out in Luton,' I lie as I hold open the door, and see her face cloud over.

'Luton,' she mutters, filling the car with the whiff of wounded pride. 'Does he take me for a right eejit?'

'One of the compressors broke down.' I look away, so that she won't see me redden. Armies of men covered in grey dust are jumping off wagons, and girls in overalls are spilling out of Baldwin's, the paint factory.

'Will you come for a meal with me?'

'A meal. You're the consolation prize, priesteen.'

'Do, and we could go to a picture after. There's a comedy on in the Odeon: *It's a Mad Mad World*, with another "mad" added on.' My attempt at humour raises only a hint of a smile.

'Or we could go to the Adelphi; there's a re-run of *Diary of a Chambermaid*.'

'How about *Trickery of a Priesteen,* who covers for his big brother and thinks I'm an eejit.' She does a playful take-back with her arm to swipe at me.

'I've to run around to the Crown to pay a few men, then we'll be right,' I say as we drive into Cricklewood Broadway.

'M.J. Galvin – always a bastard.' With a hangdog look, she stares at the teeming footpath.

While I'm checking wages in front of the Crown, Bonnie gets out for a packet of cigarettes. Striding angrily, she makes for the door where a group of fellows are leaning against the red sandstone wall, their pints golden in the evening sun.

One of them, a small chap like a jockey with hair plastered to his head, steps out in front of her. 'Could I take you to the Galty on Sunday night, Miss?' he asks, a cheeky grin on his face. The rest laugh. One of them shouts, 'Go on home, Jimeen boy, and have a sup of milk for yourself. A woman like her would blow you out in bubbles.'

But Jimeen stands his ground and keeps looking up at

Bonnie. 'Go on, give him *the start*,' they guffaw again. 'Jimeen boy, your mother won't know and I won't tell her.'

Bonnie's pout melts. Suddenly, she reaches down and grabs the front of his trousers, and half-turns to the gallery: 'Nothing. There's nothing there! I'd be wasting my time.' And she pushes him out of the way.

'Sound woman,' says a tall man, wearing his hat at a rakish angle. 'Try me, Miss, why don't you try me.'

Bonnie ignores him and disappears inside.

A few of them have made a football out of paper bags tied with twine and are kicking and jostling around the lane at one side of the pub, their hobnailed boots rasping off the concrete. Others are slouching at a window and casting baleful looks in my direction.

I set out the wages according to the list, and make my way around the football game to the door.

In a Swiss Cottage restaurant, when we have finished a bottle of wine with the meal, and Bonnie is working her way through a second, her anger returns: 'He's meeting that Grace bitch, isn't that it?'

'No. Sure, she has Roger, the chap with the moustache.'

'He dropped her. A nurse from St Andrew's told me. She won't give him his cocoa.'

She dries her eyes when she notices the owner bringing over two glasses of ouzo: 'Special treat for the Irishman and his pretty girlfriend.' She laughs, but then grows silent again. 'They fuck you, then they marry someone else. I'm great for a weekend in Chiswick.'

The letdown kindles another hurt that had blighted the flowering of her youth. As a sixteen-year-old, she had worked for the village shopkeeper a few miles outside Athenry, filling brown paper bags from the tea chest, stocking the shelves and helping his wife in the kitchen. One day his eldest son asked her to give him a hand in the store. 'He had me up against bags of animal feed before I knew it. Told me he loved me.' That was the first of many afternoons in the back of the store while the son was on his holidays from the university. Then the nightmare: sick in the morning, and wearing loose clothes to hide her shame. Finally, the discovery and the arrival of the parish priest, who took her aside in the same kitchen where he played cards on a Sunday night with the shopkeeper and a couple of well-off farmers. He whispers. 'Nuns in Dublin will take care of your baby and provide it with a good home, and then, would you think of going to England?' Yellow trace of snuff on his nostrils. 'Best way for everyone, rather than be bringing trouble to your poor father and mother.'

Her hand trembles when she raises the wine glass to her lips.

'How come you didn't – well – see the risk?'

'He was going on to be a doctor. Said he knew about these things and I was dead safe. He's a specialist now. Anyhow, I was asking for it. I had led him on. That summer, I took part in the step-dancing competition at the sports. The usual – a tractor-trailer for a stage.'

'I know.'

'Anyhow, I'd noticed him hanging around. I can tell you: when it came to my turn to dance on my own, I edged out to the front to make sure he got an eyeful.'

'I'm sorry, Bonnie – I mean, about what happened to you.'

'Men. Ah, they take what they can get, and then leave you in the lurch.'

She talks on until her anger has spent itself, then a faint smile plays around her lips.

' "Don't you know, child," says the parish priest, "that a man has strong desires and it's a woman's place to stop him." '

'The fool.'

'He wasn't the worst. Gave me a twenty-pound note when I was leaving. Told me to make sure and join the Legion of Mary when I arrived to London.'

'Which, of course, you did.'

'Of course.'

15

M.J. IS NOW DIVIDING HIS TIME between the various contracts: sometimes he stays a few days with one crew, doing everything from lifting bags of cement onto his shoulder and throwing them down beside the mixer, to grabbing a trowel and laying rows of bricks as if every day is a deadline. At other times he is deep in conversation with one of the foremen, the edges of a map fluttering in the breeze as they hold it down on the bonnet of the jeep.

Apart from the odd night when I stay at the house, we are commuters at a train station, meeting only for a few minutes while he is clearing out the safe in The Highway, or when he drops in to the site at Luton.

One evening he is home early and is unusually restive – tapping on the table, clearing his throat, humming out of tune. In a navy suit, he polishes his shoes in the kitchen after Vera has left. Over the ham and tomato salad, his conversation is fitful: asking me the same question a couple of times without waiting for an answer. At last he pushes away his plate: the easygoing mask has slipped; instead, he has the earnest look of a boy in the village shop, rummaging about in his pocket for enough to buy sweets.

'What do you know about this lad …?' – the boy in the village shop searches my face and takes two tickets from his wallet – 'Beethoven,' he says, stumbling over the composer's name.

I tell him a bit about the sonatas, the concertos and the symphonies, and how, during his deafness, he composed his best work. He loses interest. 'Double Dutch, Tommy.' He puts the tickets away safely in his wallet and smiles. 'We're off to the Albert Hall. I don't even know where it is,' he says while at the mirror, attaching a starched collar and a red tie to the new shirt he had bought that day.

'See you tomorrow.' He gives me a poke on the shoulder, and goes out humming.

'Good luck.'

The evening before I leave, he takes me to the Black Angus restaurant in Chiswick. 'I've hardly had time to talk to you and you've been killing yourself working.' We have a drink first in the bar. His head is almost touching the beams that support the low ceiling. Wearing a white shirt open at the neck which sets off a healthy glow to his skin, he conveys with lively gestures a store of energy inside his burly frame. As always, he is wrapped up in his work: this evening it's the twelve houses he has bought in Finsbury. He rattles off his plan: some are in bad shape, but he'll convert them into apartments. When Finsbury has spent itself, the compass of his interest turns to Ardglass and Gerry.

I tell him the good bits – 'the heifers you bought for him are the envy of the neighbours' – and omit their begrudgery: 'That fella must be robbin' banks over there in London.'

When he's into his third whiskey, he begins to pick at an old sore. 'My own mother selling me down the river.' He had been taking the harness off the workhorse one fine summer's evening when he'd overheard her in the cowshed; above the steady beat of the milk hitting the galvanized buckets, her voice had rung out with a dreadful clarity. 'England or the depot. One or the other. He has a good head on him, so he'd get the guards' exam, no bother, but, he has to go. Too many mouths to feed.'

'But I'd be lost without him,' our father is pleading. 'Aren't we doin' all right?'

She won't budge.

'She had the whip-hand, of course.' M.J. says, knocking back his drink.

'I know. D'you remember when he used to come home drunk from Scanlon's: "I'm only a lodger here. Only a lodger. I'd be better off dead." '

'Your table is ready now, sir,' says the waiter.

'She was trapped, you see,' he says when we are seated.

'Trapped. How?'

'I was on the way, and, in those days, they had to get married. She'd have sold the few acres in Ardglass when her father and mother passed away and returned to Chicago. Used to throw it in my face: "Only for you, I'd be in America for myself." '

'What?'

'Don't you remember the way she used to go on: "Wasn't I the fool to let that drunkard into the house? I should've gone back to where I was happy." Now you know: she couldn't go back! I could've followed Eddie to the depot and spent the rest of my life tramping the streets of Dublin. Maybe become a sergeant.'

The table shakes with his jerky movements. He begins to study the hard-cover menu in front of him, but I know he is back in that stable with the workhorse. 'One thing I'll have to say for her: she was better than any man to do a day's work.' He puts the menu aside: 'I was going out to school one June morning, and I saw her lift a tank of milk onto the donkey's cart. There could be twelve, thirteen gallons in that tank. *On her own.* Of course, himself was still three sheets to the wind after the night before.' His face tightens in a surprising likeness to hers. 'Darning socks and sewing patches until twelve or one at night with the oul tilley lamp brought low, so that she could see.'

The evening is still bright when we leave the restaurant, so he makes a detour to show off the houses in Finsbury. We drive through the redbrick street: bay windows, and wooden verandas on the ground floor. 'Seery put me in the know.' He stops the Wolsey and we get out. 'I've a chance to own the whole street. The oul landlord, a retired banker, left the wife and family and is off to live in the South of France with a slip of a girl.'

' "The older the goat, the giddier." What the Da used say.'

We drive around the corner to see the pub – a mock Tudor building at the top of Beech Hill Road. 'A lick of paint and a few things to the inside and it should be fine,' he says. 'I thought for a long time about a new name, and now I have it. Only one name.' He spreads his two arms to describe an imaginary signboard: 'The Crab Apple Tree.'

'He'd be proud to think he named a pub in London.'

He does a take-off, playing out a scene that stirs up the embers of a shared past: 'Did ye ever see a pub like that, lads? Sure, there isn't a pub in the whole of London as good.'

'You wouldn't think you're taking on too much,' I venture on the way back.

'Can't stop. You see your houses going up, you get an oul thrill out of that, man, or an MP phones you to talk about a cable-laying job.' Creak of leather when he settles himself behind the wheel; streets of redbrick sweep by. 'And at times you wonder how it all happened. Is this a dream? Will I wake up and find myself drawing turf out of Hogan's bog? Enough is never enough, you see,' he continues, when we are in the house. 'You don't want to stop as long as there's another peak ahead.'

I look out at the silent darkness, broken only by his pacing on the stone tiles of the kitchen and a car changing gears on the Chiswick Road.

'There's the oul fear I might lose it all.' He settles himself into an armchair opposite me.

'No fear of that.'

'And then the Da holding on to the counter at Scanlon's. "Come home," I says to him, one cattle fair evening. The few calves he failed to sell were out in the yard hunched up with the hunger. "Sit down there for yourself, M.J. boy; the man who made time made piles of it." "Mammy says that you're to come home." Bastards were asking him to tell them about the Ballymac ambush. And like a fool, he holds up the ashplant like you would a rifle. "I was in charge of twenty IRA volunteers, Kerry Number One Brigade, lads. Here's how I gave orders to my men." "Come on, Jack," they shout, "tell us." He tries standing to attention with his rifle: "Taraidh airm", he says and they break their arses laughing.' M.J. shakes his head. 'The same man would run a mile from a Black and Tan. I was only a gorsoon, sitting behind them with my bottle of lemonade and a couple of Geary's biscuits, but I swore I'd never end up like that.'

16

SUMMER IS SLIPPING from our grasp when I return to the seminary. The chestnuts and plane trees along by the grotto are turning brown; a smell of rotting foliage rises from the river. The class is getting smaller, but I'm glad to see Meehan is back, even though he swore before we broke up for the holidays that he has had enough of 'the pricks' who were running 'this kip'. He is still going out with Siobhán, now a teacher.

During the previous year, free spirits who could no longer endure the heavy hand of authority had sidled off down the corridor, to be met by their families at one of the front parlours. And when we trooped down to supper in double file, we stole glances through the open door of the vacant room. The same sight after every departure – the striped mattress rolled up on the bedsprings, the deserted white washing basin and the empty bookshelves.

But the Church is on the crest of a wave: fresh-faced young-sters, eager to wear Roman collars and soutanes, replace the fallen soldiers; they climb the lichen steps, the president meets them at the portico, and we help to carry their suitcases and show them around.

Bringing with him something like the sound of dry leaves blown by the wind, the bishop, in flowing purple, sweeps into Walsh Hall one evening in early October to announce the construction of another wing to the seminary. He forecasts an expanding diocese and a consequent need for a big increase in the number of priests by the end of the century. We have to pray for vocations. We do. And we are infected by his optimism: a great harvest in store for the Church. Then more dry leaves in the wind when he blesses each side on his way out, the president at his elbow. The following week, builders arrive with dumpers, trucks, heaps of sand, and shouting; they erect wire fences, so we have to go out by a side door to the football field.

Then the annual retreat before university lectures begin. For three days we roam the fields and stroll along the riverbank reflecting on our vocations. The director with a missionary's tan prescribes books that will strengthen our commitment to be good priests: *The Seminarian at his Prie-dieu* by Robert Nash SJ, *The Imitation of Christ* by Thomas à Kempis, *The Introduction to the Devout Life* by St Francis de Sales.

Wearing his cloak with its gold neckchain, the president speaks to us on the final night of the retreat. 'Like a wheel rolling down a hill, young gentlemen,' he intones, 'your years in All Saints will pass as quickly.' He is right, but no one believes him. And those of us, whether by temperament or for reasons that lie below the surface, stay, or to use a phrase that had a high currency in those days, *persist with our vocation*, and survive periodic attacks of sarcasm from Quirke, the dean of discipline.

'Who do you think you are?' he keeps reminding us, if we suggest any changes to our training. 'All Saints was here before you arrived and will be here long after you have gone.'

But my free-wheeling days of university lectures, inter-seminary football games and the annual play in Walsh Hall meet a sudden death the following June when the college is gearing up for ordinations. We have all trooped back from the oratory where the setting sun had lit up the stained-glass windows, caught the gold threads of the priest's vestments and the glittering thurible when the deacon had raised it in front of the monstrance. With the scent of incense in the air, we all sang as one: a hundred and twenty-seven male voices resounding beneath the gilded ceiling.

Veni, Creator Spiritus,
Mentes tuorum visita,
Imple superna gratia,
Quae tu creasti pectora.

In my room, I am looking over lecture notes, when a murmur of voices and bursts of suppressed laughter from Conaty, next door, disturb my concentration. The chattering sounds rise and fall, mingle with skittish laughter, and become quiet again. Then, out of the lull, a man, in splendid voice, is singing *Panis Angelicus.* When the singing dies away, Conaty applauds. Strangely, I associate his excited laughter with the flurry of dark lanes after dance-hall nights in Kilburn.

I return to my study, and some time later the door opens, and, to my surprise, I make out the hushed voice of Old Spice, a priest of the diocese, once a professor of classics at the seminary. During the following weeks coming up to exams, a pattern unfolds: the light tap on the door, the whispers, and after a while the fitful giggling.

Curiosity takes over. One evening, I tiptoe in the half-light of the corridor and hide in the cupboard that is a storage space for mops and rolls of toilet paper, and for almost an hour or so endure the smell of Jeyes Fluid, and one foot going numb in the cramped space. One after another, the fanlights go out, the corridor falls off to sleep, and with only a slight squeak of a hinge, two figures stand at Conaty's doorway. 'Good night, Declan.' Old Spice whispers, and comes towards me. And through a chink between the cubbard doors, I watch his every movement. As he passes by, the light before the statue of the Blessed Virgin shows a smile on his chubby face. Someone is giving out in his sleep; then the corridor goes dead again and I steal back to my room.

My heart is still racing when I lie on my bed, gazing at the squares of windowpane through the blind, trying to devise some course of action and wishing I hadn't stumbled on this dreadful secret. Before sleep comes to my rescue, I resolve to get Meehan's reaction.

We kick a ball around on the back pitch the following afternoon, and when the others have gone, we sit on the freshly cut grass while I tell him.

'What do you think?' I ask.

'I see what you are getting at, and you might be right. Then again you could be blowing it out of proportion, that's what I think. Maybe he's just a lonely old bastard looking for company.' The incident puts him mind of his local parish priest who used to pack a gang of children into his Morris Minor on summer days, and take them to Strandhill. Then he'd let them off to play while he read his breviary and had a snooze.

'"But don't go far," he would say to us, "I like to hear you around the place when I wake up." And even though he never went next nor near us, people started whispering, and saying he was a bent old codger.'

'Jesus! Craving for human contact. Is this what's ahead of me, Séamus?'

'Get out while there's still time, Tommy. Some guys are made for the seminary; we're different.' He nods in the direction of the gothic pile beyond the playing field. 'Actually, I never knew why you came in here in the first place.'

'I often ask myself the same question. To give up everything, I suppose. You know: *greater love hath no man than this . . . .*' I look at Meehan, but he has lost interest, and is back in Strandhill.

' "Lovely day for the strand," he would say, when we had served his Mass.

"Ah no, Father, we're wanted at home for the hay." '

'Anyway, it won't bother me – I'm pissing off out of this place in the summer.'

'Do you have to make up your mind now? Couldn't you wait till the summer is over?'

'Tommy, I've had enough.'

I make a snap decision: 'I'm going to the dean about Old Spice. Will you come with me?'

'And put my head in a halter? You must be out of your fucking mind.'

'Well, I can't live with it.'

'You'll have to go on your own. I'll not risk being shagged out of the place now. I aim to marry Siobhán inside a year, and I'll be looking for a reference from these pricks when I'm chasing a job. Two of us to think of now.'

'*You have to.*'

'There's no *have to* about it.' He stands and wipes his football boots in the grass. 'You're on your own, Tommy.'

'Right, and thanks a lot. I'll go on my own then.'

'Do, and make a right fool of yourself.'

'Ah fuck off.'

He ambles away, football socks loose around his strong legs. 'Don't be stupid, Tommy,' he says over his shoulder. 'Old Spice is powerful in this diocese. A student going to take him on? You'll never be ordained.'

'I'll take a chance on that.'

'Suit yourself.'

Two nights later the hinge creaks again. The next day I ask to see the spiritual director, a kind old man whose Thursday night talks in the chapel put everyone to sleep.

He listens from behind his desk and, when I'm finished, goes through his trademark gestures: clearing his throat and flicking back the cape of his soutane. A big crucifix hangs over the mantelpiece. Although the evening is close, one bar of an electric fire burns red beside his desk; in a corner of the room is a prie-dieu with a purple stole hanging over the armrest.

When I have told my story, he gives me one of his deep sighs – a mannerism well-acted out in the college. 'Ah no, Thomas, and is that all that's troubling you? Ah, doubting Thomas. Sure the priest is only helping a poor student to do well in his exams. He's a generous man; does that frequently, every year the same. Do you know, Thomas, he was offered a fellowship to Oxford? Oh yes, Oxford. That man could be a university professor now. Ah no, just an act of kindness. Isn't that all?' His bald head shines beneath the fluorescent light. 'First in every exam since he was knee high to a grasshopper, Thomas.' He flings back the other side of his cape. 'No. Rest assured, everything will be fine.'

'Right so Father.'

His hand is soft, like an old nun's. 'Hearing great things about you,' he says. 'Keep that up and we'll have a future bishop on our hands.'

Later that evening Conaty is loitering around the ambulatory when I go for a walk to clear my head. 'Tommy,' he calls. He is fidgety and takes a cigarette from a packet: 'Can I join you? Would you mind?'

'Not at all.'

'*Laudatur Jesus Christus*,' he says, following the prescribed greeting when one student walks with another.

'*In saecula. Amen.* Let's go down by the river, Declan.'

The white froth of meadow sweet, cow parsley and wild hemlock on both sides of the path brush against our soutanes as we make our way along by the river; sow thistles and water lilies grow wild on the mud bank. We rest on the sun-dappled garden seat and face the river; the harsh sound of ducks paddling upstream in an arrowhead shatters the quiet of the summer evening.

'Can I discuss something with you in confidence?' he asks timidly.

'Of course.'

'Did you hear anything unusual – sounds – anything at all, coming from my room lately?'

'Unusual? No. No, I didn't.'

'Are you sure?'

'No. No sounds.'

'That's all I want to know.' He points towards the ducks: 'Must be a great life for ducks. No problems.'

I laugh, but stop suddenly when he begins to sob, his graceful hands holding a white handkerchief to his face.

'Is it the exams, Declan?'

'What?'

'Are you afraid you mightn't pass?'

'I wish it were as simple as that.'

'I can keep a secret.'

Red-eyed, he looks at me: 'Are you sure?'

'It won't go beyond me.'

He twists the handkerchief on his lap, a gesture that causes a mild stir within me and invades my prayer that night in the oratory when I see him in front of me. 'I've been ... well, a priest of the diocese. Are you sure you won't …?'

'Your secret is safe with me.'

'He was helping me with revision and he put his arm around me. That's all. But now he wants us to meet during the holidays. To go to England.'

'Not a good idea, Declan.' I glance at his profile. With long hair, he would pass for a girl. 'Don't go.'

He grows silent, still twisting the handkerchief: 'I think I'm different, Tommy.'

'Aren't we all? Sure that's what makes the world so interesting,' I say in a spirited manner, but I know where he is leading.

'No. This is not the same.' He is now chewing the inside of his lip: '*Massabielle*, the Lourdes play, we put on before Christmas. Who's asked to play the part of the Virgin Mary? The same in boarding school. And more things too.'

Suddenly, I become self-conscious and look around; beyond the shimmering poplars, a few from our year are kicking a football. 'Not a word will pass my lips, Declan. Not to worry; I never repeat what I'm told in confidence.' I stand. 'Going to England with him could land you in trouble.'

'I suppose you're right.' At the turnstile leading from the cinder path, he tilts his head, a girlish smile on his face: 'Thanks for listening to me; you've heard your first confession.'

Meehan eventually agrees to go with me to Doctor Quirke. 'For one reason,' he says. 'You've helped me survive this hellhole until I could make up my mind. But I don't want to do it.' He studies me: 'For a bright bloke you're fierce thick at times. And by the way, you'll do the talking.'

'Right.'

The following morning after breakfast, we make our way in a nervy silence to Quirke's room. The traffic lights on his door show red, and a bad-tempered murmur is coming from inside – Quirke is slating a student. Doubts crowd in – Meehan could be right: 'You're as stubborn as a mule, Galvin.'

Too late. The door handle turns with a squeak and the

student comes out, red-faced. He looks at us, smiles and then gives a two-finger sign to the closed door. The light turns green.

'Yes. What can I do for you two?' With his belly stretching over the desk, Quirke is finishing off an apple. He flings the core into a waste-paper basket and licks his fingers.

'It's not easy, Doctor Quirke.'

'Well, you'd better get it out. I've work to do. And you two should be at study.'

I tell him about the proposed holiday, and my suspicions about Old Spice's visits to a student's room.

'Who is the student?' He keeps inspecting his fingernails: for a big man, his hands are surprisingly dainty. 'Who is the student, Mr Galvin?'

'I'm sorry, Doctor Quirke. I gave my word of honour that I wouldn't reveal my source.'

The inspection stops; he turns to Meehan: 'You may go, Mr Meehan. Mr Galvin, I want to speak to you alone.' When Meehan has closed the door behind him, he glares at me: 'You have a vivid imagination and a dangerous one. You won't name the student and yet you are willing to defame a man who was a highly respected member of the faculty of this pontifical seminary. A man who, out of the goodness of his heart is prepared to come in here after his day's work and help students who fall behind in their studies. And a man who is fostering vocations: something that is much needed in the diocese, and in our mission fields.'

Another quick inspection of his fingernails. 'This time I'm going to overlook your baseless accusations against a good man. And my advice to you is this: go and say your prayers and rid your mind of such nasty thoughts. Unless, of course, you want to pursue this and put your future at risk. And if I know you, Mr Galvin, you're too clever to do that. Now get out of my sight.'

After that, the creak of the door hinges and the skittish laughter from Conaty's room come to an end.

The president had been right about the wheel rolling down the hill. Three years had flown by since we had climbed the mottled steps to the front door. Three years of making the thirty-mile journey each morning to the university in the college mini bus are now over. The students who hadn't matriculated attended classes in the seminary and were told they wouldn't need degrees anyway, out in Kenya. Three years of trooping to the chapel before we leave, and the prefect reciting the prayer that will expunge the demon libido: *Averte, domine, oculos meus. Ne videant vanitatem.* If you notice a pretty girl, you turn the other way.

So, in late May when All Saints is in the grip of examination fever, the president calls me to his study. The hollow sound of my footsteps on the concrete flags breaks the silence of the warm evening as I cross the ambulatory to his rooms. All along Junior House the windows are thrown open, revealing my classmates in a last frenzy of cramming: soutanes and roman collars put aside, heads bowed over desks. Sparrows are perched on the lip of the fountain, dipping their beaks into the fresh spring water.

'Mr Galvin.' The president rises and indicates a chair in front of the mahogany desk. 'I trust you will do well again this year in the final exams.'

'I hope so, Monsignor.'

He resumes his throne, a chair much higher than mine. 'The Academic Council has granted you a place at the Irish College in Rome.'

'Thank you, Monsignor.'

'You will bear in mind that this singular honour is conferred on only a couple of students every year. A great privilege has been granted to you to study in the Eternal City and, should the Church find you worthy, most likely you will be ordained at San Giovanni in Laterano. *Deo Volente.*'

'*Deo Volente*, Monsignor.'

'I'm aware of your interest in the foreign missions, but don't foreclose on the diocese.'

On his sideboard are silver-framed photos: pride of place is given to one of himself and President de Valera in the grounds of Áras an Uachtaráin.

He relaxes and allows a weak smile to form about his thin lips. 'I trust your brother is still prospering in England.'

'He is, Monsignor, thank you.'

'An exemplary Irishman. It was very kind of him to invite me to his wedding.' He talks for a while about the Irish who are doing very well in England and yet we never hear of them: only the failures. I nod. Then, filling the air with aniseed, he stands. A gold cufflink shows beneath his soutane when he is stretching across the desk to wish me well in Rome, where, he reminds me, the world's bishops are into the final year of the Vatican Council – the most important ecclesiastical event of the century.

Senior students who are close to ordination and smoke their pipes outside a back door of the college after supper have been sounding off on the Council for a couple of years now; they predict a bright future for the Church as their sweet-smelling tobacco rises. In the dark, one evening, I linger at the edge of their discussion. They are debating complex issues such as birth control and whether the Pill is a natural form of contraception or not. 'It is,' one student declares, 'so long as the woman doesn't take it when she is about to make love with her husband. If she takes it, say, that afternoon while her husband is at work, then they are not interfering with the sexual act.' His pipe is going out, so he has to stoke up the tobacco. This gives an opening to another student, who says: 'I have no doubt but the Pope will, most certainly, come down in favour of the Pill.' They nod their heads and move on to the Doctrine of Original Sin, and the men who will usher in a new dawn: Karl Rahner, Hans Küng and Joseph Ratzinger. All the old stodgy ways will disappear forever when the Church hears what these men have to say.

'Strange that he never brought up the complaint we made,' says Meehan, when I tell him the news about Rome. The amber globes at the fountain show up like a full moon as night falls over the college; ahead of us, theology students throw monstrous shapes on the ambulatory wall.

'The exemplary Irishman's money, that's why.' I mimic the president's pompous accent: ' "Yes, and very generous to All Saints." '

'I hope it goes well for you in Rome.'

'Thanks. I'll drop you a line.'

'Do. By then I should be in the wigwam with my squaw.'

'What will you do?'

'Siobhán and myself are going to hit New York for the summer. We'll be married by this time next year. With a B.A., I'll do the diploma and get a teaching job. No bother nowadays – schools seem to be partial to spoiled priests.'

That evening, one of the deacons has organized a Gaelic football match between Junior and Senior House, but I'm in no mood for football and, instead, I kneel at the back of the oratory, the shouts reaching me through an open window. Meehan's leaving, more than any of the others, is shaking my resolve to give up everything for the imperishable prize. And for a week or so, I return to the same silent place to be tossed around in a sea of indecision.

The spiritual director sighs heavily, tosses the front wings of his cape over his shoulders, and tells me that some students worry too much and forget that God always gives us the grace to meet every situation in life. 'It is understandable that your friend's leaving would upset you, Thomas. Mr Meehan discovered he didn't have the call, but I'm convinced God is calling you. So go off to Rome and enjoy yourself.' He regales me with stories of his student days there, and then shows me to the door.

'God bless, Thomas. You'll do very well in Rome.'

'Thanks, Father.'

I return to my room, persuading some dissatisfied questioner within that the spiritual director ought to know: he has a lot of experience.

17

A T THE IRISH COLLEGE, I have a ringside view of the Vatican Council. Each morning on our sunny path to lectures at the pontifical university, Propaganda Fide, we watch a winding river of purple flowing down to the front of the college: bishops gathering folds about their knees as they climb into buses on their way to St Peter's. Priests doing postgraduate studies form a constant stream to the college every evening: they take notes and the tapping of their typewriters continues late into the night as they work on speeches for the bishops. They loiter around the marble corridors until a Cardinal or an archbishop swishes by on his way to the chapel or refectory. Over the years they, in turn, become monsignors and bishops, or at least get the best parish in the diocese. And, to be perfectly honest, from now on, my dream of digging wells in Uganda gets lost in the heady smell of episcopal brocade, and I take a keen interest at the mealtime conversations about students and priests who have managed to ingratiate themselves with members of the Curia.

After supper one evening, a young priest carrying a sheaf of notes is idling in the ground corridor. He stops and asks me my name.

'Tom Galvin, Father.'

'What diocese are you from?'

I tell him.

'You should have come to Dublin. More prospects.'

He imparts a secret. 'Never forget, Tom, that when a man is sent to Rome to study, his bishop has him in mind for higher things. We're the Coldstream Guards. None of us here are pack animals. We'd be wasted in a parish or on the missions.' He throws a shifty glance down the hallway and smiles: 'That's for the pass B.A. men.'

After ordination, he was appointed to a sprawling parish in Dublin. 'But, with the help of a monsignor, I made sure I wouldn't spend my life sipping tea and praising brown bread with old ladies after the Legion of Mary meeting. But you'll never make the top table, Tom, if you haven't someone to speak up for you. By the time I complete my doctorate, I'll make sure I'm earmarked for a diocese.' The word in my ear, he conveys with a coded wink, and when he aligns the sheaf of notes on the window ledge, the corridor echoes with a hollow sound.

'Let's go for a stroll.' He indicates the sunny courtyard. As we stroll down the loggia, past the monument that holds the heart of Daniel O'Connell, the Liberator of Catholic Emancipation, he imparts more of the commandments that ensure a successful career in the Church. 'Get to know the bishops while you're here; you have a glorious opportunity now. And most of all – the Nuncio – whenever he visits the college.' He grins: 'Some of these fellows are little runts, with egos as big as St Peter's. And by the way, Tom, theologians are ten a penny, but bishops hold all the aces, and bishops will be remembered long after theologians are dead and buried. Find one before you go back to Ireland.' Another option, he informs me, is a diplomatic post in the Vatican. 'But if you go down that road, make sure you have a grasp of at least four or five languages.' He holds up his hand, fingers splayed.

Priests visiting Rome stay in the college and worry about the rumours: the Vatican Council will be the ruination of the Church they know and love. One man, on a short break from his country parish in Mayo, shares his concerns at the dinner table: women going to Mass without a headdress, and worse – American nuns coming to Knock, wearing them scanty blouses; sure, to tell the truth, you can see ... well – most disconcerting. The next Pope might even abolish celibacy. He sighs, and, mopping his forehead, is careful not to disturb his brown wig. 'Haven't we enough on our plates besides trying to humour a woman?'

On my way back from lectures one sweltering day in October, I notice a couple of priests waylay a bishop on the via Labacana. I walk right by them, but they are too deep in conversation to notice me. One of the priests holds his hat behind him. 'Clery & Co.' shows in the silk lining. 'What's all this *aggiornamento*, My Lord?' His head is inclined towards the bishop. 'And this laity involvement?'

The bishop places a hand on the priest's shoulder. 'No changes, Father; most certainly not in my diocese. Don't disturb yourself.' He smiles like a teacher to a dull pupil: 'And remember Ecclesiastes: nothing new under the sun.'

Four years of lectures at Propaganda Fide, and sultry evenings strolling beneath the palm trees, and by the red and white-flowering bougainvillea, debating transubstantiation, the principle of double effect, and other theological questions soon come to an end. Then one glorious Pentecost, while the bells of Rome are ringing out, twenty-six of us from different dioceses throughout Ireland make our way silently across the via di San Giovanni to the Lateran Basilica for ordination. Old women in black stand and bless themselves.

Two days later, I find myself in the Gresham Hotel in Dublin thanking everyone who has helped me to become a priest. The bishop sits beside me in his violet cloak and pectoral cross. M.J. and a heavily expectant Grace with their two children, Elizabeth and Margot, also share the top table. Silent and stolid as ever, my mother in a grey dress and hat keeps a peeled eye on Gerry, who is reaching for a glass each time the wine waiter goes past.

We haven't been together as a family since my father's funeral; now we are sprinkled around the room: the twins with their wives and children from Chicago, the Leeds gang as Grace calls them, Eddie from Sligo. And before me, a sea of faces, each a part of the jigsaw of my life. While I am thanking everyone who helped me over the years of my training, Bonnie in a strawberry dress and black hat catches my attention and makes a thumbs-up sign. Earlier she had introduced me to her companion – a tall swarthy man known as The Body. Outside

The Highway one night he had stood back-to-back with his three brothers and taken on about seven or eight Connemara men, sending them hurling across the footpath.

The parish priest of Ardglass speaks immediately after the bishop. 'The priesthood is the highest calling on this earth,' he intones with his head at a slant and one hand inside the front of his tonsure jacket. 'Changing bread into the body and blood of Christ is only granted to the Lord's anointed – specially chosen men. Not even kings or potentates are granted that privilege.' His voice rises a few decibels when he adds: 'Father Thomas, if I were to meet you and an angel on the road, I would salute you first and then the angel.' He raises his glass: '*Ad multos annos*, Father Thomas.' Some of M.J.'s company men have to be nudged to stand for the toast.

At the table now littered with crumpled napkins, wine-stained glasses and the scattered fragments of cake, the bishop chats with M.J. over coffee. He would like to see a wider range of facilities for Irishmen on the building sites. He looks at M.J. 'Centres such as the London clubs where men can sit and read *The Guardian*,' he says as he massages his gold ring.

Later, while the bishop is making a brave effort to carry on a conversation with my mother about hay and the price of cattle and how the Common Market will be a great blessing to farmers, M.J. turns to me and, out of earshot of the bishop, speaks above a whisper: 'Do you think we should open a London club on the High Road?'

'Very risky. You'd have Horse Muldoon and Sputnik and Garryowen in there all day reading *The Guardian* and the *Wall Street Journal*.'

'The Crown might as well close its doors.'

After the meal, I mix with the guests, give a first blessing to neighbours from Ardglass and the dining-room staff, who form a line and get down on their knees, and, according to custom, kiss the anointed hands of the newly ordained.

Bonnie sidles up as I'm brushing ice-cream off my soutane left by a niece: 'I'd do that for you, but the bishop mightn't approve. Dab it in water. Here's a handkerchief.'

'Good of you to come, Bonnie.' I follow her instructions.

'You haven't changed a day.'

'A holy young priest shouldn't lie.'

'Let's move out of here.' I indicate the foyer where a cool breeze is drifting in from O'Connell Street. American tourists are crowding around the reception area, porters are hauling suitcases and stacking them in front of the criss-cross gates of the lift. We find two lounge chairs.

'Right,' I say, 'a full account on how things are in London.' A mistake. She launches into a tirade against M.J.: the times, when things were not going right for him and he wanted a break, she tagged along to watch Archie Moore beating the living daylights out of some poor fellow. And M.J., perfectly at home with the baying pack in hats and gabardines, sat there simulating hooks and uppercuts. When he knew no one in London, and his pockets were empty, she fed him with chickens or steaks from The Imperial. 'And more than that, but you're a priest now.'

'I am so glad that you came today.'

'I promised. You remember the night at The Highway when I said "No matter what happens, Galvin, we'll remain friends." '

The bishop, M.J. and his friend Donaghy, a member of Dáil Éireann, are approaching us. We stand to attention. A broad smile spreads across the bishop's face. 'The future of the Church. Father Galvin, you've joined the greatest body of men on this earth.'

'The very best,' Donaghy adds, his roving eye taking in Bonnie's figure.

'Bonnie Doyle, My Lord. Bonnie lives in London,' I say.

He extends his hand, palm downwards so that she will kiss his ring.

'And you've come all this way for Father Galvin's reception,' he says when she rises. 'Yes, My Lord.' She is ready to exchange pleasantries, but he ignores her, and is more interested in sharing his good news with me.

'We're extending the seminary, Father Thomas. I've just

been telling M.J. and Mr Donaghy. A whole new wing. Twenty-eight ordinations this year. Thank God, a wonderful harvest. The diocese is expanding, gentlemen,' he assures us.

'Convince this man, My Lord,' says Donaghy, winking at me, and nodding towards M.J., 'to come back and help with the expansion in this city.'

The bishop's eyes form into slits when he laughs: 'Your powers of persuasion are much more effective than mine, Mr Donaghy.' He touches my elbow: 'I want a word with Father Thomas before I go. You'll excuse us.'

We stroll into the slanting sun; the others fall back. In front of the hotel, the bishop's driver is standing by a gleaming black Chrysler. 'You will be returning to Rome in September, Thomas, for postgraduate studies,' he says.

'Thank you, My Lord.'

'I am granting you three years to complete a doctorate at Propaganda Fide.'

He gathers the trailing cloak about him and hastens across the wide footpath where his driver is holding open the car door. As he makes to step in, M.J. comes rushing out of the hotel and calls him; Donaghy stays behind chatting to Bonnie.

'My Lord,' says M.J., putting an envelope into the bishop's hand: 'something to help you with the seminary extension.'

'Oh,' says the bishop, glancing at the envelope, 'but you've been so generous already, Mr Galvin. Thank you.'

A little woman with a face like a withered orange hobbles over, does a half-genuflection and kisses the bishop's ring, and then as quickly shuffles off again, reciting a string of prayers, and disappears up a side street.

The dance afterwards is M.J.'s idea: 'It's a big day for you.' He had phoned me in Rome the previous Christmas and announced his plan for holding a reception in The Gresham. 'Why not? We're as good as the best of them now, and we can afford it.'

'I don't know about the dance. Is that a bit new in Ireland?'

'The family don't meet much. Why not?'

'OK then.'

I return to the hall and stand for a while at the door: the band is playing Glenn Miller's 'In the Mood'; couples are dancing, among them Donaghy and Bonnie in perfect harmony with the music as they quickstep on the polished maple. They are laughing, and at each corner of the ballroom or whenever they have space, he gives her a one-handed twirl and then, with a flourish, sweeps her along again. Tall and in a shiny blue suit that sets off his red hair, he winks over her shoulder at whomever catches his eye; the London crowd think he is great gas.

When the set is finished, he comes over to me and speaks into my ear while at the same time putting an envelope into my hand: 'A small gift, Father Tommy, and congratulations. You know I gave serious thought to the priesthood. The missions.'

'Did you?'

'I did. To tell you the truth, I'd have gone through with it, but,' he is winking again, 'too fond of the women, I'm afraid.'

'Ah, well.'

'But I regard what I'm doing now – public life – to be close enough.'

'You're right there. Thanks for the gift, Sylvester.'

'Not at all, Father Tommy.'

A woman with bangles comes up to congratulate me, and claims Donaghy for the next dance.

My mother sits at a side table. Even on this day, the set of life's disappointments is on her face. Her children all round her – virtual strangers to me through poverty and emigration; all, except Gerry, had taken the train out of Ardglass in the cold light of dawn. I join them, and they press me with invitations to England, America and Sligo. 'When are you going to come out to Chicago?' they ask.

'Soon. Next summer, if I can. I'd love to see America.'

My nephew Shane from Chicago interrupts his game of hide-and-seek with his English cousins: 'And we'll go out on the lake in Dad's new boat.'

We chat about the family's changing fortunes: Eily is moving to Aberystwyth where Richard, her husband, has bought a medical practice; Eddie is up for the superintendent's job in Ballina. The prettier of the two girls, Pauline – the only one without a family – is a ward sister. Nearly every summer she brings over a different man friend: the previous year it was Malcolm, whom she had met in Spain. Now it's Jeff from Bath, who wears a cream suit overspread with creases; his grey hair is in a ponytail and he smokes one cheroot after another. They had arrived the day before in a white Morgan sports car. Even in front of everyone, Jeff seems not able to keep his hands off Pauline. She jokes that she hasn't time to be thinking about marriage. Once, while parents and children are lost in each other, my mother nods in Jeff's direction: 'He's supposed to be an architect. Nice architect.' She makes clicking sounds with her tongue. 'And look at the cut of her. A right rip. Always was.'

I try to shift her bile. 'Elizabeth is like you, they are saying.'

The attempt fails. She throws a glance at the child – all froth, white silk and smiles for her Daddy, who is holding her between his knees while he speaks to Eddie.

'He's well and truly with the swanks now. The way that Grace one looks you over.' And she is about to start on the Healys and their grandeur when Harty waltzes by with Mary who was with him at the Irish Club dinner dance. 'I never in all my born days saw a priest carry on like that,' she hisses. 'I hope you don't make a fool of yourself like him.'

'I think she's his cousin from London.'

'Cousin, huh. Does he think we came down in the last shower?' She shakes herself as she always does when in one of her peevish moods.

Donaghy and Bonnie are now jiving at a corner near us. Taken up with the dance, the two of them seem to have a total anticipation of each other's movements. With a look of excitement on her face, Bonnie, in a teasing way, holds down her dress with one hand when he spins her as one might a top. Other dancers have stopped to watch; some begin to clap. And when the tune comes to an end, they applaud loudly.

'That TD.' My mother throws a jaundiced look in Donaghy's direction. 'Where's his wife?'

'I don't know. He's M.J.'s friend.'

'Ah, sure.' More shaking. 'Tell me your friends and I'll tell you who you are.'

Later, while the band is on a break, waitresses trip around with trays of sandwiches and silver pots of tea and coffee. Standing by one of the tables with his cousin Mary, Harty calls me: 'Tommy, for God's sake, why don't you get out of that soutane, and join us on the floor?'

'This is Holy Ireland, John. They're not ready yet.'

He draws closer so that the three of us form a huddle. Harty glances round. 'One of your guests, a parish priest, with a round bald head and little eyes like a pig, came over to me. "We never go on like that in this country," he says. "Out dancing like a teenager." "Is that a fact?" said I. "Well, if some of your holy men would like to join me at Euston every morning at six for the night train from Liverpool, we mightn't have as many good Irish Catholics begging on the streets of London, or young Irish women on the game, Father." That shut him up.' Harty's face lights up. He throws back his head and laughs. 'Himself and his Pioneer pin.'

His cousin excuses herself, and while she is walking away, Harty eyes her swaying hips; he turns to me, and rests his hand on my shoulder: 'Mary is sound. She'd never say a word to anyone. Tommy, you mark my words: by the way things are going at present, in ten years time we'll all be allowed marry. Crazy bloody life. The Lord never meant it to be like this.'

We chat about London. He tells me I look a bit worried; there's no need to fret. And anyway, sure whatever happens, this is a great day for your mother. Pity your father isn't alive to see it. Mary is returning. 'You'll see. Ten years.' He taps my shoulder.

The dancers are getting tired – some are putting on their coats – and my neighbours from Ardglass are stuffing ten pound notes into my hand and talking about going to Kingsbridge to catch the evening train home. When they have gone, M.J. calls me over in the foyer: 'I need to stretch my legs.'

'Give me a minute to go upstairs and take off this harness.'

We saunter down O'Connell Street where green buses are

stopping to let out bunches of young women in flared summer frocks; their high heels are clicking on the pavement as they giggle their way into Clerys Ballroom. Across the street, the Metropole is showing *The Thomas Crown Affair*. 'Donaghy is asking me to start over here,' he says suddenly. 'A big farm out near the Dublin Mountains. Planning no problem.'

'Can he be trusted?'

'In my line of work, Tommy, I never trust anyone until I see the colour of his money, but Donaghy is OK. Has the good of the people at heart. We're both countrymen, so we understand each other. He came up the hard way too.'

'He's a great dancer.'

'Oh, there's devilment in Sylvester.' He laughs. 'And some kind of oul mystery too. That's why them journalists are always prying. He'll be a minister if the party gets in at the next election. I wouldn't be surprised if he became party leader some day.'

The little woman who had kissed the bishop's ring appears out of nowhere, darts out in front of me and blesses herself. 'Any holy pictures, Father?'

I give her one of my ordination cards.

She squints at the card and kisses it. 'Ah, isn't that lovely. Blessin's 'a God on you, Father, an' I hope you'll be a bishop.'

'She may be right,' says M.J.

'Not unless they're scraping the barrel.'

But M.J. is more interested in his own future than in my career. 'This city is on the move,' he continues. 'Donaghy says there's plans for a big estate out by Raheny. And if it can be done, Donaghy is the man to swing it.' He rests his powerful hands on the parapet of O'Connell Bridge; we both look down the Liffey where a Guinness boat is docked at City Quay. The scene puts him in mind of another evening he was returning to England after his first holiday in Ardglass. 'I was on a train for Dun Laoghaire, and somewhere out near Sandymount – I think it was – blokes all in white were playing cricket. Most of those who were watching and clapping were also in white; women were sitting on rugs, eating sandwiches and drinking tea. They had a wickerwork basket open near them. And my stomach rumbling with the hunger.'

He throws a sour look at a bunch of fellows slouching towards us, their Elvis quiffs plastered in hair oil. 'Wouldn't they want a right kick up the hole?'

'A spell behind the mixer wouldn't do them any harm.'

We return to The Gresham, and all the way back he talks houses and office blocks and the money to be made in Dublin. On the northside. The country is on the move. Donaghy and the party will swing it.

18

THAT SEPTEMBER I return to baroque churches and the warm Piazza di San Giovanni in Laterano, and outings to Formia, Naples and Sorrento. I fall in love with ceremony and privilege, and grasp any opportunity that comes my way. I learn more about the Roman method for success: who wields power and might give me a leg up. I begin to nurture a belief in my capacity to lead – and all in the service of Mother Church. By now, I am fluent in Italian, conversant with German, and am able to get by in French and Spanish; so each summer I leave the sweltering heat of Rome to minister in the cooler parts of Italy or Germany.

Once in a while, I take Monsignor Boylan, a priest of the diocese, for a meal to a good restaurant in Trastevere. He had lectured in Propaganda Fide until he began to work in St Peter's. Now he makes sure I am on the invitation list whenever he throws a dinner party for prelates who have clout. And for his services to the papal household, he is made bishop. 'As soon as you get your thesis finished, I have plans for you,' are his parting words at Rome Airport. He grins. 'That's if you manage to hold on to your faith, living in the Eternal City, or should I say the Infernal City?'

Visits to Ardglass become more painful: fields wild with yellow weeds, broken-down fences, paint peeling from the front of the house. And a mother's excuses: 'He'll settle. Gerry has a heart of gold. That crowd from the village keep him all night in the pub.'

'The cows are bellowing to be milked.'

'Are they now? Those that have polished shoes and walk around with bishops needn't bother about cows bellowing.'

The next time I see her she is tipping towards the brink of death in the Bon Secours Hospital. In the corridor outside the cardiac unit, a doctor, who keeps looking at his watch, tells me that 'Mrs Galvin must have hidden her pain for a long time, Father. The X-rays show major damage to the heart muscles.' Later that morning, I say Mass facing her bed. Now and again, a student nurse checks the drip, and my mind wanders as I recite the prayers for the sick and anoint my mother's work-hardened palms with the sacred oil. Yes, *hidden her pain*. How right you are, doctor. All her life. The pain of a shattered dream – Chicago. Fragments of the past take shape: the mornings when I was leaving for All Saints after the holidays, and the stolid look she wore for the world gave way to a twitch of sadness around her mouth. And her unvarying farewell. 'Mind yourself, Tommy boy.'

A week later, I recite the Prayers at the Graveside while my brothers lower her coffin into the family tomb. Crying openly, Eily and Pauline have an arm around each other. Inside the tomb, the coffin rests on a bed of hay. When I close the Roman Ritual, neighbours shake my hand and tell me how she was so proud of me.

From then on, Gerry spends every day in Scanlon's new bar that has a pool table and a television high up over the whiskey bottles. And when he leases the land to a young farmer from across the river, M.J. phones All Saints where I have begun to teach theology. 'If that young grabber thinks he's going to get what should have been my farm, he has another think coming to him.'

'I wouldn't worry about him. I doubt if he has the money anyway.'

By the following spring the young grabber owns the few hilly acres M.J. called a farm. Everything except the dwelling house. Soon after, Gerry takes in the barmaid from Scanlon's. 'Toppin housekeeper is Patsy,' he assures me over the phone. I fail, however, to see the results of Patsy's housekeeping. The rest of the family take holiday homes in Dingle or Kenmare, and I, like a subbie with a deadline, plunge deeper into my career. The weeks aren't long enough – lectures at All Saints, weekend seminars in convents where young nuns are discovering beautiful sunsets, and the healing effect of hugging trees; theology is jettisoned in favour of interpersonal relations. Egged on by those in their communities who have returned from San Franscisco, aflame with Carl Rogers and other gurus, the young nuns get in touch with their feelings. When their older colleagues have trudged up the stairs to bed, they light candles and sit around on bean bags. Some pack their suitcases; those who remain cast off their veils and exchange friendship rings with priests. And, in desperation, Reverend Mothers ask me to come and talk sense to them.

In the years that follow, my visits to London are confined to christenings and anniversaries when I spend a couple of days at M.J.'s Victorian redbrick in Hampstead. By now he is alternating between London and Dublin, where he has bought a house in Terenure. Donaghy makes it to the Cabinet table. Very soon, M.J. acquires over seventy acres out beyond Finglas: land that had been designated for a public park. The local residents protest, but he promises football pitches, shops and a cinema: amenities such as they had never had before. When the deal is done, and the planning rezoned, the land multiplies many times in value. M.J. resells within a year.

Around this time, too, he buys a farm in Westmeath with paddocks and a racetrack. And when others like him, who had made fortunes in England, feature in the rich list, he succeeds in avoiding publicity, except for the occasional photograph in the winners' enclosure at Naas, Galway or Listowel. In one newspaper, his broad smile and Donaghy's roguish look contrast with Seery's shifty glance at the camera.

Seery returns to Dublin and sets up his own accountancy firm off Dame Street. Having played the field in London, he finally gets married – not to the doctor of his dreams, but to

Maudie, a quiet Mayo girl who worked for the O'Connell Street branch of the Bank of Ireland and is now his secretary. M.J. and the London set – those who had worked for John Lang or McNicholas and who had kept their heads, and are owners of pubs and boarding houses around Kilburn and Finsbury – arrive in new suits for Seery's wedding at the Church of the Three Patrons, Rathgar. Donaghy's ministerial Mercedes also pulls up. Afterwards we all drive out to a hotel in Wicklow where Seery, still raising himself on his toes, tells a group of us standing in the foyer: 'I got a little treasure beyond compare here.' The little treasure lowers her head and smiles. Once or twice, while a few of us are chatting, he points out to her that she should hold the white wine glass by the base. 'Look, Maudie.' He gives her a demonstration. 'Body heat takes from the quality of the wine.' She blushes and smiles again. And he proceeds to explain the difference between Chardonnay and Sauvignon.

'Did you hear him?' M.J. says, when they have moved off. ''Tis far away from white wine, or any colour of wine, he was reared. Only helping his mother to sell periwinkles after Mass.'

'Yeah?'

'Outside the chapel gate with an ass and cart every Sunday in the summer. He told me that one time, when he'd had a few too many.'

Before we go in for the meal, Seery comes over, while his bride is chatting to her sisters.

'Thanks for doing the honours, Tommy. Great to have someone I know on the altar. If there's anything ...?' And he goes through a routine of reaching for his wallet.

'Not at all, Christy. Glad to.'

'Are you sure now?'

'Glad to.'

The bride's mother, a small woman, sits beside me at the top table and tells me they had to feed the few calves at five in the morning before they left Belmullet in a hired car. She keeps repeating: 'I hope Maudie will be happy, Father.'

'She will. Maudie will be very happy. Don't you worry about anything.'

'She's a great girl. Sends me home five pounds every week without fail.'

'She'll be very happy.'

Late in the night when the floor is vibrating to Paul Jones, she begins to sob, wipes her tears with the back of her hand and clings to Maudie.

By now, the London set have thrown off their neckties and are loud around the bar and the foyer. A few of them are propping up the counter when I'm leaving. I try to get away from their offers of drink, but they won't hear of a refusal. 'A glass, Father Tommy, for old times' sake; we don't often meet.' I remembered one of them from Cricklewood; he always led the floor in the Galty. Now he's a quantity surveyor with McAlpine. I resign myself to their drunken geniality: Jack Lynch is doing a right good job as Taoiseach; so is Donaghy as a minister.

'Did you ever come across a jiver like Donaghy?' says the quantity surveyor. 'You should have seen him last night in that club in Leeson Street … what's that place called?' He turns to his sidekick.

'Club Monica, boy.'

'Oh, Sylvester did all right for himself in Club Monica. And your big brother was in top form too. Cute hoor.'

'M.J. Galvin is one right cute hoor,' the other man echoes. While the two of them are ogling a young woman in a tight-fitting dress, the quantity surveyor clamps a big hand on my shoulder, breathes Guinness into my face and gives me advice: if I've a few bob I want stashed away where the taxman won't get to it, Christy is my man. 'Now that's between me and you.'

'Right.'

'A nest egg, you know what I mean, Father Tommy. Guernsey, the Isle of Man, places like that. Remember now. Could come in handy in years to come.'

They are finished ogling. 'Christy did well, Father Tommy,' one of them chuckles. 'That fine mare will keep him warm of a winter's night. You should get one of them yourself.'

'I might.'

'Wily oul fox is Christy. Oh she'll give him babies. I'd say them hips are ripe, wouldn't you?' Then he draws closer: 'I wouldn't be at all surprised if the fox hasn't already raided the hen-house.'

He was right. Six months later I was back at the Three Patrons to perform the baptism ceremony – the first of four. And each christening party marks Seery's growing prosperity: first, it's a new extension, soon after, a conservatory, later they moved to a Georgian house in Dalkey with a tennis court, and a tiered garden sweeping down to the strand. At the last party, while women are complimenting Maudie on retaining her figure and fussing about the baby in the sunlit patio, Seery stands on the marble surround of the fireplace so that he can rest an arm on the mantelpiece and tell me, matter of factly, that the move was necessary: 'For the children's sake, Tommy. The boys will mix with the right sort; help them later on in life. I've already put down their names for Blackrock College.' His neighbours too are the right sort: well-known business people, developers, lawyers and a plastic surgeon, who has invited them to his villa in Barbados. The gilt-framed mirror shows the bald spot that Seery is failing to conceal despite the ridiculous hair-parting just above his ear. His eyes do a circular orbit around the room and he speaks out of the side of his mouth: 'Most of this was through hard work and determination and using the head.' He places his wine glass on the mantel and does a sweeping motion with his hand that takes in ormolu matching pieces, the brass fender, and paintings: 'What did I tell you in The Stag's Head many years ago?'

' "Up here for making dosh," I tap my forehead; "down here for dancing." '

'Now you're talking.'

I am there with M.J. through all the twists and turns of his life. Nevertheless, except for times when he wants my advice, Grace is the one who invites me over to England for family celebrations. Like the time their son, Matthew, was playing the part of Miranda in *The Tempest* at Downside Abbey. A couple of times during the play, M.J. leaves the hall. He had been worried about a strike pending out at Heathrow Airport, where he had a contract to extend a runway, so I assume he is phoning for an update. In the half-light, Grace sits beside me, her eyes fixed on the stage. Every time Matthew makes an appearance and prances around in a white dress with branches in his hair, his father does a nervous clearing of his throat.

At the interval, while parents daintily sip tea in the foyer and the scent of perfume mingles with cigar smoke, I make an attempt to ease my brother's abstracted look. 'There's always some hitch, I suppose.'

'What?'

'The strike. Is it going ahead? I saw you leave a couple of times.'

'The strike. What strike? Ah no. That'll work itself out.' Again he lapses into silence, and I chat with my nieces, Elizabeth and Margot, about college. Before we go back in to the hall, M.J. speaks close to my ear. 'What's Matthew up to, waltzing around with a frock on him?'

He is speaking my own suspicions, but I say: 'That's the part he's playing. Miranda.'

'Seems to me the part comes natural to him.'

I laugh in an effort to reduce the tension. 'No, he's only following stage directions.'

'Is he now? Stage directions. I see, faith.'

We have tea in the oak-panelled refectory. As he does with other families, the headmaster sits with us, his manicured fingernails working on the cape of his black habit. Didn't we think Matthew was a remarkable success? We did. M.J. stirs in his chair.

Before he leaves, the headmaster assures us that Matthew is a credit to his family. And Charlie is one of the most popular boys in Junior House, and so talented at art.

The circle of conversation breaks; Grace turns to me, and lowers her voice: 'Matthew has a vocation.'

'I see.'

'Isn't it great?'

'Yes. I suppose it is.'

'The master of novices has invited me to supper next week to discuss his future.'

M.J.'s irritation in Terenure the previous Christmas comes winging back to me. 'She's making a sissy out of him. I tried to get him out to the site. She wouldn't hear of it. Piano lessons, and tennis – sure, they're only for women.'

'Wouldn't he benefit from some experience of life first?' I offer. 'Unfortunately, many priests are dropping out now.'

The twitch over one eye becomes active. 'You didn't have much experience of life before you went into All Saints.'

'No, but it was a different world.'

'Well, the other morning I was speaking to my parish priest, Father Edward, and he says that a vocation is a great blessing from God, and God should not be kept waiting for an answer.'

On the plane back to Dublin, the sight of Matthew in a dress and green branches haunts me, as do M.J.'s sullen looks, the headmaster's fine manners and Grace's delight about her son's vocation. But I can't afford to spend much time mulling over my brother and his family: I have a diocese to run and Boylan is on another of his binges.

A man fond of company and red wine, he found the solitude of the Roman palazzo beyond his endurance. 'Winter nights are my nemeses, Tom,' he tells me. 'The Romans were right – Hibernia, land of winter.'

Every so often he invites a few of us who had known him in Rome for a home-cooked meal, and with an apron around his wide girth, he stirs the pasta sauce on the big iron stove while we stand around with glasses of Chianti. Snatches of Gigli's Pinkerton making false promises to the ill-fated Madame Butterfly reach us through the kitchen's open door.

Boylan presides at the table, and relates one anecdote after another about Popes he has worked for – the control freaks, those who suffered bouts of depression, self-doubt and loneliness – and members of the Curia who would put the Cosa Nostra in the shade. Dinners at the long table in the papal apartment – just himself and the Pope – the hollow sound of their voices beneath the high arched ceiling. And he makes every effort to keep us as the night wears on, refilling our glasses, remembering another story about Roncalli or Montini. Stories too about his friend, Monsignor Loftus, who was helping the Popes to improve their English. The first sentence he asked them to repeat several times was: *There is a vacant see in Ireland and Monsignor Loftus is the most suitable candidate.* Despite his effort at humour, his tone grows heavy, and he begins to slur his words.

I have an agenda, however, and am blind to this wreck of a man who had been a joy as a lecturer at Propaganda Fide, pacing on the dais, not once referring to notes, breaking naturally into Latin, French or German. 'Stay well clear of the fires of passion, gentlemen. Don't let your wings get burnt like Icarus,' became his parting comment at the weekend: a reference to the prostitutes who were encamped in front of the college and who lit braziers at night for the comfort of their clients.

Now Boylan is coming apart. He calls me one morning in May: he has sprained his ankle. The light switch isn't working, he says, and he missed the step down to the kitchen. Those steps can be a death trap, you know yourself. I do. A death trap. He grimaces like a fat child holding his foot, while I make coffee and put on toast. Near his radio is an empty Jameson bottle. 'You'll find my appointments diary on the desk in the library.' His hand is shaking when he raises the cup to his lips.

Apart from the odd groan when he tries to move his foot, he is silent until we pull up near the front door of the hospital. 'I want you to deal with any priest who is in trouble,' he says, while we wait for a porter to bring him a wheelchair. 'And keep Pat Nugent as far away as possible from my house. I don't trust that lackey one bit.'

'Look after yourself, and don't worry about a thing. I'll be back to collect you tomorrow' is my parting comment after an X-ray has shown up a slight fracture.

A couple of weeks later, he signs in to an English clinic, and when he returns, looks eager to resume his duties, and is full of dreams for the diocese. A false dawn, as I learn many times over the following years. I become his shield. 'His Lordship is on a commission at the Vatican,' becomes my stock excuse to school principals, architects and engineers, or parishioners who want the Church to bring back the Latin Mass. They believe, or pretend to believe, the explanation. He pays me off by giving me the running of the diocese: a conspiracy of two addicts – one to Jameson, the other to power. I get the reputation of being a workaholic; but I have their sympathy – I am carrying the diocese.

From time to time, I spend a day in St Benedict's Monastery. There, my spiritual guide is blunt: I am trying to keep step with my brother's success. Strolling through the lush fields that surround the monastery after confession, I jettison his counsel. All right for monks in monasteries to have fanciful notions; they can say their prayers in tranquillity and then milk their cows; they don't have to carry the can for an alcoholic bishop.

Work is grist to my mill. I rise at five-thirty each morning to revise my lectures, then take care of Boylan's mail: letters of complaint from parishioners – one priest is saying Mass in eight minutes, another is driving around with a young teacher who wears a very short skirt. 'She's in his house until all hours, and sometimes I see her car when I'm going to my Mass each morning,' a woman writes. In England and America, priests are pulling out of the ministry. The diocese, too, is affected – two or three each year. Priests who have found the love of their lives I try to dissuade from leaving: 'Give it another year. The experience could make you a better man.'

'No. My mind is made up.'

I meet the bullies: the Horse Muldoons who run their parishes like sergeant majors, men who are quite odd, but whose pious parishioners regard them as holy priests. I get to know the silent majority who keep their heads down, work in the trenches, and wait for their turn to become parish priests.

Despite the trickle of priests who leave, the diocese is expanding. Engineers and builders who have an eye out for the next church or school take me to lunch, and against a background of clinking glasses and silverware, and soft-spoken waiters, they repeat their offer to me and the diocesan accountant to play golf with them in Spain. Maybe later on – in July – too much on my plate at the moment, but kind of you to invite me. Priests, too, who in the past would hardly bid me the time of day, but who are itching for a foothold, invite me to the best restaurants in the county for haute cuisine. One man – we were in All Saints together – is on the lookout for a plum parish; he arrives on Christmas Eve with a canteen of Newbridge cutlery for Boylan and an invitation to me to join him for lunch at his club.

I am freewheeling down the sunny avenue of my prime, and, instead of wearing me out, non-stop meetings, lectures and appointments with troubled priests become a stimulant.

19

THAT SUMMER is devoted to the hysteria surrounding the Pope's visit in September. Priests who want to make their mark contrive to secure a place on one of the organizing committees, and lose no opportunity to show remarkable zeal about papal encyclicals, especially when the Nuncio is present.

Archbishop Marcinkos flies in from Rome on a reconnaissance mission and dominates the planning room at Maynooth – 'to check out the joint', he informs us in his East Side Chicago. We survey maps laid out on a wide table, and plan our strategy for the Phoenix Park, and the other places the Pope will visit. Whenever needed, the top brass of the gardaí join us for a briefing. At one of those meetings, the president of a seminary shows Marcinkos the configuration for the Galway Youth Mass, and during the course of the briefing mentions the word 'nuns'. Before he has time to finish the sentence, the archbishop whips the cigar out of his mouth, sweeps the room with a powerful arm, and declares: 'No broads on the altar.'

The soft-spoken president looks up, beads of perspiration on his upper lip: 'Of course, Your Grace, no br … religious in the sanctuary.'

'Save for those who are presenting the offertory gifts to the Holy Father,' Marcinkos says.

'Precisely.'

Often it is eleven or twelve before the meetings come to an end, then we drift off down by the low-burning light of the corridors to the professors' common room for a light supper.

Tables at one side of the room are laden with sandwiches, bottles of whiskey, brandy and beer, as well as tonic water and soft drinks. Bishops and monsignors outdo one another with stories of Maynooth's glorious past; how, once upon a time, they had the best brains in the country; how Ireland and indeed Europe would be in the Styx if it hadn't been for the civilizing influence of the Church. They recall brilliant students they had taught: those who got firsts in Latin and Greek, Celtic Studies and Theology. One of the bishops keeps fixing his *zucchetto* on his head and repeating that 'the media haven't a clue' and that they are no match for us because 'we're professionals'. He goes on to lambaste left-wing Jesuits and Protestants. Everyone knows his place and when to speak his lines; as by right, the bishops and the senior clerics dominate.

On one of those balmy nights, a priest, who teaches philosophy in the college and composes limericks about the bishops, whispers to me as we are filing out, high on Rémy Martin and Maynooth's golden age: 'The last hurrah, Tom, and they know it. They're afraid the bark of Peter is listing rapidly under the weight of the liberals – FitzGerald, the Cruiser and their ilk – so J.P. II is being hauled over to get us back on course.' He checks the corridor. 'Methinks it would take even more than that mighty man to keep this leaking vessel afloat. Churches will be empty in ten years, Tom, except for old people, cramming for their finals.' He disappears into the night, and I'm left with the cynical grin of his flushed face: Alice's grin without the cat.

I have a room in Maynooth, so, to clear my head, I go for a walk along the wide avenue, which generations of students have called Grafton Street or, more commonly, The Graf. The scent of cut grass mingles with a wholesome smell of earth after an afternoon shower; pigeons bedding down for the night murmur contentment from somewhere in the ancient oak trees. Priests from the various committees pass by in twos and threes, their cigarettes glowing and then fading into the night. They stop and ask me to join them; we chat for a while, but I want to be on my own. They talk plans; their tone is confident and, when they flick away their cigarettes and open a door at the back of the college, an amber glow lights up their cheerful looks.

All is quiet again. A shooting star streaks across the sky and dives behind the trees at the far end of the grounds. I want to reach out, embrace this moment and keep it for ever more young – the jubilation, the hope, the shooting stars.

Suddenly, out of the heavenly night the rolling cadences of a harp come pouring through an open window on the ground floor. I quicken my steps and stand beneath the window: a film of dew on the grass twinkles in an apron of light. Inside, a woman is singing an Irish melody: 'The Spinning Wheel'. Her flawless voice casts a spell over time and place; present surrenders to past. A Christmas night long ago. Delia Murphy singing on our first wireless – bought by M.J. for the new house; growling, the dog races around in circles and takes refuge beneath the table. *If you feel like singing, do sing an Irish song.* We all laugh except my mother, who is making clicking sounds with her tongue and muttering: 'What do we want that wireless thing for?'

Stock-still, I listen beneath the window until the song finishes, then I follow as if some crazy impulse has taken possession of me and all I can do, or want to do, is flow with the current. She is seated on a stool by the harp, halfway up the long hall; her head is tilted while she turns over the pages of her music book. Moving nearer, I estimate that she is probably in her late twenties.

'Do you come here often?' I joke.

'Only when there's a Pope in the neighbourhood.' Dark eyes peer through the harp strings.

'I was out there for a stroll, took your beautiful singing, and the harp, to be some sort of spell brought on by this glorious night.'

'You mean like the banshee. No. I'm real. At least a lot of the time.'

Later – much later – in playful moments, I would tease her, adding interest to her comment. *Oh, I'm real, all right. Oh, yes, Father, you can bet your life I'm real.*

'Are you singing at one of the Masses?'

'Galway.'

'He'll like "The Spinning Wheel".'

She laughs. 'Ah no, that was just an exercise.'

'A beautiful exercise.' I take her outstretched hand.

'Tom Galvin.'

'Lucy Campion.'

She talks about the pieces she will play at the Youth Mass. Casting aside the armour of caution I've hauled around for over a decade, I make no effort to hide my interest in Lucy Campion while she tweaks the tuning pins and we both exchange brush strokes of our lives: her studies at the Kodály Institute in Hungary, concerts in Budapest and now her part-time post at the university campus across the main road. I give her an overview: Kilburn High Road, Rome, and bits and pieces from Ardglass. And all the while the occasional nervous fluttering of her eyelashes is filling my veins with something close to the thrill of the Galtymore and the crystal bowl scattering snowflakes over the laughing dancers: excitement that I had mostly kept at arm's length until now.

'Will you sing for me?' I hear myself saying.

'What?'

'I'd love to hear you again. Will you?'

'Now?'

'Please.' I gaze in fascination at waves of dark hair reaching her shoulders.

'What would you like?'

'You choose.'

'Let me see.' When she stretches over to the stack of music books, the black lace sleeve of her dress falls over a tanned arm. 'How about a piece that might suit the occasion: it went down great with the Yanks when I was playing at Bunratty Castle last summer.'

I sit on the edge of a stool and watch while she makes more adjustments. Graceful hands coax music from the strings; she closes her eyes:

Once in the dear dead days beyond recall,
When on the world the mists began to fall,
Out of the dreams that rose in happy throng
Low to our hearts Love sung an old sweet song;
And in the dusk where fell …

At the end, the plucking slows down; for a moment, her fingers remain outstretched as if in prayer, then her hands come together and rest on her lap. I look away just in time before she opens her eyes; the lyrics and the music linger in the silence of the hall. And all I want is to sit there beside her, away from maps, cigar smoke and the slating of left-wing Jesuits; and a string of stories that hanker for the days when Browne of Galway and other muscular bishops, with one pastoral letter, were able to frighten the daylights out of government ministers.

'Thank you. Just what the doctor ordered.'

While tidying up her books, she stops and looks at me. 'You're on one of the committees?'

'Yes, I've been coming down here for the past couple of weeks.' When I tell her about the Marcinkos embargo on nuns, our laughter fills the hall so much that, like mischievous children who fear getting caught, we lower our voices. 'In that case,' she says, 'I'd better stay well back.'

'Hide behind a few tall bishops; then the Pope also will think you're the banshee.'

Afraid I might overstay my welcome, I look at my watch: 'Better be heading to my cell. It's near to the witching hour.'

'Yes, after the banshee; enough for one night without meeting a witch too. Goodnight.'

'Goodnight.' With my hand on the doorknob, I turn round: 'I have to see you – I mean, *hear* you again.' We laugh at my silly slip of the tongue.

My light footsteps echo in the empty corridor; away at the far end, one dim light burns in front of St Patrick. The door of the professors' common room is half-open and a couple of priests are standing, glasses in hand, listening to one of the bishops whose voice is in the toned-down mode of midnight.

In my room, just big enough for a bed, a bookcase and a desk, I sit and open my breviary at Night Prayer. But Lucy Campion's rich black hair and her perfume lingering on the palm of my hand come between me and the page. I put the book aside, get on my knees beside the bed and gaze at the brown crucifix over the iron bedstead. This is just a natural attraction for a beautiful woman; I'm quite capable of controlling my feelings at this stage in my life. After all, nothing much happened with Simona and we were meeting frequently that summer in Rome, when I was preparing for my *viva voce*, and she was finishing off her thesis. Well, a few harmless kisses after a meal and a bottle of wine at the Piazza Navona. And, after all, it was our last night – everyone on holidays: couples laughing and embracing at the fountains, water spouting from the mouths of baroque horses, golden lights showing up the terracotta shutters. And fireworks going off in our bloodstream.

So this is nothing to be concerned about; and nowadays, whichever book one picks up on the ministry, spiritual writers, except for those on the loony right, promote the importance of friendships in a priest's life. It's healthy. Keeps a man sane. And You always showed understanding for human weakness: look at the prodigal son. The bowed head of the crucified Christ remains impassive.

The following night, when the clock shows five past eleven, I begin to fidget with my pen, and when the meeting eventually tapers out, waste no time over the usual chat, and refuse invitations for a nightcap. A touch of a headache. Do you want an aspirin? No thanks, the night air will do the trick. Thanks. See you tomorrow. God bless. And I'm hurrying along a side path hidden by pampas grass, magnolias and lavenders; well away from the clusters of priests who are now lighting up pipes and cigarettes and taking a stroll beneath the swan-necked lights at the centre of the quadrangle, their contentment spreading over St Joseph's Square.

The back of the college is in darkness. No stranger to disappointment, I manage to nurse my blighted hopes with the prospect of meeting her again before my work with the committee is complete. I do several rounds of the football pitches, checking in the hope that light will at any moment flood the special window on the ground floor.

The day after, I run into her on my way to the chapel; she is wearing a summer frock buttoned down the front. Red-painted toenails show through the straps of her sling-back shoes.

'No serenading last night. What a let-down.' I raise my hands in mock dismay.

'I was there, but no one came to ask for an encore.'

'We were working late – some of those monsignors are in love with the sound of their own voices – but all is not lost.'

'Certainly not.'

One of the bishops is coming towards us, and, like a teenager caught red-handed, I lower my voice: 'Are you there tonight?'

With a playful grin, she falls in with my tone of secrecy: 'Will the long-winded monsignors delay you?'

'I'll make sure they don't.'

'Right, Lucy.' I return to my normal pitch and squeeze her hand: 'We'll talk about the music soon. Nice to see you again.'

'Nice to see you too, Father Galvin.'

During those weeks when the country is gearing up for the most famous visitor since JFK, we are on a merry-go-round, and neither of us wants to get off the carousel. With the final touches being put to the plans for the Pope, my work on the committee is coming to an end, and also my reason for visiting Maynooth. And despite the way Lucy Campion sidles into my daytime thoughts and invades my dreams, I cling to the self-deception about friendship and the spiritual writers, and I'll be a better man – more rounded. The inescapable truth, however, shows through weak spots in the screen of my wishful think-ing: early in the morning, or at odd times when I'm having a drink with a few classmates after golf, and I'd much sooner be with her.

But the discovery is not able to curb the energy now being

released. That night in Maynooth, a stranger woke from a fitful sleep: the same one who spent two days in the rain outside Smith's, the clock manufacturers, in Cricklewood, searching the skittish throng for Maureen from Claremorris, and who mooched around the Piazza Navona for a couple of nights after Simona had flown back to her parents in Long Island.

I ask Lucy to meet me some evening. And to ensure that our meeting place is well outside the diocese, I suggest Howth. 'It's nice out there,' I say and, fearing a rejection, rush in with: 'You're probably too busy.'

'No, I'm not too busy. And did it ever occur to you that I might have been waiting for your invitation?'

'And then we can have something in the Marine Hotel up the road.'

We walk in the chill of autumn around Howth village: smell of fish on the west pier where seagulls plunge onto the fishing boats and argue over scraps. Perfectly all right for us to walk out together: this is a friendship – nothing more. She nods. The following week we repeat the same assurances.

'It's good that we can be so relaxed with each other,' I probe.

'Great,' she says and looks away towards the rippling sea.

The evening before the Pope's visit, at a final briefing beneath the high altar in the Phoenix Park, I represent Boylan, who is working up towards a show of sobriety for the following day. In a familiar gesture, Lucy inclines her head and signals her interest in going along, and when my meeting is over we could stroll around the park. Despite my intense wish to be with her, I hedge. 'I'd love you to be there, but the security boyos are getting edgy, and anyway, I'll be down in that dungeon, beneath the high altar, and it wouldn't be any fun for you waiting round. Let's meet in The Gresham and take a stroll down O'Connell Street, have something in a restaurant.' In fact, the briefing lasts for only ten minutes, then a reception for the inner circle, but I will not run the risk of being seen with her afterwards by bishops and senior clerics who have clout.

Apart from last-minute preparations, all the work has been

done: behind the high altar, like guardsmen, tall strips of white cloth with the papal coat of arms fastened to flagpoles at both ends swell and then go slack in the breeze. Plain-clothes detectives are chatting with a superintendent in uniform. Men in dungarees are unloading bouquets of flowers from the backs of lorries, others are checking the canopy where the Pope will celebrate Mass. Priests are having a great time taking photographs of each other sitting on the papal chair beneath the high cross; a bishop is giving instructions to the sound engineers. He waves – 'Good work, Tom. See you in the morning' – and continues his instructions. A bunch of seminarians in soutanes, skittish as schoolgirls at their debs ball, are rushing around after monsignors, surveying the altar and testing microphones: a constant purr of generators in the background.

The city, festooned with saffron and white, is high on John Paul II. Street traders line O'Connell Bridge and playfully wave flags in front of our faces. Television sets in shop windows show the Pope wearing a sombrero and smiling to a million heads in Mexico; in Grafton Street, we stand close together and watch a documentary on his life. In the black soutane of a priest, he is raising his hand in blessing over a huddle of old peasant women, traces of snow on the steps of a church behind them. In another clip he is shaving on a mountain slope. And here, under the glare of Father Karol Wojtyla's penetrating look, I secretly take her hand for the first time.

Later, back in The Gresham, growing used to each other, we paint in more of the uncoloured spaces: how her father, who worked for the National Bank, was transferred every few years – Ennis, Bundoran and other towns – until he became a manager; then they acquired the three-storey limestone at the corner of The Square. Her mother – Cork city middle-class, forever moaning about backwaters that didn't have an opera society – made sure the right sort of boy was invited for lemonade and ice-cream and to play tennis in the back garden. Lucy and her two sisters had been packed off to a boarding school when she was only eleven; there she had mooched around the grounds until a nun discovered her singing voice and nurtured her love of music. The shouting of her parents late at night when they returned from the golf club. Her mother's high-pitched tone: 'I should have married Doctor Crowley, instead of a teller. Fecking moneylenders.' Her father shouting back: 'You're nothing but a drunken old bitch.' The youngest brother, a sleepwalker, who, a few years before, had been jailed for embezzling thousands from the bank where he worked. Her five years of therapy and her wedding plans for the following spring.

'Your wedding?' I stare at her bowed head. Life begins to drain from my evening.

She looks up.

'Lucy, why didn't you tell me?'

'What?'

'You're getting married.'

'Oh, no, it's all off.' She reddens and her hand brushes my arm. 'Oh no. I broke off the engagement two months ago.' She couldn't go through with it. A marriage of two families – that's all it would ever have been. 'Philip's dad was the local GP – it's what Mother wanted.' The two families used go to Kilkee or Ballybunion together every Easter.

'You gave me a start.' I have to stop myself from reaching out and taking her hand. 'I wouldn't have it on my conscience, if you were … you know, engaged.'

'Is that the only reason?' She looks up at me and waits for an answer.

'But, of course,' I tease her. 'I'm not in the habit of playing footsie with a woman who is spoken for.'

'You didn't play footsie.'

'No, just handsie.'

Her smile fades. 'This … this friendship – who're we kidding?'

'Ourselves, but let's not discuss it tonight.'

'I agree. *Not tonight, Josephine.* My Dad used to say that.'

'Napoleon.'

'OK. Not tonight, Napoleon.'

Only a couple of hours after I have joined in the celebration of the papal Mass in Galway, I fondle her for the first time. Earlier that day, in the fog-enveloped racecourse, a million screaming youngsters fell in love with the Pope after his 'Young people of Ireland, I love you' speech. Now we stand looking out through the window of her room at the Great Southern Hotel: the young people of Ireland are still high, leaping and waving flags in Eyre Square, going into pubs, and appearing again with pints of beer. With the drizzle coming down, clusters of girls in bell-bottomed jeans, their hair matted, are draped around each other and making giddy promises to visit him next year in Rome, and calling up to the sky: 'John Paul, we love you. John Paul, please come back.'

Sitting side by side, we watch a recording of the Mass on television: first, the antics of the warm-up men, Bishop Casey and Father Cleary – one letting on that he is trying to wrest an umbrella from the other; two high-spirited friends adding to the merriment. But they are forgotten when the crowd spots the Pope's red cape and a hand blessing or waving from a helicopter flying overhead. At the end, when the credits are rolling, I turn to her, and, as if under a spell, begin to stroke her long hair still damp from the rain. I do a John Paul put-on: 'Young harpist of Dublin, I love you.'

She falls in with my good-humour: 'Priest of Maynooth nights, going grey at the edges, I love you too.' This is only joking, so we can both laugh.

We talk on the phone, but with caution lest Eamon, the operator at All Saints, may be tempted to listen in. And on the off-chance of that happening, like teenagers we devise a coding system that sprinkles our ordered conversation about motets and hymns for the college chapel. The figure 8 stands for I love you; a walk in the Guinness estate at Luggala the following Sunday becomes Kestrel, recalling for us the evening in late spring when we were having a row.

'Look, Lucy,' I say, pointing to the sky, in an effort to soften her mood.

We watch a bird, a great elegant creature, drifting smoothly above us: it flaps its reddish-brown wings that glisten in the sun, then it glides smoothly. For a few moments, it stops and hovers as if suspended from an invisible thread, then suddenly it dives upon a small bird. The bird makes a futile attempt to free itself from the fierce talons; a shrill cry fills the valley, feathers drop from the sky and the predator disappears with its prey into the woods on the other side.

'That's a kestrel, Lucy.' I walk on. 'The survival of the fittest.'

Tears are streaming down her face when I turn around. 'Lucy. What?' I go back and put my arms round her.

'So beautiful and so violent.'

'It's OK, love.'

She looks away. 'My fear is that you and I are going to destroy what's between us. I know the quarrels we have aren't serious, but still, I'm afraid.'

'No we won't, Lucy love. No we won't.' Despite my brave reassurances, I am now crying with her. After a while, we grow silent, just holding each other. Then we kiss. By the time we reach the lake, her gloom has lifted and we can both laugh at our ridiculous fears of ever parting.

And like children, we play. 'Of course, *you're* the kestrel,' she says.

'No, *you're* the kestrel.'

In an effort to remove any suspicion Eamon might have, I saunter into his cubby hole near the main door one day, and in casual conversation, drop a remark about Lucy, who is doing a lunchtime concert at the Bank of Ireland. 'She's a great help with Church music, and very obliging if we need anyone at short notice,' I tell him, while fanning the pages of a telephone book on his table.

'That's good, Dr Galvin.' He nods. 'Very good.'

The ex-guard's face gives away nothing. We talk football until another call comes in; he reaches for the phone, and I turn to go, raising my hand in understanding. 'See you, Eamon.'

20

L UCY AND I are now meeting nearly every Sunday: the idle day in the seminary. Ever since the students had been given the freedom to catch a bus for Dublin, or go to a film in Drogheda, the afternoons are drained of life until nightfall. Some of the teaching staff drive off down the avenue in their cars, others pull down the blinds for a siesta, a ritual they have kept up since their Rome days. Boylan too, unless he is three sheets to the wind, visits his friend, a professor in Maynooth. There they have dinner with the rest of the staff, recalling the great brains who once taught in the college. Afterwards, they saunter around the grounds and exchange the latest Church gossip.

Sunday dinner in the long refectory becomes tedious. Along with the other professors, I take my place at the top table; the president occupies the carver at the centre, and, in two rows that stretch all the way to the far wall, the students, wearing soutanes and birettas, face each other in front of us. The conversation about diocesan appointments is leaden; now and again the president breaks off to give some instruction to Quirke: 'Tell the student down there to get his hair cut, and who is the comedian that has them all laughing?'

'He's a mimic.'

'I see. Remind him tomorrow morning that he lacks the proper disposition, and threaten that he may not receive minor orders this year. That will wipe the smile off his face.'

At long last, the president rings a bell and we stand for the Latin prayer of thanks. After that, I serve my time at the customary coffee session in the priests' parlour, and while faking an interest in the debate about Garret FitzGerald, and how he'll never win against the bishops, but Haughey's heart is in the right place, I curse them for keeping me from being with her.

Unless the weather is very bad or she is playing chamber music with the Carolan Quartet, we climb to Howth Summit, or do the headland at Skerries, where the gulls, tossing in sea squalls, screech and swoop all round us, and I discreetly hold her hand while pointing out the Cooley Mountains. Elderly women, in head scarves and sporting Pioneer pins, trundle by, deep in conversation about a bishop they know. Yes, lovely man. And so young. He did the confirmations up in Gormanston. Sure, he only looks like a boy. And he's twenty-five years a bishop this year. God bless him. Is he, faith? He is.

Our favourite walk becomes the Guinness estate in the Wicklow Mountains: over a stile at one of the farmhouses, along by a stone fence and then through dark green ferns that brush clean our boots. Sometimes, dripping wet, but deliciously jaded, we end up at the bar of the Roundwood Inn for chicken-in-the-rough, or down the connecting corridor to the restaurant for a celebration – our birthdays, Christmas, the anniversary of the Pope's visit. Any excuse.

One January evening, we have dinner in Leeson Street, and later, while the snow is falling in the front garden of her Haddington Road flat, we make love. The drapes of the high windows have been left open and the street lights throw a perfect shadow of her harp on the far wall.

That day I had said the Requiem Mass for a young woman who used to work as the college secretary; her distinctive perfume lingered each morning in the corridor after she had arrived. Vinny Lynch, whom Boylan had brought into the secretariat, claimed it triggered off his sinus attacks, and asked to have his desk moved to another part of the house.

I had been visiting the young woman for weeks in the Mater Hospital: on her locker were flowers and Mass cards beside a silver-framed photograph of herself. A tiara on her head and a sash over her summer frock, she is being driven through the main street of Celbridge on the back of a lorry. Wearing long white gloves, she waves to the smiling crowd. Now the jaundiced face on the pillow, though worn out by cancer, still bears the lineaments of the carnival beauty.

She catches me looking, and reaches out her frail hand for me to hold. 'Tommy, we're like the cherry blossom. Gone. Gone with the first strong wind. Don't waste your life.'

I recite the Prayers for the Dead at Sutton cemetery, while hailstones dance off the page of the Roman Ritual. The mourners – a huddle of black – enfold the dead woman's mother as the coffin is lowered into the grave. Afterwards, as I pick my steps over mud and wet grass, a sudden squall from Dublin Bay rushes through a row of cypress trees and sends a pile of snow crashing to the ground. People are standing around another grave; every now and again they raise their heads and look towards the main gate. A man calls me. 'Father. A word?'

'Sure.'

'Would you mind saying the prayers? The priest hasn't turned up and there are a few elderly people here.' He shakes himself. 'They're freezing.'

'Glad to.'

'The poor man is a bit gone in the head, if you ask me.'

'Right.'

The windscreen wipers are busy, clearing the glass of sleet as I make my way to the city. Dark clouds hang over the Pigeon House. My mind too is going helter-skelter. Don't waste your life. Her frail arm reaching out. The carnival queen in her summer glory. No priest. Gone in the head, Father.

Up until then, Lucy and I had managed, somehow, to satisfy our longing with kisses and holding hands in the glorious isolation of Wicklow. And with trying to convince ourselves that 'it would ruin everything', although on a couple of occasions we had crossed the boundary with fondling and probing against the door of her living-room, or on the couch before the forgotten newsreader. Once when I stopped, she grew silent, freed herself from my embrace and moved away. Staring at the television, she smoothed down her dress, then folded her arms. 'Why start something that you can't finish?'

'It would be the end of our friendship, Lucy.'

She lets fly: 'Make up your mind, because I'm not hanging around for ever.'

'It would destroy what's between us. I've seen that happen.'

'Friendship. Is it friendship when you have me jammed up against the wall?'

'I don't feel I've the right to go the full way, in deference to what I've taken on. We did agree that we would try to keep the feelings in check, if we could.'

'That was then, Tommy. I've been faithful to you for a long time now. And at the end of it all, who would be the loser? Not you. You'd have lost nothing, because I think you've no intention of leaving the priesthood, even though you say you are giving it consideration.'

Now fully clothed, we stand in the dark, inside one of the windows. The snow is still coming down; pools of amber from the streetlights rest on the clean blanket of the garden below us.

'Where are you?' Her voice is tender as she nestles closer. 'What's the deep sigh about? Was it not good?'

I stroke her hair. 'Of course, love. Of course, it was,' I lie, and kiss the crown of her head.

'Why the serious face then?'

The drop leaf of a door nearby breaks the silence with a clatter. A group of nurses from St Vincent's, who had invited us to their barbecue the previous summer, are talking loudly about drinks in Searson's as they trip down the steps; they pitch snowballs at each other until they reach the garden gate.

'What's the matter, Tommy?'

'We went the full … you know.'

'Are you sorry? It was only a matter of time.'

'No. Just the risk. If you got, well … how could I live with myself?'

'So that's it.'

I can feel her body relax. 'No worries there.' She reaches up and holds my head in her hands and looks at me. 'I've been on the Pill for the past couple of months. I knew sooner or later that we would make love. I'd been waiting for you.'

'The Pill.'

'Would you prefer I became pregnant?'

'God, no. Oh, no.'

'Look, in case you don't believe me.' She opens her bag and shows me the blister pack with several empty cells. The Pill. The subject of my lectures on sexual morality every year to young men who will, one day, whisper the Church's teaching to sin-haunted wives in the confessional. The brightest man in my ordination year left the priesthood rather than toe the party line. Others too.

We go back and, without switching on the light, sit together on the bed. The street lights shine on the heavy wardrobe and the dressing-table she had been given in her mother's will, and on the trunk from her boarding school days: *Miss Lucy Campion, National Bank House.* The remainder of the address has faded: somewhere in County Limerick.

'Will you stay?' she asks. The dark bell tower of St Mary's Church shows up the driving snow.

'Another night. I've an early start, and the traffic in the morning – you know what I mean. There'll be other nights.'

Her mouth hardens: by now a tell-tale sign of her rising anger. She gets up, closes the drapes and when she switches on a bedside light, tears are gleaming at the corners of her eyes.

I try to draw her near but she resists. 'No, I think you'd better be going. You have other commitments.'

'Lucy, let's not fight again.'

'Stay then.'

She reads refusal in my face, and turns away. 'You don't understand, do you?'

'What?'

'It makes one downright cheap. You have no idea how a woman can feel after making love. You and your theology and your seminary. Right. I don't wish to delay you then.'

As I drive back through slushy streets, and then open countryside, my head is throbbing. Many different voices are wrestling for attention, but I impose order: nothing to be alarmed about – a natural attraction between men and women. Fuck celibacy, as she once said when we were lying on the couch and I said no to the bedroom. I can see her laughing eyes, but that was early on and she was willing to be patient then.

Guilt engendered by years of sermons and retreats, however, activates a panic button and wakes me in the mornings long before it is time to rise. And despite my years in Rome and *novelle theologia*, words and phrases like *hell* and the *seven deadly sins* loom up from the Green Catechism. We will never go that far again; never again, I promise the dark ceiling.

The vow lasts until the June bank holiday when the world is out at Dollymount and Brittas Bay – building sandcastles, eating ice-cream cones and reading newspapers in the shade of windbreakers. I have sweetened the tedium of spending most of the day in the dim library by arranging to meet Lucy in the evening. On my desk is a bundle of letters to be answered. Some are from irate women who are walking out of churches because priests are making political statements about the forthcoming divorce referendum. When I'm finished, I give Boylan an update. 'The fools. How some of them were ordained is beyond me.' He shakes his head. 'They're ushering in secularism and they don't know it.'

While having tea and scones in the kitchen, we talk about the new tide of emigration. The conversation gets round to my summers in London, and, as on previous occasions, he is fascinated by my account of the men who worked on the building sites. I leave him in his rolled up shirtsleeves and braces, settling down to his well-thumbed copy of Homer's collected works in the original Greek.

When I arrive at Haddington Road, church bells all over the city are ringing out the Angelus: one following the other, as if in imitation. The laburnum trees are in full flower; rich perfume rises from the heliotrope and other plants along the footpath leading up to Lucy's flat. Here and there, white blossoms are scattered along the kerb like confetti.

In a restaurant nearby, we have dinner with a good bottle of red, and are still giddy when we return, so that resolutions are kicked aside in the privacy of her huge bedroom. And well after midnight, driving back to All Saints, when my head is in a spin, I resolve that this *will be* the last time. It's not fair to her. Over that summer, however, when the trough of desire rises again, my resolution crumbles every time we are alone in that room, with her harp casting a perfect likeness of itself on the wall.

We visit London a few times, and stay in the same Kensington hotel; knowing how Grace has become so wrapped up in religion, I arrange to meet M.J. on his own. 'Always knew you had good taste in women, Tomásheen, boy,' he says, when we are relaxing in a restaurant one evening. He looks amused as he belches and takes out his wallet to pay the bill: 'You're dead right. I don't know how you lads live like that. By the way, if ever you think about getting hitched to your woman,' he indicates with his thumb towards the Ladies, 'you're always welcome back; here or to the Dublin operation. I'll get you a place at the table, and you'll never want for anything.' He reaches across and slides a roll of notes into my top pocket, 'Here, look after Lucy while you're in London. She seems a classy bit o' goods.'

'I'll stay in M.J.'s in Terenure tonight,' becomes my stock excuse to Boylan when I sleep in Lucy's flat. On one of those nights, she gets into a fit of giggling: 'You and your resolutions.' Hair loose over her naked shoulders, she settles herself into a comfortable position beside me.

'What about me and my resolutions?' I start to tickle her. 'What about me, then, and my resolutions? Come on, Lucy Campion, speak up.' We play about on the bed; both are aware that this is grist to our rising excitement. 'Come on, Campion, answer the Grand Inquisitor, who intends to carry out a thorough search until he arrives at the truth. Don't you know, young wench, that he has the power to put you to the sword?'

Afterwards, when the rush of desire has been satisfied and yields to conversation, she begins to raise awkward questions. And, by now, I know her course of action: calm and reasonable at first, then a flare up without warning. This evening is no different.

'So what's to become of us, Tommy?'

'Give me time to think it out.'

'Time! *Give me time.* I'm sick to death of hearing *Give me time.*' She moves away and pulls the sheet over her breasts. '*Time to think it out.* You've thought it out already. You'll never change. You met someone long before me.'

'Someone? What are you talking about? I love you; surely you must know that by now.'

'The Church, career, ego – that's your first and last love. And make no mistake about it.'

When I'm leaving the following morning, she looks up at me: 'I love you, Tommy, but I'll not hang around. You want it both ways. I'll not be a walk-on part for you or anyone else.'

21

ONE AFTERNOON THAT SEPTEMBER, I am taking a constitutional around the quadrangle with Pat Nugent: the weather is unusually warm for the time of year. Walking with Nugent, then a senior member of the staff, is a grudging task because he uses these occasions to fish for any piece of information that he may have missed about the diocese or from Rome. He even takes students on the same walk and probes with a throwaway question as he draws on his pipe: 'What's Galvin up to these times, lads?' Then a harmless chuckle.

Now he stops and nods towards a long black car parked outside the bishop's house.

'The Nuncio,' he announces like a scout reading smoke signals on the horizon.

'Yes.' I put on a show of innocence. 'I think that's his car. I wonder what he's here for?' Wild shouts and the thud of a football rise from one of the playing fields below us.

We had been discussing students who would need extra tuition to bring them up to the required standard, but now Nugent's interest in the students' welfare meets a sudden death. 'Let's walk over this way,' he says, indicating the side of the quad nearest to the bishop's house. Our conversation from then on becomes patchy and disconnected, and when the front door opens and the sallow-faced Nuncio appears with Boylan towering over him, Nugent quickens his pace. 'We'll have a word,' he says. 'Just to pay our respects. I met him in Rome once.' He rushes ahead of me, his hand extended: '*Benvenuto in Irlanda, sua Eccellenza.*'

About to get into his car, the Nuncio turns around in surprise and looks at him. '*Grazie, grazie tanto.*'

'*E molto benvenuto, sua Eccellenza.*'

'*Grazie.*'

'Dr Patrick Nugent, Professor of Church History here at All Saints.' Boylan makes what seems like a half-hearted introduction and then brightens. 'And my good friend, Dr Tom Galvin, Professor of Moral Theology.'

'*Collegio Irlandese,*' Nugent wedges himself in again. 'We met on St Patrick's Day during the papal visit.'

'Ah, yes, of course.' The Nuncio takes our measure. 'I remember. You played the piano for the Holy Father.' And he runs his fingers along an imaginary keyboard.

His recent arrival as Papal Nuncio in Ireland launches a train of sympathy from Nugent for all that living abroad entails: that morning the Nuncio had accidentally stood on his reading glasses and was urgently in need of a good optician, because he always liked to have a second pair.

'Search no more, Your Grace,' Nugent rushes in. 'I play golf with a first-class eye man. In fact,' he is already reaching into his soutane and taking out a diary, 'I can phone him and take you over without delay.'

'*Sei molto gentile, Padre,*' says the Papal Nuncio.

'*Fa niente, sua Eccellenza.*'

For Nugent, the meeting is a windfall. From then on, he becomes a regular dinner guest at the Nunciature, sitting around with other fawning clerics and playing Irish airs on the piano.

Though he knows well what is happening, Boylan never opens his mouth about the Nuncio's new friend, nor about a future successor, except during a visit to Rome, when he asked me to go along with him. We are strolling across St Peter's Square one evening when he stops and looks at the basilica. 'When I hand in my gun and my badge,' he says with a nod, 'I'll expect the Cosa Nostra up there to make you the next sheriff.'

'I don't think they would make such a blunder.' I laugh loudly so that he can't hear me purr.

'You know the ropes better than anyone else by now, and the priests by and large are fond of you.' That is all he ever said.

Around the seminary, Nugent is in a combative mood against the liberal lobby that is taking root in the country. Over coffee in the priests' parlour, he declares that 'it is time to copper-fasten the legal position with regard to abortion. You see what's happening in Britain and America – killing babies by the thousand. That must never happen here. The Holy Father has challenged us to uphold the teachings of the Church. Now is the time to put the boot in.'

Whenever the Nuncio comes to dinner at the bishop's house, or for some special occasion at All Saints, such as prize-giving day before the summer holidays, Nugent repeats his conviction that it is our bounden duty to support the Holy Father. 'And Rome is right to hold out against contraception, Tom. That position has now been well and truly vindicated. Look at the way women are using the Pill as if they were taking Smarties; fornicating as if there is no tomorrow.'

'How right you are.'

Clusters of priests in tonsure suits and smoking cigars nod, and afterwards, among themselves, agree that Patrick has gravitas. Future leader there. Yes, future leader. And he has the Rome experience under his belt.

He writes articles in theological journals, with many quotes from the Pope's pronouncements on the evils of contraception and divorce. Men who have clout and money drive up to All Saints.

One evening when I'm hurrying out to meet Lucy, Nugent breaks off his conversation with a man wearing a velvet collar on his tailored overcoat.

'Tom,' he calls. 'Have you a minute?'

'I've to give a talk in Wicklow. Nuns.' I throw my eyes to heaven.

'I won't delay you.' He introduces me to a couple of businessmen, lawyers and engineers, all of whose names I have now forgotten. And when they are going down the steps, turns to me: 'They're on our side, Tom; they have power and influence. Most are members of Legio Dei. They'll do our work.' He looks pleased with himself; his hand brushes my elbow as we walk to the front door: 'Now is the time. To use a sporting metaphor, we're still playing with the wind at our backs. And they're the boys to draw blood, if needs be.'

He waves to the gleaming cars moving off down the drive-way. 'FitzGerald and his lot would make this a secular state if they were given too much latitude. Is M.J. still friendly with that minister – Donaghy?'

'Yes. I think so.'

He talks above a whisper, even though the last of the velvet collars are getting into their cars. 'I'd like to meet him sometime. His party is on our side. Say all you like about them, they have the faith.'

The Papal Nuncio makes a surprise visit as I am going through the confirmation list with Boylan. 'Enda,' he says to the bishop, 'I have found a worthy successor. Your Lordship can now retire in peace.'

'And who, may I ask, Your Excellency, is the worthy suc-cessor?'

'One of your own priests. Dr Patrick Nugent.'

I watch the colour drain from Boylan's face and another evening of trying to steer him away from the bottle of Jameson threatens. Years of Vatican diplomacy, however, have steeled him against making a hasty response: 'A good man, Your Excellency, and a fine historian. And while I don't question your sound judgment, may I say that he is a little short on pastoral experience – something priests and the people of God expect nowadays.'

'Put your mind at rest, Enda, my friend.' The brown Sicilian eyes are dancing, 'Patrick is a fast learner.'

After he has left, Boylan collapses into an armchair and sits there in a Churchillian pout, glowering through one of the high windows, while I put on a show of finishing off the confirmation list. Then, without moving a limb, he addresses the drooping willows on the lawn.' "Patrick is a fast learner". Is he now? Well, that jumped-up-Johnny will wait another while before he gets the mitre.' He turns to me: 'I need your support for this one.'

'Have no fears about that.'

'Stay for dinner,' he says when I've finished, and without waiting for an answer, picks up the intercom and phones down to the kitchen. Then he trudges out of the library to uncork two bottles of wine.

Before the television news comes on, we watch the tail end of a nature programme: two young lion cubs are learning from their mother how to keep out of harm's way, how to crouch in the long grass, bide their time and then spring on their prey. Mature lions grab weaker animals by the neck, drag them to the ground and tear them to pieces, limb from limb; blood gushes up into the blue sky. I sip a gin and tonic while Boylan dispatches a couple of whiskeys. 'That's it, Tom. Nature red in tooth and claw. We're their dressed-up city cousins. Let us go and eat in God's name.'

When his part-time housekeeper and her teenage daughter have served the food, Boylan stands and pours from one of the wine bottles. 'I was saving this for a special occasion, Tom. This is it.' He raises his glass. 'To friendship, agape, fellowship – call it what you will. I'd be dead and buried if it wasn't for you.'

We eat mostly in silence while Gigli sings 'O Solo Mio'. In the manner of an aside, Boylan asks: 'How is that sweet girl – what's her name? Oh, the memory isn't what it used to be. She played for the Pope in Galway.'

'Lucy Campion.'

'Yes. Lucy.'

So often, especially after a couple of drinks, he quotes poetry:

> For I am every dead thing,
> In whom love wrought new Alchemy

and the teacher in him sets a test for me to identify the author. He waits for an answer.

'Sounds like Donne.'

'Top of the class. "A Nocturnal upon St Lucy's Day".'

'Lucy is fine. She has a post in Trinity now.'

'My goodness, that fortress of Elizabethan perfidy.' His mouth twists in a mocking smile. 'A good young Catholic girl who sang for the Pope. My predecessors must be turning in their graves.'

'We meet now and again for a meal,' I say.

'So I'm told, so I'm told, Tom. Highly qualified, trained in Hungary: the Kodály Institute. My goodness. Top drawer.'

'Yes. The Kodály.'

He refills our glasses: 'Beauty and talent. By God,' he shakes his head, 'that's a powerful cocktail. And for any man who has a screed of humanity in him … .'

'True.'

He stops pouring and looks at me: 'And you're very human. You know that doesn't help in the Church – if you want promotion, I mean.' His wine-flushed face creases in a smile. 'The army is the same.'

Again he lapses into silence. The housekeeper, whose timing is always flawless, arrives to collect the plates and serve dessert. When she has gone downstairs, he gets up, goes for a cigar and pours us two brandies. Over the sideboard, Van Gogh's 'The Artist's Bedroom' is hanging aslant. Once, when in the doldrums, he had taken it off the wall and given me a short lecture: should be on every clerical student's room, Tom. An object lesson on solitude, and the desperate searching of the heart for companionship. Might dispel their romantic notions about the priesthood.

Now he lights up his cigar and eases himself into his chair: 'They watch everything. They're like old ones.'

'Who?'

'The priests. They have itching ears. Some of them have been gossiping since they were in All Saints fifty years ago.'

He studies my reaction: 'They talk. None of my business what you do with your life, but if you want to take over some day – and I sincerely hope you will – you'll need to think about severing your connection with Miss Campion. That's one thing the Church won't tolerate; you could have a mansion or a farm of the best land in County Kildare and they'd turn a blind eye. Mother Church has never come to terms with women. Unpredictable creatures.' He grins. 'And a distraction to monks who wanted to write their manuscripts.' The grin fades. 'That little pipsqueak in the Nunciature listens to every tittle-tattle, so at least be careful.' Then he goes back to Gigli and how he made up for lack of vocal power with the quality of his singing; I'm half-listening while he moves to John McCormack and how he could hold the melody line better than anyone.

When I'm leaving, Boylan walks with me down the wide corridor; night lights show old prints of St Peter's Basilica, the Colosseum and the Piazza Navona on the walls. No sound now except the creak of ancient floorboards beneath our feet: 'Ah, yes, Mother Church forces us to deny our natural urges and live in these mausolea.' He throws his eyes towards the high ceiling and shrugs. 'Live, hah. Live is right. But we're in the army, Tom; we wear the breastplate of Peter, who, let's not forget, had a wife to keep him on the straight and narrow.' At the great oak door, he stops and looks at me with rheumy eyes: 'Thanks for the company. You know, for all their hot passions, the Romans can be very hard-nosed about love. They have a saying … let me see now.' He scratches his thinning hair. 'Yes, I have it.

L'amore fa passare Il tempo;
Il tempo fa passare l'amore.

He cocks his head and repeats the phrase slowly, as if to himself, while I'm working out a rough translation in my head: *Love makes time pass; time makes love pass.*

'Madly in love today; gone with the wind tomorrow. Goodnight, Tom. God bless. '

I never saw anyone recover so quickly as he does after the Nuncio's visit; to a great extent he controls his drinking and manages to carry out his duties as a bishop. At the priests' re-treat in June, he announces that I am to become vicar-general of the diocese.

And the glamour of what might be: the seed planted silently in Rome whenever I passed the prelates who line the corridors of the Irish College is taking root. *Theologians are ten a penny; bishops hold all the aces.* Now Boylan is handing me the reins. Ardglass might have its first bishop. Why not? I'd be as good, if not better, than the next.

22

'I THINK WE SHOULD CALM THINGS a bit,' I say the next night when I'm leaving Haddington Road and Lucy is waiting for us to canoodle inside the wide-panelled door of her sitting-room. 'You know where that leads.'

'You had no great problem about it up till now.'

'Well then, maybe we should train ourselves, so that, you know, it doesn't happen as often.' Feeling guilty, I go to put an arm round her, but, brushing my hand away, she glares at me. 'No. I don't need your sympathy, and if this is troubling your conscience … .' She is already opening the door. 'Goodnight to you.'

'Goodnight so, Lucy.'

Apart from Sunday evening, we have been meeting whenever both of us are free; but from now on a gap is opening up. Like a secret drinker trying to hide his addiction, I become self-conscious if we meet someone in the foyer of the Abbey Theatre or at the National Concert Hall. So I have a set of excuses. Boylan, has improved, but, you know yourself – I've got to keep an eye on him. A load of exam papers to correct. The Papal Nuncio is coming to dinner. All true, but these commitments never stopped me before. In my conceit, I imagine she will be a constant in my life. And, despite fitful outbreaks when we refuse to speak for days, she seems willing to tag along. We still go to Wicklow, and, ill at ease, sip coffee in her bright kitchen when we return to Haddington Road; then, avoiding her gloomy looks, I make an excuse about having to return. Boylan … you know. Right. Well, thanks again. Thanks.

Then one Saturday evening in Luggala, I receive the broadside I had instinctively known was coming to me. We are walking back along the rugged path towards the stile when a strange silence descends upon her. I clutch at straws: how are things going in Trinity? Any chamber music concerts coming up? Easter has come and gone: how quickly time passes – the small change, with which, in the past, I wouldn't waste our rich time together. My effort fails; she lapses into silence again and, as we are approaching the stile, she stops and says, 'Tommy, you remember the lecturer I told you about. He works in the Maths Department. You met him at a lunchtime concert in the Bank of Ireland.'

'Ronan. He couldn't keep his eyes off you.'

'He's been asking me out.'

'And?'

'And … I gave this every chance. Gave you every chance, but I'm not hanging around any longer. I've to look out for my future.'

I take time to weigh up her ultimatum. 'It's over, that's what you're telling me. Over. Is that it?'

'I would have given him the brush-off. But you've another agenda.'

The rain that was forecast in the morning is now drifting across from the hills.

'I took no bloody vow of celibacy, Tommy.'

'We haven't been exactly living like pure spirits.'

'No, but I could count the number of times we were together – made love.'

'I can't live any other way.'

She glares at me, and, with a strength that is surprising, grabs the lapels of my overcoat. 'Why didn't you stay away from me then? Why didn't you pass by the window that night in Maynooth? Why?'

'Lucy, please.'

'No *Lucy please*. I'll tell you why. You want it both ways.

And another thing: I've got tired of the secrecy. That All Saints place is like the Kremlin; for Christ's sake, you have to talk in riddles in case the operator is eavesdropping. Is that what the Church does to you? Grown men living like fellas in a boarding school?'

I try to free myself, but her red fingernails have a firm grip.

'You have your Church, your priest friends, golf on a Thursday, me. In that order.'

'What?'

'I'll not be an ornament.'

I recover my balance. 'Golfing friends, yes. We know each other for a long time; been through boot camp, you might say. We're used to each other, but what do they know about me, apart from the fact that I fix things? I'm reliable. Man Friday to Boylan. Lucy, listen to me. You're the only one on this earth who really knows me.'

'Then choose.' Her voice is shrill now. I draw her close; the rain is cold on her cheek. She is trembling and I have to hold her so that we don't both fall against the stone fence. And even though we are in the middle of a valley with only sheep following a man chugging along on his tractor, I begin to whisper like a frantic youngster, to plead and repeat myself: 'You are so much a part of me. How can I? I mean, life without you ... I couldn't even bear to think ... .'

But her gaze is fixed somewhere on the hills, among the sheep and the tractor in low gear. Slowly and deliberately, she puts her hands on my arms and frees herself from my embrace. 'I haven't told you the full truth.'

'The full truth. I don't want to hear it.'

'I should have told you before now. I've been going out with Ronan.'

'No, Lucy.'

'I've been going out with Ronan. Have been for a while.'

The farmer has come off his tractor and is calling to his dog to round up the sheep. The dog crouches, the farmer whistles. Blue smoke rises from the tractor. A red tractor with one of those mechanical lifts at the front. I see it all frame by frame without making connections or sense. She keeps on talking about Ronan and herself. 'Have been going out with him for a while.' Been to meet his family. And he has asked her to go to the Trinity Ball in May – news that falls on me like a hundred dark November evenings.

'Lucy, for God's sake. I've never in all my life been as close to anyone.' I'm shaking my head and stretching out my hand, but she folds her arms. 'We've been naked together, and in more ways than one. I have never spoken about myself to anyone like I did to you. Never. Are we going to throw away everything we had – everything we've shared?'

The hood of her red oilskin has fallen down and rain is dripping from her matted hair: hair that from now on will fall loose for another man to fondle. She never looked as pretty.

'Let's go back. We're getting drenched.' Her voice is calm and controlled, and I hate her for it.

'Is it the rows, Lucy?'

'For goodness sake, everyone has rows. No, Tommy. You're just not available.'

Going to the Roundwood Inn, a place that had held such promise in the past, is a mistake. By the time we reach the pub, my shock has turned to poison. 'Such honesty. I must say I haven't experienced such overwhelming honesty for many a day. Ronan. Really?'

The poet is there with glasses perched on his nose, a mop of greying hair and the face of a friendly lion. As usual, he is buried in a book, propped up in front of him while he eats. I gave her a collection of his one Christmas: *To Lucy – my gorgeous banshee.* She hasn't noticed him seated in a corner, but I'm too sick to tell her. During coffee, she raises her head: 'It's hard for me too, you know. The least you could do is say something.'

'Is there something to say? Oh, there is. I'd forgotten. Yes, there is.'

She looks up, her face softens, but I air my spleen. 'Yes, how could I be so churlish? Of course there's something to say. Please forgive my lapse. I hope you and Ronan have a great life together, and I'll go back to nursing a boozy bishop. And another thing, Lucy.'

'Yes.'

'Thank you for being so candid with me.'

She lowers her head, and the ache to ignore whomever may be watching grips me. I want to go round the table and hold her, while we put together the splinters of our world. But I insist on nursing a hurt, and anyway, we both know we've passed the point of no return.

The rain gets heavier, causing the traffic to slow down as we make our sullen journey to the city, and in the bitter silence I am tempted again to break the deadlock, but foolish pride won't allow me. Let her make the first move. When she is looking away, I throw a side glance at the set of her profile: the deep red lipstick freshly applied, the hair still wet and shiny from the rain. I long to stop the car, cast aside my wounded pride, and tell her I'm sorry for being such a bastard. And that she can't go to Ronan. When all is said and done, no one gives a tinker's curse for me. I've no one else, Lucy. I'm there to cover for a washed-out bishop and bolster up priests who are teetering on the brink of despair. I was never as open with anyone as I was with you.

Instead, I bury the desperate appeal in my chest, switch on the radio, and whenever the traffic is free-flowing, increase the speed. When I stop at Haddington Road, her harp shows through the net curtain.

'I suppose you won't … .' With one hand on the door handle, she half-turns to me.

'Go in. No, I don't think so.' Now I want to make her suffer. 'Ronan might drop around and we wouldn't want Ronan to worry that there's anything going on between us, because there isn't.'

Staring straight ahead, I know she is looking at me, but I sink the knife even further. 'How should I have taken it? Oh, Lucy, that's fine … Ronan is it? Ah well, so long as it's Ronan.'

'You knew this was coming; I gave you every chance, but you made your choice, and I'll play second-fiddle to no one.'

She bangs the door and storms across the footpath towards the wicket gate.

Sleep is fitful for the next couple of weeks. At three or four I'm staring into darkness – wouldn't I be better off leaving the priesthood, and starting out a new life with her if she would still have me? Some of the best priests in my ordination year have left and got married. The Church is sinking anyway. I torment myself by going over the good times, and the times we fought. Like the Sunday morning when it was teeming with rain and she took me to the airport, though she had a concert that night with the quartet and needed to practise. And when she couldn't stay for coffee, but had to leave me at the set-down bay, I rounded on her as I was taking my bags out of the car. 'You know how I hate it when there's no one to see me off. Of course, you think only of yourself. That's you all over.' Filling up with remorse during the flight, I phone as soon as I arrive at the Irish College in Rome with a bundle of apologies, and later search the shops until I find her special perfume.

Through those wakeful hours, tormenting pictures spring up of her and Ronan together in that big room. When he turns over in the night, will he delight in the steady beat of her contentment, and the sheer beauty in her wavy hair, slack and loose over her naked back? The fantasy goes out of control and clouds of guilt hang over me in the morning when I recite the divine office:

> Against you, you alone have I sinned;
> What is evil in your sight I have done.

Not since my father died do I go about my work in such a gloom; by the same token, work becomes my salvation. Apart from my golfing day, I fill each moment with lectures and meetings, and with dictating instructions to Vinny Lynch and the women in the secretariat. Boylan, though he has his own struggles to stay off the drink, tells me I look a bit peaky, and asks if I have something on my mind.

'No, just a bit tired. I'll be as right as rain in a few days.'

'No wonder you're tired – you're like a driven man for the past few months: seven days a week non-stop.'

Some days I'm fine until I turn a corner and collide with the past: such as the glorious Sunday in June when I come upon a harpist at the bottom of Castle Street. She is no Lucy though. Pale and tired-looking with wispy hair. When she notices me lingering I move away slowly. Images well up without notice: the way, while playing, Lucy used to toss her head when her hair fell over one side of her face. A postcard she sent the time the quartet was doing a St Patrick's concert in New York falls out of a book – *Missing you, and by the way, 8 more than ever.*

Gradually work numbs the pain and I reach a kind of healing, though the scar tissue remains – even to this day. I start going back to the weekly game of golf and staying on for the leisurely meal of steak and wine and clerical gossip. Up until then, I had been making credible excuses: a meeting in Maynooth, or I've to check on Boylan, lads – a dumb show of hand to mouth in a drinking movement.

'They were full of sympathy: 'God help you, Tommy. See you next week, if you can make it.'

23

BOYLAN GOES TO ROME with Vinny Lynch to present the *ad limina*: the report on the diocese for the Holy See, submitted every five years. The evening before, he asks me to join him for dinner, and when his housekeeper has served coffee, he goes to the sideboard and takes out a bottle of Chivas Regal and two glasses.

'Don't get alarmed,' he says, 'not a relapse,' when he notices me following his movements. 'A toast.' He raises his glass and I fall in with his mood.

'Who or what are we toasting?' I ask him.

He is already taking off his ring and placing it on the table. 'I got this from a member of the Curia – and, hard to believe among that set – a walking saint, if ever there was one. Take it. You'll need it more than I will from now on. I'll be seeing Cardinal Bartoli. He's the kingmaker now, so – as they say – it's in the bag. Anyway, you're way ahead of the field as the priests' choice. *Salute.*'

'*Salute.*'

'I think I still have some friends in the land of Machiavelli.'

Despite my meek protest – guff about several other priests being worthier – my heart is at full throttle.

At Dublin Airport, while Vinny Lynch is at the check-in desk with passports and tickets, Boylan turns to me and speaks above a whisper: 'It won't be long until you are the *de jure* man. And you're welcome to it. *Arrivederci.*'

The following week, I go to meet Boylan. He is cock-a-hoop, waddling across the arrivals floor. Vinny Lynch is behind him, pushing their bags on a trolley. From his inside pocket Boylan takes a letter and waves it in the air: 'The rescript, Tommy. What did I tell you?' I glance at the envelope with the official Vatican seal intact. 'I didn't get to meet Bartoli himself, but he sent this by his secretary to the Irish College.' He is in the same excitable state all evening, and when Lynch leaves after supper, he tells me that I should now take off for a few days until the official announcement the following Tuesday in All Saints. 'You'll have a round of appointments and you'll need all your energy for them. I'm not allowed open the rescript until Sunday.'

As with so many priests who study at the Irish College and who fall to the charms of Gregorian chant – church bells tolling in the evening – and the whiff of power, I am drawn back to Rome, like the swallows to Capistrano. So for the few days before the announcement, I traverse the narrow streets and sit in the cool of ancient churches, drafting speeches and preparing for interviews. I even look at sets of episcopal robes in Gammarelli's, but decide that I can get those in Dublin. Before I leave the shop, however, I buy a *zucchetto*, which I still have as a reminder of my vanity. My golfing friends had offered to go with me to Rome, but I knew from experience how many bottles of wine would be emptied at our dinner table each night, and I needed a clear head for the following weeks.

Each morning as I hurry to the chapel for Mass, past the memorial to Daniel O'Connell where a young theologian had informed me that 'we who study in Rome are meant for higher things', a cock crows beyond the high walls of the college. Breakfast afterwards in the refectory with students and professors revives memories of the Council and aspiring theologians offering to type up notes for bishops. After weeks of grey skies and drizzle back in Ireland, I set off on my daily walk to wallow in the dry heat: up the via Merulana towards the basilica of Santa Maria Maggiore – baroque splendour against a blue sky. Rome is already heating up for the summer: hordes of tourists with cameras are beating a path to St Peter's to file past the tombs of the Popes. In the setting sun, while they are dining alfresco in narrow streets where paint is peeling from walls and shutters, I take a taxi to a favourite restaurant in Trastevere. One evening, I go back to the Piazza Navona, and linger over coffee as darkness falls and memories of another time begin to take shape until I pull myself up, and make my way through the streets, now settling down for the night.

At Dublin Airport, I pick up the *Irish Independent* at a newsagent and sit for a moment at the arrivals section to see if there is any mention of the appointment. Banner headlines declare 'Reynolds in Fresh Row over Passports'. Taking up two columns to the side is a piece headed 'Engineer Claims Priest had an Affair with his Wife'. Speaking at his home in Galway during the week, the engineer had said that the priest was a gigolo and he was going to sue the Vatican because the priest had been the ruination of his marriage. Jack and the Irish soccer team wave from the steps of a plane on their way to the World Cup in the United States.

I leaf through the pages and then stop. *A source close to the diocese has informed this newspaper that the Reverend Dr Patrick Nugent, Professor of Church History at All Saints Seminary, has been appointed to succeed Bishop Boylan, as* … I smile. They've got it wrong again. You'd think they would check their story. Typical. Always *a source close.*

Nugent's picture below the report is the one taken at the Nunciature that first evening of the papal visit. Chomping on a big cigar, Marcinkos had growled that the Holy Father would catch his death of cold in light shoes if he were to walk on the grass 'of this sodden land'. That night Nugent combs the city, gets every shopkeeper he knows out of bed and is back the following morning with a pair of white galoshes. In one of the parlours of the Papal Nuncio's residence, Marcinkos removes the tissue paper from the shoe box and bellows into the Dublin archbishop's ear: 'Make that man a monsignor this week – before the Holy Father leaves this country. And I ain't kidding.'

Then I see it. *Fr Vincent Lynch of the bishop's staff confirms the truth of this story and informs us that the official announcement will be made today by the Papal Nuncio at All Saints Seminary.* I stare at the page. No. Sure, Bartoli ... he's Boylan's friend. That nitwit Lynch must have got panicky with the press – that had happened once, while I was in Rome with Boylan. Only two weeks before, the bishops at Maynooth were welcoming me into the fold. All you need now is the rescript, Tom.

They joked. 'You'll never be short of a good dinner. But you'll never again hear a word of truth from your priests.'

I let the paper drop on the seat beside me. Pilots and laughing stewardesses pass by, flirting with each other. Trolleys are pushed over the shining tiles. 'How was your flight?' Duty-free plastic bags and hugs. Someone is called to *please go to the Aer Lingus information desk.* How could Boylan have got it so wrong? And now having to face the priests at All Saints and sit there and watch that little Sicilian runt make the announcement. I want to cry, like the time when, as a small boy, I got seperated from my mother in town, and was lost in a forest of legs.

A man sits down beside me. 'Is that your paper, Father?'

I look at him.

'The paper, is it yours?'

'Yes. Please take it.'

I haul my bags out into the merciless sun. There would have been one more to haul if I had bought episcopal robes at Gammarelli's.

'Where to, Father?' the driver asks when I'm seated in the back of his taxi.

'What?'

'Where are youse goin', Father?'

'Where am I going?'

He turns round, a baffled look on his face, and I rush in with: 'Malahide Station please. For the train.'

He switches on the meter and joins the stream of traffic. Once or twice I see him glancing in the mirror.

'A bit of oul jet lag, Father, wha'?'

'Jet lag? Oh yes, jet lag.'

On the way to Malahide, he is anxious to talk again: 'You guys. Priests. Rough station.'

'Very rough.'

'Not fair.'

'No.'

'The missus gives a dig-out to the local parish priest. I'm … well, you could say, lapsed.'

'Understandable. Yes, very understandable.'

He answers a call from the crackle and hangs up.

'Did you know the singin' priest?'

'I did.'

'Did a gig for us one time; fundraiser for the football club. Gas man. All the same, sure 'tis only nature comin' out, d'you know what I mean?'

'Yes, I know well. You're dead right.' And I wish you would shut up.

With Vinny Lynch at his side, Boylan is slouching in front of All Saints when I arrive at the main gate. Cars are parked on both sides of the avenue, and by the new wing. The football pitch has been opened for the overflow.

'Sorry, Tommy,' is all he is able for as we climb the steps. 'That quisling Bartoli knew — must have — and that's why he didn't meet me. I should know better than to trust those wretches in the Curia. So sorry.' He is shaking his head: 'You deserved it much more than that cringing acolyte.'

'Not to worry. You did all you could. Thanks.'

Egan Hall is a blur of clerical black, hoots of laughter and cigar smoke, and the tinkle of glasses when waitresses swerve through the crowd. Standing at the top of the hall, close to a huge oil painting of Judas betraying Jesus, is a group of senior priests with Nugent holding court. He is flanked by two canons of the diocesan chapter; a couple of young priests are pirouetting around them. And, like at a funeral, when people are ill at ease with the bereaved, priests come up to me, and, in a clumsy way, mutter words of consolation: 'The diocese's loss,' then a tap on the shoulder, or a wink. 'Keep up the heart, Tom.' One man who runs a farm in his country parish speaks close to my ear: 'They'd sell their own mothers.'

'What?'

'Them hoors in Rome.'

When I go to congratulate Nugent, the room seems to quieten for a moment. '*Ad multos annos*, Patrick,' I say, shaking his hand.

'Many thanks, I look forward to working with you.'

That night, when they have gone and the palazzo is silent, Boylan asks me to join him for a drink, even though when he had stood at the dinner to congratulate Nugent and to wish him every blessing, he was slurring his words. Priests were shifting in their chairs and keeping their heads bowed. With a swaying motion, he walks ahead of me down the corridor to the kitchen. On the table are leftovers: rasher rind on a greasy plate, a tea-stained mug and a milk carton. While I clean off the table, he slams shut the door, removes his Roman collar and stock, and sinks into a chair in front of the big stove. 'Open it, Tommy,' he says and jerks his stout hand towards the bottle of single malt. 'You'll find the glasses in the press.'

For every tumbler I drink, he is throwing back at least two. He grows silent, and raises his glass. 'Fill that, Tommy.' Through his thinning hair the pink head glistens beneath the ceiling lights. 'A toast to the scholarship boy.'

'The scholarship boy?'

'Six miles along the railway track, morning and evening, running barefoot from one sleeper to the next, saving the shoes until I got to the outskirts of town.' He holds up the whiskey to the light. 'I had to be first, you see. As soon as the Leaving Cert results came out, *The Tribune* had it.' He runs his hand along an imaginary banner headline: 'Local boy is first in Ireland'. A drunken smile spreads across his tired face. 'Seduced, Tommy. The scholarship boy is seduced by power and promise: the bones of St Peter buried beneath the basilica, twenty centuries of history, trattoria, purple and brocade. Your teachers become bishops and Cardinals – you see that the way is clear if you play your cards right.' He finishes off the glass and reaches for the bottle. 'I could have spoken out against *Humanae Vitae*, like Curran and others theologians who had balls. I'd seen the terror in women's eyes when they came for guidance, but I did a Pilate.' He turns away his head. 'No. I wanted part of the action, and knew that speaking out was the kiss of death to the mitre.'

'It wasn't your fault.'

A look of contempt on his fat face, he stares at the big range: ' "The fault, dear Brutus, is not in our stars, but in ourselves, that we are underlings." So Tommy, the bogtrotter knew he was far smarter than the others.' Nursing the tumbler close to his broad chest, he gives a cynical twist to his mouth. ' "You'll pass out the big shots, if you keep at the books, son, and I'll be the proudest woman in the chapel." My mother, God rest her.'

'What's that?' It has been a long day, and a fog is clouding my brain.

'She used to say that when the reports came home. First in Latin, first in Greek – the same in Maynooth.'

Boylan, as always when he has consumed most of the bottle, is in full swing. 'Bad to think too deeply; that's when the doubts set in or else you turn to this. Nugent – now there's a man who will never be troubled by doubts.' He rests the tumbler on the arm of his chair; his head drops. 'No. I'm afraid the sea of faith has ebbed away from me, Tommy.'

'I'm sorry to hear that.' I search for a palliative. ' "There lives more faith in honest doubt," ' I quote.

'Yes, but Tennyson was long before Ypres or the Somme or the microchip. No, I started doubting a long time ago. Long time ago in the Infernal City.' He grins and drains the tumbler.

On his retirement, Boylan moves to a bungalow in Bray, and, at first, gains a new lease of life, controls his drinking and goes back to Homer. Gigli, Caruso and McCormack sing again. After a few months, however, he begins to wander off. On one occasion, a young couple find him trundling aimlessly, in his dressing-gown, close to the sea's edge. He tells them he is looking for Monsignor Galvin to make out the confirmation list. I get him into a nursing home nearby, and from then on until his death, he keeps asking me if Tom Galvin is doing well as a bishop.

'Very well. Yes, he's doing very well.'

'The son I never had, you know.'

'Really?'

'Yes. Well, you'd better be getting back to your wife.'

'Right so. See you next week.'

Nugent asks me to continue as vicar-general: I would still deliver the odd lecture here and there, and remain a friend and confidant of the priests. 'Your experience of the diocese is indispensable,' he assures me in the selfsame library where I updated Boylan on diocesan events. One of the golfers sums it up while we are waiting to tee off: 'The old story – better to have you pissing out than pissing in.' Nugent also brings in Father Henry Plunkett, who had cleared off a huge debt in one of the biggest parishes in the diocese. Within a fortnight of arriving there as parish priest, Plunkett had let go the paid catechist, sacked the sacristan and replaced him with an old nun who was willing to work for a trifle. He then closed down most of the parish groups. 'Gossipers,' he called them. 'Drinking tea and coffee, and wasting heat and electricity in the basement.'

'My predecessor, God love him, and his advisers, had many talents, but housekeeping wasn't one of them,' Nugent tells his classmates the night they present him with a crozier; he boasts that, with Plunkett's help, he will clear off the diocesan debt in five years.

24

A S HIS WEALTH GROWS, M.J. and Grace grow apart. The children shoot up. Holy Communion, confirmation, and then, suddenly, the girls, Elizabeth and Margot, are at university. Much to his father's disgust, Charlie is in art school; Matthew is a year away from ordination at Downside Abbey, and Grace is driving down there every Saturday and staying at the guesthouse for Sunday Mass. And, like photos dipped in solution where the features gradually are revealed, echoes of their parents' manner come to the surface.

Elizabeth, once a thumb-sucking child brushing against her Dad's knee, walks like him, clears her throat like him and wears her father's charm when she wants her own way with the board of directors. Margot, my godchild and favourite – who was left with the small change of her parents' affections – sails into St John's College, Oxford with straight As. All she learns there, however, is how to drink one gin and tonic after another in dark-panelled pubs.

'Come over, Tom,' she phones in desperation one night. 'I need to talk. You always listen.'

That visit becomes the first of many. In a snug at The Eagle and Child, surrounded by ancient boarded walls and plummy accents debating Shakespeare, American foreign policy, or Thatcher, I try to talk sense, but it falls on deaf ears despite fervent promises. Next week. Next month. The New Year.

One May, during Eights Week, we walk around the honeystone quad at St John's where she spells out the feverish course of her life: the hotel rooms with tutors – married and single – some she'd only met in a bar earlier.

'If you became pregnant … .'

She shrugs.

'Having a child would change the whole course of your life. You'd be tied down then.'

'There are other options.'

Afraid of what she has in mind, I hold my tongue. She tosses her golden head, and a young troubled version of Grace walks beside me beneath the archway leading to St Giles Road. 'Anyway, there's always the "morning-after".'

'Providing you're sober enough to remember.'

'Who cares?' The puffed-out look of the drinker saddens me; I stop preaching and invite her to The Randolf for lunch.

The following September, during a duty-bound week of concerts and galleries with Nugent and Plunkett, I visit her apartment in Bayswater. She has scraped a third-class honours and has got a job with a publishing house off Charing Cross Road.

Everything is fine now, Margot assures me while she rushes around the kitchen, preparing a salad. A man's jacket hangs over one of the chairs. 'Yes, everything has worked out fine.' While we eat out on the terrace, a soft breeze drifts in from the Thames; she drinks one glass of wine after another, and then opens a second bottle. Her hangdog look returns. 'What's the use in pretending?' she cries. Nothing has changed – if anything it has got worse. She had woken one morning after a heavy night's drinking and had no recollection of where she was, or who she had been with the previous evening.

'But your Oxford degree, your job … .'

She isn't listening, but keeps mumbling how she'd be better off dead.

'Would you think about seeing a doctor – a consultant?'

'A psychiatrist with a pipe, and glasses perched on his nose who would listen behind a desk and make a diagnosis? Then he'd put me on tranqs or sleepers, and I'd walk the streets of London a smiling imbecile. No, Tom. You remember the rhyme:

"All the King's horses and all the King's men couldn't put Humpty Dumpty together again." Nor Margot.'

During the idle times – such as summer holidays – when the papers are short on news, M.J. features once or twice, along with other Irishmen who have made fortunes building up and restoring services to war-torn London. At first the papers applaud his success: he is 'a down-to-earth Irishman who never lost his native accent'.

Then the tide turns. The cruellest blow comes when a tabloid headlines Margot's death only two days after I had said her funeral Mass. 'Irish Millionaire's Daughter Throws Herself under Train at Paddington'. She had tried to do the same the previous Christmas week, but a man had grabbed her as she lunged towards an incoming train.

To his eternal credit, Nugent goes with me to the funeral. 'Stay on for as long as you wish,' he says, when I drive him to Heathrow for his flight back to Dublin. 'Your brother and his family need you at this tragic time. And if there's any way I can help, remember to phone.'

After the funeral, M.J. asks me to go with him to the old house in Chiswick, now an office; there he drinks day and night, and raves about Margot, how he has now caused another death by neglect. Then his tormented brain switches to Ardglass. He mutters something about climbing Brandon. And milking cows. 'They need to be milked, Tommy. We'll go and do it now. 'Tis getting dark.'

I glance out at the sunny street. 'Right. First drink the coffee. We'll do it then.'

'And we'll cut the hay in the Mill Field.'

'Next week, but drink that first.'

He holds the cup like a deranged child, and I manage to calm him until the next fit of crying. 'Where did I go wrong?'

'You didn't. You did well. Very well.'

'Money. Fucken money. You make a few bob, and before you know where you are, you're a junkie. And those poor devils I wronged.'

'You gave them work.'

'I'll make it up to them. I will.'

For three days we hide away in that house, while he lances his guilt, his sadness, his life's frustrations. And despite my efforts to keep him afloat, he seems to be sinking and is dragging me down too.

'So much oul sadness in the family. Mossie, and now poor Margot. I hardly know the twins, or Eily and Pauline. And the Da. Boasting one minute about all the money he'd make out of the few hungry calves at the November fair, crying the next minute. "What are you crying about, Da?", Pauline used to ask him. Do you remember, Tommy?'

'Too well.'

' "Yerra, go away girl, sure, I'm not crying at all, something went in my eye." '

At night, M.J. walks the corridor with a glass of whiskey in his hand, or tramps up and down the stairs, talking to himself. I switch on the light and stare at the ceiling. He is asking questions of me too; more serious than any retreat has ever done: about who I am, or where I am going, or, indeed, how I got into the priesthood.

Then, the morning before I leave, as if nothing had happened, I can hear him making phone calls while I shave. The radio is playing in the background. And like the men who climb into the lorries at Cricklewood Broadway, deadlines come to his rescue.

'We're survivors, Tommy. Survivors,' he says with a sigh, and then as usual, the wad of notes appears on the kitchen table and is stuffed into my side pocket. It is futile to protest. 'Take it,' he insists, 'and you'll say the Mass for poor Margot in Dublin.'

'Of course.'

'Now I want you to do something for me.'

'What?'

'Hear my confession.'

'Now?'

'Yes. Now, Tommy.'

'But, could you not wait, and go to one of the priests around here? And anyway, I'm your brother, and I don't know....'

'You're a priest aren't you?'

True to form, he won't hear of a refusal, even in this most intimate of rituals. He kneels beside my chair and confesses his sins. No mention of *dead men* or hard rock, or bribing borough officials – just women. Women he had met on business up in Manchester, or on visits to Dublin. I raise a hand in absolution over his wavy hair, now turned to silver.

He holds a reception at the Berkeley Court after the Month's Mind Mass. I sit with Jody in the lounge beneath the sparkle of chandeliers, while important-looking waiters weave their way around groups of agents and engineers: family members, a few of Margot's friends from Oxford, and people from the building trade. In a suit that looks too big for him, Seery is standing at the bar with M.J. and Donaghy.

'Christy has done alright for himself,' I remark while I study a bald version of the cocky young man who had held whispering conferences with English blokes smoking cheroots, and was given bulky envelopes at The Stag's Head. 'His own accountancy firm in a select part of town.'

Jody gives a discreet look towards the bar; the little man is rocking on his heels while he talks. 'The bagman,' he chuckles. 'He's your man if you want land rezoned, so long as you grease his paw. Offshore accounts are his speciality. And, by the way, he's not Christy any more. Chris now.'

Even though he had pumped my hand when we met earlier, Seery comes over to top up his condolences. 'You've an ally in heaven, Tommy. Lovely girl. Too good for this world.' He then takes a Mass card from his pocket. 'This is for your dear niece. I didn't want to bother you that day at the funeral.' He removes the card from the envelope. 'I didn't manage to get it signed. Will you do the needful?'

'Certainly, Chris.'

'That's grand.' And he makes to reach into his back pocket.

'What's the damage, Tommy?'

'Ah, don't bother about that.'

'But I'd like to give you some offering.'

'I wouldn't hear of it, Chris.'

While I'm raising my hand in protest, he is already putting away his wallet. 'Are you sure?'

'Good of you to come, Chris.'

He spots a waitress with a tray of drinks passing by and calls her: 'I'll have one of them, girl. Might put a bit of life back into me.' He gives her a leering look, but she ignores him.

Just back from Spain with his family, staying in one of M.J.'s apartments – the one in Marbella, Seery boasts that he had lived on Galtee cheese and sliced loaves for a week. Hardly spent anything.

'That's great.'

'I learned how to keep my head above water, Tommy, had to, from an early age. Thirteen of us, head to toe in the beds; oul empty sacks for quilts down on us in the winter.'

'You're all the better for it.'

'Did I ever tell you about the gabardine coat?' He did, but he tells me again. Six of them in succession had taken the *Princess Maud* with the cattle down in the hold; all had shared the one gabardine. 'Send back the coat when you get paid,' had been the final instruction at the railway station; several times the gabardine crossed the Irish Sea until it was in tatters.

'Ah, too soft they have it now,' he says, but he has exhausted the poor childhood, so he changes gear. 'You play a tidy hand of cards if my memory of Kilburn serves me right.'

'We gave him every educational advantage you could think of,' says M.J., who had left the others at the bar and had come to sit with us: a strong smell of drink from his breath.

'Great,' says Seery. 'He can join us some night.' He turns to me. 'Give you a break from them serious books. Why don't you set it up, M.J.?'

'I will.'

Though limping after another attack of gout, M.J. does a round of hand-shaking, as the gathering begins to file away. His eyes are red-rimmed, and the intense ruddy colour of his cheeks and the broken veins on his nose suggest someone who could do with a check-up. When they have gone, he sits opposite me; worry lines have worked their way into his forehead.

'Grace had to go early: she's visiting Matt in Downside.' He has a glass of mineral water resting on the arm of his chair.

'I see.'

'He's doing some play with the students,' is spoken with tired resignation. 'Ah, I don't know.' He begins to tap the arm-rest. 'Things aren't working out between herself and myself. More so since poor Margot's death.'

'Sorry to hear that.'

'Haven't been for a long time. You might hear rumours. I'm sure 'tis all wrong in your books, but I didn't bargain for marrying some sort of a nun. I go my way, she goes hers. She says she should've married that doctor fellow. Blames me for it. Blames me for everything.' He releases a heavy sigh, and takes a sip from the mineral water. 'You never saw the like of all this washing and cleaning. Door handles, bathrooms. Off to the dry cleaners after one wear of a dress. The housekeeper has to change the bedclothes twice a week.' He shakes his head. 'Not healthy. And the way she's turned to religion. Confession every Saturday.'

'All that can't be easy for you.'

'Women – I'll never understand them.' He goes through a noisy clearing of his throat. 'Your crowd are right to keep them away from the controls.'

The poker sessions are only a disguise for the main agenda. Donaghy and Seery and a couple of the party hacks arrive late and fill the room with loud laughter and the smell of drink; they make references to a meeting they had had earlier with county councillors in a pub off out in Raheny.

A well-known mimic in the bar at Leinster House, Donaghy adds to the high spirits with his hilarious take-off of a woman deputy and her posh accent. 'I know what she wants and she's not getting it.' He raises his glass: 'Anyway, here's to a man who cleaned up half of London after Hitler, and who is now changing the face of this city.'

'Hear, hear,' say the party hacks. We all turn to M.J., who shakes his head and waves us away in mock protest.

While we play, the conversation gets back to land development and planning proposals. Whenever there is a doubt, Seery has the answer. The grandfather clock in the hallway strikes eleven and M.J. begins to stretch and yawn in an overdone way: 'Right, lads,' he says, 'a last hand, and may the devil take the hindmost.'

We leave the table and the pall of blue smoke hovering beneath the light shade. 'A bit of a shark we have here, Chris,' says Donaghy, gesturing at me and winking.

'Ah, they learn more than their prayers in the seminary, Sylvester.' Seery is bitten by the loss of a few pounds.

'Our daily prepared these for us. Now dig in, lads,' says M.J., bringing a tray of sandwiches and chicken limbs from the kitchen.

'Up to her usual standard, I trust, M.J.,' says Seery.

'Give us this day our daily bread,' one of the hacks says, reaching for a sandwich.

Through the open door of the kitchen, I can hear M.J. scalding the teapot.

While we are eating, Seery, with a magician's flourish, whips up a leather briefcase, clicks open the metal locks and takes out a folded map. 'Gentlemen,' he declares as he lays the map on the card table, 'come over and take a gander at the city of the future.' He rocks on his heels. 'This,' he says, standing aside, 'is an outline sketch of the plans for the next ten years.'

M.J. traces a line across the north suburbs and comes to rest around Swords. 'That's all for agricultural use, I'm told.'

Seery removes his glasses and peers at the map; then he straightens, and throws cunning looks around the room: 'M.J., you know by now, my contacts in the department are open to – shall we say – my power of persuasion. Amn't I right, Minister?'

Munching a sandwich, Donaghy puts down his cup and clears his throat: 'Sure, M.J., Chris has the damn planning department by the short and curlies.' When he laughs, particles of food splutter from his mouth and come to rest on the map. The party hacks join in the laughter. Seery, whose lips are pursed, casts a cold eye on each man's reaction.

'Didn't I swing the Rathfarnham site for you, M.J.?'

'Fair play to you, Christy, you did so, boy.'

We return to our seats and chat. Seery turns to me and drops his voice, as if he is imparting a secret. 'The city needs houses; young couples want their own place. They can afford it now. And an expanding economy means more government offices.'

'Right,' says Donaghy, finishing his tea, 'can't keep the little woman waiting all night, hah, lads. You know yourselves.' Before he leaves, he comes over and shakes my hand: 'You'll have to join us again, Tommy. Give us a chance to win back our money.'

When Donaghy and his henchmen have left, I help to clean up. Seery hooks his thumbs inside his braces and paces the room. 'You know,' he grins at me behind M.J.'s back, 'poor boys like me who got a buckshee education from the Brothers will rule this country before long.'

'And what about poor boys like me, Christy, who never saw the inside of a Brothers' school? Two years in the Tech and then finishing school in John Bull.'

'Ah,' Seery taps his forehead, 'you have it up here. You're a cute Kerry hoor.' He goes over to the table, folds the maps and puts on his jacket. 'When those old English dames put up for sale in Cabinteely, I'll be on to you first thing.'

'Will they sell?' M.J. asks.

'They'll sell. They need the money. Living in squalor in one room of that mansion. Freeze their arses off in the winter.'

'You'll be able to swing it?'

'Did I ever fail? A gold mine there. Eighty acres. My man in the planning department never let me down yet. He'll expect the usual, of course – mad for the readies. And you can count on Donaghy to swing it.'

'I know that.'

While M.J. is seeing Seery to the door, I clear away the rest of the glasses, put the bottles of whiskey and brandy back in the cabinet and empty the ashtrays. Then, spotting one of Seery's maps on the table, I rush to catch him, and reach the hall just as M.J. is putting a package into his outstretched hand. They stop dead: two boys caught stealing apples in a neighbour's orchard.

'Your map, Chris. You left it on the table.'

For a moment both are thrown off guard; M.J. is the first to recover: 'Ah, the first signs of old age, Christy. You'd want to watch it from now on, boy.'

The eyes dance in Seery's head: 'Now, where would any self-respecting servant of the people be without his map, Tommy, I ask you?'

'We'll go over the accounts next week,' says M.J., one hand on the door lock.

'We'll do that. And have no worries. Cabinteely is in the bag. You have my word.'

After he has left, I leaf through the newspaper, aware of M.J.'s fidgety movements: one minute he is tapping on the armrest; the next he is pacing the floor, a glass of wine in hand, then back to the armchair. Watching his movements out of the corner of my eye, for a moment I'm back in the days of *dead men*, hard rock and borough council officials on freebie holidays in Killarney. He stops tapping: 'The next fellow will do it if I don't.'

'What?'

'Oil Seery's palm. Someone else will. People need houses. Easy for them journalists to talk. Oul blather.'

'You have a point there.'

No fight now; instead, a shared understanding that this is the reality of building houses for young couples looking for their own place, and old ladies with freezing arses in winter who need ready money. And M.J. gets the 'oul thrill' out of it all.

He drains his glass. 'You know how it was in London, Tommy. Same here. Same everywhere. *In saecula saeculorum.* I'm going to my bed.'

As we speak in front of his house the following morning, the orange and rust of autumn from the maples and beeches set off the redbrick avenue. A light mist covers the roof of my car. 'Don't be a stranger,' he says. 'You need a break from all that trouble ye'er having with them court cases. I'll get tickets for the All-Ireland. Bring Lucy.'

'I'm afraid Lucy and I have gone our separate ways.'

'I see. Ah, well, more fish in the sea, Tommy. God bless.'

'God bless.'

He holds open the gates, and the tyres crunch the gravel driveway before I join the morning traffic.

My ticket for the final is only a few rows behind the president, who sits with her husband and the head of the GAA. As he does nearly every year, M.J. brings with him some of the London crowd – those who had served the company for years – gangers and quantity surveyors; Jody also, who is now running a haulage business in Watford. Whenever there's a break – when the ball goes wide or a player is down with cramp – the president's free-and-easy northern tones rise above the excitement of the crowd; at half-time she works her chatty way through the hospitality room. There we run into Donaghy and his poker players: I make promises to play cards again.

Wearing linen suits and holding glasses that sparkle in the harvest sun, politicians and their wives stand around talking. At a corner of the bar, a member of Dáil Éireann, towers above his circle of admirers and dominates the conversation; his loud laugh can be heard above the tinkle of glasses, the TV monitors and the backslapping. With mouse-coloured dye reaching his hairline, he holds his golfing umbrella in front of him with both hands and scans the room, looking for notice. When he comes over, the circle around him moves as one like a bonded mass. After introductions and jokes, and brief comments about the standard of play, he quickly falls into conversation with M.J., Donaghy and the hacks about Dublin Bay developments. Then, after assuring us that Kerry will be no match for Mayo in the second half, he turns as he moves off, and shouts over his shoulder: 'Maurice Fitz is past his sell-by, M.J.' Gold fillings show when he laughs.

I saunter down by the dining area and see a team of dark-skinned waiters serving drinks at the tables; Jody is standing on his own outside one of the glass panels smoking, and squinting at the sun-washed chimney stacks of Drumcondra. 'Linen napkins and bottles of wine in Croke Park, Jody,' I say, indicating the dining-room.

'The Tiger,' he draws on a cigarette. 'No more wedges of bacon, and bottles of milk straight from the cow for Paddy.'

'Nor the ghost train from Dingle.'

'And the misfortunate blokes who sent home their postal orders every week are now riddled with arthritis, and are trying to hobble up and down Cricklewood Broadway.'

'D'you think Mick O'Connell was the greatest ever, Jody?'

He looks at me and chuckles: 'The poor bastards. Hard to believe how they beat the living daylights out of each other over Seán Purcell and Mick O'Connell.'

Seeing him again quickens my curiosity about London. He has an update: Garryowen fell and hit his head against a door frame one winter's night in Richmond Street, and was frozen to death when he was found the following morning.

'All night. My God, the poor man.' Images flood my mind. The books in his bed-sitting-room, the way he fell to his knees beside the dying Deano, and recited the Act of Contrition, he who boasted after pints in The Highway that he was a Marxist and didn't believe in heaven or hell. Dan McGrew.

'They say he willed whatever few bob he had left to one of the ladies in Richmond Street,' Jody adds.

'He was right. Sure, he got the only bit of comfort ... anyway, the poor man. God rest him.'

We fall silent, looking out over the chimney stacks.

'How's Bonnie?' I ask after a while. 'She didn't turn up at Margot's funeral. I send her a card every Christmas, but for years now I've got no reply. Has she moved?'

He draws on the cigarette and looks at me.

'Is she still at The Victoria, Jody?'

'You haven't heard?'

'Heard what? I told you. No word for donkey's years.'

'I don't think you'd like to know.'

'Is she all right?'

'Bonnie … I'm afraid. Well, Bonnie has slipped, Tommy.'

'Slipped?'

'She's in around Kennsington – good hotels: she's been at it for a long time now. Started off in the usual way: businessmen away from their wives, but now, just lonely old jossers. They can pay well for the comforts of the night – so I'm told. And Bonnie's no spring chicken anyway.' He sees the look on my face. 'She's not the only Irish girl to go like that.'

The lounge has grown silent. Through the glass panels, I can see the staff clearing off the tables and calling to each other in their own tongue, and am half-aware of the referee's piercing whistle for the second half.

'A few of the Athenry crowd she used to hang around with in the Galty tried to do something. They even asked Father John to talk to her – that's before himself and Mary rode off into the sunset.' He throws his cigarette butt on the concrete and crushes it with his heel. 'We'd better be going back in. I'll talk to you after the match.'

'Which hotels, Jody?'

'The Somerset, The Devonshire … others, where well-off old gents stay.'

Maurice Fitz is even better in the second half, and when the Kerry team comes to receive the Sam Maguire right in front of us, I stand with everyone else; M.J.'s gang cheer and punch the air. But Jody's words puncture the cheers and the speeches. The Somerset. The Devonshire. Well-off jossers.

25

I'M STILL NOT SURE why I decided to search for Bonnie: guilt perhaps at the way M.J. had treated her, or some remorse of conscience for failing to keep in touch, except for a Christmas card sent at the last minute. So, while the students are on a short retreat during mid-term, I catch a plane to Heathrow, and spend hours sipping coffee in quiet corners, behind pillars and in the lee of palm branches, until an older version of the Bonnie image in my head strides out of the revolving doors of The Belgrave. In a well-fitting suit and carrying an umbrella, she has ripened into the upper limit of middle-years; her hair is cut short and she has lost weight.

I put down the cup as she hurries by. 'Bonnie,' I call.

She swings round. 'Who are *you*?' Then, after a moment's recognition, her look of anxiety gives way to a scowl; she makes to dash off, but I go after her. 'Bonnie, come back. Can we talk? Bonnie.'

A commissionaire with two rows of buttons down the front of his red uniform and wearing white gloves eyes me.

'I've nothing to say to your crowd any more,' she says over her shoulder. 'Sorry I ever set eyes on the lot of you.' Her accent has become distinctly English.

I lay my hand lightly on her forearm: 'Bonnie, remember what you said: "No matter what, Galvin, we'll always be friends."'

'Don't think I ever said that.'

'Have something with me.'

She glances at the reception. 'Not here.' And without another word being spoken, she stamps out of the hotel; anger in every movement of her body. 'Who told you?' she asks over her shoulder.

'Jody.'

Silence then until we reach a restaurant off Kensington Gardens.

'I know what you and your Church think of what I'm doing.'

'We knew each other before I ... before I joined the Church.'

'In case you're shocked, it's no different from what the men who work for your brother are doing. They sell so that he can get richer. They sell, I sell. The only difference is – I get well-paid.'

Under the light of the table lamp, I notice grey roots at the parting of her hair, and her overdone make-up fails to cover the wrinkles that have scored her face and neck.

She catches me looking. 'You're shocked.'

'No, no. I respect everyone's decisions about their life. Enough to do to make sense of my own.'

'Why did you look me up?' She raises her head from the menu chart. 'To go after the lost soul, is that it? Well, Tommy, save me your pity.' She looks nervously around. 'Yes, sure, I've been treated like an object. No promises. Money up front.'

'I'm not going after any lost soul, but I am anxious to know how you are. That's why I ... well, I was in London just to browse around a few bookshops and call to see M.J., and decided to look you up.'

She picks at her food, and, like a broken record, falls into the same groove: M.J. and the times she went with him to stupid cowboy films, and he fell asleep on her shoulder, and she wouldn't move in case she'd wake him. Took his washing with her to the hotel; his shirts were ironed as good as the prime minister's. And all the while he had another English dame who worked for Nat West. Anyway, rich blokes like him are used to getting their own way. He was only a couple of years married when he asked her to take up where they had left off. 'How about that now, Father Galvin?'

She dries her eyes, and is silent for a while as she emerges from her troubled world, and, for the first time that evening she looks directly at me. 'You're getting thin on top, and you had a fine mop; they must be pushing you too hard.' She studies my face in a way that causes me to redden. Her tone softens. 'You've suffered too, Tommy. I can tell.'

'Who doesn't?' I try to wriggle away from her gaze. 'Isn't it a vale of tears?'

'I've met all sorts, and I see their eyes at close range, and I know when the light has gone out.'

'You should be a counsellor, or a spiritual director.' I force a laugh and take refuge in describing my work with Nugent: visiting the priests, trying to encourage them to keep going; the drinkers and those who are fiddling the parish accounts; the career men who know what buttons to press for a reward.

'You should be good at that.'

'Why?'

'Seems just like the building sites.'

'Ah, not *that* bad.'

She softens and we rake over the ashes. The last she'd heard of Sputnik, he had gone off to Sale with Scunthorpe Peggy, whose teenage son had then stabbed him eight or nine times one night and had brought him to death's door. Horse Muldoon had bought a pub, and a hundred acres of land outside Castlerea and had married a local barmaid twenty years younger than him: six children, one of them going on to be an engineer. Not bad for an ignoramus who could just about write his name.

'You wouldn't know the place now. Well, the Crown and The Highway are much the same, but the men have cards – nearly all of them. Have to, government regulations. Hats and gloves and proper rainwear.'

'Do you remember the steam rising from their wet clothes when they sat in The Highway. Drenched after a two-hour journey?'

'Yeah, wrecks now around Kilburn and Holloway – those that are still alive. That's all they ever got out of building the skyline and sending home their postal orders.'

Though rarely making eye contact, she relaxes and begins to talk about her customers: most of them are at the stage of life where they just want someone to listen to their stories. She gives a half-smile: 'I probably hear more confessions than you do, Tommy.'

'That would be easy. Not many go any more in Ireland.'

'One chap – an elderly gent from the West Country – brings a framed photo of his mother he takes out of a briefcase and talks about her all the time. Then goes back to his wife in Bournemouth.'

'You would imagine the sea air should be enough for him.'

She laughs for the first time.

When I spot her stealing a look at her watch, I call for the bill. 'If you're ever across the pond,' I say as I write down my address and telephone number and hand it to her, 'I'd love to see you.'

At the door, I am using the rain as an excuse to linger and fill the leave-taking with idle talk and questions: which Tube should I take back to my hotel, the bookshops I have left to visit. London is changing. She begins to tap her umbrella against the concrete. 'Nice of you to take the trouble to find me, but don't worry, I can look after myself.'

'OK. And phone me if ever … you know … you need … well, anything.'

'I will, I'll phone.'

I know Bonnie; she won't phone.

Suddenly, she puts her arms around me, kisses me on the lips, and says: 'I met the wrong Galvin. Goodbye, Tommy.' And she is gone, merging with the indifferent crowd jostling for the Underground. Instead of taking the train, I trudge back to my hotel, vaguely aware of young couples meeting and going into restaurants, or taxi drivers smoking cigarettes and laughing together at a rank.

I have a late flight back to Dublin the following evening, so, after a quick visit to a bookshop or two, I take the Jubilee line to Kilburn Station and walk as far as Quex Road Church, where I stop and let the past flood my thoughts. The spot by the low wall where they sold the newspapers is now a bus shelter: dead leaves lie on the top of a wheelie bin. The place seems smaller, the road narrower. Even the church has shrunk. On the red seat two old men are cross with each other. One is resting his hands on a walking stick, and is giving out in an Irish accent about this new fellow, Blair, to the other man, whose shirtsleeves hang loose outside his shabby overcoat. Another old man sitting apart from them throws a bloodshot look in my direction, and then begins to poke aimlessly with his crutch at a sweet wrapper on the footpath.

Buckram-flared summer frocks, the smell of Brylcreem and wild promises well up in my imagination: a forest of hands is reaching for the Irish provincial papers. Wearing a cravat and sports jacket, Deano is smiling again and is slipping an arm around Kim Novak. Over the tannoy, the priest is announcing a Pioneer outing.

> *I'll sing a hymn to Mary,*
> *The mother of my God …*

The world is young; we shall never die.

Passing by Halal shops, and the smell of fruit, I make my way up Kilburn High Road. Scattered among the coffee-coloured skins of Eastern Europe, and women in swathes of orange and brown saris, are old men from home who still carry in the set of their walk the memory of struggling against bleak November hills.

My compass becomes the State Cinema, now a bingo hall, where I'd taken a Galtymore girl to see *Saturday Night and Sunday Morning*. We had fish and chips afterwards at the Green Rooster; over its doorway is a sign in red plastic: Popa-dom Indian Restaurant. A swarthy man in a turban looks up and down the street, throws me a look and disappears inside.

With Deano's ghost, I catch the bus for Cricklewood, past stalls selling soap, umbrellas and shoes, once drapers' shops with striped awnings where men bought shiny suits the day before

Christmas Eve to wear on the boat for the North Wall.

At a café opposite the Galtymore, I have coffee while staring across at what was the gateway to unmixed joy, but now, in the clear light of day, is just a shabby building with brown paint peeling from the walls. Near me a man is growling his way through a soggy mass of baked beans, runny eggs and rashers. He calls roughly to a waitress, and bygone mornings of gulping down food when whistles are blowing outside come tumbling back to me. 'Don't shout, Jimmy,' says the dark-skinned waitress with the firmness of a well-intentioned nurse. He splutters that he wants more cuts of bread, and throws a cautious glance in my direction.

I nod towards the dance hall.'Not like it used be.'

For a moment, he raises his mane of bedraggled hair and looks out with rheumy eyes. 'They're goin' to knock it down. Apartments.' Then back to his runny eggs.

'Pity.'

'Ah, that day is gone.' The tone – pure Connemara – has softened.

'No one around here now. Caribbeans.' The knife he holds in his knobbly fist jerks in the direction of the girl who has cast the cuts of bread on his plate.'No manners.' Hunched over the table, his broad shoulders suggest what must have been a powerful frame; his comments come out in throwaways.'Them Latvians. They're done too by the subbies, same as our crowd were. Nothin' changes.'

'Paid into their hands, I suppose.'

For the first time he looks straight at me, and is about to speak, when his eye falls on my briefcase and he stops, as if remembering the old law of guarded speech with outsiders. 'Did you work here?'

'I did. A long time ago.'

'One of them engineers, I suppose.'

I hedge. 'While I was a student.'

'What are you doin' now?'

Fearing that my profession might cause a strain in our conversation, I say, 'Personnel management.'

'What's that?'

'Seeing that the workers are looked after.'

He shows rotten teeth when he grins. 'You did all right.' Every now and then, while he slurps his tea out of a saucer, he makes barking sounds with his throat, then struggles to his feet and reaches for his stick. 'The pauper's grave for the rest of us. Good luck.' He shuffles off to pay the waitress.

Before I get the bus back to Kilburn Station, I look around for one last landmark. The dark alley where Maureen from Claremorris had led me that first night at the Galty is no longer an alley; instead, a cyber café fills the space that once was Eddington's Lane. On a blue-painted metal hoarding, a sign over the door says: Internet City: Mobile City. I get on the next bus and hop off at Kilburn Station, where a man with several days' stubble and plastic bags tied around his shoes holds out a box in front of me: 'Give us a little help, sir, to buy a cup o' tay.'

He stares at the pound coin I fish out of my pocket, and as it settles in the box, he looks at me. 'May you never be short, sir. You're a dacent man and all belongin' to you.'

26

FOR THE TUESDAY LUNCH with M.J., I hurry up Grafton Street. A city girl in a suit, resolutely neutral to the world, is speaking into her mobile; she does a neat side-step when a sallow-faced woman wrapped in folds of clothing holds up a child and copies of the *Big Issue* before her. In the open doorway of a newsagent, a display board shows a headline: 'Government Minister and Planning Official for the Heaslip'.

M.J. is waiting outside Brownes. He has one foot resting on the granite base of a railing and his head is raised as if in the act of listening. 'Look.' He points to the skyline over St Stephen's Green. 'I can count six cranes from here, and one of them is on a Galvin site. Not bad for an oul bogtrotter from Ardglass.'

In a grey suit and a wine-coloured tie, he looks fit and well; his high colour could be mistaken for a healthy glow, but after his two heart attacks, a cardiologist in Harley Street had issued an ultimatum: slow down or you'll be in a box within six months. Since then, he takes the odd week at the stud farm in Westmeath. Even there, he can't rest and spends the time in wellingtons, pounding paling posts with a sledgehammer and tightening fence wire.

The headwaiter at Brownes greets us: 'Lovely day, Mr Galvin. And Monsignor, good to see you again.'

We are about to sit at our table when a Minister of State stops on his way out and, in a low voice, sympathizes with M.J.: 'After all you've done for this city. No gratitude.' Between his teeth, he makes a speech about 'these bloody tribunals'. 'Waste

of money, if you ask me. Making millionaires out of the lawyers.' Then a handshake, a tap on the shoulder, and he rejoins
the two men near the door.

Settling the linen napkin on his knees, M.J. nods towards
the departing politician: 'A great support when I started here.
Himself and Donaghy never let me down, especially when
them Trinity boyos were writing to the papers about how I was
destroying Georgian Dublin. Pampered bastards. Never did an
honest day's work in their lives. Many's the time, Tommy, when
I was going back to London, I saw nothing except boarded-up
houses as soon as I left Ardglass until the train reached
Limerick. And crying at every railway station. Tradesmen
couldn't get a day's work for love or money.' He pokes with his
thumb: 'His party – say what you like about them – they always
got the building trade moving.'

Anger at being called a tax cheat surfaces during the meal.
He lowers his voice: Seery is a jumped-up little fucker for
landing him in the shit. And all because the lousy bastard
wouldn't pay one of his staff a promised bonus.

While he speaks, I remember the news report from earlier
in the week. After securing immunity from prosecution, Seery's
junior partner had blown the whistle. The firm of C.F. Seery
and Co. was organizing offshore accounts for fat cats in the
construction industry. A thread had been pulled and the whole
garment was now coming apart.

'Put money into the pockets of them that would spend it
in the boozer, is it? Or run around to the nearest Ladbrokes. I
didn't take the boat with only a pair of wellingtons in a case for
that sort of caper. A bob or two back from every hard-earned
pound when that fellow with the eyebrows – Healy – was
chancellor. And nearly as bad here.' His colour is rising.

I nod in agreement to what seems like a rehearsal for the
judge. 'You did well,' I try to reassure him.

'Did I? A mother who blamed me for Mossie's death. A
wife who can't bear to be in the same house as me. And then
Margot.'

'Stop torturing yourself.'

'A son who tells me he became a priest to hide the fact that he's a homo.' He leans forward and speaks in a hushed tone. 'I sold cabbage, turnips, hay – anything to make a few bob. My two buckos rubbing shoulders with earls and viscounts at Downside Abbey. Now they're two layabouts.' He sinks into a gloomy silence and begins tapping the tablecloth.

After a while, he raises his head: 'Where in God's name do dreams come from? I'd love to know.' A few nights before, he dreamt about being back in Ardglass chapel, and the parish priest is thumping on the altar, and knocking over candles. 'What shall it profit a man', he roars, 'if he shall gain the whole world and lose his own soul?' The people in the seats laugh out loud; M.J. joins them. And now he can hardly hear the priest, even though he is still shouting. Flames are rising and spreading to the altar rails and the front pews. The old priest keeps on shouting: 'It is easier for a camel to go through the eye of a needle than for a rich man to enter into the Kingdom of Heaven.' M.J. is laughing because no one there, apart from the Healys, or Scanlon the publican, has more than maybe fifty pounds in the post office.

'You haven't lost your soul.'

He looks at me in a distracted way. 'It all happened so quickly. I've office blocks in this city and in London; I've pubs, farms and horses. What's the use? I wanted it all and I got it. And it hasn't turned out like … I wanted to prove to them at home – to her – that I could make it. And that no one would make a fool of me like they had laughed at our father.' He stops tapping. 'You remember that night in the Irish Club. The night Grace …?'

'When she played the piano. And you couldn't take your eyes off her.'

'I'd made the millions – now I wanted to be connected to the Great House crowd. To be married to Grace, well, sure that would be the icing on the cake.'

'Anyone's marriage could go on the rocks. It happens every day.'

He is deaf to palliatives.

'Two sons – strangers to me.'

'Is Matthew going back to the monastery?'

'No. Downside was a phase, he said. I declare to God, I always thought when a fellow took on something like that, he stayed with it.'

'They're like that nowadays.'

But he is lost in his own world: 'A son of mine a nancy boy. Then the other bucko – good-time Charlie – is pedalling his great works of art around the streets of Paris. And when the oul ticker started acting up last year, do you think one of them would come to see me in the hospital. Tommy, have they any nature in them at all?'

A couple of nights later, I listen to a radio programme on the Heaslip. An actor does a flawless impression of M.J.'s broad accent, how he had to emigrate or draw the dole and that he would never take the soup. His senior counsel adds that he had given employment to hundreds of Irishmen and had gone beyond the call of duty as an employer by taking a personal interest in the welfare of each worker.

I switch off the radio, but the actor's voice plays on in my head. Sleep is broken and at around four I am wide awake, my head teeming with images. Among them is M.J. striding across the cobbled yard of Dublin Castle, hordes of photographers shoving cameras in his face. He is nodding and smiling. Alone.

The morning he left comes back in sepia from a peasant land of paraffin lamps and Fair Isle jumpers.

'You'll be grand, M.J.,' my father is saying in the pony and trap. 'Go on there, girl, go on, girl.' He tugs on the reins to hurry along the pony. The cardboard suitcase rubs against my bare knees; my hands are sore and numb from holding the lantern, but I want to do something for my brother who is crossing the pond, as the grown-ups call it. The pony treads on potholes and leaves behind a shattered moon on ice, and in the breaking dawn is the outline of my mother's bulk, her scarf pulled tightly around her head.

Steam from the train rises in clouds against the dim lights of the station and fills the cold air with a bitter smell. Girls wearing Woolworth scarves, folding lines still showing, crowd around the ticket office. Clutching tickets, they brush tears away with the sleeves of their coats as they return to their families. Above the noise of the engine and the din of conversations, I hear their brave efforts to be casual. 'Yerra, haven't I an aunt in Slough? What need I care?'

A youth squares his broad shoulders, yet steals a glance at an ageing couple hunched beside him. 'Sure 'tis only a few miles across the pond. I could swim it on a fine day.' He laughs and draws on a cigarette; the old man wipes his nose. My father takes out his pocket watch and checks the time against the big clock hanging from the cold iron girders.

'Look at that,' he gets excited, 'will you look at that? Not a minute out in thirty years. Did ye ever see a watch like that?'

'No, never.' I catch M.J.'s eye; he returns a weak smile.

My father puts the watch into a black purse: 'There,' he says to M.J., 'you'll need that more than I will.'

'Ah, no.'

'Take it, boy, in God's name. Take it. You'll need it in the evening, so that them subbies don't fool you. This little watch keeps good time.' His voice is breaking. 'And think of me.'

'I will, Da.'

Hands deep in her Chicago coat, my mother stands in silence, but as soon as the guard throws open the carriage doors, she turns to M.J.: 'Listen to me: don't let anyone or anything stop you. You can make your fortune in London, if you keep your head. But you'll have to earn it.'

'Ah woman,' my father pleads, 'now is not the time for that.'

'Hold your tongue. Now *is* the time.'

An icy wind of Brylcreem and whiskey cuts through the station. I pull up my socks and do a brave jumping exercise from one foot to the other. High in the railway cabin the stationmaster is pulling long levers; a whistle pierces the grey morning. With much slamming of doors and false cheer, a guard moves through the reluctant crowd: 'Come on now, lads and lassies, next stop Camden Town. You'll be dancing in the

Glocca Mora on Saturday night. Can't you come on, lads? McAlpine is waitin' for you at London Bridge.' His attempt at humour gets lost as the crying gets louder and the awkward gestures of farewell rise above the hissing train.

'Write soon.'

'I will, I'll write as soon as I get over.'

'Mind yourself, boy, and go to Mass every Sunday.'

'Goodbye so.'

I look away towards Eason's kiosk, and, on the cover of a glossy magazine, the blurred image of someone called Ava Gardner gives me a dreamy look.

Belching plumes of smoke, the dark monster trundles out of the station, death rattle of the carriage couplings as my father hobbles beside it. 'M.J.,' he calls. 'My son, don't stay if you don't like the place, boy.'

'Listen to the fool.' My mother tightens the scarf around her neck.

The train snakes its way into the countryside and all we're left with is a glimpse of the hungry-looking fields that are Ardglass, a bitter wind and the defeated voices all around us. My father keeps on waving in a clumsy manner.

'God go with them,' a woman says.

'Amen,' others chorus.

'And he was a great little worker. What'll I do?' says a man who slouches away towards the granite archway, and who is fidgeting with the peak of his cap. As at a wake, other men console him.

My father has to plead with my mother to stop for a drink at the Railway Bar. The shafts of the pony-trap jerk and put strain on the harness as we cross the train tracks and enter the yard behind the pub. Bicycles are thrown three deep against a wall.

The inside is loud and dim and smells of porter; men in brown suits and collarless shirts stand at the bar. My mother stamps her way to a snug, and through the open door I watch the publican fill jugs of Guinness from wooden barrels.

'We're all in the same boat, Jack,' says a neighbour to my

father. 'What's to become of this oul country?' They curse 'them hoors of politicians who are only for the big shots'.

On his bony fingers, my father lists the children he has lost: two in Chicago, Eddie in the depot. Soon the girls will head off. Then only Mossie and Gerry, and the boyeen there. He points to me.

My father's face is flushed. 'And I suppose it won't be long before they go off too. Come over here, Tomásheen. Come over here, boybawn.' He draws me between his knees; his overcoat smells of pipe tobacco and the cow house. 'You'll never leave your oul da, sure you won't?'

'I won't. Never. I'll milk the cows, and save the hay for you, Da.'

They laugh, and order drinks.

Just then the door latch clicks and a young man in a priest's black coat and a red scarf knotted around his neck steps in and brings with him a perishing current of air. He begins to sing:

> Lonely I wander through scenes of my childhood.
> It brings back to memory the happy days of yore,
> Gone are the old folk ...

'Shut the door, Dinny, or I'll throw you out on your arse,' the publican roars as he puts full pint glasses on the counter. 'Isn't it early in the morning you're wandering lonely? But you can sell them oul ballads if anyone is foolish enough to buy them.' My father buys three. 'There Tomásheen,' he says. 'Learn a few songs for yourself.' I look at the pink, blue and yellow sheets: 'The Moon behind the Hill', 'Galway Bay', 'The Castle of Dromore'.

'Look, Mammy.' I hold them up. 'I've ballads.'

She shakes herself: 'The oul eejit. Very free with our few bob.'

27

THE MORNING AFTER I had lunch with M.J., Nugent calls the autumn meeting to complete the clerical appointments for the year: a tidying-up exercise, since the bulk of the diocesan changes had been filled in May. As every year, the personnel board – priests favourable to the bishop, who like to believe they have power – sit around a polished table at All Saints and prescribe the changes. Unknown to them, however, Nugent presides in his library while Plunkett, Vinny Lynch and I go through the list of priests, and single out those who will receive a letter of appointment within a week. In that room with the roller blinds down, because Nugent's fussy housekeeper has a hang-up about the sun fading the carpet, we decide each priest's future. The green-shaded light on the bishop's desk casts a sickly pallor on the books, the wallpaper and the heavy furniture. We send out the standard letter that obliges each priest to gather up his belongings and within two weeks stand before a sea of nameless faces.

Over the period of Boylan's binges, I had got to know most of the priests, and during that time their confidence in me grew: they poured out their stories of drink and women, once in a while, young men – while on continental or American holidays. They mourned their loss of faith in life and in God, and yet asked for confession. And in the basement kitchens of city presbyteries, or in dark-panelled sacristies, I raised the hand of absolution over heads tousled with confusion. I assured them of God's grace and forgiveness.

I knew who was in and out of hospital with depression, and who was spending three or four days away from the parish each week. Boylan, and later, Nugent, sent me to do the dirty work: reprimand the parish priest who never let his curate know how much was in the collection, and who even came back from his holidays each Sunday evening to count the money. I sorted out the mail, and dealt with complaints from cranks and insomniacs about curates who 'have no respect for the Holy Father, or Our Blessed Lady'. The occasional letter from a scorned woman Nugent handed to me. 'Tom, try and deal with that as well as you can,' was followed by a weary sigh: 'Good God, why they won't say their prayers and stop chasing after these women is a mystery to me. And most of them aren't worth chasing after.'

'Hard to fathom,' I nodded in sympathy. I was a good civil servant, or maybe a reliable hiring-foreman.

This particular morning, with half-lenses perched on his nose, Nugent surveys Vinny Lynch's list: 'What's this Collins fellow like? He's asked to get out of Knockbawn.'

Plunkett raises his head: 'Can't make up his mind whether he wants to serve the Church or his mother.'

'Send him to Canon Corrigan,' says Vinny Lynch, giggling.

'Canon Corrigan, then.' Nugent makes a note in the margin.

The longest any curate had survived with Iron Corrigan was two years: one young priest left after four months – he said the ten o'clock Mass one morning, and then caught a plane for Boston, where he became a high-school teacher.

Next on the list is a priest who has applied for laicization. 'Now there's a man who should have more sense,' Nugent declares: smack of his ring when the back of his hand strikes the page. ' "Can I have your blessing?" he asks. And he can't keep his trousers on.' He throws his arms in the air. 'I offered him a sabbatical. "No," said he, "I've prayed for guidance and the Holy Spirit is leading me to share my life with Monica. And Monica agrees with me." '

Plunkett winces in sympathy with the bishop: 'He came to me looking for severance pay, no less. Two thousand for every year of his priesthood, nearly fifty grand. "Are you mad?" I said. "Wouldn't there be an exodus if we forked out good money like that?" ' He glances at Nugent for approval and receives a dry laugh.

We move on to those who are in line for a parish. Nugent appoints to the well-off parishes priests who have gained a reputation for fund-raising and who have never caused him trouble. His right to do this we never question. He browses through my draft, purring as he ticks: 'Yes. He's a good priest. Good man.' Then he stops and draws a line across the page. 'Not as long as I'm bishop. He'll never get a parish.'

'With respect,' I venture, 'they think highly of him in Assumption.'

'No, Tom.' He fixes on some spot over my head. 'My sources tell me he refuses to read out my letters in full to my people.' Again he slaps the paper with his ring. 'And he had a general absolution in the secondary school – that, as we all know, is strictly forbidden by the Holy See. The nun in charge should have known better, but of course, nowadays … nuns … I give up.' He throws his hands in the air.

'Now, that man' – more smacking with his ring – 'he's a buffoon. An embarrassment to me at a confirmation dinner. Acting like a clown in front of the teachers with a hideous mask he'd brought from America.'

After lunch we have to tackle child abuse cases: a series of long-running sores that shows no sign of healing. For a couple of years I have been handling questions from journalists, consulting lawyers, visiting priests in prison, and opening the morning papers to accusations about Church secrecy. And then having to endure the stale air of the basement archives, staring now and again through the window bars as I try to piece together a horrible jigsaw.

'Where are the written statements, Angela?' I ask one of the secretaries and hold up a letter. 'This woman claims she has already sent a report.'

Angela removes her glasses so that they hang from a chain around her neck. 'They were never filed.' She speaks in a low tone: 'A long time ago, Monsignor, things were different then.'

I pitch the letter back into the file.

On the nine o'clock news a priest accused of multiple offences appears handcuffed between two guards. For weeks he becomes a hated figure – ugly photos in the tabloids, a torrent of phone calls, hostile to the Church, floods the chat shows.

The first complaints about him had come in while Boylan was bishop, and I was his right-hand man. As soon as a boy and his mother had finished their deposition and we closed the big doors behind them, Boylan, in the dim light of the library, poured himself a double whiskey.

'What'll we do, Tom?'

'We have to send him to a psychiatrist. That's the recommended course of action.'

'Psychiatrists. I don't know. They never cured me of this,' he mutters, looking at the whiskey glass, 'asking how did I get on with my father. But as you say … .'

I make an appointment with one of the top men in Fitzwilliam Square.

Shuffling along the corridor one morning, a few months later, Boylan, unshaven, waves a letter in the air from the psychiatrist. 'He's fine now. Fine. He won't offend again.' One end of his dressing-gown belt trails along the carpet; traces of toothpaste show on the front of his pyjamas. 'Sure, putting his hand on a boy's shoulder on confirmation day, only a peccadillo, Tom. Didn't the Greeks … you know what I mean. And look at what they've given us – philosophy, architecture, drama – the foundations of our civilization.' A look of satisfaction on his red swollen face, he puts the letter back into the envelope. 'A nice quiet parish for him, Tom.'

'Are you sure?'

'Sure, I'm sure. A nice parish.'

I stare at the bulky figure wobbling off into the darkness, and to my shame, like Pilate, I washed my hands. Boylan had a vicious side, especially when on a binge, and my chances of succession might have been put at risk if I had opposed him. Nugent's mood swings from rage to depression. The journalists round on him one morning before a confirmation ceremony, and, to save face, he lays the blame at the feet of 'those who have come before me'.

They keep prodding. 'You mean Bishop Boylan?'

'Bishop Boylan was a good man, but he had lost control.'

'Who then?' Microphones are being pushed in front of his face, and like a cornered dog, he shows his teeth to protect himself.

'Others?' They keep pressing him.

'Others, yes. I'm afraid so.'

'Including the vicar-general, Monsignor Thomas Galvin?'

'Yes. A fine priest, but he was misguided.'

The newspapers pick it up. 'Bishop Nugent Blames Senior Cleric for Cover-up'.

During a daylong meeting at Maynooth, a bishop who had been in my class in Rome, and who is regarded as the only independent voice in the hierarchy, spells it out for me. Whenever the Pope makes a statement about gays or cohabiting couples, this bishop is the one the journalists descend on for a comment. 'We're sinking faster than the *Titanic*, Tom, and every man is jostling to save his mitre or his arse, I'm not sure which. You saw it yourself this morning at the opening session.' He gestures towards the grim building, rigid against a hellish sky. 'We're headless chickens. Nugent needed a scapegoat; you fitted the bill. That little Roman gadfly, the Nuncio, is breathing down his neck. Do you get my drift?'

'Only what I suspected.'

'Anyway, he was always jealous of you. Watched like a hawk in case you'd get the Yellow Jersey.' We are strolling around the grounds after the lunch break. Red of autumn in the Virginia creeper, shining and tremulous along one side of St Joseph's Square: crows are swooping, plunging and landing on bare branches, wonderment in their sidelong glances; beyond the quadrangle, more crows are raising Cain in the beeches. A sudden gust sweeps through an opening at the corner of the square and causes the bishops ahead of us to sink deeper into their scarves and the upturned collars of their overcoats while they give full attention to the pipe-smoking Cardinal. In front of them, press photographers scramble backwards on the lawn, and, on one knee, brazenly take shots from different angles: shots, they hope, that will depict the bishops as comical or even sinister in the newspapers.

That morning, a Vatican expert on child abuse had delivered the keynote address. He was credited with cleaning up one or two dioceses in America, and was speaking to the hierarchy at Nugent's invitation. Priests who are dragging the Church into the gutter must be expunged without delay; he hammers home his message by thumping on the lectern. 'This is an evil, this is leprosy. Zero tolerance, My Lords, the same as we decreed at the Dallas Conference,' he booms in his American drawl. The green-shaded light on the podium deepens the lines on his suntanned face. At the coffee break, flanked by the Cardinal and Nugent, with Plunkett bringing up the rear, he struts around the room, and, towering over grey heads, informs every group that the only way to deal with this poison is to remove forthwith any Judas against whom a claim is made. And gays must be rooted out of our seminaries; pussyfooting and all the soft talk about love is what has brought us to this sorry state. Farmers' and shopkeepers' sons who, over the years, had learned the skills of Church politics and were rewarded with the pectoral cross and a gold ring, look up in awe, and nod to everything the Pope's man says. He checks his watch and tells us he can't stay for lunch: he has to be in Geneva by six. Trouble there too.

'Did John Wayne impress you?' my bishop friend asks me as we approach the archway leading to the conference room.

'Let priests swing in the wind: isn't that the gist of it? We've come to a sorry pass. I'm not talking about a challenge to the civil law.'

'No.'

'This is about putting a poor bastard in the stocks who hasn't been convicted of anything.'

'Precisely, but you see, Tom, nothing has changed. The institution comes first. The institution.' He gives one of his nervous laughs. 'For the last forty years, bishops have been casting a blind eye on priests who have offended, in order to save the image of the Church. Now Rome wants to show the world that we are squeaky clean. So, as it was in the beginning, is now, and ever shall be.'

'And did you hear him? "Sing it from the housetops, My Lords, sing it from the housetops: the Church is not a safe haven" – even though a man is still innocent until proven guilty. Ah no.'

Other bishops and canon lawyers are passing by; the sound of their laughter deepens when they go through the archway. They smile: 'So glad to see you. We'll have to meet for lunch.' Veneer of good manners to hide what they say behind his back: 'Should never have been given a diocese. Babbling to those journalists about a married clergy, and how he could live with the ordination of women.'

When they have gone by, he touches my elbow. 'Come down this way, we've a few more minutes.' We do another lap of the square. 'Tom, if I were you, I'd go easy on that; I mean what you've been saying there now,' he says when we are clear of everyone.

'What?'

'You're still a front runner for the next vacant see, but that line wouldn't help your cause, I can assure you. We need people like you, and when you get a diocese, well, then you'll be better placed to speak out. Take a fool's advice.' Behind the rimless glasses, he studies my reaction.

'Even though the reputation of good men may be the issue.'

'They couldn't give a fiddler's for the poor bastards in the trenches. A bad sign. If there isn't trust between priest and bishop … . Did you know that Napoleon attributed his success to his respect for the troops? Ordered trees to be planted along the roads of France to protect them from the summer's heat. How often was it drummed into us in Propaganda: *Roma locutus est, causa finita est*? The window design has changed, but in the shop the wares are the same. The Curia will make whatever decisions it likes, and neither you nor I can stop it.'

He glances around again. 'Power, Tom. Power always wins out in the end. And never forget the Lord's words, *be wise as serpents and innocent as doves.'*

'You're hardly the one to talk about caution … .'

'And I pay for it. Make no mistake about that, I pay for it.'

The Cardinal, Nugent and Plunkett are approaching, so he speaks above a whisper: 'Don't forget what I said.'

We exchange smiles and greetings in the vaulted corridor, and agree that the weather is atrocious as we pass by paintings of proud-looking bishops in purple and fine linen.

In the conference room, the Cardinal, a hangdog look on his face, sits bent over the top table and opens the discussion for the afternoon. He refers to the excellent keynote speech. When he leafs through a stack of papers, his gold ring catches the watery sun through the high windows. This plenary session is devoted to formalizing the guidelines and procedures for child protection, and also for devising ways of dealing with priests who have offended. Along with other theologians, canon lawyers and advisors, I sit behind the bishops.

The Cardinal's opening remarks are about complying with the letter of the civil law in matters that relate to 'this cancer that must be rooted out of our Church'. A few bishops mutter sympathy. With glasses perched on his nose, he runs his eye over handwritten pages: 'I have a draft made out by Doctor Nugent here, ably assisted by Father Plunkett. It is a very accurate summary of the recommendations made this morning in the keynote address. I suggest we give them careful consideration in implementing a policy to deal with this scourge that has been visited upon us. It goes without saying that each bishop is the sole authority in his own diocese.'

He reads:

> Any priest against whom an allegation has been made shall be asked to step aside from his ministry for the duration of the garda inquiry.
>
> Having been notified about the allegation, he shall be asked to leave his residence forthwith.

A prepared statement shall be read at all masses in the parish where the accused priest was ministering. The bishop, if he wishes, may visit the parish and explain the priest's sudden departure.

The room darkens and a shower of hailstones crashes against the high windows so that it now becomes difficult to hear the Cardinal's doleful voice. My Roman classmate rubs his eyes; without his glasses, he is a tired old man.

Despite the way Nugent had falsely laid the blame at my door for the mishandled abuse cases, and the fact that he holds meetings without my knowledge, I still remain firm in my resolve to accept a diocese if such an offer is made. So every morning after saying Mass in the cathedral, or in a convent nearby, I leave my rooms in All Saints, and walk up the cypress-lined driveway to my office in the palazzo. And yet, despite my resolve and the encouragement I get from priests on the golf course, or during a chance meeting at the Veritas bookshop – how my style of leadership is needed in these awful times – I know my desire is waning.

Nugent's scowl deepens with each new revelation of what the newspapers call clerical scandal: his clothes hang off him; now and again, at meetings, he gives out a heavy sigh, causing his slouched shoulders to rise and then collapse beneath the avalanche. 'What's happening? What's happening to my Church?' he keeps repeating, and searches the broad leaf of the gleaming table for an answer. His despair seeps through the house and worms its way out into the diocese where it infects priests like a poison. Some lash out at the newspapers. They hate us because they know we have the truth, a young priest informs me at a deanery meeting. Others throw in the towel: they no longer visit schools, or help to coach football teams, and will not hear of having altar servers in their parish. They limp along: provide Mass and the sacraments, visit the housebound with communion, nod and make pitiful sounds when some old woman deplores what the newspapers are doing to 'our lovely Church'.

Journalists and photographers hide behind the trees that line the driveway and watch every visitor who drives up to the front door of the bishop's house. Inside, Nugent disappears for hours; priests who are working on diocesan projects, women from the marriage tribunal, the staff in the chancellery – all of us tiptoe around the grey corridors, and, until we hear his beautiful rendering of Bach sonatas on the baby grand, we are whisperers in a wake house.

The allegations of child abuse continue to be a torment. We take depositions and summon the accused priests to All Saints. And in a futile effort to lighten the threat hanging over them, priests invent a catchphrase: *You're only a phone call away from doomsday.* We sit behind a table. Flanked by Plunkett, who takes notes, and myself, Nugent in full robes presides. The child protection officer for the diocese sits next to me. Our backs are to the light from the stained-glass windows. Vinny Lynch meets the accused at the front door, ushers him in, and then disappears into the silence of the house. On the wall behind the accused priest's head is a print showing the compassionate father embracing The Prodigal Son: hands of forgiveness on the son's shoulders, one shapely, the other powerful – male and female incarnations of divine pardon. At the far end of the room, over the marble fireplace, is a tall photograph of an incandescent Pope in the Phoenix Park; he is holding high a rose and waving to the crowd from the popemobile.

The first interview after the Maynooth conference is with a man who was only a year away from ordination when I was a first-year student in All Saints. Every June, he won the Victor Ludorum prize at the inter-seminary sports, and even made the Tipperary hurling panel, but the dean of discipline invoked the ban on all such activities for seminarians.

'Before God, My Lord, I can tell you, I have failed many times to keep the rules.' His face is pinched, his eyes are red-rimmed, but he looks straight at Nugent. 'Interfering with children was never one of them.'

'That may be so, but we have to carry out the requirements of the law, Father.'

'I'm being thrown out of my house. I'm disgraced in front of the people.'

'You are entitled to legal representation from now on, and, of course, it is a convention of the diocese to defray legal costs unless a case goes to the High Court,' says the child protection officer, a former hospital matron. 'And if you wish, Father, you have the right to remain silent.'

'Silent? Am I being tried already then? Can I not trust my own bishop any more? My Lord, you have to follow the law, I know that. I've no argument there. But, putting my name up on Sunday morning as a child molester ... .' He leans towards Nugent and appeals with raised hands, 'I could swear to you now on my knees, on a Bible – right now – I never did such a thing. Not in all my born days.' He turns to me: 'Get a Bible, Monsignor Galvin, and I'll swear right here and now.'

'No, Father,' says Nugent, his eye fixed somewhere on 'The Prodigal Son'. 'The law has to take its course. But I'll appoint a good priest of the diocese to help you over this period, and may the Lord support you.'

'Do you have to make it so public, My Lord?' His knuckles turn white when he grips the armrests. 'I always worked honestly; never gave you any trouble, did I?'

'Then, Father, I'm asking you to see this as another way of serving our Church in these trying times, and I'm also asking you to unite your suffering with that of our Saviour.'

To indicate that the interview is over, Nugent begins to tidy up the priest's file, and when the ordeal grinds to a halt, I, like the chaplain who walks a condemned man to the gallows, accompany the accused priest along the wide corridor to the front door.

'Remember now, this is just at the level of allegation,' I try to reassure him. The big clock chimes the hour of four, and breaks the silence of the hallway. 'Take every day as it comes.' I watch him descend the limestone steps, and call out to him: 'I'll see you on Sunday.'

'Yes, to blacken my name forever.' He throws me a look of contempt.

'Lord no. No, not at all. Just to give you a hand and help you in any way I can.'

'Thanks. Thanks ever so much.'

That Sunday I do Nugent's dirty work for the last time. I announce to the parishioners that their priest has been accused of improper behaviour and the police are investigating the case; that he is innocent until proven guilty, and that he will be leaving the parish the following week until this matter has been cleared up.

Like the day when Deano fell out of the sky, I get sick in the toilet of the sacristy after Mass, refuse cups of tea, and without even thinking of lunch, drive across country to Clogher Head. There I pace the strand until darkness is falling and the lights beyond the village are defining the contours of the hillside. All day I rehearse my challenge to Nugent; all day my anger rages against this inhuman way of treating someone who is still innocent before the law. And on that Sunday strand, I erase forever any wish for the crozier.

When the priest opens the door the following Wednesday, his stubbled face is lined with worry; his clerical shirt is open at the neck, the plastic band that is a Roman collar hangs loose.

'Tea?' he asks, and turns towards the open door of the kitchen without waiting for an answer.

'Sure, I'll have a cup.'

Following him into the kitchen, I notice a photograph of a hurling team in the hallway; behind the team is a sea of flags and sunny faces. I recognize the Hogan Stand. 'Anyone to help you move out?'

'Anyone? A lot you fellows care.'

'Your family. Do they know?'

'Haven't been near them.'

'Only a matter of time before they find out. Better to … .'

'I'm going over tonight to my brother.'

Wagging its tail, a collie dog appears from the living-room, looks at me and licks his master's hand while the priest is filling the kettle. In front of the washing machine is a heap of clothes; the table is strewn with the remains of a pizza still in a cardboard box, a carton of milk, unwashed cutlery and plates. In the cold air, dog smell mingles with stale food.

The priest brushes aside an empty Panadol box, an ashtray loaded with cigarette ends, and takes cups and saucers, and a biscuit tin from a cupboard. Every gesture is ponderous.

In the living-room, we sip tea beneath a picture on the mantel that shows him raising a hand in blessing over a middle-aged woman. She is kneeling on a prie-dieu in front of the sun-drenched chapel at All Saints. In the background are girls in summer frocks, children squinting up at the camera, a man with a peaked cap, braces showing over his white shirt.

He notices my interest. 'At least she – God rest both of them – *they* won't have to put up with this. Aren't they better off dead?' He rubs the collie's back. 'Better off dead.'

The dog wags its tail, yawns and nestles its head against the priest's arm. 'The other evening I was mooching around the house, trying to make sense of all this,' he says to the empty grate. 'When I spotted a bunch of schoolchildren out there. I could hear them talking. "He lives there," says the ringleader. "What'd he do?" a little boy asks. "He likes kissing young fellas like you and doing other things to them." "Ring the doorbell. Go on," says the little boy. "No, you go and ring the doorbell." The ringleader pushed the little boy, "I can see him, look he's coming for us. Run." "Where?" "Look, see there, he's hiding in that hedge." They scampered up the road, shouting: "He's after you." '

The priest draws deeply on a cigarette. 'I'm now a bogeyman. Tom, I've made my share of mistakes. Women, yes, but what priest hasn't? Never children. Never, and I could swear that in any court in the land. And now.' He rubs the dog's head. 'How can I ever? You can't clear your name. They'll always say – you know, no smoke without fire.'

'As a citizen you have your rights. Due process.'

He looks at me.

'I don't want to put words in your mouth, but the law courts are there to protect people's privacy until a judgment is handed down.'

'Take the bishop to court?' He draws on the cigarette.

'It's an option.'

'No.' He shakes his head. 'Priests are caught there.'

'How?'

'The skeleton in the closet. Many priests – well – a woman somewhere, or a man maybe, unless he hasn't grown up, or he likes dressing up in silk and waltzing around with bishops in Rome. Fear of the skeleton popping out with publicity. That's why.'

About a month later, the sergeant in charge of the investigation tells me that the Director of Public Prosecutions is going to throw out the case; they have some more work to do, but it seems almost certain that the priest is innocent. The complainant is a woman who, a few years before, had gashed her arm, gone into a hardware store and claimed she had stumbled against the edge of a saw.

'As I say, Monsignor, we've nearly finished, and from where I stand, and more importantly, the DPP, he's a free man.'

Two weeks later the same sergeant comes to tell me that the charges are without substance. When he has gone from the bishop's house, I sit at my desk staring out at the grey sky and the larches dripping with rain in the front garden. What rankles most is that other innocent priests have been put through the same misery. A couple of whiskeys in my room that night sharpen my resolve to confront Nugent at a meeting the following day.

In the morning, I say the seven o'clock Mass at the cathedral; a scent of incense lingers in the big sacristy after the previous day's funeral. I glance at the age-darkened oak of the vesting bench, and at the throne, once in the sanctuary, where the bishop presided for Holy Week and Christmas. While the sacristan is lighting the candles on the high altar, I put on the garments of preaching and healing, and catch a glimpse of myself in the long mirror. Suddenly, an urge to fling off each vestment flashes across my mind: throw them on the throne, and be done with cathedrals and bishops, and priests jockeying for position. Instead, I rest my elbows on the vesting bench and stare at the liturgical calendar. Today is the feast of the Sacred

Heart, the great Catholic symbol of love. Love, always love.

Swift as a shooting star, Lucy invades my head, and a chance meeting in Grafton Street the previous Christmas Eve comes winging back to me. I hadn't seen her since she'd sung 'Pie Jesu' and 'In Paradisum' at the Cardinal's funeral. Ronan and their two daughters wrapped in Christmas colours stand beside her: in mock-desperation, Ronan asks my advice on how to cope with three women who are on a spending spree. Lucy gives him a playful thump on the arm. Carol singers in front of Bewley's are belting out 'Have Yourself a Merry, Merry Christmas'. 'Great meeting you again.' She smiles. 'And you'll have to come around for dinner,' but she is buttoning up her coat, and shifting from one foot to the other.

'Indeed. And great meeting you all.'

The reverie has such force that I whisper her name.

'I beg your pardon, Monsignor. Did you say "Lucy"?'

Caught out, I swing around to see a look of concern on the sacristan's face. 'Oh yes, yes of course,' I say. 'Today is the feast of the Sacred Heart. What was I thinking? Sure, St Lucy's feast day is in December. Let's go in God's name.'

Nugent is in Rome when news of the accused priest's death reaches us one evening in the bishop's house. Two guards arrive with the details, and to offer their condolences. While Vinny Lynch is showing them out, Plunkett broods at the long table where we are making arrangements for the diocesan pilgrimage to Lourdes. Gilt-framed photos of former bishops line the walls.

When Vinny Lynch returns, he is fidgety: 'Poor guy. Goes to show, doesn't it, one can't be careful enough on the roads nowadays. One slip and you're a goner.'

Plunkett, who never smokes while Nugent is in the house, now lights a cigar. 'Yes, slippery surface,' he says. 'I've to contact the Boss immediately. Get him back. That's all them bastards in the media. Can't you imagine the spin they'd put on that?'

'He was alone.' My own voice sounds like a cold stone hitting the base of a metal shaft.

They look at me.

'Yes,' he says. 'Alone. Priests are usually alone in their cars.'

'Straight stretch of road, the guards said, and he crashes into a wall,' I say.

'Ah no,' Vinny Lynch taps the table, his small eyes are darting. 'Ah no, Tom, ah no. He wouldn't do anything – you know – anything foolish.'

Plunkett glares at me through a cloud of smoke. 'God, what a thought. The poor man, God rest his soul.'

The following morning, Nugent takes the first flight out of Rome, and at the funeral, preaches about the dead priest's many talents and how his death was such a huge loss to his family and the diocese.

That afternoon, when I have left the mourners and friends at the Castle Hotel, I phone the guards to talk about the accident. The sergeant invites me to drop up to the station – just beside SuperValu, he tells me. I park outside the single-storey redbrick with venetian blinds and a well-kept garden of marigolds and hydrangeas. Over the front door is the stern crest of the Garda Síochána. The sergeant is at a computer in the day room; a ban garda with a short back and sides is seated on a table, her stout legs dangle while she talks into a mobile phone. She throws me a cold glance, and turns away.

In a room at the back, the sergeant leafs through a file on the table: here and there, initials have been carved into the white deal: faint whiff of sweat and stale cigarette smoke lingers. He removes his reading glasses and looks at me: 'Yes, a straight road, Monsignor Galvin. No oncoming traffic, and driving conditions … well, a bit of rain earlier – nothing much. God rest his soul.'

'Amen.'

He looks at me: 'None of my business, Monsignor, and this is just between ourselves, but he was never the same after what happened.' He closes the file.

'I know. And thanks for your time, Sergeant.'

'Every week he reported here. At this very table I saw him age in a month. Ten or twelve years ago when he came here –

fine figure of a man. Trained the hurling team. In God's name, Father,' he leans towards me, 'have you no union? That man was condemned from the day you made that announcement.'

'I was only following instructions.'

'Oh, I know that.' He stands.

'No. No union.' Children are having a great time on a swing in the back garden. 'That would be against the grain – promises to the bishop at ordination, father-and-son relationship. That sort of thing.'

The sergeant shakes his head: 'You are now doing the guards' work, Monsignor.' And he goes on about how his organization would not tolerate that for one moment, but I'm jaded from the funeral and mourners, and broken sleep.

'We're now doing the guards' work to show the people and the media that we're purer than the driven snow,' I say at a meeting with Nugent, Plunkett and Vinny Lynch.

'With respect, Tom, that makes no sense.' Plunkett comes to the defence of the bishop.

I hold out. 'Sealing a priest's fate before he has a chance to defend himself?'

'Look here. We're following the regulations laid down by the statutory bodies. Take it or leave it. Now more than ever, this calls for all priests to be loyal to their bishop.'

Vinny Lynch squeaks his support, and then looks at me: 'Our hands are tied, Tom. We'd never live it down if we didn't take this course of action. We've got to show we're not doing what was done in the past. The cover-up.'

'I have no argument with the requirements of the statutory bodies, none whatever. If someone is accused, he has to step aside while an investigation is going on, but I know of no other organization that makes a public statement about an allegation, and then evicts a man from his house.'

'Look,' says Plunkett, raising his voice, 'this is a mutual agreement between the priest and his bishop. You know that.'

'Mutual agreement, my foot. Neither mutual nor an agreement.'

'For the good of the Church, Tom,' says Vinny Lynch. 'We save money. We can show to the claimants that we have dealt with the matter.'

Nugent, who has withdrawn into a brooding silence, is massaging his ring and looking out through one of the tall windows. The stroking stops. When he addresses Vinny Lynch and Plunkett, his tone is measured. 'This is something I never thought would happen: the day when a colleague, my vicar-general, would cause me such grief as I have suffered in the past while, and who now tries to put another obstacle in my way.'

His frail look shakes my resolve, yet I can't give in now. 'Why not invite in the legal experts then – canon lawyers – to argue the case, in front of the priests? If I am wrong, I will publicly apologize to you.'

The silence is intense; Vinny Lynch jumps up. 'I'll put on coffee. We're all tired.' He makes for the door.

'Come back, Father Lynch.' Nugent rounds on him. 'Sit down.' His eyes are fixed on the far wall where John Paul is still waving to the crowd with a rose. 'This is outrageous; such gross defiance of my authority. Monsignor, you choose the darkest hour in the history of this diocese to inflict a wound on your bishop. You know full well that the policy adopted by the hierarchy has been found to be successful in America and other countries. So are you placing yourself above the authority of the Church?'

Plunkett makes a growl of indignation. 'Well said.'

Vinny Lynch keeps shifting, and polishing the wooden armrest of his chair with delicate fingers.

'In the long history of the Church, you wouldn't be the first, of course, to do something like that.' Nugent closes the stiff-backed folder where he keeps his notes.

A cynical grin appears on Plunkett's face: 'There was that monk.'

I stand my ground. 'Anyone with a screed of common sense can work out what the Church is now doing: trying to make up for past sins. Priests are the new victims.'

A scowl shows on the bishop's face. 'That is a monstrous

allegation to make. I've had enough of this,' he says and rises from his chair behind the desk.

From then on, he cancels the morning conference and, instead, consults with Plunkett and Vinny Lynch in the library; I can hear the murmur of their voices on my way to the basement. Whenever I come upon them in the corridor, their conversation freezes.

As always, when I'm distressed, my ulcer flares up. I am waking at ungodly hours and staring into the dark until light begins to show at the edges of the curtains. Plunkett avoids me. Vinny Lynch, who tries to keep in with everyone, tells me that maybe, just maybe, I'm a little hard on the bishop, and when he smells sulphur between Nugent and myself, disappears with Caesar to the riverbank.

I meet him alone one morning in the stone corridor. 'All I'm asking, Vinny, is that the diocese provide a proper forum where this issue can be discussed in front of the priests.'

'They wouldn't attend, Tom. My classmates said the other night that if there's one more discussion on this at the deaneries, they won't go.'

'Even though it concerns human rights.'

As if his circulation is bad, he is hopping around on one foot, and keeping a lookout up and down the corridor. His psoriasis is acting up again: red blotches show on his neck and on the back of his hands. 'Come in here for a minute.' We step into one of the parlours: old and dark, there is a smell of neglect in the air: pictorial books on the Pope and on Rome lie on the round table.

'It's way worse than we think, Tom. Everyone is scared. And you'll get nowhere with his nibs, unless you go easy on him.'

'Too late, Vinny. Too late.'

'Oh, that's a shame. Behind it all, his nibs has a high regard for you.'

He opens the door again, looks up and down the corridor, and touches my arm: 'Tom, this will blow over in time. Don't let it get you down. God love you, I admire your courage.'

28

MY DOCTOR talks me through the latest in tranquillisers while she takes my blood pressure: they aren't
addictive, and you could go off them whenever you
like, she tells me. 'You know you're in bad shape, Monsignor.
And nowadays many people take them to steady their nerves,
if they're going through a difficult patch, say, making a speech
or attending an important meeting. There's nothing to be
ashamed of. You'd be surprised who is on them nowadays. And
something to help you sleep also.' Womanly compassion in her
brown eyes.

'And with respect, Monsignor, may I suggest you think
about a holiday, or else you'll run yourself into the ground.
Heed my advice. The graveyards are full of people who could-
n't take a break.'

I follow her advice. For two weeks, I wander through the
fields around St Benedict's Monastery, where high in the
October-tinted oaks the screeching of rooks penetrates the
valley. Every morning I rise at four-thirty and make my way
beneath gothic arches to the chapel, hearing only soft footfalls
or a door being closed – monastery sounds in the low-burning
lights of the corridor. When going by the sacristy, I catch the
smell of polish and incense.

In the chapel, I sit and drift in and out of prayer. Ageing
monks with wholesome faces shuffle into the stalls to pray or
to sing the divine office. After daybreak and again in the
evening, I wander down to the farmyard where the murmur of

pigeons rises now and again above the steady beat of the milk-ing machine. Honest hands that hold breviaries in the chancel work to fit on stainless steel cups to the cows' teats.

I ransack every corner of my mind with one of the monks who had taught Shakespeare in the boarding school beyond the sweeping driveway; his rough habit gives off a slight whiff of the dairy. He is mostly silent: rubbing his farmer's face or looking through the guestroom window at the tall oaks as though lost in thought. After a few days, he gives me a pene-trating look: 'Where did the youth who went up that lane ... what did you call it?'

'Eddington's Lane.'

'Where did he go to? And the man who fell in love with Lucy Campion?' Again he rubs his face and looks out over the fields, waiting for an answer.

'I have to say, I'm a bit lost here, Father Albert.'

'The urge, Monsignor, the urge.' The creases on his face deepen when he smiles. 'It never leaves us. It's like a river. But if you block the course of the flow, or deny it ever exists, it will take another route. For us priests, it might be the desire to be in the driving seat. One of our men here' – he laughs – 'if anyone else uses the sit-up mower to trim the lawn, he's in a bad mood for the day.' Standing now, he talks as if to himself: 'The pectoral cross, of course, could make up for a lot of lonely nights.' He chuckles: 'That's the way the Creator made us; in Him we trust, Monsignor.' He looks at me: 'Luke, chapter four, verse five for tomorrow.'

'The temptation of Jesus.' I want to delay and discuss the scriptural passage, and Eddington's Lane, Lucy and *the urge*, but his hand is already on the doorknob. 'The same time tom-orrow.'

I hurry to my cell to look up the reference. Power. Wealth. The devil. *All this will be yours if you worship me.*

As with a jigsaw, I am putting together the pieces, and discovering that for most of my life, despite retreats, and – once in a while – reading books on the spiritual life, I had managed to live as a stranger to myself. Falling for Lucy should have cured me of my blindness. Indeed, the way I made demands, and used her subsequently, should have brought me to my senses; but, like M.J., deadlines and the desire to breast the tape caused me to avoid paying close attention.

For most of the time, Father Albert is silent, looking away into the distance through the guest-room windows. Towards the end of the two weeks, he talks a bit more. 'That's the difference between the Lord and us. We all want our hands on the tiller. It's human. But priests especially. No one else, you see, to tell us that we're such great fellows. No one else to turn to when we wake in the small hours. You know about all that now.' His face becomes boyish when he laughs. 'You've a big decision to make. Jesus was born in a stable; His successors have lived in some of the finest palaces in Europe. He didn't seek power or possessions. God go with you, Monsignor.'

As soon as I seal my resolve to ask Nugent for a country parish, the ferment in my brain ceases; I sleep as if I'd been ploughing all day with a pair of horses. And in that mysterious city of the night, disconnected images surface: Deano is tumbling to his death; Lucy is playing the harp while Ronan and the children stand around the Christmas tree in Grafton Street; the train is leaving Ardglass station and M.J. is demanding answers from the monk who is standing on the platform: 'What does it profit?' he keeps repeating. But the monk keeps a steady gaze on the Ardglass hillside.

When I return to All Saints, Nugent, true to a clerical code of chilling silence, says nothing about my letter from the monastery, apart from a comment one day after lunch: 'I'll process your request for a parish without delay, Tom. And I'd be grateful if you would take in hand your successor; he'll be here on Monday.'

'Of course.' From then on, we relate according to the way of middle-class manners, and give each other a wide berth, while I train in my replacement – a young man just back from Rome with a canon law degree and a gleaming Alfa Romeo.

Each night I listen in to the Heaslip Tribunal, and M.J. gives me an update on the phone – he curses the media, and them smart-alecky lawyers, and most of all Seery for being such a stupid bastard to get caught and land him in the shit. I hear actors' impressions of voices I had known so well forty years ago and, to satisfy my curiosity, I leave the gloom of the bishop's house and drive down to Dublin Castle. Over a shirt and tie, I wear a scarf to escape the curiosity of the journalists.

In the public gallery of the tribunal, they are still chatting after the lunch break. Beside me, two elderly women recall their nurses' training in London. 'And do you remember Matron,' she chuckles, and does a high-pitched-Matron take-off: ' "Do not on any account, young ladies, go near that Galtymore place. Only by the grace of God do those navvies keep their trousers on." ' I look around. Just as the papers had said, the retired find it the best matinee in town.

Mr Bartholomew Muldoon is called first. Stooped and with a head of white hair, Horse fills the witness box and swears on the Bible that he will tell the truth, the whole truth, and nothing but the truth. By now his colourful tussles with the lawyers have made him into a likeable clown with the public.

'You are the owner of a big farm and a luxury bungalow in County Roscommon, am I right Mr Muldoon?' Counsel for the State, a weedy little fellow with rimless glasses and a bulky folder in his arms, sweeps the room with a smirk.

'Not as much luxury as the barristers who live around Dublin 4, Mr O'Shaughnessy.'

Laughter explodes from the gallery; the smirk dies. Horse looks around with the same menacing grin I had remembered from that morning in Stevenage after he had kicked the youth up the backside, and the lad had to make his own way back to Kilburn.

'And you were a trusted member of Mr Galvin's work-force, both in London and here in Ireland.'

'That's right, sir.'

'Did you have any knowledge that Mr Galvin may have been making deposits to an offshore account?'

'I was a hirin' foreman, not a bank manager. Mr Galvin

wasn't in the habit of askin' his hirin' foreman for bankin' advice. That's for experts like you; not for the likes of me.'

'Come now, Mr Muldoon. Surely you would have been aware of the culture of salting away money in foreign banks.'

His tie loose around his bull neck, Horse gives the impression of one who could tear apart the witness box and fling it across the room. 'Mr O'Shaughnessy, I know about buildin' houses and gettin' men to work, the same as you know about the law. But I know nothin' about saltin'. The only thing I ever salted was a slaughtered pig when I was slavin' for a farmer before I took the boat.'

Again, the put-down causes a ripple of laughter to spread through the gallery, and the silver-haired judge's head to appear above the bench and threaten that he will not tolerate disturbance at his tribunal. And for Mr Muldoon to please answer the questions.

The crosscurrent of accents comprises two streams that have shaped the course of my life: the echoes of Ardglass and, later, the clipped tones of parents at the annual school outing to the opera festival, and at garden fêtes.

M.J.'s defence counsel calls him back to challenge the evidence of the Revenue Commissioner, which has shown him in a bad light: it claims bank accounts in Guernsey had suddenly disappeared when rumours of the tribunal began to circulate.

M.J. stands defiant in the witness box, telling how he had left Ireland just after Christmas in 1952. In a strong voice, he recalls selling hay, turnips, mangolds and potatoes at the market in town. Frosty mornings when people were still in their beds, he was out snaring rabbits. And, after all that, he had only a pair of wellingtons in a cardboard suitcase, his father's pocket watch and a five-pound note when he stepped off the cattle boat at Liverpool.

Like a radio interviewer favourable to his guest, the defence lawyer cites a list of his achievements. 'Am I right in saying, Mr Galvin, that in lean times your workers sent on substantial remittances to this country, which laid the foundations for the prosperity we enjoy today?'

'They certainly did. Every week they sent home the postal order, or the five-pound note in the envelope.' M.J. pauses, and glares at the Revenue Commissioner. 'In fact, there might be no Celtic Tiger only for those men.'

The silver head appears again over the bench and reprimands the defence counsel: 'This manner of discourse is not *ad rem* to the substantive issue of a non-resident account. Please don't waste the tribunal's time canonizing your client.'

'Just to establish Mr Galvin's creditable contribution to this country's economy, Your Honour.'

With a throwaway motion of his hand, the judge dismisses him. 'Get on with it.'

I have to be back in All Saints for a meeting, so I leave quietly and return to my car. The stippled Liffey waters reflect a blue sky and tall flags secured to poles that battle with the wind, and draw attention to another new hotel across in Ormond Quay.

Within a week, I receive a formal letter of appointment from Nugent. 'Thank you for your work in All Saints. I have pleasure in appointing you to the parish of Kildoon, taking effect from 29 October.' The rest I skim over – my contribution to the diocese and my support for his predecessors. In accordance with tradition and good manners, Nugent hosts a dinner in my honour and presents me with a canteen of cutlery. Afterwards, he plays the piano, and when I'm leaving, calls me aside: 'I regret we didn't see eye to eye, Tom, and while we disagree fundamentally, I admire your spirit.' He throws a tired glance around the room: Vinny Lynch is hopping up and down taking photographs, Plunkett is recharging glasses. 'I'm surrounded by fawning incompetents, and I relied on your experience. God bless.'

'God bless, Pat.'

29

BEHIND THE PRESBYTERY here in Kildoon is the cemetery. The graves of my predecessors since before the Famine line a stone wall in the church grounds. Once, Boylan sent me down here to straighten out a parish priest who was on a bottle of Powers a day. In the selfsame kitchen in which I write this story, I had asked him to consider St Camillus's for a couple of months. His father, a retired schoolmaster, had played 'The Cualann' on the concertina, and when he had finished, he had cried and knelt on the bare flags, pleading with his son to give up the drink. The priest vowed to take the pledge. 'I will, Dad, right now before Monsignor Galvin.'

'Promise me, son. As a priest of God, promise me.'

'I promise, Dad. As a priest. I'd like Monsignor Galvin to give me the pledge.' He kept that pledge and, by all accounts, no journey was too far for him, if asked to go and persuade someone to sober up.

My curate is a young man who lives near the chapel of ease two miles away. He is chaplain to two community schools and a technical college, and is so busy that the day isn't long enough for him.

Nearly every Friday, he festoons the church with schoolchildren's drawings in gaudy colours, and, instead of giving a sermon, sits with the pupils on the steps of the sanctuary and talks about his mother, and how 'Jesus is full of love for all of us'. At present, he is on a high concerning a parish website; and, although I fail to see what benefits will come to Kildoon from a website, I go along with his zeal. We meet for lunch each Monday at The Kildoon House, and, in between answering calls on his mobile, he tells me about dinner parties he has been to with bishops. It is his considered view that 'Henry Plunkett would make a great successor to the Boss. He has the gravitas, you see.'

'Yes, he has. The gravitas.'

While he lists the virtues of Monsignor Plunkett, now the vicar-general, a night after an ordination at All Saints looms up in my mind. The brandy had been flowing in the bishop's house, and in a haze of well-being and cigar smoke, Plunkett had dropped his guard: 'Before I leave this house, Tom, I intend to be a bishop, make no mistake about that.'

'The Boss wants me to become the vocations director for the diocese, but I'm not sure if I can fit it in with all my other commitments,' my curate confides, and I remember a whisper from his last parish priest: 'Look after him, Tom, he's inclined to sink. Takes to the bed.'

Every morning, I say the ten o'clock Mass for a handful: the two old haberdashery ladies who ritually touch the hands and feet of the Sacred Heart statue when they arrive, and again when they are leaving the church. And Kevin, who hides the bell when he is away in Knock, or in Medjugorje.

For the past while, I have been helping a group of local men to clean up the cemetery; they are surprised I can use a pickaxe so well. The plot around the presbytery we also cleaned of alders and briars, and overgrown bushes that had hidden the house and had almost closed in the pathway to the front door. While he is showing me around, my predecessor makes a half-apology for the condition of the place. 'But don't worry, Tom, you'll have few callers here, except for the postman, and an old dear who wants to consecrate her virginity.' He laughs as he hands me the keys to the house and the church. Parishioners tell me he was full of ideas when he arrived first to the parish, but for the past few years had been disappearing after Sunday Mass and not returning until the following Saturday, leaving the weekday Mass to the curate.

Today the sacristan and I work at a pace that is comfortable for us both. He hobbles around dragging bushes and brambles to the centre of the long garden for burning. At first, I tried to talk him out of doing any work, but then discovered that he wants to feel he's giving a helping hand. 'This is therapy for me, Monsignor,' he tells me. And for me too: my ulcer has cleared up.

The sacristan leans on his garden fork and takes a piece of newspaper from an inside pocket: it is a cutting from the *Bedfordshire News* about Irish builders who, last month, were found guilty of exploiting Polish workers at Dunstable Crown Court, and of not paying tax or social insurance.

I half-listen while he reads the judge's decision: 'This blatant transgression of the law in a civilized country, I will not tolerate. I will hand down a judgment one week from now after consultation with Her Majesty's Inland Revenue.' The sacristan crushes the newspaper into a ball and throws it onto the fire where it is consumed by the flames.

' "Nothing new under the sun," ' I quote as I heap up more brambles.

'What's that, Monsignor?' He is studying the blaze.

'Ah, just something. A long time ago. Can't even remember where I heard it. Let's gather up the branches in God's name before the rain comes.'